THE *Man* IN THE BLACK SUIT

SYLVAIN REYNARD

ARGYLE PRESS

❄ Praise for *The Raven* ❄

"A fabulous Gothic treat of a book filled with ancient vampires, dark vendettas, and star-crossed love."

❧Deborah Harkness,
#1 New York Times bestselling author
Discovery of Witches trilogy

"This book knocks over genre and swirls it into an addicting mix of mystery, romance and fantasy. With nearly lyrical prose and magical characters that step right off the pages, *The Raven* is going to make SR diehards and newcomers alike nurse an epic book hangover."

❧Christina Lauren,
New York Times bestselling author
Beautiful Bastard series

"Reynard never disappoints, especially when it comes to creating well-developed characters and granting readers an invitation to use their imaginations. This dark, sexy tale is nestled in the mysterious city of Florence and will amaze and enchant readers throughout. The author tries the paranormal genre on for size and, not surprisingly, it's a perfect fit."

❧RT Book Reviews

"I'm loving this series…Sylvain Reynard's writing is exquisitely beautiful and it evokes such emotion and vivid imagery…Compulsive reading as the reader is swept away in an intriguing sensual romance set in the heart of Florence. Raven and William's story is addictive and mesmerizing as new meets old with humour, passion, danger and mystery."

❧Totally Booked Blog

"Sylvain Reynard's dark and mysterious world of The Florentine and its vampires is sensual, passionate and deadly."

❧The Reading Cafe

Argyle Press

First edition, December 2017

ISBN: 978-0-692-94883-5

10 9 8 7 6 5 4 3 2 1

Cover Design by Heather Carrier Designs
Interior Book Design by Coreen Montagna

Printed in the United States of America

✳✳

Thank you for
reading,

S.R.

✳✳

Prologue

Cassirer Foundation Museum
Cologny, Switzerland
December 2007

"Stop pestering me," the museum curator scolded. She smiled at the telephone handset. "I'm almost finished."

She was careful not to groan as she surveyed the files that covered her workspace. Her office was dark, illuminated only by the old-fashioned banker's lamp on her desk. But the lighting was as she preferred it. Fluorescent lights gave her headaches.

"*I'm coming to get you.*" Her younger brother's voice through the phone was tinged with exasperation. "*We've been waiting an hour.*"

"*We?*" All thoughts of files and their contents evaporated. The curator straightened in her chair, and the vertebrae in her spine snapped to attention.

Her brother paused, and she fancied she heard the sound of footsteps as he walked to a more private area. "*There's someone I want you to meet.*"

The curator grinned. "You brought someone home? Have you introduced her to *Maman* and *Papa?*"

"*Yes, and I would have introduced her to you already if you'd arrived home when you said you would,*" he huffed. "*Is the security system on?*"

"I always keep it on after hours. Thierry is here, doing his rounds." She glanced at her desk once again. "As soon as I hang up, I'm on my way."

"See you soon. Drive safely."

She could hear the smile in her brother's parting words, and she chuckled as she hung up. He worked in London while she curated the family art collection in Cologny. Clearly, he'd met someone special.

She was happy for him.

She tidied her desk and organized the files into three neat stacks. She called Thierry, the security guard, and asked him to escort her through the building and outside to her car.

With a last look at her desk, she retrieved her handbag and coat. Ten minutes later, she glanced at her watch. Thierry still hadn't appeared.

She dialed his extension again, but he didn't answer.

Conscious of the fact that her brother and his evidently serious girlfriend were waiting, the curator quickly switched off the desk lamp. She walked to the door and entered the hallway. Thierry was still not to be found.

She checked the doorknob to ensure the office was locked and made her way down the dark corridor. The museum lighting was always dim, so as to preserve the collection. Individual pieces received special, targeted lighting during regular hours but were left to repose in darkness afterward.

"Sleep well, old friends," she murmured as she passed one of the exhibition rooms.

Her heels tapped across the floor as she pulled on her coat and adjusted her handbag. She flicked her long, red hair over her collar as she approached the main exhibit hall.

Something flickered in her peripheral vision. Startled, she turned her head.

Flashlights streaked the pitch-blackness of the hall. She could just make out the outlines of figures—some holding flashlights while others tore artwork from the walls.

They were dressed in dark clothing and wore ski masks. A beam of light glinted off a long knife as an intruder slashed a painting from its frame, damaging the masterpiece irreparably.

The curator cried out at the carnage. She clasped a terrified hand over her mouth as the sound escaped her lips.

One of the figures turned and shone a flashlight into her eyes.

Blinded, she jerked backward, unsteady on high heels.

Loud footsteps echoed as the intruder raced toward her. She fought to regain her balance and turned, preparing to run.

He grabbed hold of her hair and yanked her backward.

"No!" She dropped her handbag, arms flailing, and tried to free herself. She screamed and sought to elbow him in the ribs.

He avoided her elbows and struck her with the flashlight. She continued to scream and clasped her hands over his, struggling violently.

He lifted the flashlight and brought it down on her head.

Her hands went slack as she slumped against him. She felt herself fall to the floor.

Everything went dark.

Chapter One

The man in the black suit exited the limousine in front of the Hotel Victoire on the beautiful Avenue George V, a short distance from the Champs-Élysées.

Dark sunglasses shielded the man's eyes. He surveyed the area as he buttoned his suit jacket before walking in step with his bodyguard. The man's cell phone buzzed as he entered the hotel.

He removed his sunglasses and stared at the screen. His footsteps ground to a halt, as did his bodyguard, who stood watch.

The man's thumb skated across the screen as he scrolled through a series of photographs. His expression darkened. He jabbed a finger at the phone and placed it to his ear.

"Freeze Silke's accounts and change the locks on her flat." He spoke in German, his tone low and commanding. "No, don't notify her. She's violated the terms of our agreement in the most egregious way possible. She knows what she's done."

The man ended his call and continued his walk toward the reservations desk. He moved with the kind of fluidity and command that caused heads to turn — as if he were a professional athlete.

He was very tall with dark hair, large, dark eyes, and a lean, athletic form. With the exception of one glaring deficiency, he would have been termed attractive, even handsome.

Céline, one of the front desk agents, smiled at him widely. "Welcome back to Hotel Victoire, Monsieur Breckman." She spoke in French, taking care to look straight into his eyes. "We've prepared your usual suite."

The man nodded.

Céline glanced behind him and noted the presence of the large, burly bodyguard. "Will Mademoiselle Rainier be arriving later?"

"Mademoiselle Rainier will not be arriving." The guest glared. "Strike her name from the reservation."

He pivoted, and his handmade leather shoes tapped against the marble floor as he crossed to the concierge's desk. The agent stared after him, stunned.

Settling himself in an ornate chair in front of the concierge's desk, the man slid his finger across his cell phone screen. "I need to speak with Marcel."

"I'm sorry, Marcel isn't in today," the concierge replied. "My name is Acacia. May I be of service?"

The man lifted his dark eyes to meet hers. He was displeased. "I spoke with Marcel yesterday. He was arranging a meeting."

"Of course. And your name?"

The man huffed impatiently. "Pierre Breckman."

The woman turned to her laptop and pressed a few keys, her hazel eyes scanning. "I'm sorry, Monsieur Breckman. There's nothing in your records about a meeting. Would you like me to reserve one of our salons?"

"No, I would like you to produce Marcel." He stared at her with mounting hostility.

Acacia's gaze strayed to the left side of his face.

A long scar curved across his cheek and edged toward his mouth. It was white against his tanned skin and very deep, as if someone had attempted to cleave his face in two. He was an elegant man in all other respects, which made the scar that much more jarring.

His dark eyes narrowed. "Find Marcel. Now."

Acacia jolted, her hand moving instinctively to the curls at the right side of her face. She gave him a repentant look. "I'm sorry."

The man leaned forward. "Keep your eyes on my accounts. I'm sure you won't find them repulsive."

Acacia glanced over at the bodyguard, who stood at the end of her desk. He was even taller than Monsieur Breckman, standing at six-foot-six and weighing at least two hundred and fifty pounds. His head was shaved, and he had pale blue eyes.

She consulted her laptop. "Marcel booked your usual table at Guy Savoy's at eight o'clock this evening. Will you be needing a car?"

"No." The man sat back in his chair. As if in retaliation for her perusal, he shamelessly assessed her intelligent hazel eyes, her tan and flawless skin, and the black, curly hair she wore in a bob. His upper lip curled. "Marcel said he'd be on duty."

"Yes, monsieur. I was called in to replace him."

"Why?"

"I'm a member of Les Clefs d'Or." Her fingers brushed past the jaunty scarf she wore at her throat and touched the gold keys pinned to her lapel. "Marcel is my senior colleague, but I can assist you with whatever you may need."

"I don't need your assistance. I *need* Marcel." The man tapped his phone with short, staccato motions. When his call connected, it went to voicemail. "He isn't answering his mobile. Ring him at home."

"I'm afraid Marcel cannot be reached." Acacia's voice was strained. She tried to hide her distress by consulting her computer. "He arranged for champagne and fruit to be delivered to your suite, and he noted your allergy to strawberries. Shall I arrange your usual breakfast for tomorrow morning?"

"I ask you about Marcel and you reply with strawberries." The guest's eyebrows snapped together angrily. "Has Marcel left the country?"

Acacia looked up in puzzlement. "No, monsieur."

"Is he dead?"

"Certainly not!"

"If Marcel hasn't left the country and he isn't dead, then why isn't he here?"

Acacia forced a smile. "Monsieur Breckman, I would be more than happy to —"

The man stood abruptly and returned to the front desk, where he addressed Céline. "Tell the manager to find Marcel and send him to my suite. The concierge on duty seems to have difficulty fulfilling the simplest of requests. I asked for Marcel no less than four times, and she refused to assist me."

The man strode toward the elevators with his bodyguard, his footsteps echoing angrily through the lobby.

Céline gave Acacia a smug look.

Acacia rose from behind her desk and tried to hide her distress. She watched with gritted teeth as Céline dialed the hotel manager and reported the guest's words. Paul, the other reservation agent, didn't bother to conceal his eavesdropping on her conversation. He seemed amused.

Acacia had been a concierge at the Hotel Victoire for only a few months. She worked hard to provide exceptional service without attracting undue attention, hiding behind her navy blue uniform and her desk. Most guests treated her as they treated the furniture: with benign indifference. Monsieur Breckman had been in the hotel less than fifteen minutes and had already made her conspicuous.

She straightened her navy jacket, sat down, and ignored the desk staff and their reactions. She outranked them in the hotel's hierarchy but had always treated them with respect.

Now they were enjoying her embarrassment a little too much.

She turned to face the manager's office and steeled herself for his appearance. She was in trouble, she knew. She just didn't know how much.

Chapter Two

A cacia watched Jacques Roy, the hotel manager, approach her desk via a series of heavy, foreboding footfalls. He wore an expensive blue suit and a paisley tie that contrasted with the violet of his dress shirt.

Acacia thought he resembled a blueberry.

Monsieur Roy waited until he was close enough to speak to her without attracting the guests' attention. "What happened with Monsieur Breckman?"

Acacia rose from behind her desk. She was five-foot-eleven in her two-inch heels and looked down at her five-foot-four supervisor. "He was adamant he speak with Marcel. When I explained Marcel was unavailable, he ordered Céline to contact you."

Monsieur Roy's features grew harried. "Did you explain that Marcel is in the hospital?"

"No, monsieur. You instructed us not to answer uncomfortable questions about his whereabouts."

The manager sniffed. "Your discretion is appreciated, but nothing is more uncomfortable than upsetting a *highly valued guest*. You could have told him Marcel had an accident."

Acacia bit back a rude reply. "Yes, monsieur."

The manager straightened the red rose he wore pinned to his lapel. "I will speak to Monsieur Breckman. You will apologize and convince him you can provide the same level of service as Marcel. Be sure to ignore his scar."

She swallowed hard. *Too late*, she thought.

Monsieur Roy drew himself up to his full height. "This is the second time you've had a conflict with a valued guest. I had high hopes for you, Acacia, but you won't remain at the Victoire if this pattern continues."

The manager strutted away like a short, corpulent peacock, while Acacia tried very hard not to unleash her favorite Brazilian profanity.

After he visited the penthouse, Monsieur Roy returned to the concierge desk and escorted Acacia upstairs. She felt as if she were a criminal awaiting sentence.

Monsieur Breckman had reserved the penthouse suite, one of the finest rooms in the hotel. The suite featured a terrace that provided a three-hundred-sixty-degree view of Paris. At dusk, one could relax outside and gaze at the Eiffel Tower as it became illuminated.

Monsieur Breckman's bald and expansive bodyguard answered the door. In the distance, the guest could be heard in heated conversation. "We've lost our intermediary. Replace him or find another buyer. I'm not going to risk—"

Without comment, the bodyguard closed the door in Monsieur Roy's face.

The manager passed a hand over his eyes. He took a deep breath and knocked again.

A moment later, the bodyguard reopened the door. Monsieur Breckman stood next to him and looked down his nose in irritation. "Yes?"

"Acacia wishes to speak with you." The manager glanced at her out of the corner of his eye.

Acacia gripped the leather-bound journal she held in her hand. "I apologize for not disclosing Marcel's situation, monsieur."

The guest frowned. "His hospitalization is not a state secret."

Acacia's chin lifted. "I didn't wish to alarm you."

"Information about Marcel's assault might be crucial to your guests' safety. To *my* safety, mademoiselle."

"I apologize," she repeated.

The man regarded the much shorter manager with distaste. "What about you, Jacques? Why wasn't my security detail advised that Marcel was assaulted mere steps from the hotel? I should have been notified before my arrival."

The manager appeared taken aback. He lifted his hands in a conciliatory gesture. "We want to be sure you have all the information you need. But as Acacia mentioned, we didn't wish to alarm you."

"Of course not, that would be bad for business. I might have decided to stay at the Ritz instead." Breckman gave the manager a shrewd look. "So you marched mademoiselle to my suite so she could apologize for your decision?"

"Monsieur," Acacia intervened. "Now that you know about Marcel's situation, I hope you'll allow me to assist you during your stay."

The guest peered down at her.

"You have courage." He turned and glared at the manager. "More so than you."

The manager began to sputter, but Monsieur Breckman interrupted him by nodding at Acacia. "You have my attention, mademoiselle."

"I was educated at the Sorbonne and speak six languages. I have contacts all over the city and pride myself on opening doors for our guests. As I mentioned downstairs, I am a member of Les Clefs d'Or."

Immediately, the man's expression grew less severe. "The Sorbonne?"

"Yes, monsieur." Acacia resisted the temptation to glance at his scar.

The guest looked at her intently. "There may be something you can assist me with."

"Excellent." The manager extended his hand to the guest and they shook. "Welcome back to Hotel Victoire."

The manager gave Acacia a pointed look and waddled off down the corridor.

Monsieur Breckman stood next to his massive bodyguard. Neither made any move to invite her in or to dismiss her.

"How may I assist you?" Acacia asked.

The man addressed his bodyguard in English, with an Oxbridge accent. "It's all right, Rick. I doubt mademoiselle is a threat."

Rick opened the door more widely and allowed Acacia to enter. After he closed it, he stood to the side, between her and his employer.

The employer turned abruptly and walked down the hall.

Acacia's eyes followed him. His unhurried pace and squared shoulders spoke of confidence and control. When he disappeared from sight, she refocused her attention on the bodyguard.

Rick offered little in the way of acknowledgment, apart from a blank stare. Acacia placed her hand on the doorknob, intent on escape.

"Rick, escort Mademoiselle Santos to the living room." Monsieur Breckman's voice carried down the hall.

Acacia startled, surprised the guest knew her surname. Monsieur Roy certainly hadn't used it.

Rick jerked his chin in the direction his employer had gone.

She walked toward the living room, feeling anxious. She had no idea what the guest would say or do next.

The penthouse living room was elegantly decorated in gold brocade and pale blue, with ivory silk window hangings and stately furniture. Large arrangements of fresh cut flowers had been placed artfully in various locations and impressive art volumes were stacked imperiously on the table in front of the sofa.

Monsieur Breckman stood at the bar—a well-stocked affair set atop an antique wooden cabinet. He had a short, whispered exchange with Rick, who disappeared into the adjoining conservatory and left the door between the two rooms ajar.

Rick's departure drew Acacia's attention to the floor-to-ceiling windows, whose curtains had been pulled back. She could see the impressive terrace and beyond it, the Eiffel Tower.

Acacia tucked her concierge journal under her arm. She wondered how Monsieur Breckman had discovered the truth behind Marcel's absence. *Monsieur Breckman must have sources in the police prefecture.*

The guest placed ice cubes in a highball glass. He poured vodka from a bottle of Grey Goose and swirled the mixture before adding tonic water and a slice of lemon.

He lifted the glass to his lips and paused, his attention drawn to the elegant mirror that hung over the bar.

Acacia watched as the man shifted minutely, so he could no longer see his own scar.

She looked down at her shoes, embarrassed at having witnessed so private a moment.

"I've decided to increase my security detail," he announced. "When they arrive, I'd like them escorted here. I'll use the rear entrance to the hotel from now on."

"Of course," Acacia replied. "I expect your security will want to liaise with hotel security. I can arrange a meeting."

"Absolutely not. Hotel security failed Marcel."

Acacia bristled. "I assure you, we're all very upset about what happened. The management is taking steps to address the situation."

"Forgive me if I don't trust the management." The man leaned against the bar, his back to the mirror. "I'm curious. When did you learn of the assault?"

Acacia hesitated.

The man cocked an eyebrow at her.

She swallowed. "Last night. Monsieur Roy rang me at home."

"Did Marcel have any enemies? A jilted lover? Anyone who might wish him harm?"

"I'm not familiar with his personal life. Some of our guests are… challenging." Acacia carefully avoided looking at the guest at that moment. "But Marcel is respected. The police said it was a mugging."

"If that's what the police said, they lied. A mugging is a crime of opportunity, conducted swiftly with minimal violence. Marcel sustained several broken bones and a head injury. He was assaulted shortly after his shift ended and dragged around the corner, out of sight of the hotel doormen. That sounds premeditated, not opportunistic."

Acacia's eyes widened. "How do you know?"

The man lifted his glass to his lips. "Research."

"Why would the police lie?"

"Did you speak to them directly?"

"An officer interviewed me when I arrived this morning, but he wouldn't tell me anything. Monsieur Roy is the one who addressed the staff." Acacia came a step closer. "Why would someone want to harm Marcel?"

"That is a very good question." The guest swirled the contents of his glass.

"Someone needs to speak to the police. Marcel could still be in danger."

"The Parisian police aren't fools. They know this without being told."

Acacia pondered his words. She had a contact in the Brigade de Répression du Banditisme, but she wasn't keen to speak to him. She wondered what contacts Monsieur Breckman had.

She tilted her head toward the hall. "I should return to my desk so I can greet your security detail."

The guest retreated to the sofa. He sat and stretched out his long legs. "Are you from Portugal, mademoiselle?"

"Brazil."

"Monsieur, your reservation is at Guy Savoy's at eight o'clock. I'm sure you wish to relax before dinner. If there isn't anything else, I'll wish you a good evening." She forced a smile and turned to go.

"How long have you lived in Paris?"

Acacia stopped. She avoided sharing personal details with guests, but she was all too conscious of the manager's threat. Monsieur Breckman was a *highly valued guest*.

She faced him. "I came to Paris as a student."

"Did you study languages?"

She examined his expression. If the guest was feigning interest, he was an exceptionally fine actor.

"Among other things," she hedged.

"Such as?" His dark eyes pinned her to the spot.

"I studied art." Her posture stiffened.

The man's eyebrows lifted. "Which period?"

"Impressionism."

Breckman gestured to a print of Edgar Degas' *The Ballet Class*, which hung on the wall opposite. "Are you responsible for that?"

She smiled to herself. "No, the hotel has an interior designer who is responsible for the furnishings."

"I sense Degas is not your favorite."

"I prefer Monet."

"Monet is very popular."

"One could argue that Degas is even more popular, if you take into consideration the number of his works that have been stolen."

"Stolen?" the guest repeated, his eyes suddenly alert.

"There was the theft from the Gardiner Museum in America. And the Musée d'Orsay lost *Les Choristes* when it was stolen while on loan in Marseilles."

"Yes, but *Les Choristes* was recovered. Unfortunately, the Gardiner works have never been found." The guest finished the rest of his drink. "What do you think of Matisse?"

Acacia frowned. "Matisse is post-Impressionist."

Monsieur Breckman's mouth turned up. "Really?"

Acacia's frown deepened.

"I'm only teasing," the man said gently.

When Acacia's frown didn't abate, his smile faded.

He moved to the bar. "May I offer you a drink?"

Acacia blinked. "Thank you, but I'm on duty."

"Of course. I forgot." He prepared another vodka and tonic for himself. "Did Monsieur Roy initiate any new protocols with respect to staff leaving the hotel after dark?"

"No. He told us what happened to Marcel. We agreed to cooperate with the police investigation."

"He didn't suggest anyone receive an escort?"

"No." She shifted her journal to her other hand. "You think we're in danger?"

The man looked at her via the mirror. "What do you think?"

"I can't imagine the kind of criminal who would attack a concierge." She touched her lapel pins self-consciously. "We're in the business of helping people."

The man turned around. "Do you take the Metro to and from the hotel?"

"Not usually."

"You have a car?"

"I drive a motorcycle."

"A motorcycle?" The dark slashes of his eyebrows lifted almost to his hairline.

She smothered a smile. "Yes."

"I hope you wear a helmet. Paris drivers are mad."

"Yes, monsieur." She adopted a serious tone. "I always wear a helmet."

His dark eyes met hers. "When you leave this evening, make sure one of the doormen escorts you to your motorcycle. Insist he remain with you until you're safely away."

Acacia shifted her weight from foot to foot, surprised by the guest's show of concern. "I will be more vigilant traveling to and from the hotel. But I should mention we are in a safe part of the city."

"The management's lack of regard for their staff is truly staggering." The man focused on his drink. "Unless…"

When the guest didn't continue, Acacia prompted him, "Monsieur?"

He placed his drink on the bar and disappeared into the bedroom, leaving a bewildered Acacia behind.

He returned from the bedroom a moment later, holding a distinctive red box, embossed in gold. He regarded it solemnly. "Today was not the best of days."

"I'm sorry, monsieur."

"Not as sorry as I am. I'm afraid I've been a fool, and it has caught up with me." He sighed. "Can you be discreet?"

"Absolutely. As a concierge, discretion is essential."

"Marcel made certain…arrangements, which must be undone." He held the box out to her. "Can you return this to Cartier, in person?"

"Yes." She took the box and carefully schooled her reaction. She wondered if she was holding an engagement ring.

She felt a twinge of compassion for the guest. She'd seen in his records that a female companion was supposed to have accompanied him. Perhaps his short temper was related to matters of the heart.

She looked at Monsieur Breckman with new eyes. "Is there anything else I can do?"

"There are other items." He inclined his head toward the bedroom. "I need them returned."

"Of course. Should I remove them now?"

He nodded.

She walked past him into the bedroom and saw three large shopping bags sitting on the bed, bearing the logos of Chanel, Louis Vuitton, and the lingerie designer Modiste.

The guest had spent a great deal of money on lavish gifts and possibly an engagement ring, only to have to ask a stranger to return them. Acacia pressed her lips together to avoid making a comment. She doubted the guest would appreciate her sympathy.

She gathered the bags with both hands, juggling the Cartier box and her journal, before she returned to the living room. "Will there be anything else?"

"No." He placed his hands in his pockets.

"I hope you enjoy your evening at Guy Savoy's. I should mention that his artichoke soup with black truffle is highly recommended."

Monsieur Breckman retrieved his drink from the bar. He turned and made eye contact. "Thank you."

"You're welcome." Acacia ventured a small smile before leaving.

Chapter Three

Modiste would not accept returns of custom-made lingerie. Monsieur Breckman's taste could not be faulted; he'd chosen a basque in pale blue satin, edged with sheer black lace, as well as two sets of brassieres and panties, in red and in black. The items were finely made and crafted for a tall, thin woman with small breasts.

Monsieur Breckman was going to have to keep his lingerie. Acacia hoped he'd enjoy them.

She returned everything else, including an enviable pair of diamond earrings from Cartier. At each of the boutiques she visited, she made a point of introducing herself to the manager, some of whom she'd met previously via telephone. Acacia's success as a concierge was linked with her outlook: she approached her tasks not as toil but as opportunities, cultivating friendships and always being polite and professional.

At the end of her shift, she changed into jeans, a leather jacket, and motorcycle boots. Yusuf, one of the doormen, was kind enough to walk her to her vehicle and wait until she departed. She was confident in her ability to take care of herself, but her confidence was wedded to wisdom. Having an escort could deter a potential attacker.

It was summer in Paris. The weather was warm, and the sun was still shining as she sped down the tree-lined Avenue George V and turned right on the Champs-Élysées, moving in the opposite direction of the Arc de Triomphe. Acacia revved her motorcycle as she weaved in and out of traffic on the multi-lane avenue.

She could have avoided the heavy traffic on the Champs and taken a more efficient route, but she didn't. She enjoyed the view along the avenue and suffered the traffic because of it.

The wind whipped her face and fluttered the curls that had escaped her sturdy helmet. With a glance or two of appreciation, she shot past the Grande Palais, the Petit Palais, and approached Place de La Concorde before heading south toward the river Seine.

Acacia had to fight to keep her eyes off the river and on the traffic in front of her. The Seine was mesmerizing. She'd spent hours walking its banks and bridges, sometimes with friends and sometimes alone.

Boats carrying tourists traveled up and down the river. But the Seine was high this summer, owing to two weeks of heavy rain. As she approached the Pont des Arts, one of her favorite bridges, she saw a tourist boat turning around. The bridge was too low for it to clear.

She nodded to the Louvre on her left before she continued to Pont Notre Dame, crossing over to Île de la Cité and heading to the Left Bank.

Before she left the island, Acacia took a detour alongside Notre-Dame cathedral, slowing her speed to an almost unacceptable level. The thirteenth-century structure was smaller than one might expect, especially if one had seen it in films. But it was very impressive, with its twin towers and intricately carved portals on the western façade.

Acacia wasn't a Christian, but she made a note to herself to attend Mass at the Cathedral the next time she was able. The aesthetic experience fed her soul, and she couldn't admire the rose windows from her motorcycle.

She turned away from Notre-Dame and headed north so she could drive by the historic house of Héloïse and Abélard. Acacia disliked their story. In her estimation, Abélard was manipulative and controlling, and Héloïse had been foolish and co-dependent. But Acacia honored their love, even if she couldn't understand it. So with a hand on her heart, she paid her respects to the lovers who had been dead since the twelfth century.

She circled back to Petit Pont and crossed to the Latin Quarter, where she lived. She smiled at some of the buildings of the Sorbonne, her former university, before turning onto Rue Soufflot and parking her motorcycle.

Acacia lived in a small studio on the third floor of an old but beautiful building on the corner of Rue Saint-Jacques and Rue Souf-flot. A friend's parents owned the studio and because of her friendship with their daughter, they blessed her with affordable rent. Acacia had lived in the flat since she was a student.

There wasn't an elevator in the building, but few if any of the older buildings had them. Acacia trudged up the staircase, carrying her backpack.

"Hey." Kate, Acacia's American neighbor, greeted her in English as she approached.

"Hi." Acacia paused as Kate locked the door of the flat she shared with her roommate, Violaine.

"What's happening?" Kate pushed her riot of red hair back from her face. "I haven't seen you in a while."

"I've been working. How are you?"

"Tired. Graduate school is kicking my ass." Kate pulled her knap-sack over her shoulder. "Bernard is having a party Saturday night. You should come."

"I'd like that." Acacia smile was carefully neutral.

"You mean it, right? The last time you said you were coming, you never showed." Kate made a face.

"I was called in to work. I'll try to make it this time."

"Great. Bernard throws the best parties, and he'll be happy you're coming." Kate squeezed Acacia's arm as she passed. "Give Claude a hug from me."

Acacia chuckled and shook her head. Kate was lively and gener-ous with her friends, of which she had many. She'd even tried to set Acacia up with Bernard, who was a journalist with *Le Monde*.

Bernard threw the best parties, it was true. He liked food and fine wine and always invited an interesting and diverse array of guests. But Acacia felt no spark of attraction with him, and getting involved with a journalist was far from safe.

She entered her flat. Claude greeted her with a meow and rubbed himself against her legs until she lifted him for a proper hug. He had large, yellow eyes and soft, black fur. She'd found him on the doorstep one wet and rainy night. With the exception of Acacia and Kate, he hated everyone.

"*Olá, Fofo.*" She murmured endearments to him in Portuguese before she fed him and opened her mail.

After a modest dinner and a generous glass of white wine, she pored over a printed copy of Monsieur Breckman's guest profile, which she'd smuggled home in her backpack. It was possible he was embarrassed about asking Acacia to return the gifts for his girlfriend and that was why he'd preferred to deal with Marcel. But something about the hypothesis didn't sit right with her.

"Marcel was supposed to set up a meeting." Acacia addressed Claude, who was curled up in her lap as she sat at the kitchen table. "But there was nothing attached to Breckman's reservation. It isn't like Marcel to forget something."

Claude blinked his yellow eyes, as if in acknowledgment.

"Unless Marcel tried to set up a meeting and failed," Acacia thought aloud. "But wouldn't he have notified Breckman before he arrived?"

Marcel was the senior concierge, and he took great pride in his work. He wouldn't have forgotten a task for an important guest. And there was the matter of his assault. Acacia was inclined to believe the Paris police over Monsieur Breckman, but his assessment rang true. Marcel had been beaten badly, which didn't seem to align with a random mugging.

She wondered if Monsieur Breckman spent much time watching American police dramas. He seemed to have a curious understanding of the criminal mind.

According to the smuggled file, Pierre Breckman was a business-man from Monaco. The nature of his business was not disclosed. He'd been accorded a four and a half star rating by the hotel, which Acacia found surprising. Five stars were reserved for royalty and heads of state. Four stars were usually given to celebrities of one sort or another. Pierre Breckman was neither, but clearly—as the management emphasized—he was a *highly valued guest.*

He was thirty-eight, had a fondness for jazz and Michelin-rated restaurants, and visited Paris several times a year. According to Marcel's notations, it was not uncommon for Breckman to socialize with the world's elite. He also enjoyed sporting events such as European football and the French Open.

During his stays at the Hotel Victoire, three different female companions, all significantly younger than him, had joined him in the past five years. Monsieur Breckman was not considered difficult or troublesome, which made his behavior earlier that day puzzling. Understandably, he was sensitive about his scar. But his file didn't mention tantrums or outlandish behavior.

Silke Rainier, a Swiss model, had been Monsieur Breckman's latest partner. Their separation must have been recent, as Marcel had included her in his remarks on the current reservation.

Acacia put the printed pages aside. She knew the reservations agents and housekeeping staff could have told her far more than was recorded in the file. But she wasn't on friendly terms with the former and she didn't want to make herself conspicuous to the latter, who were notorious for gossiping.

She opened her laptop and Googled "Pierre Breckman," which yielded only enough information to confirm what was listed in the file. Strangely, none of the entries included photographs.

Googling Silke generated hundreds of entries. Although Acacia didn't recognize her, photographs of Mademoiselle Rainier were splashed across the internet, including recent images of her sunbathing topless with an American film star on the deck of a yacht. The way she caressed her new man's unmarred face seemed calculated, if not punitive to Monsieur Breckman, who would no doubt see the photos.

"What a cruel display," Acacia whispered.

Claude responded by rubbing his head against her stomach, as if in agreement.

While Monsieur Breckman had been busy purchasing gifts for his girlfriend, she'd been topless with someone else. Acacia closed the browser window.

Monsieur Breckman was not the kind of man who would welcome pity. He'd reacted in anger when she'd apologized for staring at his scar. Of course, he'd probably seen the photos of his erstwhile girlfriend. No wonder he'd been so irritable.

But Monsieur Breckman's interest in the attack on Marcel seemed of a personal nature, as were his questions about Marcel's associates. Again, she scoured the reservation notes for information about a meeting, but found nothing.

Acacia took her membership in Les Clefs d'Or very seriously and would never disgrace the organization by participating in anything illegal. Not all concierges were as scrupulous. She'd never caught

Marcel committing an infraction, but since he was her superior and discreet in the extreme, it was quite possible his compromises had gone undetected.

Acacia slid her hand under the neckline of her T-shirt and withdrew the hamsa amulet she always wore. She never took off this pendant of protection. However, given the antagonism in France toward religious symbols, she was careful to keep the necklace hidden.

Much later, she lay in bed while Claude curled up on top of the blankets next to her feet. She gazed sleepily at a print of one of her favorite paintings, Monet's *Twilight, Venice*, which hung over the bed.

The Bridgestone Museum of Art in Tokyo owned the painting's original. Although she'd never seen it in person, Acacia had fallen in love with it when she began studying Impressionism.

The painting featured the church of San Giorgio Maggiore, an island haven surrounded by water and sky. Monet had used oranges and pinks to convey the light of the setting sun, darkening to blues and greens at the edges of the painting. The church appeared like a floating city, dark and shadowy against the warm light.

She studied the brush strokes, admiring the way Monet had used wavy lines here and there to give the impression of gently moving waves.

If she focused very hard, she could forget everything around her and disappear into the painting. She could feel the fading sunlight dance across her skin. She could smell the scent of the sea.

Acacia was not an idealist. Any ideals she'd had were killed years ago in Amman. Of course, no one in her current life knew about that. She was determined to keep it that way, which was why she hid behind a navy uniform, serving a transient clientele and never letting anyone get too close—not even Luc, her former boyfriend.

Acacia shut her eyes. She didn't like thinking of Luc and how things had ended with him. She didn't like thinking about lying next to him in this very bed, his hand smoothing across her naked skin while he whispered to her. She hadn't had a lover since.

As much as she tried to deny it, Acacia was lonely. Rarely did she admit it and rarer still did she dwell on it. But like many, she longed for love and companionship. She longed for honesty and intimacy, even though she'd lived without them for years.

Acacia opened her eyes and rolled over. Claude meowed his annoyance at being discommoded.

Her position at the hotel paid well, and she received thousands of Euros in gratuities on top of her salary, which enabled her to support her mother in Recife. In addition, she was slowly building her savings—her exit strategy—and hoped someday she could work in a gallery.

By chance, her gaze landed on her work journal, which rested on her nightstand.

Every well-trained concierge kept a record of the requests made by hotel guests. She carried her journal at all times, which was why it was on her nightstand. The contacts and comments inside were too confidential to be left at the concierge desk or in her locker at the hotel.

If Monsieur Breckman had asked Marcel to set up a meeting, Marcel would have recorded the particulars. Indeed, any work he'd done for Breckman would have been written down, with the possible exception of illegal activities. No doubt Marcel had the journal with him when he was attacked, which meant it could be lying on the street near the hotel. Perhaps the police had overlooked it.

Acacia resolved to look for the journal before she began work the next morning.

Chapter Four

Pierre Breckman sat on the exceptional terrace of his suite and stared at the brightly lit Eiffel Tower. He sipped vodka without tonic and wondered how all his plans had gone to hell.

Silke had ended things in a very public manner. His blood pressure increased as he recalled the photographs of her and her new lover. She was beneath his contempt for such a narcissistic display, but he was still angry. She'd wounded his pride, although he was loath to admit it. It hadn't been the first time.

He strode to the edge of the terrace and leaned over the railing. He could hear Rick's evening replacement step outside, simply to keep an eye on him.

Then he thought of the tall, Brazilian woman with the striking hazel eyes. She'd stood in his suite and argued the virtues of Monet.

There was an earnestness about her that piqued his interest. She was professional and honest, or so she appeared. Given the moral state of her colleagues, he had his suspicions.

Pierre sipped his drink. Corruption could be enticed and drawn into the open with a few well-placed suggestions.

As his anger retreated, he was conscious of the weakening effects of rage. It made one rash. It made one foolish. He'd vowed never to be those things again.

The Eiffel Tower winked at him, beckoning him to visit her. To do so, he'd need a companion worthy of so beautiful and romantic a location.

Sometimes it seemed as if he were surrounded by vipers. Nowhere was the kind of woman worthy of the Eiffel Tower.

He turned his back on her and went inside.

Chapter Five

The next morning, Acacia visited her local dojo much earlier than usual so she would have time to search for Marcel's journal.

She kept secret the fact that she studied martial arts. Luc had known, of course. When they were together, her daily visits to the dojo had coincided with his time at the gym.

Her mother had enrolled her in Brazilian jiu-jitsu classes as a child, in the hope it would enable her to defend herself. Indeed, the classes had proved successful. When she came to France, she switched to karate. Acacia prized the quiet confidence martial arts gave her as much as the strength it gave her body.

She arrived at the hotel forty-five minutes before her shift and parked her motorcycle near one of the pedestrian entrances to the Victoire's underground parking lot, which was across the street from the hotel.

She took care to survey her surroundings before she switched off her bike. Avenue George V was always busy—cars parked here and there, traffic consistently moved down the street, and pedestrians dotted the sidewalks. She was cautious as she approached Marcel's motorcycle, which was parked nearby.

The Avenue ran through a neighborhood that housed luxury boutiques, including Hermès, Bulgari, Givenchy, and Saint Laurent. The street had two medians shaded by mature trees. Tall buildings lined both sides. Owing to the number of parked cars and vans, there were many places to hide.

Other motorcycles flanked Marcel's. Remnants of police tape could still be seen clinging to his bike, but the area had been swept clean.

Acacia looked under the motorcycles and Vespas in search of his journal. She looked on the street, the sidewalk, and checked the gutters. She even peered into a nearby garbage bin. The journal was not to be found.

It occurred to her as she scanned the area that there was something odd about the attacker's choice of location, which was across the street from the hotel. Given the busyness of the street, the assault must have been seen. But no witnesses had come forward, with the exception of the person who'd stumbled upon Marcel's bleeding body and called the police.

Being a concierge was in some respects like being a detective. One had to solve problems, find things, and on occasion, locate people. Acacia wondered if Marcel had found something that put him at risk.

She walked the short distance to the hotel's service entrance and changed in the staff room, arranging her concierge pins with pride on her navy blue uniform. At the beginning of her shift, she sat behind the concierge desk and placed her journal next to the hotel's laptop. She checked the day's calendar and reached for her pen. It was gone.

Thinking she'd knocked it to the floor, she pushed her chair back and looked under the desk. The pen sat on the floor to the right, underneath one of the desk drawers. She reached forward to retrieve it and as she withdrew, her hand brushed against the drawer.

But instead of the solidity of wood, she touched something else. Puzzled, she felt along the bottom of the drawer. Someone had attached what seemed like a book to the underside.

"I need the concierge." An imperious voice sounded above her.

Acacia sat up and pushed her chair closer to the desk. She smiled at a well-dressed, elderly woman. "Yes, madame."

Out of the corner of her eye, she saw Monsieur Breckman enter the lobby, dressed in another black suit and surrounded by a security detail that had swelled to six men.

She wondered if he always wore black suits. She wondered if the Earth would cease moving on its axis if he wore, say, navy blue.

He was headed toward the reservations desk. When he caught sight of her, he switched direction, as did his security detail, who trailed like a series of large, dark-suited ducklings after their mother.

The elderly woman sniffed, as if Acacia's momentary distraction was a waste of her valuable time.

Acacia widened her smile and gestured to one of the chairs. "I am the concierge, madame. How may I help you?"

The woman refused to make eye contact and adjusted her Chanel jacket. "I don't want to speak with someone from Spain. I want a *French* concierge."

Acacia kept her smile firmly in place. "I'm from Brazil, but I live here in Paris. I would be happy to assist you."

"Go and find a French concierge." The woman settled herself in one of the chairs, not bothering to look in Acacia's direction.

"Good morning, mademoiselle," Monsieur Breckman addressed Acacia as he approached the desk. He looked down his nose at the elderly woman. "When you're finished with the concierge, I need to speak with her."

"I don't deal with foreigners," the woman said primly. "I'm waiting to speak to a *French* concierge."

The man rocked back on his heels and his dark brows snapped together. "Foreigners? And where are you from, madame?"

The woman brushed her fingers across the gold insignia of her Chanel handbag. "I am from Lyon."

"Really?" Breckman's eyes glittered impishly. "Then you must be familiar with Lyon's history."

The woman frowned up at him. "Certainly. I've lived there my entire life."

"Then it's almost certain you, too, are an immigrant." The man examined the ceiling, as if deep in thought. "If I remember my Lyonnais history correctly, Roman immigrants arrived from Vienne in the first century. Were you there then?"

The woman sputtered, but Monsieur Breckman continued. "What about the Burgundian refugees who escaped from the Huns in the fifth century? Surely you remember them, given how long you've lived in Lyon?"

"How dare you!" The woman reddened in outrage.

"How dare you, madame." The man glared. "As the revolution taught us, to be French is to be devoted to the principles of liberté, égalité, and fraternité. Since it's you who has abandoned those principles, it's you who has ceased to be French."

Acacia rose from behind the desk and interrupted. "Madame, I can introduce you to one of my colleagues, if you prefer."

"Fascism and xenophobia have no place in France," the guest continued, his brown eyes glittering. "They have no place in the world, although it appears, sadly, they've taken residence in Lyon."

"I'll be speaking to the manager about this outrageous conversation." The elderly woman stared daggers at Monsieur Breckman. "I've never been so insulted in all my life."

The man bowed. "Please give Monsieur Roy my best regards. He knows where to find me."

The woman gave him a haughty look and followed Acacia to the reservations desk, where she was introduced to the blond, blue-eyed Céline.

When Acacia returned, Monsieur Breckman was already seated in the chair opposite her desk. His security detail had drawn back, with the exception of Rick, who stood at his elbow.

She sat down and opened her journal.

The guest angled his head in the direction of the reservations desk, his gaze sharp. "Does that happen often?"

"Monsieur, I—"

"Mademoiselle?" His eyes met hers, his tone more of a command than a request.

She shrugged, all too conscious that the lobby was filled with guests and other staff. "How was your evening?"

The man ignored her question as he surveyed the other guests. "Anti-immigration sentiment is on the rise in Europe. I didn't expect to find it here."

"Paris is the whole world." Acacia attempted to defuse the situation with humor.

"So they tell me," he responded, his eyes finding hers. "You're more restrained than I."

"A concierge provides service through friendship."

"Friendship with a xenophobe? Sounds unlikely."

"We cannot choose our guests, but we can choose how we respond." Acacia looked toward the desk, where the woman from Lyon appeared to be giving Céline a difficult time.

Her eyes moved back to the man sitting in front of her. "If someone hates me and I respond with hatred, all I've done is reinforced their hate. If I respond with kindness, I've changed the conversation. Perhaps on the receiving end of kindness, the person who hates me will see a better, peaceful way."

Monsieur Breckman made a sound that came perilously close to snort. "You censure me for deriding her?"

"No, monsieur."

The guest gave her a hard look.

Acacia lifted her pen pointedly. "How was breakfast this morning? Was everything to your liking?"

"Now that I think about it, the hotel staff isn't very diverse." He turned in the direction of Céline again.

"There's diversity in the staff, I assure you." Acacia's gaze strayed to her desk. She was eager to retrieve the mysterious item attached to the drawer, but not in front of him.

"Am I keeping you from something?" The guest's eyes moved from her face to the desk.

"No, monsieur." She flushed. "How was dinner at Guy Savoy's last evening?"

"A work of art. The chef himself greeted all the patrons. Have you met him?"

She smiled wistfully. "I've not had that pleasure."

"Really?" Monsieur Breckman seemed surprised. "I was told you send guests there regularly."

"That's true."

"You've never dined there yourself?"

"I toured the restaurant once. I was impressed with the location. The building they occupy used to house the French mint."

He studied her. "It must be vexing to arrange all these lavish experiences for your guests but never experience them for yourself."

"I prefer to think of it as an opportunity." She leafed through her journal to the previous day's entries. "With respect to the items you gave me yesterday, I was able to return all of them except the gifts from Modiste. I'm sorry, but they don't accept returns of custom-made items."

"Damn." He met Acacia's eyes. "They're of no use to me."

She bit the inside of her cheek to avoid making an impertinent remark. "If I may make a suggestion?"

"Certainly."

"Since the items are unworn, they could be donated to charity. There is a local organization, Vision du Monde, that would auction the items, discreetly, and give the proceeds to children in need."

"That's an interesting proposal." He scratched at his chin. "Fine."

"I'll see that the items are delivered, along with a short explanation. The receipt will be issued in your name."

"Absolutely not."

"You'd prefer the donation be made anonymously?"

He gave her a look that was its own reply.

"Very good." Acacia made note of their conversation in her journal, ignoring the feel of his eyes on her.

"I hadn't thought of donating the *items* to charity. Do you encourage guests to make charitable donations?"

"Many of our guests are already involved in philanthropy. Sometimes when I'm problem solving for a guest, an opportunity arises to help a charity. It's up to the guest to decide, of course. I simply present a range of solutions."

"I see. Obviously the clientele here can afford to be generous. But those who can afford to be generous seldom are, in my experience."

"A donor needs to be sufficiently motivated." Acacia smiled. "They need to see value and purpose in donating to charity."

"You missed your calling. You should have gone into philanthropy."

Acacia's smile widened. "We can all do our part to help others, no matter our occupation."

The guest frowned.

"Is something wrong, monsieur?"

"You're very different from the concierges I usually deal with. You mentioned yesterday you speak several languages. How many?"

"Six."

Monsieur Breckman looked impressed. "And they are?"

"French, Portuguese, English, Spanish, Russian, and Arabic."

"Arabic?" the guest repeated. "Why Arabic?"

Acacia's response was a reflex. "Arabic is important in the service industry in Paris."

"And you studied art at the Sorbonne?"

"Yes." Acacia had no intention of expanding on her response.

For a moment, she contemplated mentioning Marcel's journal. It was possible it contained private and unflattering things pertaining to Monsieur Breckman and other guests. If the contents of the journal were made public, it could be embarrassing for him.

But then he spoke. "How old are you?"

She turned to her laptop and pressed a few buttons. "Monsieur, I don't think—"

He interrupted her. "I could find out through other means, but I'm giving you the courtesy of asking directly. How old are you?"

"Thirty-five." Acacia's words were clipped. She drew a deep breath through her nose and fought the urge to squirm.

"Thirty-five," he repeated, as if the number were a revelation. "Then you wouldn't have been at the Sorbonne at the same time as…" He rearranged his position in the chair. "I've decided to extend my stay. Since Marcel is unavailable, I thought I'd avail myself of your services."

"How can I assist you?" Acacia positioned her pen over her open journal.

The man consulted his expensive wristwatch. "I want a new, bespoke suit."

"Would you like to visit the tailor or have him see you in your suite?"

"Have him come here. Tell him I'm looking for a black suit, and I'd like it finished in time for a dinner engagement this evening."

Acacia restrained a laugh and resisted the urge to point out that he already possessed at least two black suits, according to her observations.

"I'm sorry, but a respectable Parisian tailor will require at least two fittings and a minimum of seventy hours of work. Some of the tailors require more."

"Really?" The man tried to sound surprised, but failed. "Monsieur Roy made it sound as if you were a miracle worker."

"I'm a concierge, not a saint."

The guest's eyes took on a new intensity. "Nor am I, mademoiselle, I assure you."

Acacia felt something flare between them — a spark of attraction or warning, she wasn't sure which.

She lowered her gaze. "I can recommend a couple of tailors from Rue de la Paix and you can choose, or would you prefer I choose for you?"

"You choose, but pick the best. I'm in need of a couple of custom shirts and a new tie, as well. I'd like the tailor to get started as soon as possible. I'm not sure how long I'll be in Paris."

Acacia recorded his requests in her journal. "I shall do my best, monsieur."

"I'm sure you will." He looked as if he were resisting the urge to smile.

"Will there be anything else? Do you require dinner reservations? Or would you like tickets for a show or to a museum?"

The guest grew thoughtful. "There may be one or two other things."

"It would be my pleasure."

The man scowled. "I don't see how this could give anyone pleasure. You speak six languages and studied art at the Sorbonne. Wouldn't you rather be employed in the art world? Not being abused by racists?" He waved at her uniform. "Or trotted around as a minion to the manager? I fail to see how someone with your intelligence and education could be content to work in such an environment."

His speech pierced her. Anger, hot and violent, burned in her middle.

A torrent of ugly words stood gated at the back of her throat. He had no idea, no idea why she did what she did. Or that she had an exit strategy.

She clutched her pen so tightly she thought it might break.

The man's gaze fixated on her pen, his expression morphing from displeasure to something else.

Acacia focused on her breathing, a technique she'd learned through her martial arts training, and moved her hand to her lap.

As she breathed, she noticed Monsieur Roy had chosen that moment to walk through the lobby. She was grateful she hadn't given voice to the anger fighting to escape her pursed lips.

The manager nodded at Monsieur Breckman, who returned his nod, and disappeared in the direction of the marble courtyard, seemingly unaware of Acacia's show of temper.

"I spoke without thinking." The guest's voice was low.

Acacia kept her hand and her pen in her lap. She avoided his eyes. "You had additional requests?"

"*Mademoiselle.*"

"Monsieur?" She took a deep breath.

The guest placed his hand flat on the desk, next to her open journal. "Acacia, I apologize."

She visualized her anger as a wave, watching in her mind's eye as it retreated with the outgoing tide. She felt her body begin to relax.

She lifted her pen to the journal. And waited.

In her peripheral vision, she could see the guest move his hand, bypassing his scar to rub at his forehead. "Everything about this visit has gone straight to hell. First Silke. Then Marcel."

Now Acacia's eyes ventured to meet his.

"I apologize," he repeated firmly. "You've been nothing but professional in the face of ugliness, mademoiselle. I'm sorry to have contributed to that ugliness. It's not who I am."

There was something open about his expression at that moment. The man looked contrite.

Acacia glanced up at Rick, who didn't bother making eye contact. She wondered what he'd do if she spoke to him directly. She wondered what he'd say if she dared criticize his employer.

"The Victoire is very fortunate to have you," the guest continued. "I doubt they realize precisely how fortunate."

Acacia ignored his compliment. "I'll be sure to make arrangements with the tailor. Now, if there isn't anything else…"

"A round of drinks for you and the staff, with my compliments."

Acacia's eyes widened. "That isn't necessary."

"It is." Monsieur Breckman's tone was firm.

Acacia elected not to argue with him. A gift of drinks for the staff would certainly improve morale, in the wake of the attack on Marcel. "I'll make arrangements with the bar."

"Thank you." The guest smoothed the silk of his tie. "Out of curiosity, have you ever received a request you were unable to satisfy?"

"A guest once asked if I could provide a bespoke suit in a couple of hours."

He grinned, and his smile almost obliterated his scar. "Touché."

"You mentioned you have a dinner engagement this evening. Will you be needing a table here at the hotel or would you like me to make a reservation elsewhere?"

"I believe my associate has already made arrangements." He gazed at her thoughtfully. "There's one more thing I'd like you to help me with."

"Yes?"

"In my travels, I've been searching for a relic of St. Teresa of Avila. I'd like you to acquire one for me."

Acacia's mouth fell open.

She shut her mouth quickly and recorded the request, deciding she would not be mentioning Marcel's missing journal.

"Can you help me?" His eyes were searching.

Acacia kept her expression neutral. "I will research the matter and present the options to you."

The man's face showed signs of admiration. "Thank you. That's all for now."

He stood and buttoned his suit jacket.

She looked up at him. "Monsieur, as I mentioned yesterday, I was unable to find any notes from Marcel on your meeting. Were you able to discover the details?"

He looked over his shoulder swiftly, so swiftly he'd turned back to Acacia before she'd even realized he'd moved.

He placed his hands on top of the concierge desk and leaned over her. "Forget about the meeting," he barked in a whisper. "Don't mention it again, to anyone."

Acacia moved her chair back, out of reach of the guest's long arms.

Rick grabbed his employer's elbow.

Evidently his touch was enough to capture the guest's attention. He withdrew immediately.

Monsieur Breckman smoothed his hair back from his forehead and adjusted the sleeves of his suit. He marched through the lobby toward the rear of the hotel, his security detail forming an impenetrable wall around him.

Rick glanced over his shoulder, his eyes trained on Acacia.

She was frozen in place. A guest had never threatened her before. There was no mistaking his tone or the look in his eyes. The fact that Rick had to intervene made the situation all the more menacing.

Acacia didn't waste any time. She ensured no one was watching her before leaning over to retrieve the item from under the desk. It took several tries to dislodge it as it had been attached to the drawer with wide, sticky tape.

Acacia placed the item in a file folder, away from potentially prying eyes. She carried the file folder to the staff room and barricaded herself in the adjacent bathroom. Only then did she examine the contents.

It was a leather-bound journal, remarkably like the one she owned. She undid the clasp on the cover and opened it. On the flyleaf, in Marcel's handwriting, was his full name and contact information.

Her thoughts moved to her colleague, lying unconscious in the hospital.

She leafed to the last page. There was an entry that included today's date and the following words:

Breckman 10 PM. Important. V.

Acacia scanned the previous entries and searched for any reference to Pierre Breckman. He was named, along with Silke Rainier, but there was nothing unusual in Marcel's notes — just remarks about breakfast preferences, an allergy to strawberries, the gifts Marcel had been asked to procure for Silke, and a dinner reservation at Guy Savoy's.

There was no indication as to who Breckman was supposed to be meeting that evening at ten o'clock, unless one of the person's initials was a *V.*

What was Marcel doing? And why was he attacked?

Monsieur Breckman might have threatened her, but he couldn't control her thoughts. And at that moment, she was thinking the connection between him and Marcel was something sinister.

Chapter Six

Hotel Victoire was a five star hotel that enjoyed an excellent reputation and attracted a wealthy clientele. However, some of its guests took pleasure in testing the concierges with ridiculous requests, simply for amusement. Monsieur Breckman's need for a relic of St. Teresa appeared to be one of those requests.

Acacia wasn't in the mood to devote her time and attention to indulging him, especially since he'd threatened her. Instead, she spent most of her day assisting guests with genuine needs.

During her breaks, she hid in the staff room, poring over Marcel's journal. To her frustration, she found nothing out of the ordinary. Many of his entries were written sparsely, with full names and details omitted. Since she didn't know what she was looking for, the search seemed hopeless.

At the very end of the day, she turned her attention to relics.

Some of the relics of St. Teresa were housed in Avila, while some were housed in the town of Alba de Tormes. The Church would never sell the first-class relics. However, one could acquire a third-class relic — a piece of cloth that had been touched to a first-class relic — quite easily. Somehow Acacia knew a piece of cloth was not what Monsieur Breckman had in mind.

At the end of her shift, she changed out of her uniform and made her way to the sumptuously decorated hotel bar — its walls paneled with gleaming wood—where she'd set up a tab for the staff on Monsieur Breckman's account. As on most evenings, hotel guests populated the bar. With the exception of the bartender, Acacia was the only staff member in sight.

"Good evening, Carlos." She greeted the bartender in Spanish as she sat inconspicuously at the very end of the bar. "Where is everyone?"

Carlos greeted her with a wide smile and replied in Spanish. "Everyone from the day shift already stopped by. I have something special for you."

She gazed at the rows of bottles wistfully. "What is it?"

"Champagne." Carlos retrieved a bottle of Louis Roederer Cristal that had been chilling and presented it to her.

Her eyes widened when she saw the label. "Are you sure?"

"The guest chose this vintage personally. And he told me to give you the bottle." Carlos winked.

She shook her head at the extravagance, but she wasn't about to reject the gift. "I want to share."

"I'm on duty." He looked around the room.

She placed a finger to her lips.

Carlos opened the bottle and poured a glass for Acacia. Then he lowered the bottle below the bar and poured himself half a glass.

Acacia lifted her champagne. "Cheers."

"Cheers, beautiful."

She closed her eyes as the tiny bubbles filled her mouth. The taste was almost magical—there was fruit and spice and something almost floral. It was an unexpected delight.

She opened her eyes and sighed. "It's very good."

"It should be, for the price." Carlos turned his back to the room and sipped the champagne discreetly.

"That's good," he said as he turned around. He placed his glass out of sight and reached under the bar. He handed her a gift bag. "For you."

"For me? Why?"

"It's from the guest." Carlos nudged the bag closer.

Acacia reached into the bag. She retrieved a finely made brioche, wrapped in cellophane and tied with a bow. A tag indicated the treat came from Guy Savoy's restaurant.

"Is there a note?" She looked into the empty bag.

"No, but Monsieur Breckman delivered it himself when he chose your champagne." Carlos smiled and moved to the other end of the bar to fill a waitress's order.

Acacia thought back to her earlier exchange with the guest, and his surprise at her remark that she'd never visited Guy Savoy's restaurant. It was thoughtful of him to bring her a treat from the famous chef.

Then she thought of his insulting words about her profession and the way he'd threatened her.

She put the brioche back in the gift bag.

She wasn't a psychologist. It wasn't her job to try to analyze guests and their behavior. Breckman's recent actions were at odds with the way he'd been described in the guest records. Clearly, brioche and top shelf drinks were his way of making amends. But no gift, however generous, was enough to cause her to forget what he'd said.

She took her time sipping the exquisite champagne and chatting with Carlos before finding a doorman to escort her and the carefully concealed bottle of Cristal to her motorcycle.

At the end of her shift the following evening, Acacia approached the penthouse suite. Two bodyguards flanked the entrance. She stated her name, and one of them repeated the information into a communication link inside his shirtsleeve.

Rick opened the door, unfriendly and unsmiling as always.

She lifted her eyebrows at him.

Without a word, he led her down the hall and into the living room.

Monsieur Breckman stood in front of a round, glass table. An unframed painting lay on top of the glass. He held what appeared to be a white sheet, which billowed from his hands like a cloud and came to rest on the backs of the chairs that had been pushed flush against the table.

The sheet dropped over the chair backs, obscuring the painting from view, but not coming into contact with it.

Before he covered it, Acacia caught a brief glimpse of the work. It seemed familiar. She took a step forward.

The guest turned and blocked her path. "Mademoiselle?"

Acacia found his expression unsettling. His dark brows were knitted together, and he examined her closely.

Over his shoulder, she could see a pair of bodyguards out on the terrace. The men had shed their suit jackets, which made the handguns they wore visible in their holsters.

Her heart rate increased. Tension radiated from the guest, who continued to watch her. She began to feel as if she'd intruded on something dangerous.

Instinctively, she relaxed her body and shook her hands out at her sides. She looked around the room and made note of all the possible exits should she need to flee.

"You wanted to speak with me?" The guest removed a pair of white gloves and stuffed them into the pocket of his suit jacket.

"Yes, monsieur." She dragged her gaze from the door that led to the terrace. "How are things proceeding with the tailor?"

The guest crossed his arms. "They're proceeding well. Unfortunately, I've had to cut my visit short. I'll see him on my next visit."

"Please let me know if I can be of further assistance on that matter."

"I had difficulty sourcing the relic you requested," she continued. "Third-class relics are easy to obtain, but according to my research, the Church owns all the first-class relics of St. Teresa. They aren't for sale."

"Perhaps," Monsieur Breckman said slowly. "Perhaps you haven't been looking in the right direction."

She was puzzled by his subdued reaction. He didn't seem surprised by her report. Instead, he looked as if he were waiting for something.

Acacia felt as if she'd been cast in a play and forgotten her lines.

The guest stared at her, and she stared back. She wasn't looking at his scar. Indeed, she'd almost forgotten it existed. But her eyes strayed to the gloves, which were hanging out of his pocket.

She positioned her concierge journal under her arm. "I would be happy to secure a third-class relic for you."

"I want a first-class relic. Obviously I don't expect to acquire it from the Church." The guest rubbed his thumb across his chin. "As long as there's a buyer, there's a market and a means of acquisition. This applies to everything, mademoiselle. *Everything.*"

"Respectfully, I disagree. The Church owns the relics, and they have a policy—one might even say a theology—that forbids selling them."

"Again, mademoiselle, you've been looking in the wrong direction." The guest gave her a knowing look. "Marcel was extremely *creative* in his problem solving. Perhaps you could be similarly creative?"

Acacia resisted the urge to respond with sarcasm. Marcel's creativity had probably put him in the hospital. She would not make the same mistake.

"I'm sorry, monsieur. As I said, third-class relics are easy to acquire, but first-class relics belong to the Church. If you wish, I can contact Church authorities."

"There's little point in doing that." The guest continued to examine her.

Acacia's attention was drawn back to the painting beneath its shroud. She visualized it in her mind's eye. The brush strokes were almost Impressionistic.

What work of Impressionism could Monsieur Breckman have in his possession?

He moved quickly and obstructed her view. "Thank you, mademoiselle. That is all."

He smiled, and when he spoke again, his voice was smooth as silk. "I'm leaving tomorrow. Rest assured you'll be well looked after."

Acacia recognized the coded language of the guest's last sentence; he'd leave a gratuity. "My colleague François is on duty now. If you need anything, he'll assist you. Enjoy your evening and safe travels."

She faced the hall and took a single step. Then, for some unknown reason, she turned toward the painting.

She thought of the Musée d'Art Moderne. A lone thief had broken into the museum a few years prior and stolen five priceless paintings. One of them was by Henri Matisse.

Hadn't Monsieur Breckman mentioned Matisse two days ago?

Acacia's eyes narrowed as she envisioned the brushstrokes, hidden from view by the sheet.

Monsieur Breckman crowded her immediately, his arms outstretched. "Thank you, mademoiselle. Rick will walk you to the door."

Acacia forced herself to make eye contact, her mind a whirl.

The guest seemed to search her eyes. "I believe you told me you pride yourself on being discreet."

"Yes, monsieur," she managed.

He leaned forward. "Your discretion will be rewarded."

Rick appeared beside her. He didn't touch her, but began to herd her toward the door.

Acacia gave the guest a single, backward glance and focused her attention on the carpet in front of her. She ignored the presence of the other bodyguards as she entered the hall and walked quickly to the elevator. She pressed the button and looked over her shoulder.

Rick remained in the doorway, watching her.

Acacia entered the elevator and pressed the button for the lobby. Her thoughts raced.

Monsieur Breckman is a wealthy businessman whose photographs don't appear on the internet. He was supposed to attend a meeting Marcel arranged, possibly with someone called V. Before the meeting occurred, Marcel was attacked.

Breckman asked me to source a relic and said I should be creative in doing so. Was he asking me to find someone to steal one?

He has a large security detail and what could be a stolen painting. And he wants to pay me to keep my mouth shut.

Once the elevator doors closed, Acacia leaned against the back wall and covered her mouth with her hand.

Monsieur Breckman appeared to be in possession of one of the most famous pieces of stolen art in French history. And he was about to leave the hotel with it.

Chapter Seven

Acacia was cautious. She worried about making mistakes and drawing attention to herself. Monsieur Roy had already warned her to be careful with highly valued guests, which indicated her position at the hotel was not entirely secure.

For these reasons, she was the picture of decorum as she bade her colleagues good evening and entered the room that housed the staff lockers. She changed into casual clothes and forced herself to behave as if nothing were wrong.

Inside, her stomach rolled.

Acacia checked her backpack and breathed a sigh of relief when she realized Marcel's journal was still hidden. Putting the bag over her shoulder, she fled through the back hall past the kitchen to the receiving doors. She burst through them into the alley where trucks and vans delivered supplies. She needed privacy to think, and as expected, the alley was empty.

She used her cell phone to search for information about the famous theft from the Musée d'Art Moderne. A few clicks on her web browser and she was staring at Matisse's *La Pastorale*, one of the stolen masterpieces.

She'd only caught a glimpse of the painting in Breckman's suite. But her memory seemed to match the image on her phone.

Still, she took her time searching, looking for news of the stolen painting's recovery. There was no such news. Indeed, none of the paintings stolen from the Musée that fateful evening had ever been recovered.

She put her phone in her pocket and hugged her backpack.

She recognized the painting. The painting had been stolen. Was this what Marcel's creativity had produced for Monsieur Breckman? Was this why Marcel had been attacked?

She squinted at her watch in the dim light that shone from above the receiving doors.

Monsieur Breckman was leaving in the morning, provided he didn't change his mind and depart sooner. He was returning to Monaco, presumably with the painting.

I'm a concierge, not a policeman.

Acacia gave careful consideration to the thought, but discarded it. Although she still carried a Brazilian passport, France was her home, and she loved it. The theft of paintings from the Musée had been a national scandal. She wasn't going to allow a rich businessman to leave the country with one of its treasures. She just needed to find a way to report him without making herself conspicuous.

You need to speak to Monsieur Roy.

This thought had merit. But what if she was wrong? The hotel manager would not take kindly to her accusing a *highly valued guest* of theft, especially on the heels of angering him with her vagueness about Marcel.

If the painting were a reproduction, wouldn't Monsieur Breckman have said so? Why would he handle it with white gloves?

A loud bang sounded behind her.

Acacia whirled around, hands lifted, feet planted in a fighting stance.

"Sorry." One of the kitchen staff held up his hands. He was holding a package of cigarettes and a lighter. "I just came out for a smoke."

Acacia straightened and gave the man a tense smile. "I'm heading back in." She brushed past him and went inside, looking over her shoulder as he propped open one of the doors with a crate.

He sat down, lit a cigarette, and inhaled deeply. He blew a plume of smoke toward the heavens, and his shoulders relaxed.

Acacia envied him.

She gathered her thoughts and realized she had to do something about the painting, even if she just shared her suspicions. Unfortunately, the last person with whom she wished to speak was precisely the person she needed to call.

She walked down the empty corridor to put some distance between herself and the open door. She was careful not to come too close to the kitchen, for fear of being heard.

She dialed a number and waited for the line to connect.

"*Ma belle.*" The man answered on the second ring, his voice a caress.

"Luc." Acacia's breath left her body in a rush. She looked around to ensure she was still alone.

"*What is it? What's wrong?*" Luc's tone changed immediately.

"I—" Acacia paused and backed into a corner.

"*Caci? Are you hurt?*"

She closed her eyes. The sound of her old nickname in his earnest, concerned voice caused her insides to twist.

"I just finished my shift, and I think…" She paused, uncertain. "It may be nothing. I shouldn't have bothered you."

Footsteps emanated from the phone, along with the loud clang of a door being shut.

"*Are you at the Victoire?*"

"Yes." She frowned. "How did you know where I work?"

"*I had drinks with Yves and Véronique the other night. What might be nothing?*"

Acacia grew flustered at the thought of being the subject of a conversation between her friends and her ex-boyfriend, but she pushed the concerns aside. She had more important things to worry about. "I think one of the guests has a piece of stolen art in his room."

The footsteps came to a halt. "*Stolen from where?*"

"The Musée d'Art Moderne."

Luc's voice grew muffled. "*What makes you think it's stolen?*"

"It looks like the Matisse."

"*None of those paintings have surfaced. Are you sure?*"

"No. No, I'm not. I just saw it for a moment, before the guest covered it up. It wasn't in a frame; it was just canvas on top of a table. But he handled it with white gloves."

"*The paintings from the Musée were cut from their frames. What's the name of the guest?*"

"Pierre Breckman, from Monaco. He's a regular at the hotel, but I've never met him before."

Luc grunted into the phone, and Acacia heard his fingers tap against a keyboard. "*Tell me everything you know about him.*"

"He's thirty-eight. He's a wealthy businessman, but I don't know what kind of business he's in. He comes to Paris several times a year and stays at the Victoire. He was involved with Silke Rainier, a model, until recently. When he's at the hotel, he deals exclusively with Marcel, the senior concierge."

"*What does Marcel do for him?*"

"Football tickets, dinner reservations, shopping. The guest mentioned a meeting Marcel was supposed to set up. But before the guest arrived, Marcel was attacked."

The tapping stopped. "*What?*"

Acacia checked her surroundings once again. "Marcel was attacked a few nights ago, while he was walking to his motorcycle after a shift. He's in a coma."

The sound of a desk chair rolling and striking something solid echoed in Acacia's ears.

"*You could have called me.*" Luc's tone was censorious.

"Why would I call you? The city police told us Marcel was mugged."

Luc huffed. "*I'm in the BRB.*"

"That's why I'm calling about the painting." Acacia resisted the urge to roll her eyes.

The Brigade de Répression du Banditisme, or BRB, was a special law enforcement unit under France's Ministry of the Interior, outranking the Paris police. Art thefts were part of their jurisdiction.

"*The BRB also deals with armed robberies, Caci. Most muggings don't result in comas.*"

Acacia heard the sound of quick footsteps through the phone.

"I'm not your problem anymore," she said softly.

Luc ignored her remark. "*You say the mugging occurred just before the guest and his painting arrived?*"

"Yes."

"*When you saw the painting in the guest's room, how did he react?*"

"He covered it up. He told me my discretion would be rewarded. Then he had one of his bodyguards escort me to the hall."

Luc swore. "*Did they touch you?*"

"No."

"*Did they threaten you?*"

"No, but he implied I should keep my mouth shut."

The sound of footsteps quickened. "*Are you at the concierge desk?*"

"No, my shift is over. I'm hiding in the back hall near the kitchen."

"*Are you alone?*"

"Yes."

"*Go to the lounge. Sit at the bar and order a drink. Don't allow yourself to be alone.*"

"I need to tell the hotel manager what's going on."

"*Fine.*" Luc's voice was strained. "*Tell the manager agents are on their way. No one is to approach the guest or his suite unless he tries to leave the hotel.*"

"You're sending agents?" Acacia looked around frantically. "I just wanted to ask you about the painting."

"*I have to report this. You've provided a lead for one of our major cases, not to mention the fact I'm concerned for your safety. Art thieves, like muggers, are usually petty opportunists; buyers of stolen art are far more dangerous.*"

Now it was Acacia's turn to swear.

Luc interrupted her. "*Tell the manager the guest will probably try to remove the painting, if he hasn't done so already. When did you last see him?*"

"About twenty minutes ago." Acacia kept the phone to her ear as she moved down the hall and toward the lobby.

"*It may be too late. Can you see other people now?*"

"Yes, I'm entering the lobby. I'll head to the night manager's office." She rounded a corner and shifted her backpack awkwardly on her shoulder.

"*Has anyone else connected with the hotel been the victim of a crime recently? Or had an accident?*"

"Not that I know of. Monsieur Breckman has a large security detail with him. They're armed."

"*How many men?*" Luc's voice lifted and Acacia heard a door close.

"Six."

"*What kind of weapons?*"

"I don't know—hand guns."

"*Stay with the manager or head to the bar. Act as if nothing is wrong. If the guest or one of his men approaches you, call me. I'm on my way.*"

"You don't have to do this."

"*Stay there*," he commanded. "*I'm in my car.*"

He disconnected, and Acacia stared at her cell phone, wondering what she'd just done.

Chapter Eight

Acacia sat at the bar and positioned herself so she could watch the door.

She knew better than to involve Luc in her suspicions, but she'd done it anyway. Now he was on his way over *with agents*.

She took another drink, fearing she'd destroyed her anonymity in one unguarded moment. She wrung her hands as she glanced around.

Luc appeared in the doorway.

At five-foot-eleven, he was only two inches taller than Acacia. His hair was sandy brown and needed cutting, and his handsome face was shadowed with scruff. He'd been attractive when they were students and was even more so now, wearing dark pants, a blue shirt, and a black leather jacket. He looked more like an actor than a policeman, although he surveyed the lounge with sharp eyes before he entered it.

"Caci," he murmured as he approached her. He kissed her cheeks.

The greeting itself was innocuous. Friends greeted one another like that all the time. But Acacia felt a wave of nostalgia, made all the more poignant by the speed with which he withdrew.

She felt her face flame. "Luc, I—"

"Not here," he interrupted, his blue eyes focused on hers.

He reached in his pocket and pulled out a few Euro notes, placing them next to her half-empty glass. He nodded at the bartender and retrieved Acacia's backpack from the floor.

As soon as she stood, he guided her to the door. His hand hovered at her lower back, but he didn't touch her.

Acacia appreciated his professionalism but felt an underlying sadness. She'd given him up even though she'd loved him. She'd had her reasons, and they still existed. She needed to remind herself of them.

"Is there a place we can speak privately?" He kept his voice low as they walked toward the lobby.

"We can go to the staff room." Acacia glanced around. "But you aren't supposed to be in there."

"I just need a minute." Luc was in policeman mode and would not be deterred.

When they approached the staff room, Luc entered first and searched to see if anyone was inside. Once satisfied the room was empty, he beckoned to Acacia.

She closed the door behind her. "I called you about the painting because I was worried it was stolen. I didn't expect you to come over."

"You're a witness." He returned her backpack. "I wanted to see for myself that you were all right."

Acacia rubbed her forehead in agitation. "I am in so much trouble. You have no idea what this could cost me."

Luc's blue eyes met hers. "The lead investigator of the Musée robbery is on his way. My colleagues are already in the building, and you're with me."

Her eyes flashed. "The hotel is going to be swarming with agents. The night manager was furious when I spoke to him. My supervisor will be apoplectic."

"You did the right thing." Luc spoke reassuringly. "The night manager is being interviewed as we speak. I can't be involved with the investigation because of my connection with you, but I had to report what you told me."

She crossed her arms. "What happens next?"

"The lead investigator, Philippe, will interview you. I'll speak to him about assigning someone to keep an eye on you, as a precaution. I doubt your interview will take very long, although he may want you to come down to thirty-six Quai des Orfèvres to make a formal statement. One of the officers will drive you home afterward."

"I have my motorcycle."

"Too risky."

Acacia tugged at her hair. "This is bad. This is very, very bad. I should have spoken with my supervisor before I called you. This will be all over the news!"

Luc's expression grew grim. "We're talking about possession of a masterpiece, not a case of stolen towels. If we recover it, you'll be a hero."

"I don't want to be a hero!" She gesticulated wildly. "I don't want my identity made public. Do you have any idea what this means?"

Luc came a step closer. "We aren't going to plaster the name of a key witness all over the media. I've already told Philippe you're a friend. He'll treat you right."

"Sure," she murmured, unconvinced.

"Without question," Luc said firmly. "If you help us close this case, you'll have the thanks of the BRB."

He reached for her, then stopped abruptly. He thrust his hands in his pockets. "I'll make sure everyone understands you don't want your name in the media."

His expression softened. "I know it's shit timing, but it's good to see you."

Acacia looked down at her shoes. "It's good to see you. How's Simone?"

Luc rubbed the back of his neck. "She moved out. That's why I was having drinks with Yves and Véronique. They wanted the whole story."

Acacia lifted her head. "I'm sorry."

"Things weren't working out." He gave her a half-smile. "How about you? Are you seeing anyone?"

She lifted her backpack over her shoulder. "I work a lot. But I like my job, which is why I hope Monsieur Roy is understanding about having the BRB all over his hotel."

Luc cleared his throat. "Leave it to us. I'll take you to Philippe now." He gestured for her to precede him through the door.

She paused. "I know things didn't end on the best of terms. I'm grateful you came to check on me."

His expression tightened. He nodded.

For a moment, Acacia considered turning over Marcel's journal. The longer she held on to it, the more she was in jeopardy of withholding evidence. But the Paris police were handling the investigation of Marcel's assault. She needed to turn the journal over to them.

With gritted teeth, she stepped into the hall, and Luc followed.

As they rounded the corner to the lobby, Acacia could see the beautiful space crawling with BRB agents.

All the air seemed to flee from her lungs. Luc didn't know the source of her deepest fear or that his actions might have put her life and the life of her mother in jeopardy.

But it was too late.

Chapter Nine

Acacia did not sleep well.

Late into the night, a BRB agent had driven her back to her apartment. She'd then spent an hour staring at the ceiling above her bed, turning the events at the hotel over in her mind. Finally, she'd given up on sleeping and made *pão de queijo* instead.

Shortly before sunrise she'd returned to bed, exhausted, and slept for a couple of hours. She'd just finished making breakfast when there was a knock at the door.

Claude meowed.

Ignoring the cat's pique, she peered through the viewer. Luc stood outside, his hands in the pockets of his leather jacket, his face grim.

She picked up Claude and opened the door.

"Morning." Luc smiled at her tightly.

She frowned. "It's seven thirty."

"It's important." Luc looked beyond her, into the apartment. "Can I come in?"

Claude meowed unhappily and began to struggle. When Acacia released him, he shot across the floor and disappeared under the bed.

She opened the door wider and invited Luc in. He kissed her cheeks, and this time his hand lingered on her shoulder.

"What's going on?" she asked.

"Have you spoken with the hotel?" He ran his fingers through his hair, which looked as if he'd rushed out the door without combing it.

"No. My shift doesn't start until nine. I was just having breakfast." She gestured to the small table and twin chairs in her efficient kitchen.

Luc took a seat and she poured him a cup of coffee from a press.

"You're still wearing your good luck charm." He gestured to her hamsa pendant.

"I never take it off." She pulled the edges of her robe closer together as she sat across from him. "Your colleague Philippe wasn't nice."

"Philippe is a good detective, but he's under a lot of pressure from the Minister of the Interior to solve the Musée case." Luc sipped his coffee.

She offered him the plate of *pão de queijo*.

"I've missed this." He smiled and wolfed a piece of cheese bread.

"I made them this morning." Acacia wrapped her hands around her coffee cup.

"I miss a lot of things."

She drank her coffee, unwilling to engage him.

"How is your mother?" He looked over at her.

"She's fine. Thanks for asking."

"Give her my best."

Acacia nodded stiffly.

Luc's gaze wandered over her posture. He looked stricken. "Was I so terrible?"

"No," she whispered.

"I loved you." His voice was gentle. "I treated you well. I was faithful."

"Yes."

"If you were with someone else, I'd respect that. But all these years later, you're still alone. I worry about you, Caci."

Now her spine straightened. "I can take care of myself."

"I know that." He made eye contact. "I don't think you've ever needed anyone. But why should you be alone? You're an intelligent, beautiful woman with a good heart."

"It isn't easy being an immigrant in this country." She fixed him with a stern look. "It isn't easy being caught between two worlds and never fitting in. For now, I'm focusing on my career and supporting my family."

He rubbed his hand across his unshaven face. "I worry about a backlash against immigration in this country. Every time there's a terrorist attack in the world, the anti-immigration groups ratchet up their campaigns."

"I know. The other day a guest at the hotel told me she wouldn't speak to me because I wasn't a French concierge. And she was from Lyon."

Luc swore. "I'm sorry, Caci. You're still sending money back to Brazil?"

She nodded.

"You're a good daughter." He glanced in the direction of her sleeping area. "I can't believe you're still living in this tiny apartment. The bed is lumpy, and it creaks. You could afford something better."

"I like it here. I like the neighborhood, and I like my landlords."

"I forgot about Anouk's parents. They're good people." An unhappy expression took up residence on his face. "Philippe released Breckman an hour ago. He called me at home to tell me. That's why I'm here."

Acacia put her coffee cup down with a loud thump. "Why did they release him?"

"Experts from the Musée examined the painting and said it's a reproduction."

"Why wasn't it in a frame? Why was he wearing gloves and being so secretive?"

"They examined the painting they found in the hotel," Luc clarified. "It's possible he removed the original after you saw it."

Acacia went very still. "Will he come after me?"

"He's supposed to be leaving Paris today. He wasn't told you were the witness, but he's probably figured it out.

"You'll have someone shadowing you for the next few days, just in case. And I'm only a phone call away."

She touched her pendant absently. "What about the media?"

"There's a media blackout. The press knows something happened at the hotel, but they've been told simply that the BRB was following a lead. No one will mention your name." He stretched his hand across the table, and Acacia squeezed it. "Breckman was cooperative. But you should be careful. The attack on the other concierge is suspicious, and according to a contact of mine in the Paris police force, they don't have any suspects."

"I think we're missing something."

Luc nudged her arm. "No more Commissaire Maigret, Caci."

She laughed at the mention of her favorite French detective.

"That's fine with me." She offered him more cheese bread.

"Thank you." Luc took another piece. "I agree, we're missing something. So I pulled Breckman's records."

"What did you find?"

"You have to keep this conversation confidential. Philippe knows I'm here and that I'm telling you Breckman was released. I'm not supposed to be pulling his file, and I'm certainly not supposed to be telling you about it."

Acacia frowned. "You know I can keep a secret."

He chuckled ruefully. "That's why I'm risking it.

"I didn't find anything unusual in Breckman's records, but you saw his security detail. Why would a legitimate businessman need so many men? Why would he hide a reproduction of a stolen painting and tell you your discretion would be rewarded?" Luc shook his head. "Organized crime has been known to use works of art as payment or insurance. The more powerful the crime boss, the smaller the footprint. He can afford to have others do the dirty work."

"Monsieur Breckman didn't seem like a crime boss, but I guess it's possible." Acacia pushed her hair back from her face. "What should I do?"

Her cell phone rang, interrupting Luc's response.

"Excuse me." She crossed to the counter where her cell phone rested and answered it. "Hello?"

"*It's Céline at the Victoire. Monsieur Roy is requesting you meet him in his office at eight thirty.*"

Acacia cleared her throat. "Did he mention the reason for the meeting?"

"*No.*" Céline's tone was smug. "*That's all.*"

"Goodbye then." Acacia disconnected and placed the phone back on the counter.

Luc rose to his feet. "Work?"

"The manager wants to see me before my shift."

Luc combed his fingers through his hair. "I'll take you."

"I can take a taxi. My motorcycle is still at the hotel."

Luc placed his hands on his hips. "I'm not letting you walk in there alone. I'll take you to the hotel, and then I'm going to look around."

"Thank you, but no. I'm capable of getting myself to work."

"Breckman is still there. If I take you to work and make my presence known, it sends a message."

"How many people know about me?" Acacia clasped her hands together.

"Only those involved directly in the investigation, apart from me." Luc stuffed his hands into his pockets. "Do you want to stay somewhere else for a few days? You could call Yves and Véronique."

"No. They live too far away from the hotel."

He lifted his shoulders casually. "You could stay with me."

"Absolutely not."

"You didn't even consider it." Luc frowned. "I'm not infected with plague."

"It's kind of you to offer, but we both know that's a terrible idea." She unclasped her hands.

"Fine. If you see something suspicious, call Philippe or me. Did he give you a card?"

"He suggested I program his number into my phone. I did that last night."

Luc cleared his throat. "Am I still programmed into your phone?"

A long look passed between them.

Acacia turned and disappeared into the bathroom.

Chapter Ten

Luc insisted on parking his Renault illegally in front of the hotel. He opened Acacia's door and helped her to her feet, guiding her toward the front door.

Acacia eyed the doorman before she whispered, "I'm supposed to use the service entrance."

"You're using the front door today." Luc flashed his identification to the doorman, who scurried ahead to open the door.

When Luc and Acacia entered the lobby, a frowning reservation agent greeted them.

"Don't bother changing into your uniform," Céline said, ignoring Luc. "Monsieur Roy wants to see you immediately."

"And you are?" Luc held his identification under her nose and began asking a series of pointed questions.

Acacia didn't bother to restrain her smile as she turned away.

At that moment, Monsieur Breckman exited the elevator with his security detail. Once again, he wore an expensive black suit, paired with a white shirt and black silk tie. A man Acacia did not recognize stood next to him, speaking very insistently in hushed tones.

Luc abandoned his interrogation and positioned himself in front of Acacia.

Monsieur Breckman's eyes met Luc's, and his eyebrows lifted. He made no effort to approach Acacia, but his gaze sought hers.

He stared at her as the man next to him continued to speak. Breckman gave no indication he was listening.

He didn't look triumphant or arrogant. He seemed worried.

He glanced at Luc and gave Acacia a very unhappy look. Then he and his entourage turned and walked toward the back entrance to the hotel.

Once they were out of sight, Luc touched Acacia's elbow. "I'm going to follow them."

Acacia mumbled her thanks before she walked to Monsieur Roy's office. She rapped on the door.

"Come in, Acacia." The manager didn't rise from behind his desk when she entered his office.

"Good morning." She waited for him to offer her a seat. He didn't.

Instead, he sat back in his chair and regarded her with small, beady eyes. "I spent last night on the telephone, explaining to my superiors why the hotel was swarming with BRB agents."

"I'm sorry, monsieur. I'm sure that was upsetting." Acacia adopted her most sympathetic tone.

"Upsetting?" Monsieur Roy's normally pale face reddened. "Are you familiar with the employee handbook?"

"Yes, monsieur."

"Apparently not. Because if you'd been familiar with the hand-book, you'd have known it was your responsibility to inform *me* of any suspected illegal activity in the hotel."

"I informed the night manager."

"The night manager is not me!" He slammed his hand on top of the desk. "You called the BRB. You might as well have engaged an anti-terrorism unit. Guests were panicked and upset."

"I am truly sorry, monsieur. I contacted a friend who happens to work for the BRB, simply to ask about the painting I saw in Monsieur Breckman's suite. The BRB recognized the painting from my description and came over, hoping to recover it."

"And did they?" The manager's tone was mocking. "No, they did not. You discommoded a *highly valued guest*, failed to follow proper procedure, and caused an extreme amount of embarrassment not only to the company that owns the hotel but also to me. And you did all of this because of a reproduction!"

Acacia folded her hands. "Monsieur, I'm sorry for the inconvenience and will be more than happy to apologize to all the affected guests. But time was of the essence. I was worried the painting was genuine and that it would never be seen again."

"This isn't the first time you've caused a problem." He glared. "I've grown tired of your attitude and your insubordination. Go home. You will be paid for today's shift but starting tomorrow, you will work the night shift. I've decided to switch your schedule with François. He'll be working days from now on, in Marcel's absence."

Acacia gasped. "But I've always worked the day shift. You're demoting me?"

The manager smiled. "Of course not, that would be illegal. You will still be a concierge; you will simply be working the night shift. A formal reprimand will be forthcoming in writing. The next time you commit an infraction, you'll be dismissed."

"Dismissed?" Acacia moved forward. "Monsieur, you can't punish me for doing my civic duty."

"Perhaps not. But you can be reprimanded for not following procedures. I am the one who will decide whether to contact the authorities. Not you," he said with a huff. "In view of what's happened, you may wish to search for other employment. I understand your work permit is tied to your contract here?"

"Yes." Acacia swallowed. "Please, monsieur. This has been a misunderstanding."

"I understand precisely what's happening. Report for the night shift tomorrow evening." The manager opened a file on his desk and began to write in bold, angry script. "Go home."

Chapter Eleven

Acacia was so rattled by her conversation with Monsieur Roy that she agreed to spend the morning with Luc. He took her to Notre-Dame and walked with her around the great cathedral, a favorite pastime of theirs when they'd been a couple. He even accompanied her to the house of Héloïse and Abélard. Then he took her to lunch at one of her favorite cafés in the Latin Quarter.

He drove to her apartment building and accompanied her to the front door.

"I can stay," he offered. The light in his eyes shone unconcealed hope.

She shook her head. "I'm fine."

Slowly, oh, so slowly, he leaned forward, his hand cupping her cheek. "You're my biggest regret."

She grimaced. "Why would you regret me?"

"I regret that I didn't fight for us."

Acacia closed her eyes. She didn't want to have this conversation. She already felt raw from the day's events. Her job and possibly her residency permit were in jeopardy. She didn't want to add Luc to the mix.

He brushed the curve of her cheek and kissed her lightly.

Sadness and longing washed over her. She fought for control, not wanting him to see what she was feeling.

"Call me." He touched her cheek, waiting for her to open her eyes.

When she did, he gave her a small smile and walked to his Renault. He lifted his chin to his fellow BRB agent, who sat in an unmarked car nearby.

Luc climbed into his Renault and drove out of sight.

A lone tear streaked down Acacia's cheek. She'd done what she needed to do in the past. She wasn't going to second-guess herself. At least not today.

She touched her chest, willing the pain to subside. Then she unlocked the door to her building and began to climb the stairs.

Her thoughts turned to the day's events. With one act of civic duty, she'd practically ended her career. She could only hope Monsieur Roy's anger would wane and she would be able to work herself into his good graces once again.

Luc had been furious when she'd dragged him from the lobby and explained in hushed tones what had happened. He'd wanted to speak to Monsieur Roy himself, but Acacia had dissuaded him. She needed to fight her own battles. And she didn't want to lose the possibility of receiving a reference for future job applications.

I hope Monsieur Roy doesn't fire me.

She was so deep in thought she almost didn't hear the voice behind her.

"Mademoiselle."

Acacia startled and clutched at the metal railing of the staircase.

"Careful." Monsieur Breckman approached from several steps below. "You'll fall."

"Stop!" Acacia lifted her voice. "Don't come near me."

The man stopped, Rick at his side. He frowned. "There's no need to be alarmed."

Acacia retrieved her cell phone from her pocket. "Leave or I'll call the police. There's a BRB agent parked outside."

"Yes, I know. With an agent close by, you're perfectly safe." Monsieur Breckman turned to his bodyguard and addressed him in English. "Rick, wait downstairs, please."

The bodyguard moved, his gaze trained on her.

"I don't know how you got in without the agent seeing you." Acacia watched Rick's departure over the edge of the railing.

"Rick is very resourceful," Breckman said drily.

He cleared his throat. "I had hoped to speak to you at the hotel. When I checked out, they told me you'd been sent home."

Acacia waited until Rick was out of sight and turned her attention back to the former guest. "Were you hoping I'd be fired?"

"Of course not." The man inspected her features. "I hoped we'd have a chance to talk."

She bristled. "I'm not interested in talking to you. Why are you here?"

"I mean you no harm." His voice was gentle. "I'm sorry about what happened."

She clutched her cell phone, poised to dial. "I had you arrested and you're apologizing to me?"

"I wasn't arrested." The man sniffed. "I was merely interviewed."

"*Merely*." Acacia scoffed. "I was sent home and demoted to night concierge. Monsieur Roy is threatening to fire me."

"That's why I'm here." The man climbed a step. "I defended you."

Acacia made a derisive noise. "Why?"

"We had a misunderstanding." The man thrust his hand in the pocket of his coat. "I should have told you the painting was a reproduction. Still, you did what any decent person would do. I admire you for it."

"I don't believe you."

He gazed at her with admiration. "Your suspicious nature will serve you well."

Acacia retreated a step, still clutching her phone. "I want you to leave."

The man lifted his hands. "I'm leaving Paris, but before I go, I wanted to encourage you to fight your employer. Concierges are supposed to report illegal activity to the authorities. Roy knows that."

"I embarrassed him. He's already heard from the corporation that owns the hotel. They aren't happy."

"They'd be more unhappy if someone alerted the press to their hiring practices. You're the only visible minority in the entire hotel who has a rank above bartender."

Acacia pressed her lips together. "Why would anyone speak to the press about that?"

"Because *'injustice anywhere is a threat to justice everywhere.'*"

Acacia's eyebrows knitted together. "Your commitment to justice, if genuine, is admirable. It's still inappropriate and intimidating for you to appear at my building."

"I don't disagree. As I mentioned, I had hoped we'd speak at the hotel. But you were sent home." The man opened his trench coat and retrieved an envelope. He held it out to her.

"What is it?"

"Your gratuity."

"No, thank you."

The man opened the envelope and showed her the cash. "I thought I could smooth things over with Roy. I was wrong. He intends to fire you, even though he has no legal means of doing so. Use the money to hire a lawyer."

"If he fires me, it will be too late for lawyers. Concierge positions are difficult to get, especially in Paris."

"Then resign your post and use this until you can secure another position." The man extended the envelope once again.

"No." Her refusal was firm. "I don't want your money."

"It isn't my money," Breckman protested. "It's yours. You earned it."

"I won't accept it." Acacia ascended the stairs, cell phone in hand. She kept a watchful eye on the former guest.

The man lowered his arm. "I'm simply rewarding you the way I've always rewarded Marcel. Stop being stubborn."

"Stop following me." She began pressing numbers on her phone.

"Who are you calling? Your boyfriend from the BRB?" His tone dripped with disdain.

Acacia ignored him.

"Wait." Breckman paused a moment, then cursed. "The Paris police still haven't discovered who attacked Marcel. It's possible you're in danger."

Acacia lifted her head. "Why?"

Breckman shifted uneasily. "You're Marcel's replacement."

"I don't know anything about his activities. The only suspicious guest I've had to deal with is you."

A muscle jumped in the man's jaw. "If I wanted to hurt you, I wouldn't warn you in advance."

"No, you'd just accost me at my apartment and issue threats."

He placed the envelope on one of the steps. "I am a lot of things, mademoiselle, but I am not without honor. I'm not a thug, and I'm certainly not a thief." He gestured to the cash. "The money is yours."

Acacia's thumb hovered over the screen of her cell phone. "Take the money with you."

Breckman stood still. "Whether you believe me or not, I didn't mean for you to be demoted. Quite the opposite."

"Get out." Acacia completed her call and ran as fast as she could up the stairs. She glanced over her shoulder to see if the man followed her.

From below, she could hear quick footsteps and Breckman cursing.

She leaned over the railing and caught sight of the man and his bodyguard as they exited the ground floor hallway through the back entrance.

As her call connected to Luc, she burst into her apartment and bolted the door.

Chapter Twelve

"I agree. This is the best bridge in Paris." Kate grinned as she leaned over the railing on the Pont des Arts. Her long red hair twisted into a single braid that hung down her back. She wore a T-shirt and jeans, her feet clad in sandals.

Acacia surveyed the crowded bridge from behind her dark sunglasses. "But today there are too many people."

Kate groaned, still leaning over the edge. "Forget the padlocks, the lovers, and the tourists taking selfies. Just look at the Seine."

Acacia followed her gaze. The river flowed beneath them, dotted here and there with riverboats. Since the water was still too high, many of the boats approached the bridge slowly before turning around and sailing away.

"People come, people go. The river flows." Kate sighed. She rested her chin on her upturned hand.

Acacia removed her sunglasses. "Why so melancholy?"

The breeze blew a strand of red hair into Kate's mouth, and she pulled it free. "I'm homesick, but I can't go home. I have to earn some money, and I have to haunt the library, researching my thesis."

Acacia replaced her sunglasses. "I only go home at Christmas. Even then, Recife doesn't feel like home anymore. It's funny. I get homesick for Brazil, but every time I go back, it isn't like I remember it."

"Yeah, Boston is the same way. I just miss my mother and my brother." Kate turned and placed her back against the railing. She squinted in the bright sunlight. "How's the job search?"

"Not good." Acacia continued to look down at the Seine. "I've sent out applications, but only two of them were for concierge positions. I received rejection notices almost immediately."

"Why?"

She lifted a shoulder. "It could be because I haven't been at the Victoire very long. It could be because my manager is blackballing me."

"If he wanted to get rid of you, wouldn't he help you get another job?" Kate gave her an apologetic look. "No offense."

"I haven't earned his respect, so he won't vouch for me. His voice carries a lot of weight, and unfortunately, the hospitality world is surprisingly small."

"I'm so sorry." Kate gave her a pained look. "How's the night shift?"

"It's all right." Acacia closed her eyes behind her glasses, suddenly feeling tired. "Even though I wasn't the senior concierge, I always worked the day shift. Depending on the day or the time of year, sometimes I worked with other concierges and sometimes I worked alone."

Acacia opened her eyes. "The night shift concierge always works alone, and the workload is less, which means it's often boring—until it isn't. The requests I'm receiving from guests are rather…exotic. And I don't mean requests for tickets to Le Crazy Horse or Moulin Rouge."

She and Kate exchanged a look.

"I've been on nights for two weeks, and I still can't adjust. Sleeping in the day, working at night—I feel like a vampire."

"Is there such a thing as a Brazilian vampire?"

"Some of the most dangerous vampires are Brazilian." Acacia gave her a solemn look before laughing.

"What are you going to do?"

She joined Kate at the railing. "Hopefully, find another job before the manager fires me."

"I thought it was almost impossible to fire someone in France."

"It is, if the firing is done legally. In my case, the manager knows my work permit is tied to my job. I have to find another job in order to get another permit. That jeopardizes my residency in France, and it also puts me at a disadvantage with other employers. They'd have to apply for a permit for me."

"Isn't that what happened before?"

"Yes, but when I started at Le Méridien Étoile, I was on a student visa. They applied for a work permit for me just before I graduated. When the Victoire recruited me, they modified my existing work permit. I've never been between jobs here, and I've always had legal immigrant status."

"My brother is a lawyer in Boston. Do you want me to ask if his firm can recommend someone here?"

Acacia shook her head. "I'd likely be deported before I could pursue a lawsuit, and my manager knows it. He's just biding his time until he can give the personnel office a plausible reason to let me go, even if it isn't entirely legal."

Kate's green eyes sparked. "Won't the personnel office intervene?"

Acacia leaned over the railing. "I'm just the night concierge now. And not everyone is sympathetic to the plight of immigrants."

"That's ridiculous. We're all immigrants or descendants of immigrants. People act as if contemporary nation-states were handed down from heaven, borders intact." Kate gazed down at the river once again. "What about returning to the Sorbonne? You could switch to a student visa."

"I could, but I think I'd have to go back to Brazil while I applied. I'd have to give up my apartment." Acacia shook her head. "I love that apartment. I don't want to lose it."

"What about the hot BRB agent who's been dropping by? Can he help?"

"He's my ex."

Kate put a hand to her heart. "The hot BRB agent is your ex? Are you kidding?"

"We dated when we were students." Acacia focused on one of the tour boats that sailed beneath them.

"I can't believe you have an ex with that level of hotness." Kate pretended to fan herself. "Why are you exes? Is he a jerk?"

Acacia rubbed the toe of her shoe against the railing. "No. And yes, he's hot. But he's a BRB agent."

"I wouldn't want to date a cop, either. But when his hotness is enough to power the city of Paris, I think I'd make an exception. Holy cow."

Acacia stifled a laugh.

Kate shaded her eyes with her hand. "There's a story there, but we need lots of chocolate and a bottle of wine for me to pry it out of you." She rummaged in her pockets and withdrew a few Euro coins. "What's the cop's name?"

"Luc."

"Since he's your ex, I'll dub him Agent What-A-Shame, because again, that level of hotness should be illegal."

"I could introduce you," Acacia said quietly.

"Absolutely not. You're my friend." Kate closed her fingers over the coins and brought them to her mouth, blowing on them before muttering a few words in English. She threw them over the side of the bridge, where they barely missed a barge.

"You're going to get arrested." Acacia looked over her shoulder and scanned the bridge. "You aren't supposed to throw things into the Seine."

"No one noticed. If someone comes by, we're tourists and neither of us speaks French. Or perhaps we can ask Agent What-A-Shame to bail us out." Kate winked. "I just made a wish. I asked the river to help you."

Acacia fought a smile. "You think the Seine is going to find me another job?"

"Yes."

"You're thinking of the Trevi Fountain in Rome. You throw coins into it and make a wish."

"Fountain, river, whatever. I made a donation to the river gods and asked them to help. I'm pretty confident they'll do something, or they'll have to refund my money."

Acacia snickered. "I appreciate the thought."

"I'm here to help." Kate cupped her hands around her mouth. "Come on, Seine. Don't let me down."

Over the sound of Acacia's laughter, her cell phone rang.

She glanced at the screen. "I'm sorry, Kate, I should take this. It could be someone calling about a job."

Kate waved her off and continued to lean against the railing.

"Hello?" Acacia stepped a few meters away.

"Good afternoon," a mature female voice said. "May I speak with Acacia Santos, please?"

"This is she."

"This is Madame Bishop of KLH. We represent a number of corporations and assist them in finding exceptional employees."

The mere hint of hope caught in Acacia's throat. She moved the phone away from her mouth to cough quickly. "Yes, madame. May I ask how you got my name and number?"

"We are an executive search firm and have contacts in the hospitality industry. At the moment we are assisting a number of clients who are looking to hire persons with concierge experience. I understand you're currently employed as concierge at the Victoire?"

"Yes, madame."

"Would you be interested in interviewing with us? This isn't an offer of employment. But if your interview is successful, we can attempt to match you with a client company. Our client list includes multinational corporations as well as French companies, and they all offer generous remuneration and benefits packages."

Acacia shut her eyes tightly and tried to contain her excitement. "Yes, I'd like to interview. Thank you."

"Could you come in Friday afternoon, say at two o'clock?"

"Yes, I'm available then."

"Excellent. We are located in the financial district of La Défense. When you arrive, tell reception you have an appointment with me. I'll be expecting you promptly at two."

"Of course. Thank you, madame."

"In the interim, I'd suggest you look at our website and familiarize yourself with the guidelines for prospective employees. Please email my assistant a cover letter and your curriculum vitae, along with any supporting documents." Madame rattled off the email address of her administrative assistant.

"Yes, madame. Thank you again."

Acacia ended the call and tucked the cell phone under her chin. Her heart beat quickly, and she found herself smiling.

It wouldn't do to be excessively optimistic. A job in the corporate world would be different from one in hospitality. Still, it was too good an opportunity to turn down.

Acacia dug into the pockets of her jeans and withdrew a handful of coins. She crossed over to where Kate stood and surreptitiously dropped them into the river.

"What was that for?" Kate asked as she watched the Euros breach the surface of the water.

"I'm just showing my thanks to the river gods." Acacia lifted her hands into the air. "I think my luck has changed."

Chapter Thirteen

Despite her ray of hope, Acacia remained anxious.

She worried her identity would be leaked to the media in the aftermath of the BRB's descent on Hotel Victoire. She'd set up a Google alert for any mention of her name or, God forbid, a photograph. Dread filled her every time she checked her email.

She hadn't mentioned the situation to her mother, foregoing their weekly telephone calls in favor of emails. It was impossible to hide her anxiety over the telephone. If Acacia lost her job, she wouldn't be able to support her mother. But she didn't want to worry her unnecessarily.

By the time Friday arrived, Acacia was more than eager to quit the hotel. Monsieur Roy had recruited other staff to watch her, eagerly looking for any misstep or hint of customer dissatisfaction. Acacia knew it was only a matter of time before he found something he could manipulate into an infraction worthy of termination, which was why she'd delayed turning over Marcel's journal to the Paris police.

She'd researched KLH and found it to be a well-respected employment firm. She had no idea how she'd come to their attention, but she was grateful she had.

Acacia had to cut her sleep short on Friday in order to prepare for the interview. That morning, she took extra care with her appearance.

She was fortunate her tanned skin was clear and required little in the way of cosmetics. Her parents had gifted her with beauty and an attractive figure that wore clothes very well.

She had to remove her jacket and shoes when she went through security as she entered the building, a modern high rise in the financial district. Their setup rivaled that of the airport.

As she waited outside Madame Bishop's office, she carefully smoothed her black skirt. She wore a suit and her lapel pins, her hair and clothes intentionally conservative.

"Madame will see you now." The administrative assistant approached Acacia and ushered her into a large corner office that featured floor-to-ceiling windows.

A diminutive woman with black hair pulled into a severe bun at her nape and oversized, red-framed glasses rose behind the desk.

"Mademoiselle." She extended her hand.

Acacia shook it and took the seat that was offered to her.

Madame Bishop returned to her seat and retrieved a file. "I've reviewed your curriculum vitae, mademoiselle, and I've spoken with the Paris branch of Les Clefs d'Or. They noted that you received several commendations during your tenure at Le Méridien Étoile."

"Yes, madame."

She gazed at Acacia from across the desk. "Some of our clients are looking for more than just an experienced executive assistant. I know the tradition of the concierge is tied to the hotel industry, but we've been successful in recruiting talented concierges to work in the corporate sector. For example, we recruited one of the junior concierges at the Shangri-La Hotel to serve as the personal concierge for the CEO of a major technology firm. Both our client and the concierge are happy with the arrangement. Would you be interested in becoming a personal concierge?"

Acacia hesitated, but only for a moment. "Yes, madame. I believe the skills I have are transferable to assisting an individual client."

Madame Bishop opened the file and uncapped a pen. She made a few notes. "It's possible the position would require travel. What would you do to ensure you maintain a consistently high level of service outside Paris?"

"In both of my positions I've worked with concierges from hotels in other countries to assist guests, so I already have an international network. I'd be more than happy to cultivate that network. I believe my facility with languages is also an asset."

"Have you traveled much?"

Acacia shook her head but forced a smile. "No, madame. But I'm enthusiastic about the possibility. I enjoy learning about other cultures."

"According to your paperwork, your citizenship is Brazilian, and you are on a work permit tied to your position at the Victoire. Why do you want to leave?" Madame's blue eyes grew razor sharp.

Acacia thought very quickly, maintaining her smile. "The Victoire is an excellent hotel. But the senior concierge is firmly entrenched, and for the time being, there isn't room for promotion. I'm eager to expand my experience so I may apply for senior concierge positions someday."

"So you wouldn't see yourself as a personal concierge in the long term?"

"That would depend on the position."

"I see." The woman gazed at her sharply. "Do you possess any other talents that aren't listed in your curriculum vitae?"

"I enjoy sports and try to stay physically fit. I studied art history."

"Anything else?" Madame persisted.

Acacia developed the impression that Madame Bishop was expecting something in particular, but Acacia didn't know what it could be.

"I think that's all." Acacia forced another smile.

"As with any prospective employee, we have to conduct a background check. Also, we would need you to sign a non-disclosure agreement. Our clients expect confidentiality with respect to any information you might glean while in their employ, even with regard to the interview process."

Acacia's smile didn't falter. "As a concierge, I'm committed to confidentiality."

"Excellent." Madame produced several pages that were stapled together. "Please take a few moments to review this agreement. If you accept it, please sign and date at the bottom.

"May I see your passport? I'll ask my assistant to make a photocopy."

Acacia retrieved her Brazilian passport and work permit from her briefcase and handed them over.

The woman excused herself and exited the office, leaving Acacia to read the form.

The non-disclosure agreement appeared to be fairly standard, although she noted that the form expected her to keep confidential the names and identities of any potential employers she might encounter. She read the agreement twice and signed and dated it.

In the end, Acacia wasn't sure how the interview had gone. Certainly it was very different from other interviews she'd had.

She knew a search of her passport or fingerprints would find nothing damning. Even if KLH somehow pulled her birth certificate from Brazil, there wouldn't be a problem. Still, she lived with the fear that someday someone would discover who she really was and *he* would find her.

The office door opened and madame returned.

"Did you sign the form?" She returned Acacia's passport and work permit.

"Yes." Acacia placed the signed agreement on the woman's desk.

"Good. One of our clients is in the office today and has expressed an interest in meeting you. Would you object to a second interview?"

Acacia turned in her chair. "Not at all."

"This way, please." Madame waited for Acacia to pack up her briefcase and escorted her down the hall to what was labeled a conference room.

She opened the door. "Monsieur Nicholas Cassirer, I'd like you to meet Mademoiselle Acacia Santos of Hotel Victoire. Mademoiselle, Monsieur Cassirer has a few questions for you."

Madame guided Acacia into the conference room. "You can ring my assistant when you're finished, monsieur."

"Thank you." A deep voice spoke from the other end of the conference room.

Madame closed the door.

"Bonjour, monsieur." Acacia greeted the broad back of a tall man who stood at one of the windows, gazing at the financial district with his hands in his pockets.

"Bonjour, mademoiselle." He turned.

Acacia placed a hand over her mouth as she realized the man who stood in front of her was none other than Monsieur Breckman.

Chapter Fourteen

Acacia retreated and put her hand on the door handle.

"All I ask is a moment of your time." Monsieur Breckman remained by the windows.

"You're stalking me." She cast him an accusatory look.

"Far from it." He gestured to a chair, but Acacia refused to take it.

"Who are you?"

"Nicholas Cassirer." He stepped toward her and extended his hand.

She spurned it.

"We've gotten off on the wrong foot." He lowered his voice. "I regret this."

"You changed your name. And your appearance." She gestured to his face, which was now bearded. His scar had been covered, presumably with some kind of prosthetic that blended into his beard. His dark hair was combed differently.

"I'm still scarred." He gazed at her coolly. "I just choose to cover it on occasion."

Acacia had to fight the urge to touch her temple, where the skin was marred but hidden. "Why the name change?"

"I'll explain in a moment. I've made several missteps, which I mean to correct. The gratuity was not intended as a bribe, but rather a reward for excellent service."

"Wrongs can't be rectified by money."

"I agree." Nicholas's tone was sincere. "I'm not here to give you your gratuity. I'm here to offer an explanation."

He gestured to one of the chairs again.

"Thank you, I prefer to stand."

"Very well." He placed his hands in his pockets once again. "My family owns a number of different corporations. I'm involved with their oversight. A few years ago I began devoting much of my time to the recovery of stolen art."

Acacia's gaze sharpened.

Nicholas smiled. "I knew that would pique your curiosity. Because of the nature of the black market, I assume different identities. I have the support of several governments and sometimes travel on diplomatic passports."

"Why would a government support you?"

"My goal is to return stolen art to its rightful owners. National governments view me as an ally."

Acacia looked at him curiously. "Are you a spy?"

Nicholas's dark eyes twinkled. "I inhabit the corporate world, while dabbling in black market art and antiquities." He extended his arms. "Think of me as Robin Hood in a suit."

"There was a theft at the Uffizi in Florence a few years ago; someone stole a collection of illustrations of Dante's *The Divine Comedy*. Later on, they were recovered. Was that you?"

"No." He lowered his arms. "But you heard about that."

"It was all over the news."

"I know the Emersons, the present owner and his wife, because my family sold them the illustrations. But I was not the Robin Hood who returned them."

"Robin Hood was captured by the Sheriff of Nottingham."

"I have powerful friends who assist me in evading capture."

She squinted at him. "Is that why the BRB released you?"

"They released me because I was on the trail of a stolen painting. I was undercover, which is why I couldn't explain myself to you. Marcel was the intermediary between an art dealer and me. Unfortunately, he was attacked before he could give me the location of the meeting or the name of the dealer."

"I didn't know Marcel had those kinds of connections."

"Probably because those connections run through the black market." Nicholas took a step closer. "A couple of years ago, I expressed interest in an artifact I knew was illegal to acquire. At first, Marcel refused. Later, he said he might have a source that could help me. I've been using Marcel ever since."

"Did you ask him for a relic?"

Nicholas chuckled. "No."

Acacia waited, expecting him to expand on his answer. But he didn't.

She clutched her briefcase. "Marcel is still in a coma."

"I've been trying to discover who attacked him. You should know, mademoiselle, Marcel has been procuring illegal goods and services for his clients for years. I'm convinced Monsieur Roy has some awareness of these activities and probably takes a commission. His animosity toward you suggests he sees you as a threat."

"I'm not a threat to anyone."

Nicholas gave her a pointed look. "You're a person of integrity who has a friend in the BRB. Roy doesn't want their scrutiny. He has to get rid of you or risk exposure."

Acacia's shoulders slumped. "Then there's nothing I can do to keep my job."

Nicholas guided her to a chair, and she finally sat down. He walked over to the conference table and lifted a bottle of sparkling water. He poured some into a glass and presented it to her.

"Thank you." She sipped, her mind racing. "I didn't know about any of this."

"I thought as much."

"If law enforcement ever investigated the Victoire and made arrests, my reputation would be tarnished. No other hotel would want to hire me."

"That's why I'm here."

Acacia tasted the water again. "I don't need rescuing."

Nicholas's expression tightened. He pulled up a chair and sat facing her.

"My executive assistant is unable to travel. I need someone who can accompany me on business trips and help with local arrangements. I also need an interpreter."

"I'm sure there are many potential executive assistants who could fill the position."

"I don't want them. I want you."

Acacia arched an eyebrow.

Nicholas leaned forward and rested his forearms on his knees. "You have concierge experience, fluency in several languages, and a background in art."

"Why not contact me directly rather than using Madame Bishop to lure me out here?"

Nicholas stiffened. "There's no *luring*. KLH is a respected employment firm. I asked Madame Bishop to mediate our contract because I wanted to be open and above-board. She will ensure there's a paper trail, and she can assist you in contacting my references."

"Who are your references?"

"The Minister of the Interior, for one."

Acacia restrained a laugh. "The Minister of the Interior would vouch for you?"

"Yes." His dark eyes focused on hers. "In one of our conversations you mentioned the theft of a Degas while it was on loan in Marseilles. You're probably aware the painting was recovered."

Acacia nodded.

Nicholas smiled. "I was involved in the recovery.

"I can offer you a contract through one of my Paris offices. You'll receive an excellent salary and benefits, which Madame Bishop will outline. The contract would only be for one year. After that, my current executive assistant should be able to travel."

"If I leave the Victoire, I lose my work permit."

"As I said, the Minister of the Interior is a friend. I can secure a temporary work permit for you and apply for an EU blue card."

"An EU blue card?" Acacia couldn't keep the longing out of her voice.

"Yes. Usually EU blue cards can only be secured after a year, but given my connections, we'll try to fast track it. Once you have a blue card, you'll be able to live and work in the European Union indefinitely. KLH can act as your reference and help you find work as a concierge after your contract with me is complete."

"This is all very generous, but I still don't understand why you're offering me a job. We had very little contact at the hotel and much of it was unpleasant."

"I apologize for my unpleasantness." Nicholas's eyes took on a new intensity. "Even in the face of such challenges, you manifested several qualities I admire."

"Such as?"

"Honesty. Integrity. Civic duty."

Acacia was tempted to offer sarcasm, but Monsieur Cassirer's expression was earnest. "You made at least two outrageous demands at the hotel. A bespoke suit in a matter of hours? A relic? I'm not keen to work for a person who treats his staff in that way."

Nicholas's dark eyes narrowed. "I wasn't sure I could trust you."

"Those tasks were a test?" Acacia lifted her voice.

"In my life, I've known precious few people I can trust. Given Marcel's activities, it was highly likely you were also involved. I had to know for certain."

Acacia stood, hands shaking, and placed her empty water glass on the table. "I don't appreciate being a test subject."

"I would feel the same way. But you called the BRB." He smiled. "I was impressed."

She scowled. "Is that why you threatened me when I mentioned the meeting Marcel was setting up? Because you found me impressive?"

Nicholas's smile fled. He stood. "I was worried you'd get hurt."

"So far only two people have threatened me: you and Monsieur Roy."

"Roy is a snake." Nicholas made a fist with his right hand. "You're a person of integrity in a workplace surrounded by vipers. I'm offering you a way out. Further, I'm offering you an opportunity to work with me to restore stolen art to the great galleries of Europe. It's a tremendous opportunity."

"What if I don't like working for you?"

"Then quit. This isn't indentured servitude, mademoiselle. You can quit at any time, provided you give adequate notice. But I believe we will work well together. Certainly, working for me will be more secure than working at the hotel."

"Wouldn't I just be leaping from the frying pan into the fire? I'm still not sure who you really are, Monsieur Cassirer, assuming that's your real name. And your work is dangerous."

"I don't take unnecessary risks, and I'm not a thief. Money usually exchanges hands in these transactions, which is why I've been successful. I have excellent security, which would protect you as well."

Acacia remained unconvinced.

Nicholas studied her features. "There's risk in everything, Acacia. Right now, you are in a position to choose what happens to you before someone like Roy takes that choice out of your hands."

Acacia picked up her briefcase. "Thank you for your offer, but I cannot accept it."

Nicholas placed his hands on his waist, flaring out his suit jacket. "You'd prefer to stay at the Victoire than work for me?"

"You tested me for your own amusement, and as a result of that test, I've been demoted and my career is in jeopardy. I need to find another job as soon as possible, hopefully one where my employer doesn't treat his employees as lab rats."

Something flared in his eyes. He was silent for a moment. "I should remind you that you've signed a confidentiality agreement, which means you aren't to speak about anything we've discussed."

"I understand." Acacia retrieved her briefcase. "Goodbye."

Nicholas didn't reply.

Acacia felt his eyes on her as she walked to the door.

Chapter Fifteen

I t was a quiet evening on the night shift.

Acacia attended to her list of tasks and made notes for the daytime concierge. Then she sat at her desk, deep in thought.

Madame Bishop had been surprised when Acacia declined Monsieur Cassirer's job offer. She'd mentioned the salary and the prestige attached to becoming his executive assistant.

Diplomatically, Acacia had said she wasn't a good fit. Madame Bishop made no secret of the fact she thought Acacia was being foolish, but she accepted her decision.

Sitting at her desk in the empty lobby of Hotel Victoire, Acacia wondered if Monsieur Cassirer's new identity was itself a fiction. It was possible Madame Bishop was colluding with him to deceive her. Perhaps he was still angry over his arrest and fixated on revenge.

Acacia decided to Google him.

Googling Nicholas Cassirer provided very different results than when she'd searched for Pierre Breckman. There were pages and pages of entries on Nicholas, centering on his family and their vast financial empire. The Cassirers were involved in a variety of charitable and philanthropic endeavors.

Acacia found several photographs of a youthful, unscarred Nicholas at black tie functions, including a few images of him with a petite blond woman who was identified as his girlfriend. In more recent photographs, the blond was absent and his face was bearded, his scar concealed.

Acacia puzzled over Nicholas's choice to appear unshaven and scarred while assuming the identity of Pierre Breckman. From what he'd said during their encounter at KLH, the scar was genuine. He seemed to have gone to great lengths to hide it while appearing in public as Nicholas Cassirer.

She clicked on a news item from 2007. The article made reference to the theft of several works of art from the Cassirer Foundation Museum in Cologny, Switzerland. Scanning the story, Acacia focused on three lines:

"The curator of the museum, Mlle. Riva Cassirer, was attacked during the robbery and died as a result of her injuries. Mlle. Cassirer's great-grandfather, Édouard J. Cassirer, founded the museum. She is survived by her parents, Armand and Hélène, and her brother, Nicholas."

Acacia stared in mounting horror. *Nicholas's sister was murdered.*

The photograph that accompanied the news story showed a young, smiling red-haired woman with warm, brown eyes. The article referenced her education at the Sorbonne, as well as her devotion to public art education and the use of art therapy. She'd founded a number of scholarships and had opened the doors of the museum to children for several programs.

In that moment, Nicholas's quest to recover stolen art took on new meaning. Art theft was a crime that almost never involved violence. The murder of Riva Cassirer was shocking, her life and good works snuffed out.

Acacia searched the internet for more information, but a recent article in a Geneva newspaper confirmed that the stolen items, which included a Degas and a Monet, had never been recovered. Riva's murder remained unsolved.

Acacia closed her laptop. Now that she'd seen the smiling face of Riva Cassirer and learned of her tragic death, the image would haunt her. How much more did Riva's death haunt the Cassirers.

Nicholas's work had to be propelled by the loss of his sister. Perhaps he viewed his activities as a tribute to her, or at the very least, an attempt to right one of the wrongs that had been done to his family. Acacia wondered how far he'd go in his quest. In any case, he probably gave little thought to exacting revenge against her. He had a far more important, far more dangerous mission.

Her meeting with Monsieur Cassirer had been a revelation. Not only did she learn his true name, she'd learned the truth about what was going on behind the scenes at Hotel Victoire.

Marcel had arranged a meeting that, according to Nicholas, was related to a stolen painting. Then Marcel had been viciously attacked. Acacia wasn't an expert on crime, but it was clear that both the attack on Marcel and the attack on Nicholas's sister were atypical in the art world. Nicholas was the common link to both crimes.

Acacia reflected on his overreaction to her mention of the meeting Marcel had set up. She could accord Nicholas some compassion, given the loss he'd suffered. No wonder he traveled with such an extensive security detail. No wonder he'd been so persistent she quit the hotel.

When Acacia's shift ended the following morning, she was still thinking about Riva Cassirer and her brother. She changed into jeans and motorcycle boots and exited through the service entrance at the back of the hotel.

It was after seven in the morning, and the sun had already risen. She'd parked her motorcycle illegally behind one of the dumpsters, having persuaded hotel security to turn a blind eye. Nicholas had warned her to be cautious when traveling to and from the hotel, but his warnings were superfluous. She didn't want to end up like Marcel and would do anything in her power to avoid it.

Acacia hadn't told Luc about her interview with Monsieur Cassirer, but he'd continued to provide her with BRB surveillance when she traveled to and from the hotel. As she walked toward the dumpsters, she looked for the unmarked car that had been parked in the alley when she arrived at work that evening.

The car was gone.

She looked toward the street, hoping to see the previous car's replacement. But the alley and what she could see of the street were empty.

She stopped, puzzled.

Without warning, someone grabbed her from behind. A hand gripped her throat while the other tightened across her abdomen.

Acacia tensed as her worst fears were realized.

"Where's the book?" the man whispered in French.

Relief flowed through her at the sound of the familiar language. He was not who she feared he was.

Acacia dropped her backpack and helmet and dug her elbow into the man's side. She plowed into his kneecap with her foot and scraped the sole of her boot down his shin before stomping on his toes. He released her, howling curses in a language she did not understand.

Acacia whirled around and punched the man in the throat.

He dropped to his knees and clutched his neck.

"Get on your bike and get the hell out of here!" a voice shouted in English.

Acacia turned and saw Rick, Nicholas's bodyguard, running toward her. Ahead of him by a few strides was another man, large and powerfully built.

Acacia gaped at Rick, then grabbed her backpack and hopped on her motorcycle. She kept her eyes trained on the two men as she switched on the vehicle.

Rick tackled the man from behind before he reached Acacia.

With a rev of the engine, she piloted the motorcycle around the dumpsters. She raced onto the street and wove in and out of traffic as adrenaline flooded her system.

She was halfway home when she realized she'd left her helmet behind.

Chapter Sixteen

Acacia parked her motorcycle in front of her building and ran inside; she climbed the steps to her flat as if the Devil himself were chasing her. Inside her jacket, her cell phone rang.

She ignored it.

Once she was locked safely in her apartment, she sank to the floor, her body shaking. She covered her chest with her hand and took a deep breath, willing her heart to slow.

No one had followed her from the hotel to her apartment. No unmarked car sat downstairs in view of the front door to her building. She was completely unprotected.

Claude meowed his greeting and rubbed his ear against the side of her leg. She kissed the cat's head and pulled him into her lap.

When her cell phone rang again with an unknown number, she hoped it was Luc. "Hello?"

Acacia could hear movement on the other end of the line — the echoing of footsteps and then a low, gravelly voice. "Rick called. Where are you?"

Acacia's heart quickened. "How did you get this number?"

"You listed it on your curriculum vitae. Are you hurt?" Nicholas's tone was clipped.

"No."

"Good." He let out a loud exhalation. "Rick failed. No one should have gotten close enough to touch you. He said you handled yourself well, however."

"What was Rick doing outside the hotel?"

"I asked him to keep an eye on you when the BRB pulled their surveillance."

"They pulled their surveillance? No one told me."

"Probably because the person doing the surveillance was paid off."

"Why?" Acacia breathed.

The man paused. "You know why."

Acacia shut her eyes. "Did you set this up? Is this some kind of game?"

"I'm not a thug, mademoiselle," Nicholas snapped.

Acacia placed Claude on the floor, stood, and double-checked the locks on her door. She peered through the viewer. The hall was empty.

"Thank you for your concern, but I'm fine. Goodbye."

"Wait!"

The footsteps that had sounded in her ear ceased, and Acacia heard a muffled sound, as if Nicholas was covering his phone with his hand.

A few seconds later, he returned. "You aren't safe in your apartment. The man who attacked you may have followed you there. Rick is on his way."

Acacia looked through the viewer again. "You think they'll come here?"

"One of your assailants escaped. If he knows your work schedule, he probably knows where you live."

"What do they want?"

Nicholas's voice grew soft. "They want to solve a problem. I'm sorry to say it, but you appear to be that problem.

"Rick expected hotel security to intervene because they have cameras covering the back of the hotel. No one appeared, and no one called the police. The man Rick wrestled with had a gun."

"They had guns?" Acacia slumped against the door.

"Yes."

She made a noise in her throat. "I spoke to one of the security guards before I started my shift. He let me park my motorcycle behind the dumpsters, even though it's against the rules."

"Precisely."

"He told them." She placed her hand on her forehead. "He told them where I parked and then sat back and watched."

"You have to leave Paris." Nicholas's tone grew urgent. "Rick will escort you to the airport, and one of my men will accompany you to Geneva. You'll be safe there."

"Is this what happened to Marcel? Hotel security told someone when Marcel was off duty and where his motorcycle was parked?"

"I don't know." Nicholas breathed a heavy sigh. "It's possible."

"If I go to work tonight, I'll end up like Marcel." She tugged at her hair. "If I don't go, I'll lose my job and my work permit."

Monsieur Cassirer made an exasperated noise. "I can put a security detail on you, but Roy will ban them from the hotel, and you'll be unprotected. They underestimated you this morning; they won't repeat that mistake."

"You want to help me get out of Paris?"

"Yes."

"Why?"

Nicholas lowered his voice. "I don't want your blood on my conscience."

Acacia felt a chill travel down her spine as she remembered what had happened to Riva Cassirer.

She heard footsteps through the telephone. There was a pause and they began again. Nicholas was pacing.

"The hotel isn't safe. If security saw Rick this morning, they'll discover his connection with Pierre Breckman. Whoever is looking for you will start looking for me. I'm not waiting until I'm found."

"You think they'll come after you?"

"I'm not sure what they want. But if you quit the hotel, they may wash their hands of you."

It's the journal, Acacia thought. *There's only one book these men would want, and that's Marcel's journal. The security cameras in the lobby must have caught me retrieving it.*

Acacia didn't share her realization with Nicholas. She listened to his pacing and his agitated breathing. He wasn't giving up.

Claude looked up at her and meowed.

"What's that?" Nicholas almost barked.

"That's my cat."

"She has a cat," he murmured. "Of course she does."

He cleared his throat. "You can take your chances at the hotel, but since you can't rely on their security, you'll be at risk. You can go to the police, but again, it will only be a matter of time before the persons who are after you elude the police. It's possible they've already paid off the BRB."

Acacia picked up Claude. "If you're worried they'll come after you, then we have a common enemy."

"All the more reason for us to work together."

Acacia buried her face in Claude's fur.

Fatigue began to overtake her as the adrenaline in her system waned. She could call Luc, but he'd involve the BRB. At this point, she couldn't trust them. They'd left her unprotected precisely at the moment she'd been attacked.

An ugly memory flashed through her mind. Acacia remembered a previous attack that had almost been successful. She'd escaped and fled Rio for Recife.

Paris was supposed to be safe.

If she wanted to continue living and working in France, she had to avoid both her attackers and the police. Remaining at Hotel Victoire and involving Luc would jeopardize that. And there was the small matter that she still had Marcel's journal. She could be charged with obstruction and possibly sent back to Brazil.

The enemy of my enemy is my ally, she thought. *At least for now.*

"All right." She shut her eyes in resignation.

The sound of Nicholas's pacing ceased. "Rick will arrive at your apartment shortly. I'll meet you in Geneva. Call me if there's trouble."

"Fine." Acacia was angry. She didn't like feeling powerless.

"And Acacia," Nicholas's tone was grave, "remove everything you value from your apartment. If they decide to look for you there, they won't be gentle."

She whispered her acquiescence and ended the call.

Claude meowed at her again. She hugged him tightly.

What have I done?

Chapter Seventeen

A short time later, Acacia knocked on Kate's door, with Rick at her side. He looked slightly the worse for wear, with cuts and abrasions on his hands and face. He wore dark sunglasses and an earpiece and had appeared at Acacia's door holding her motorcycle helmet.

With the exception of Claude and his things, Acacia had packed everything she valued into a rolling suitcase and a briefcase, including Marcel's journal. Claude meowed in protest from behind the walls of his carrier, scratching at the sides.

Kate opened the door to her flat wearing only a bathrobe. She rubbed her eyes. "What time is it?"

"Early. I need a favor." Acacia addressed Kate in French, partially because she'd only heard Rick speak English and hoped his French was poor.

"Whoa." Kate started and took a step back as she caught sight of Rick. "What's that?"

Acacia addressed the large man in English. "I need a minute."

He grunted. "You aren't out of my sight."

"Fine. I'm not talking in the hallway." Acacia pushed past him and entered Kate's apartment. He followed and closed the door.

Kate gave Rick a dirty look. "Who's the giant?" she whispered in French.

Acacia turned her back to Rick. "He's a security guard. There was an incident at the hotel. I'm leaving the city for a few days."

Kate looked horrified. "What happened?"

"Someone jumped me." Acacia gestured over her shoulder toward Rick. "He's a private security guard for one of the guests, and he came to help me. Security at the hotel ignored the incident, so I'm not going back to work. Can you look after Claude for me?"

Kate examined Acacia more closely. "Someone jumped you? Are you okay?"

"Just a few bruises." Acacia placed the cat carrier on the floor. "I'm sorry, Kate. I don't have a lot of time. Can you take care of Claude while I'm gone?"

Kate looked down at the cat carrier. "Of course." She blinked in confusion. "Why would hotel security ignore you? Did you call the police?"

"Something is going on at the hotel." Acacia handed Kate a shopping bag that contained cat food and toys. "I'm going away until I figure out what to do next."

Kate put the bag aside and faced her friend. "This is ridiculous. You need to call Luc."

Acacia shook her head. She glanced over at Rick, who scowled. "I have to go. We're on our way to the airport."

Kate took Acacia's hand. "Give me Luc's number. I'll call him."

"I'll contact Luc after I leave the city." Acacia's tone was firm. "I'll text you."

"Just blink if you're doing this against your will," Kate whispered.

Acacia stared back at her.

"Okay." Kate narrowed her eyes at Rick. "I'd better hear from you every day, or I'm tracking Luc down."

"If you don't hear from me, tell Luc to speak to Madame Bishop at KLH. It's the firm I interviewed with the other day." Acacia glanced over her shoulder, toward the door that led into the hall. "The men who came after me may come here. Be careful going in and out of the building. Please keep Claude with you."

"I will." Kate's gaze moved to Rick again. "I hope you know what you're doing."

"We have to go," Rick announced. He walked toward the door.

Acacia hugged her friend and took a moment to say goodbye to Claude before she exited the apartment with her luggage.

Chapter Eighteen

Acacia wasn't foolish; she knew she was taking a risk.

On the way to the airport, she texted Nicholas's name and alias to Kate, along with a short explanation about KLH and Madame Bishop. Acacia also forwarded Luc's number, asking Kate to alert him if for some reason she didn't maintain contact.

Kate responded immediately:

Okay. Be careful.

No sooner had Acacia read Kate's text when another text arrived, from Luc:

Where are you?

Acacia sat back in her seat. Obviously, whoever was supposed to be protecting her that morning at the hotel had checked in with Luc, saying he'd lost her. Although she was confident Luc wouldn't hurt her, she didn't trust his colleagues.

She ignored the text.

A few minutes later, when Luc called, she let the call go to voicemail.

Acacia wasn't entirely confident she was making the right decision. But Rick had come to her aid, as had Nicholas. If they meant her harm, they'd gone to an extraordinary amount of trouble to do so. On her analysis, they were the lesser of two evils—the greater evil being the risk of returning to the hotel.

Rick escorted her inside Charles de Gaulle Airport where he introduced her to Kurt, one of his associates.

When she queried Rick as to why he was staying in Paris, he muttered something about working. Acacia hoped that meant he was on the heels of the men who'd attacked her.

Acacia and Kurt flew business class on Air France to Geneva—a very short flight—and were then met at the gate by another security guard and an airport agent. They were whisked through customs and accompanied outside the Geneva airport to a waiting limousine.

Kurt held the door open for Acacia. She climbed in.

"Good morning." Monsieur Cassirer's smooth voice greeted her.

She startled.

Kurt slipped around her and sat opposite his employer, leaving Acacia to sit near Nicholas.

Monsieur Cassirer was dressed in one of his ubiquitous black suits. His purple tie hung loose around his neck, just a shade darker than the purple of his dress shirt. His hair was carefully combed and he was clean-shaven, his scar miraculously invisible.

Acacia lowered her gaze to her seatbelt. She pondered his disappearing scar and wondered why he'd worn it as Pierre Breckman but covered it every other time she'd encountered him.

"I trust your flight was comfortable."

"Yes. Thank you."

Nicholas handed her a bottle of sparkling water. "You look tired."

Acacia took the bottle gratefully. "I am."

She was too exhausted to reflect on her denim jacket and white pants, or the state of her hair. She'd worked the night shift at the hotel before the terrifying events of that morning. On the short flight from Paris to Geneva, she'd only been able to sleep for a few minutes.

She opened the bottle and sipped, her gaze drawn to the landscape outside the car. "Where are you taking me?"

"Just a moment." Nicholas lifted his hand as the driver pulled out of the airport and onto a small side road.

The driver pulled the car to the shoulder and parked behind a small, black van. The door to the van opened, and an Asian man exited the vehicle.

"What's going on?" Acacia asked.

"It's all right." Nicholas spoke in a soothing tone. "He's part of my security detail. He's going to sweep you for surveillance devices."

Acacia's mouth dropped open. "Is that necessary?"

Nicholas wore a grave expression. "It's for your safety, as well as mine."

Acacia thought back to the events at the Victoire earlier that morning. She certainly didn't want to see her assailants again.

"All right." She squared her shoulders and followed Kurt and Nicholas out of the limousine.

The Asian man appeared to be in his late twenties. He was slender, with dark hair and dark eyes. In his hands, he held a silver briefcase and what looked like a portable metal detector.

He smiled at Acacia. "Hi there," he greeted her in English. "This will just take a minute."

Acacia stood still as the young man meticulously scanned her with the wand. Then he repeated the procedure on Kurt and Nicholas.

Acacia stared at the man, wide-eyed.

When he was finished, he nodded at Nicholas and hopped back into the van.

Nicholas piloted Acacia into the limousine. "That was Wen. He's part of my security team. He's already scanned in here, so we can talk now."

"I don't recall you scanning me for bugs before I met you at Madame Bishop's office."

Nicholas smiled patiently. "Don't you recall going through security when you entered the building?"

Acacia blinked. "What about at the Victoire? No one scanned me there."

"My advance team scanned the suite before I arrived, and they continued doing so as people came and went." Nicholas gazed over at her thoughtfully. "You weren't bugged."

Acacia straightened. "I didn't know you had an advance team when you stayed at the Victoire."

"Hotel security was aware of it, and so was your manager." Nicholas's lip curled at his mention of Acacia's former supervisor. "I didn't have you scanned individually because I was concerned you'd spread information about my anti-surveillance practices."

Acacia frowned. "Did your team ever find anything?"

"Always. On my last visit, there were six devices in the penthouse suite."

Acacia took a drink from her water bottle. "Why would someone want to listen in on your conversations?"

"It wasn't limited to audio. Some of the devices recorded video as well. Interested parties might be looking for blackmail material, as well as information about my business dealings."

"Who would do that?"

He shrugged. "We all have our enemies."

Acacia muttered a low curse. "Now that we've been de-bugged, where are you taking me?"

"My parents' house. My team is investigating the men who attacked you. I hope to discover who they're working for soon."

"Your parents?" Acacia swung her head to face him.

Nicholas broke eye contact and looked straight ahead. "They aren't at home. They spend most of their time abroad."

"Do they live near the airport?"

"They have a house in Cologny, which has a full staff and excellent security."

She exhaled. "You don't even know me."

"I take responsibility for my actions, mademoiselle. You're in danger because of me." Nicholas set his jaw. "I may not enjoy the view, but at least I can look at myself in the mirror."

Acacia examined his profile. "How did it happen?"

He ignored her question.

She couldn't fault him. Whatever had caused his scar had surely been traumatic.

She decided to change the subject. "How long will it take to find out who attacked me?"

"Not long. I have my suspicions; I just need confirmation."

"And what are your suspicions?"

"Organized crime. They're probably running things through the hotel, using Marcel and Monsieur Roy. It's possible the attack behind the hotel was designed simply to frighten you. But given what happened to Marcel..." Nicholas's voice trailed off.

"They're expending a great deal of effort to get rid of me. Seems a disproportionate response."

"Are you familiar with the iceberg principle?"

She shook her head.

"When you see an iceberg, you're only seeing one-tenth of it. The rest of the iceberg lurks below the surface. We're only seeing ten percent of what's going on at the hotel."

Acacia shivered. "I have to tell Monsieur Roy I'm not coming to work tonight."

"There's wireless at the house. What will you say?"

"I don't know. I'm not in a hurry to quit, but for the sake of my reputation I'd rather not be fired." She smoothed a crease from the front of her white jeans. "I suppose I could claim to be ill."

"Seems like a good idea." Nicholas gazed at her thoughtfully. "Apart from me, did you have any peculiar exchanges with other guests?"

Acacia shook her head. "No, nothing unusual."

"None of the other employees approached you with anything suspicious?"

"No. That's why this is so strange."

Nicholas looked beyond Acacia and out her window. "We're almost there."

A few minutes later, they pulled up to a set of iron gates. The driver spoke briefly with a security guard, and the gate opened.

They drove down a long, winding road and approached an elegant three-story stone mansion with gabled windows and a tiled roof. Next to it stood a two-story carriage house with large, circular windows on both levels.

From the car, Acacia could see the grounds were impeccably landscaped, with grass, manicured hedges, and carefully tended rose bushes and potted flowers.

The driver parked the limousine at the front entrance and opened Acacia's door. He retrieved her luggage from the trunk and followed as Nicholas escorted her toward the front door.

A mature woman dressed in a green suit waited just inside the entryway. She had lively blue eyes and gray hair, which fell in straight locks to her chin.

"Good morning, Juliet," Nicholas greeted her in French. He kissed her on both cheeks. "It's been a long time."

"Too long." The woman pressed his hand between hers.

Nicholas stepped back. "This is Mademoiselle Santos. She'll be staying for a few days. Acacia, this is Juliet. She's been the housekeeper since I was a child."

"Welcome, mademoiselle." Juliet bobbed her head.

"Thank you, Juliet." Acacia returned her smile and tried not to gawk.

The entranceway opened into an expansive hall with hardwood floors covered by Persian rugs. The wood-paneled walls were hung with oil paintings set in heavy, ornate frames. A large and elaborate crystal chandelier was suspended from the center of the high ceiling.

Juliet gestured toward a wooden staircase in the center of the hall. "Allow me to show you to your room. Breakfast will be served in the dining room."

Acacia made eye contact with Nicholas before shaking her head. "I'm sorry; I was awake all night. What I'd like most is to sleep."

"Of course. I'll ask the chef to send up a tray." Juliet turned to a young woman who stood in a doorway nearby. Nodding, she disappeared.

"That's Gretle. She will assist you with whatever you need," Juliet explained as she led Acacia toward the staircase.

Nicholas cleared his throat. "I have some business to attend to. Shall we meet for dinner? At seven?"

Acacia was uncomfortable. She wanted to participate in the investigation, but she was too exhausted. "Yes, see you at seven," she managed to say. "Before you go, I want to know more about the security on this property."

"Armed guards with dogs patrol the grounds. Cameras cover every inch of the perimeter, along with motion sensors. At night, the house is locked and additional alarms and motion sensors are activated at all windows and entrances. There are tunnels beneath the property that allow for evacuation in the event of an emergency." He paused, noting her continued discomfort, and came a step closer. "You're safe here."

"What about the tunnels? Could someone access them to get in?"

Nicholas's eyes glittered. "They could try. But they'd have to use a large amount of explosives to blow open the doors. Any intruder would give himself away before gaining access to the tunnels."

"Thank you." Acacia ducked her head so he wouldn't see the emotion in her eyes. She followed Juliet up the stairs.

Chapter Nineteen

Acacia's room was on the second floor and had a balcony that overlooked the swimming pool and the tennis courts. Through the windows, she had an exceptional view of the Alps.

Juliet drew back the curtains and opened the balcony door, allowing a refreshing summer breeze inside.

She unfolded a luggage rack and gestured for Gretle to place Acacia's suitcase atop it. "Thank you, Gretle."

She bobbed her head and withdrew.

Juliet switched on a lamp that sat on a side table adjacent to the large bed. "Gretle will bring your breakfast tray and unpack for you."

"That isn't necessary. I didn't bring much." Acacia smiled at Juliet and placed her briefcase on a desk that stood near the floor-to-ceiling windows. The view of Mont Blanc was breathtaking.

"Very good." Juliet opened a door to the left of the bed. "This is the closet. If you need anything pressed or cleaned, please speak to Gretle."

Juliet crossed over to the desk and touched the telephone. "Line one is an internal line and will ring downstairs. Line two is an external line. The wireless password is recorded here." She pointed to a piece of paper on the desk.

"Thank you," Acacia murmured.

"The dining room is downstairs, and dinner will be served at seven o'clock. Do you have any dietary restrictions?"

"No."

Juliet gestured to a doorknob that seemed affixed to the wall near to the bed. "The bathroom is behind that wall. Just turn the knob.

"Rest well."

Acacia thanked Juliet again and watched as she exited and closed the door soundlessly behind her.

She heaved a sigh of relief, unaccustomed to being on the receiving end of service.

She removed her jacket and walked out onto the balcony. A trellis, covered with vines, climbed the outside of the balcony. She tested its strength. It wasn't clear it would support her weight, but it was the simplest way of escape, should she need it.

She surveyed the grounds before she went inside and closed the door. She locked it and pulled the curtains. It was a shame to block such a view, but she needed darkness in order to sleep.

The room was very large, with cream-colored walls and heavy, blue damask curtains. An expansive rug that matched the window dressings covered the parquet floor.

The furniture appeared to be antique. The bed had a high, tufted, blue velvet headboard. Something resembling a crown was situated above the bed, from which blue damask curtains fell, draping to the floor in two large swags.

The bed coverings were blue silk, and at the foot of the bed was a small, backless couch with rolled arms, upholstered in blue velvet.

Acacia was admiring an antique gold clock on top of the marble mantelpiece when there was a knock at the door.

"Come in," she called.

Gretle, who appeared to be in her early twenties, entered the room carrying an elaborate breakfast tray.

Acacia greeted her with a smile. "Thank you. If you'd just place it on the table."

Gretle nodded shyly and completed the task before she withdrew.

Finally left to her solitude, Acacia yawned. She was exhausted, but not too tired to make sure her room was secure. She checked all the windows to ensure they were locked, and she locked the door to her room and braced the desk chair under the door handle.

Satisfied that anyone wanting to get in would find it difficult, she opened her laptop and connected to the wireless network. She typed a short, polite email to Monsieur Roy, copying the Human Resources department, which stated that she was ill and wouldn't be at work that evening.

She wondered what kind of reaction that would elicit.

She texted Kate and told her she was in Cologny and provided her with the telephone number she found printed on the house telephone.

Luc had left more than one message. In each, his voice grew increasingly alarmed. Acacia felt a pang of regret at worrying him, but only a pang. Her safety was her chief concern.

She typed out a text and sent it to him.

**I needed a break from everything.
I've left Paris for a few days.**

Acacia knew he'd call her as soon as he received her message, so she switched off her phone.

She regarded her breakfast. There were eggs and toast, fresh fruit, chocolate, and a carafe of coffee. Acacia skipped the coffee and drank the orange juice, but she only nibbled the food. It was possible, she reasoned, that the items had been tampered with.

Afterward, she began unpacking. She retrieved Marcel's journal from her briefcase and looked around, trying to find a hiding place. Eventually, she lifted the mattress and placed it on top of the bed frame. The mattress would hide the journal well enough.

She needed a shower.

In Brazil, it was common to shower several times a day. Acacia averred that Brazilians were probably the cleanest people on Earth.

She reached for the doorknob, which turned easily in her hand, and a door swung inward.

Acacia stepped into a bright, white marble bathroom with a spacious, modern shower.

"Heaven," she whispered.

For the moment, at least, she was safe.

Chapter Twenty

At ten minutes to seven, Acacia left her room.

She assumed Nicholas dressed for dinner but was unable to do so herself. The contents of her rolling bag had been gathered in a panic and were entirely haphazard. She had underwear, but only the bra she was wearing; cosmetics, but no shampoo. For dinner, she opted for black jeans and a black T-shirt, since they matched.

She hadn't slept well. In her dreams, she'd been chased through the streets of Paris and had hidden inside a darkened corner of Notre-Dame. Her attackers found her and dragged her outside. She'd woken up only to fall back to sleep and suffer a variation of the same dream — faceless men chasing her on foot through the Latin Quarter of Paris.

Acacia was halfway down the stairs when she realized she'd forgotten her purse and her cell phone. She quickly returned to her room.

She opened the door and stepped through it. Light shone from the enormous windows that looked out over the terrace, the curtains opened wide.

It took a moment for her to realize it was not her room.

This room was larger and sat on the corner of the second floor. There was a large canopied bed, a desk and a chair, a couch, and an easel that sat near the balcony door.

Acacia approached the easel. A half-finished watercolor of Mont Blanc looked back at her. Palettes of paint and a series of brushes had been carefully placed on a nearby table.

The room was clean, and the bed was made. Open books sat on the desk where a cluster of Post-it notes decorated the wood. There was a framed photograph of two teenagers, a girl and a boy, dressed in white tennis outfits. The boy was tall and gangly, his arm around the girl's shoulders. Acacia recognized his unscarred face.

She stepped back in dismay, realizing she was in Riva's room. A portrait of her hung over the fireplace — a smiling woman with dark red hair and brown eyes.

A throat cleared nearby.

Juliet stood in the doorway, wearing a severe expression. "Excuse me, mademoiselle. This is one of the family rooms."

"Of course." Acacia approached the housekeeper, flushed with embarrassment. "I opened the wrong door by mistake. I'm so sorry."

Juliet waited until Acacia had passed into the hall before closing the door firmly.

"I need to get my purse." She glanced around the hall, confused. She wasn't sure which room was hers.

Juliet slipped past her and opened a door. "Nicholas has requested that dinner be served on the terrace. I can escort you." Her face was decidedly unfriendly.

"Of course. One moment." Acacia entered her room and quickly switched on her cell phone before she put it in her purse.

"Thank you for waiting." She re-entered the hallway and closed the door to her room.

"This way, please." The housekeeper gestured to the staircase, and they began their descent.

Over the railing, Acacia saw Gretle carrying a large tray. The young woman paused before a closed door and vainly juggled the tray in an effort to reach the doorknob.

"Wait." Nicholas's long strides crossed the cavernous hall. He opened the door and held it as Gretle passed through.

Acacia regarded the scene with interest. As Monsieur Breckman, Nicholas had been abrupt and demanding. Now...

As if he'd heard her thoughts, his eyes strayed upward. He straightened and gave her an appreciative look.

He'd shed his tie and was clad in the purple shirt and black suit. He met her at the base of the stairs and extended his hand. "Did you rest well?"

"Yes, thank you." Acacia allowed him to assist her down the remaining stairs. She eyed Juliet, hoping she wouldn't mention her mistake with the rooms.

Nicholas nodded at Juliet. "I'll escort mademoiselle to the terrace."

"Very good." Juliet turned and disappeared through another door.

Acacia's shoulders relaxed.

She turned to Nicholas and whispered conspiratorially, "Do you always wear black suits?"

He raised an eyebrow. "Not always, no. But in my opinion, gray or navy suits look inferior."

Acacia shook her head.

He gestured to the door through which Gretle had entered and held it open. Acacia accompanied him through an elaborate sitting room and dining room before they exited through a set of glass doors.

The terrace was situated under the balcony to her room. She recognized the vine-covered trellis that climbed skyward.

From the terrace they could see the great expanse of green lawn that disappeared into a copse of trees. Above the forested area, the snow-covered Alps were visible, including the awe-inspiring Mont Blanc.

What a beautiful place to grow up, Acacia thought.

A long table had been set for two. A bar was situated next to the doorway with a bottle of Pastis and a silver pitcher of water at the ready.

Nicholas pulled out her chair. "I hope you don't mind dining outside. It's a warm evening, and the view is incomparable."

"I don't mind."

"I asked the chef to create something special—an homage to Guy Savoy, because I recalled you hadn't had the chance to visit his restaurant. We have weighty matters to discuss, but at least we can have an enjoyable meal." Nicholas crossed over to the bar. "Can I offer you an apéritif?"

"Please."

He poured Pastis into a tall glass and added water before handing it to her. It was customary to enjoy the spirit mixed with cold water on a very hot day.

Gretle appeared with another tray. When she saw Nicholas at the bar, she grew flustered. "I'm sorry, monsieur."

"I decided to serve myself, Gretle. Not to worry." He gave the young woman a smile and filled his own glass.

When he returned to his seat, he lifted his drink. "To alliances."

Acacia lifted her glass in return. "To safety."

Pastis was an acquired taste, but Acacia liked it. She sipped her drink and noticed the bar was stocked with several bottles of wine.

"My parents have an enviable wine cellar." Nicholas's voice broke into her thoughts.

"Are you sure they won't mind?"

Nicholas was quiet while Gretle served the amuse bouche and waited until she left the terrace before he spoke. "My parents are seldom here. The staff aren't used to the house being occupied."

"It's a beautiful home. Has your family lived in it long?"

"The house was built in the nineteenth century by one of my ancestors. Cassirers have lived here ever since."

At that moment the chef appeared in his white coat and hat. He introduced himself and said a few words about the evening's menu before wishing them *bon appetit.*

After his departure, Acacia turned to her host. "I'm grateful for your hospitality, but I have questions."

"Ask." His unruffled response surprised her.

"*Cassirer* is a German name."

"Someone has been doing research." The edge of his mouth turned up. "We're related to the more famous branch of the family, but my ancestor quit Germany in the 1860s and settled here. My father was born in this house."

"You don't live here?"

"I live in Zurich."

"Why didn't you take me there?"

"Someone in search of both of us would scour Monaco for Pierre Breckman. If they uncovered the link between Breckman and me, they'd travel to Zurich. We're at least two steps ahead of them by being here, and the security is better. In addition…" He paused and broke eye contact. "We're chaperoned."

Acacia felt the sudden urge to laugh, but caught herself.

His eyes met hers. "Perhaps I'm old-fashioned."

"It's very thoughtful of you," she admitted. "Thank you."

"How are you feeling?"

"Working nights takes its toll. I find it difficult to sleep during the day."

"You're a strong person, Acacia. But I'm conscious of the fact your experience at the hotel this morning was traumatic. I should have asked if you needed a doctor."

Acacia was dumbfounded. She hadn't expected this level of consideration.

Her thoughts strayed to Luc. She squirmed. "No, I don't need a doctor. The man who grabbed me frightened me, but I'm not hurt."

"I'm relieved to hear that." Nicholas's tone was genuine. "If you're feeling up to it, I'd like to show you my family's art collection after dinner."

She smiled. "I'd like that, monsieur."

"I think we're passed the formality of titles."

"Very well, *Nicholas*."

"Rick tells me you've trained in martial arts."

Acacia tasted her amuse bouche, which she found delicious. She avoided Nicholas's eyes.

He persisted. "What forms of martial arts do you study?"

"I started in Brazilian jiu-jitsu. When I moved to France, I changed to karate."

Nicholas hummed. "I began studying martial arts a few years ago."

Acacia lifted her head. Her host was a man of many layers. "I want to know more about the meeting Marcel was arranging."

Nicholas rubbed his chin. "I believe I answered this question before. Marcel set up a meeting between me and one of his contacts who was interested in selling a painting."

"What painting?"

He finished his amuse bouche and wiped his mouth with his napkin. "The details weren't revealed. You don't announce that you have a stolen painting for sale; you make it known that a rare work is available and wait until you find an appropriate buyer. That's why we use intermediaries—someone has to vouch for both parties. Names are rarely exchanged."

"Have you discovered who attacked me at the hotel?"

"Two Bosnian men."

Acacia nodded. The man who attacked her must have muttered in Bosnian, which was why she hadn't understood.

"Who were they working for?"

"I'm still looking into it." He gestured to her empty plate. "How was it?"

"It was delicious." She sipped her apéritif as Gretle appeared and removed the used plates.

She served the appetizers and presented a bottle of sherry to Nicholas, who perused the label and nodded. She opened the bottle and poured a glass for the two guests, then placed the bottle on a nearby table.

Acacia waited until Gretle was out of earshot before she continued. "Is this sherry?"

"Yes. The chef recommended it to pair with the gazpacho." Nicholas lifted his small glass in salute.

Acacia mirrored his actions. It was theater of the absurd to sit in such a beautiful place, drinking and eating expensive delicacies while her attackers roamed free. Or perhaps Nicholas knew more than he'd revealed.

"I have a theory about why Rick remained in Paris."

"Oh, really?"

"When I left the hotel this morning, Rick had one of my attackers on the ground. I doubt he released him."

"I don't deny it." Nicholas tucked into his gazpacho.

"Did he turn the man over to the police?"

"No."

She rested her spoon on the edge of her bowl. "Why not?"

"Because I ordered his release."

"Good God, why?" Acacia wrung her hands.

"So he would deliver a message to his superiors. The men who attacked you are one rung in a ladder. We want the message to climb higher."

"What message is that?"

"Anyone who fucks with you, fucks with me."

Acacia's eyes widened. His sudden and forceful profanity surprised her.

Aside from a look he exchanged with her, Nicholas appeared unperturbed and continued to eat his soup with gusto.

She took hold of the edge of the table. "I thought you used aliases in order to avoid detection."

"Once Rick was seen at the hotel, Monsieur Roy would have pointed the assailants in Breckman's direction. I thought it important to send a message."

"As soon as I return to Paris, I'll be in danger again."

"You don't know anything damaging. As long as you stay away from the Victoire, I expect you'll be forgotten."

Acacia thought of the journal hidden under her mattress upstairs. The people who wanted it weren't going to give up so easily. "They may have forgotten me, but they won't forget Breckman."

Nicholas lifted a shoulder. "If they dig any deeper, they'll discover Breckman is an arms dealer. That should give them pause."

Acacia went very still.

Nicholas continued eating his gazpacho, oblivious to her reaction.

"The BRB must have looked into you." She held her voice steady. "Did your boyfriend tell you what they found?"

Acacia opened her mouth to correct him, but thought better of it. "The agent who interviewed me seemed very thorough."

"Yes, but evidence that Breckman is an arms dealer was planted today, after you were attacked."

Acacia stared. "Won't that ruin your alias?"

"Silke ruined it already by placing herself in the tabloids." His tone was subdued.

"I'm sorry."

His eyes bored into hers. "Don't be."

"I saw the photographs. What she did was disgusting and cruel."

Nicholas looked away. "We didn't have a traditional relationship. No doubt I'd shock you if I described what we really had."

"I don't shock easily."

At that moment, her cell phone chirped. She smiled apologetically. "That's an incoming text. I should probably check it."

The phone chirped three more times in rapid succession.

"Go ahead. I'll tell the chef to hold the next course." Nicholas stood and walked into the house, leaving her in privacy.

Acacia retrieved her phone and found two voicemail messages from Luc. She ignored them.

Kate had also sent several texts.

Your apartment was trashed.

**I'm so sorry. Don't know when it happened.
Didn't hear anything.**

Door is wide open. Everything on floor.

Should I call police/Luc?

Acacia sat back in her chair.

A new text arrived with photographs of the inside of the apartment. Clothes were ripped from the closet, dresser drawers pulled out and their contents dumped. Even her mattress had been slashed and upended.

Every cupboard and drawer in the kitchen was open; glasses and dishes lay shattered on the floor.

Acacia stifled a gasp.

Footsteps sounded behind her.

"What is it?" Nicholas's voice came from over her shoulder.

Wordlessly, she lifted her phone.

He took it and scrolled through the images. "That's your apartment?"

She nodded.

He cursed and handed back her phone. "Was anyone hurt?"

"No. My neighbor is taking care of my cat. She didn't hear anything, but saw that my door was open."

He passed a hand over his mouth. "Someone didn't take my message seriously."

"What do you mean?" she whispered.

"I told you, Acacia, anyone who fucks with you, fucks with me." His expression hardened. "We'll make them pay. I swear it."

Chapter Twenty-One

"No," Acacia said resolutely.

Nicholas peered down at her. "What?"

"I don't want them to pay, because I don't want this to escalate." She picked up her phone and tapped out a quick text to Kate.

Nicholas turned on his heel and walked to the bar. He retrieved a bottle of wine and showed her the label. She nodded, and he opened it, pouring the cabernet sauvignon in generous portions.

Acacia took the wine gratefully. "Thank you." She swirled her glass, her mind a jumble.

"What are you afraid of?" Nicholas asked.

Her eyes met his. Concern was etched across his strong features.

"I know what happened to your sister." Acacia tried to make her voice as gentle as possible. "I'm so sorry."

Pain flashed across his face. "Your situation is completely different."

"Until we know who is behind this, we don't know what kind of situation this is."

Nicholas lifted his glass and took a long drink. "Do you want to call your boyfriend?"

She shook her head. "I texted Kate and asked her not to call anyone yet."

He seemed surprised. "What about the Paris police?"

"No."

"Why not?"

Acacia forced her voice to remain even. "If I want to continue in the hospitality industry, I have to stay out of the media. It's going to be difficult enough for me to find another position once Roy fires me."

She placed a hand over her mouth and removed it quickly. "I forgot about my landlords. They'll need a police report for the insurance, and so will I. I need to go home."

He leaned against the bar and faced her. "You left Paris so you'd be safe."

"You saw the pictures. There's thousands of Euros in damage."

Nicholas regarded the currant-colored liquid in his glass. "I'm puzzled as to why you wouldn't call your boyfriend."

"That's none of your business," Acacia snapped.

He lifted his head and his dark eyes glittered. He nodded, as if affirming something to himself.

Something clicked in Acacia's mind as well. "You knew," she whispered.

"What did you say?"

She thrust her chair back and stood. "When we spoke on the phone, when you were convincing me to leave Paris, you warned me to remove everything valuable from my apartment."

"I did." Nicholas seemed unruffled. "The man who attacked you escaped. If I were he, I'd have followed you to your apartment.

"You told me you had a cat, Acacia. Men who would attack a woman wouldn't hesitate to harm a pet."

She stared at him incredulously. "You were protecting my cat?"

He frowned. "Not just your cat. They would have taken anything of value, anything you couldn't afford to lose."

She gestured vaguely, her mind racing. "Did you set this up?"

"Acacia," he said softly. He waited until she made eye contact before he continued. "I have no reason to attack you or to ransack your apartment. I was worried something like this might happen, which is why I told Rick to keep an eye on you. It's a good thing I did, since the BRB was nowhere to be found this morning."

She grabbed her phone. "After Rick dropped me off at the airport, did he go back to my apartment?"

"Of course not." Nicholas gave her a pointed look. "While we're on the subject, what do you think those men were looking for?"

"What makes you think they were looking for something?"

"The ransacking appeared systematic."

Acacia lifted her chin. "Maybe they were looking for you."

Nicholas stretched his arms wide. "I'm not in your apartment."

"You were in the building."

"They could have come after me then. They didn't."

"Because you had a large, armed security detail, and the BRB had me under surveillance." Acacia froze. "It was a diversion."

"I beg your pardon?"

"You wanted me to see the painting in your suite and call the BRB. You wanted the diversion."

Nicholas shook his head. "I was using an alias. Why would I invite scrutiny?"

"Because of the meeting Marcel arranged. You said names are never exchanged. What if the art dealer learned your name before you arrived? He found out you recover art for various governments and sent men to attack Marcel in order to derail the meeting."

"The thought had occurred to me," Nicholas said. "That doesn't explain why he'd send men after you—assuming the men who attacked you are the ones who assaulted Marcel."

"I'm leaving." Acacia yanked her purse from where it hung on the back of her chair.

Nicholas stepped between her and the doorway. "Kurt will take you to the airport, but you'll be running back into a burning house. You're safer here."

At six-foot-three, Nicholas was taller than Acacia. But her years of training had settled steel into her spine. She stood toe to toe with him and flashed angry eyes. "If they know who you are, they'll know who your parents are. That will lead them here."

He grew very, very still. "Even if they discovered Breckman's identity, they won't necessarily connect him with me."

"But they know my name. They could trace my passport. They could find my information in the passenger manifest from the flight."

"They could, if it was there."

"What do you mean?"

"It means my security team deleted your name from the manifest."

"That's illegal."

"A computer malfunction." He gestured to the door. "You can leave at any time. But if you want to avoid the police and the media, you should stay. The next time these men approach you, they'll be even more vicious."

She stopped; his observation had merit.

Nicholas's hand curled into a fist. The muscles in his arm bunched beneath his suit jacket. "You know what happened to Riva. What you don't know is that she's the reason I became involved in the black market. Everything I do is because of her. Everything I do is an attempt to right those wrongs. I'm not the enemy, Acacia. I'm your ally. Be mine, as well."

Acacia glared. "You're withholding information."

"So are you." He gestured to the dinner table but Acacia crossed her arms. He huffed impatiently. "For an alliance to work, information needs to flow in both directions. What were those men looking for in your apartment?"

"Oh, excuse me." Gretle's voice broke into their conversation. She stood nearby with a large serving tray.

"It's all right, Gretle." Nicholas turned back to his houseguest. "Are you staying for the main course? The chef has prepared Chateaubriand."

Acacia looked from Nicholas to Gretle and back again. If she returned to Paris, she would have to go to Luc. He was the only one who could protect her.

But Luc's colleagues had failed him. They'd left her unprotected because they'd been paid off or for some other reason. It was possible he'd find himself at odds with the BRB if she went to him for help.

There was also the matter of her personal connection to him. Returning to Luc would mean undoing the most difficult decision she'd had to make.

She couldn't do it.

Acacia took her seat and glowered at her host. At the moment, at least, he seemed her best option.

Gretle served the main course and topped off their wine glasses before she returned to the kitchen.

"I'll stay for now. But I want answers." Acacia lifted her fork.

"So do I." Nicholas speared his steak aggressively. "I've already shared some of my information. It's your turn."

"How do I know you've been telling me the truth?"

"I've been open with you, Acacia. My alias appears in the hotel records. The Minister of the Interior knows who I am, and so does Madame Bishop at KLH. Would someone intent on deceiving you leave behind so many breadcrumbs?"

Acacia shifted in her seat. He had a point.

"I brought you here, to my parents' home, where you'd be safe and where we'd be chaperoned. Again, why would someone intent on harming you involve so many potential witnesses?

"You were assaulted." Nicholas's voice grew soft. "Your home was invaded, and your possessions destroyed. But I can help."

She moved the food around on her plate.

His large hand slid across the tablecloth but stopped just shy of touching her. "I'll send a team to repair the damage and clean up the mess. I'll ask them for an inventory so you can see what's damaged and what's missing. You won't have to go through the insurance. I'll replace everything."

"Why?"

"If the art dealer is the one behind this, then I'm the true target. I feel responsible for what happened to you." He stared at her intently.

She pushed her hair back from her forehead. "The superintendent will see the damage. She'll call my landlords."

"Then I should make the call right now." He pushed his chair back.

"It's after hours. You won't be able to hire anyone tonight."

He gave her a half smile. "What if I were a guest at the Victoire? Could you find contractors that work at night, for me?"

She shook her head. "I could find someone who would be there first thing tomorrow morning, but not tonight."

"Let me see what I can do."

She pondered his offer and thought about the journal she'd hidden upstairs. She hadn't locked her room. It was possible someone had already searched and found it.

If the men who attacked her knew she had the journal, perhaps Nicholas knew as well.

"Fine." She cleared her throat. "I'll tell you what the men were looking for. Rick doesn't speak French, does he?"

"Not really."

Acacia grasped the stem of her wine glass and toyed with it. "When the man attacked me at the hotel, he spoke to me in French. He asked for *the book*."

Nicholas leaned forward. "What book?"

She sighed. "Marcel's journal."

"Do you have it?" His tone was eager.

She searched his eyes. "You know about it?"

"I'd noticed Marcel's journal on previous visits but didn't think anything of it. It only occurred to me to wonder about it after I saw you recording things in a similar book."

Acacia felt her lungs constrict. It was possible he had brought her to his parents' house in the hope of wresting the journal from her.

But Rick could have let the men harm her at the hotel. Or he could have come to her apartment and demanded the journal. Nicholas didn't need to fly her to Geneva.

The journal was of no use to her. It was evidence related to a crime, and she was eager to be rid of it.

"I found Marcel's journal at the hotel. He'd hidden it in the lobby."

Nicholas pursed his lips. "Did you tell anyone?"

Acacia hesitated. "No. I intended to turn it over to the Paris police, but I haven't had the chance."

"So your boyfriend doesn't know about it?"

"No."

"Is it with you?"

She nodded.

"I'll make the call about your apartment." He stood. "Excuse me."

Acacia watched him leave then quickly texted Kate.

If you don't hear from me in the next few hours, phone Luc with the information I gave you.

Chapter Twenty-Two

Nicholas had been subdued upon his return to dinner. He resumed his meal and made no mention of the journal.

Acacia found his behavior peculiar. She expected him to demand she retrieve the book immediately.

"Not hungry?" Nicholas finally addressed the issue after she'd rearranged the food on her plate twice.

"I've lost my appetite."

"I'm sorry. Workmen are on their way to your apartment." He turned his attention back to his food.

"How is that possible?"

"My parents have an apartment in Paris. Juliet had the contact information for the contractor who recently renovated their place. He agreed to inspect your apartment tonight, as a favor."

"Thank you." Acacia swallowed a lump in her throat. "Please thank Juliet as well."

"What's so interesting about Marcel's journal?"

"I don't know." Acacia pushed her plate aside. While Nicholas's attention was focused on his meal, she placed her purse on top of the steak knife. "I read every page more than once. Marcel used a short form in most of his notes. The entry on your meeting had the letter *V* next to it."

Nicholas pushed his empty plate aside as well and gestured to Gretle to remove the dishes.

Acacia had mere seconds to decide whether to steal the steak knife and hide it in her purse, or leave it for Gretle to remove.

It would be good to have a weapon, she reasoned, eying Nicholas.

But her martial arts training had eschewed weapons. *She* was the weapon, her sensei had said. She had to have confidence in her training and her instincts, otherwise no weapon could help her.

Nonchalantly, Acacia slid her purse off the table to her lap, leaving the steak knife behind.

"Would you prefer dessert or cheese? Or both?" Nicholas asked.

"Neither, thank you." She lifted her napkin and touched it to her lips.

"Coffee or tea?"

"Coffee, please. Black."

Nicholas nodded in Gretle's direction, who cleared the table and left to retrieve the next course.

He fidgeted with his napkin. "You're sure the letter was *V?*"

"Yes. I can get the journal for you." Acacia moved as if to stand.

"After dinner."

She studied his profile. She had expected a more vigorous reaction, but he was almost relaxed.

"I suppose *V* could stand for Victoire," she surmised. "Perhaps Marcel intended to introduce you to the dealer at the hotel."

"Not likely. These meetings are usually scheduled on neutral territory, with ample time for both security teams to inspect the area."

"So *V* is a person?"

"Or a number."

"Of course, the number five." She sighed. "I wish I could ask Marcel about the people who attacked him."

"I have contacts keeping an eye on his progress. They'll get in touch, if necessary."

"Are you sure you aren't an arms dealer? You have more contacts than a concierge."

Nicholas laughed.

She'd never heard him laugh before; the sound was deep and happy.

He smiled broadly, and for a moment Acacia realized just how handsome he was. He had an intelligent forehead, high cheekbones, an angular jaw, and an expressive mouth. His smile lit his entire face.

"I doubt arms dealers would self-identify. But for the record, again, I am not an arms dealer." He chuckled, as if the thought were incredibly amusing.

Gretle appeared and brought espresso, a plate of cheese and fruit, and a sliced baguette.

Despite the fact that she'd refused dessert, Acacia helped herself to the cheese and bread.

"Are you still interested in seeing the art collection?" Nicholas's tone was casual.

Acacia sipped her espresso. "Sure."

"Good. I can give you a private tour of the gallery."

"The gallery?" Acacia blinked. "I thought the collection was inside the house."

The edges of Nicholas's mouth turned up. "Prepare to be amazed."

After dinner, the duo exited the terrace and walked on a path that led from the back of the house to the driveway at the side. There, two black cars were parked in tandem.

"I don't usually travel without security." Nicholas gestured to the Range Rover. Kurt and another man stood next to it. "But my father doesn't like anyone driving his car, besides me." He led her to the passenger side of a Porsche 911 Turbo S and opened the door.

Acacia stepped into the car. He closed the door behind her.

"Where's the gallery?" she asked Nicholas as he settled into the driver's seat.

"A few streets over. Kurt will follow us, and when we arrive, security will let us in."

The Porsche roared to life.

Acacia congratulated herself on texting Kate. If, for some reason, Nicholas and his minions decided to hurt her, she'd do her best to fight them off. If she failed and wasn't able to text Kate again, Kate would call Luc.

"*Just because you're paranoid doesn't mean they aren't after you,*" Acadia thought, channeling Joseph Heller.

She'd always thought her paranoia served her well.

They exited the gates and turned left, then drove down a tree-lined road populated by other large estates.

Nicholas glanced in her direction. "Would you rather go back?"

She tore her gaze from the window. "Why do you ask?"

With his right hand, he gestured to her lap, where she clutched her purse with both hands.

She forced a smile. "You're driving a bit fast."

"And this from a Parisian driver." He grinned.

He took his foot from the accelerator and slowed the car.

"In Paris you have to keep up with the flow of traffic, or you'll end up in an accident." She looked over her shoulder and saw the Range Rover had slowed as well. "We're in a residential area."

He flashed a wide smile. "I'd like you to take me for a ride on your motorcycle."

"Really?"

"Rick says you handle it well." Nicholas slowed the car again as they approached a roundabout. They took the first exit and drove along another residential street and up a hill. Two more turns and they traveled a private road.

Acacia's phone buzzed with a text.

She removed the phone from her purse and looked at the screen. The message was from Kate.

You're scaring me. I'm calling Luc now.

Nicholas peered over at Acacia. "Something important?"

Discreetly, she hid the screen from view. "Just my neighbor fussing about the damage done to my apartment. I'll assure her it's being looked after."

Acacia replied to Kate, keeping the screen from Nicholas's prying eyes.

**Don't call Luc unless you don't hear from me
for several hours. I'm okay.**

"I thought your neighbor was your friend," Nicholas remarked.

"She is, but she worries."

"Then she's a good friend."

"Yes." Acacia's phone buzzed again.

Okay. But be careful.

Acacia could barely restrain her sigh of relief at Kate's reply. She muted her phone so she wouldn't be disturbed.

Nicholas pulled the Porsche in front of a set of high iron gates. The gates opened, and they passed through.

The gallery was actually a small estate that overlooked Lake Geneva. There were several buildings, all connected, with a large and elaborate fountain situated in the beautifully landscaped quadrangle.

"This is where your family houses their art collection?" Acacia asked in amazement.

Nicholas parked the car near the fountain. "Yes. It was opened to the public in 1951."

Acacia noted that some of the large windows in the buildings were shuttered, probably for conservation purposes.

Nicholas helped her out of the car and accompanied her to the central building. "I told the curator we wanted to tour the collection privately. Or would you prefer he be our guide?"

"A guide isn't necessary." As she entered the building, Acacia noticed the interior lighting was very low. The display cases and exhibits, however, were well lit.

They shook hands with the curator, who welcomed them and made a few remarks about the collection.

Nicholas and Acacia turned a corner into the first exhibition.

Acacia stopped so suddenly Nicholas walked right into the back of her.

"My apologies." His hands gripped her arms from behind, steadying her. He took a very large step back.

Acacia barely noticed their collision. She was at a loss for words.

"Is that…" She took a step forward. Before her hung a famous portrait of Dante Alighieri. It was an image she'd seen a hundred times on the cover of her copy of *The Divine Comedy*.

Nicholas strode past her. "Come closer."

She approached the painting with wonder. "I didn't know you owned it."

"One of my ancestors had a fondness for Florence. I told you we used to be in possession of a set of illustrations of *The Divine Comedy* that were copies of Botticelli's. This is an original, painted by Botticelli around 1495. Of course, Dante died in 1321, but it's considered a very good likeness."

"Incredible." She looked closely at the colors, at the way Botticelli spread the tempera over canvas.

"I've always liked this painting," he mused as he followed her gaze.

"Me too," she admitted.

"I thought you liked the Impressionists."

"I do." She gave Nicholas a sheepish look. "Botticelli has always moved me."

He searched her eyes. "Look as long as you like. We have the entire gallery at our disposal."

He moved away and left Acacia to admire the piece.

She joined him a few minutes later. "It was such a surprise to find that painting here. I thought it belonged to the Uffizi."

"No, we've owned that work for generations. We don't publicize our best pieces. Not since the theft."

She cleared her throat. "Do you mind if I ask about the paintings that were stolen?"

His shoulders tightened. "*The Mante family*, a pastel on paper by Degas. *Ice Floes on the Seine near Bennecourt* by Monet. We also lost a Renoir, *Dance in the Moulin de la Galette*."

Acacia made a sound of shock and covered her mouth momentarily.

"I'm so sorry. I'm not familiar with the Degas, but I know the Monet. It's lovely. But the Renoir…" She shook her head. "That's a very famous piece. I didn't know your family owned it."

"We used to own it," Nicholas said bitterly.

Abruptly, he stepped back. "In addition to artwork, the gallery houses a library. There's an extensive collection of papyri, manuscripts, early printed books, and letters. Would you like to see some of them?"

Acacia bobbed her head. The Cassirers' loss was tragic on many levels. She wondered how Nicholas was able to enter the museum, which represented so much grief.

He led her through room after darkened room and pointed out some of the more important items. The collection of papyri alone was priceless. Acacia couldn't believe how impressive the holdings were. And one family owned them all.

Acacia paused in front of a beautiful manuscript of the Qur'an. Unthinkingly, she touched her hamsa pendant.

The manuscript was open to the fifth Surah. Acacia read aloud in Arabic, "...cooperate in righteousness and piety, but do not cooperate in sin and aggression."

"You read Arabic as well as speak it." Nicholas's voice intruded on her reading.

"Yes." She avoided his eyes.

"What does it say?"

She translated the line for him, and he nodded. "There are significant differences between Islam, Judaism, and Christianity. But I'm always struck by the way the traditions mirror one another."

"That's true."

When she'd finished admiring the manuscript, Nicholas steered her to another display case. According to the printed sign, the papyrus inside was the oldest copy of the complete Gospel according to Saint John. It dated from the second century.

Acacia studied the Greek letters in wonder. "How did your family acquire these treasures?"

"My ancestors were people of the book. Most of the family was Jewish, although there were a few converts to Christianity here and there. I believe this piece was acquired by one of those converts."

Acacia looked at him with interest. "And your family?"

"Jewish." He studied her face, as if looking for a reaction.

Acacia offered none.

Nicholas's shoulders relaxed somewhat. "My family was part of the Reform movement in Judaism in the nineteenth century. But at this point, we celebrate the high holidays and that's it."

Acacia nodded and followed him to another display case.

"This is a medieval manuscript of the Zohar. Do you read Hebrew?" Nicholas glanced over at her hopefully.

"No." She moved closer to the case so she could admire the writing.

"The books are at peace." Acacia gestured to the series of cases, featuring Islamic, Christian, and Jewish works side by side.

"Sometimes I wonder if they speak to one another when the museum is closed, sharing their secrets." Nicholas smiled.

His whimsical reflection surprised Acacia. It also pleased her. "Maybe they will share their secrets with us."

"One can only hope." He winked.

She turned in a circle and surveyed the exhibit hall. "It's an incredible collection."

"You'll notice the entire gallery is accessible by wheelchair. We have ramps at all the entrances and an elevator for the upper floors." Nicholas's pride was evident.

He pointed to a sign in Braille posted next to a display case featuring *Le Terze Rime*, a first edition of the works of Dante dating from 1502. "The visually impaired can read the signs posted next to each item. We also have a guide book that features raised illustrations so they can experience the works with their hands."

"That's amazing." Acacia ran her fingertips over the Braille sign. "You have raised illustrations of each work?"

"At least part of each work, yes."

"I wish more museums and galleries would accommodate visitors' special needs." Acacia touched the Braille once again. "Art should belong to everyone."

Nicholas's smile slipped. "My sister agreed. She was very passionate about increasing access to art. She founded several educational programs for various groups, including children."

Nicholas led Acacia into the corridor.

"Tell me more about the programs you have." Acacia looked up at him.

"We've continued them in my sister's memory and expanded them. The programs for those suffering from dementia or Alzheimer's are particularly successful. Caregivers and patients come to the museum once a month and are given comfortable places to sit so they can admire the artwork. We play music through the sound system, or sometimes we have musicians perform. The atmosphere is very relaxed and..." Nicholas paused as if he couldn't quite think of the correct word. "Joyous. The patients and the caregivers seem to experience a great deal of joy."

He grew somber as they approached a large, open doorway. "There was a time when we wondered whether there would ever be joy in these halls again. My sister's programs ensure that there is."

His black shoes stopped just shy of the entrance. "This is the central exhibit hall."

She entered the room, but turned around when she realized he wasn't with her. She lifted her eyebrows.

He shook his head.

Puzzled, Acacia faced the room. The walls were blank, with the exception of a single painting. Low lighting shone from overhead and washed down the brick red walls. Empty frames were strewn haphazardly on the floor.

Acacia didn't understand what she was looking at. It was very odd to have so avant-garde an art installation in what seemed to be a conventional gallery.

Her gaze was drawn to the painting. She gasped.

She twisted her neck in order to find Nicholas. He remained standing near the threshold, his body still.

"We left it as it was found," he whispered.

The painting of Riva Cassirer was hung high on the back wall—too high in Acacia's aesthetic judgment. It had the effect of enabling the former curator to look down on the carnage. She wasn't smiling, although her face was both regal and beautiful.

Acacia counted three empty frames on the floor, three works of art that had been stolen and never recovered. Bits of canvas were still visible at the interior edges of the frames. The works had been slashed and cut before they were stolen.

Her stomach pitched.

She exited the hall, her footsteps echoing. She reached out to Nicholas but didn't touch him.

He looked over her shoulder. "My parents commissioned the portrait. They wanted her presence to be the focus."

"It's a beautiful painting."

His lip curled. "I hate it. Riva was always smiling—especially here, inside the gallery. Of course we couldn't have her smiling down on this."

Acacia withdrew her hand. "Are you close to finding the thieves?"

Nicholas's entire body tensed. "Close. Far. Who knows?"

She noted his reaction and moved to his side. "We should go."

It took a moment for him to focus on her. When he did, he seemed puzzled. "You haven't seen the whole collection."

"You're upset."

"You want to forego seeing the rest of the gallery because I'm troubled?" He sounded incredulous.

"Yes."

His focus sharpened. "You're unselfish."

"No, just human."

Nicholas rocked back on his heels. "You are most unexpected, mademoiselle."

She looked up at him sadly. "I'm sorry the world is so dark that embracing one's humanity causes shock and surprise."

"I don't know why I continue to be surprised by you. You've demonstrated over and over again that you have an admirable character."

She lowered her gaze. "Thank you."

"Would it surprise you if I told you I can't remember the last time someone denied themself for my benefit?"

"You need new friends."

Acacia cringed at her own words. "I apologize. That was rude."

"Your observation was correct."

His acknowledgment didn't seem to require comment, so Acacia refrained.

"Suffering is the great equalizer," he observed and turned his attention once again to the exhibit hall.

"I agree. Through empathy we can try to have a better understanding of our fellow human beings."

"Riva would have agreed with you." He faced Acacia. "You and she would have much to talk about."

"She did an excellent job with the gallery."

"She did. She found items in my parents' house that we'd overlooked, including the Degas that was stolen."

Acacia's eyes widened. "You didn't know it was there?"

"It hung on a wall in the master bathroom for decades. No one knew it was a Degas. It's pastel on paper, not an oil painting. Whoever framed it covered up his signature."

"Your sister recognized it?"

"She had her suspicions. When she removed it from the frame, she found the signature." He regarded Acacia solemnly. "We should continue."

He gestured to the far end of the corridor.

For the next hour, they viewed more of the Cassirer collection, until Acacia could no longer disguise her fatigue.

Nicholas checked his watch. "It's after midnight. I'm sorry I've kept you so long."

"Thank you for bringing me."

He bowed his head. "I never come here. To me, the place is a tomb. But I knew you'd appreciate the artwork."

He escorted her to the entrance, where they were once again greeted by the curator. Kurt and his associate stood outside by the vehicles.

Nicholas opened the car door for Acacia, but waited to speak to her until he was in the driver's seat. He pointed his chin in the direction of the gallery. "I was at my parents' house when it happened. We were having drinks, waiting for her to come home."

"I am so sorry," Acacia whispered.

He wrapped his fingers around the steering wheel. "Although I tried, I was not in a position then to do anything about what happened. I've led a fictitious life since, quietly acquiring information and contacts."

He turned his head, his eyes meeting hers. "I'm no longer the prey. I'm the predator."

The Porsche roared to life, and they sped out of the compound.

Chapter Twenty-Three

Acacia had slept most of the day, so her insomnia wasn't surprising. She wanted to sleep. She craved the bliss of slumber, but it eluded her.

She'd texted Kate after the visit to the gallery, assuring her she was all right. She'd tossed and turned in her darkened room long after she'd bid Nicholas good night and placed Marcel's journal in his hands.

He'd thanked her, a look of triumph flitting across his face. Then he'd put one of his large hands on her shoulder and wished her a good rest.

But her rest had not been good.

At three o'clock in the morning, she'd had enough. She threw off the covers, dressed quickly, and turned on her computer. She Googled the Degas that had been stolen the night Riva Cassirer was murdered.

It wasn't an especially striking piece, although she liked it. It featured a young ballet dancer, whose mother was fixing her hair. Another young girl stood next to the pair, holding a handbag.

The subjects of the works stolen from the Cassirers were all different. There wasn't a single thread that linked the three, other than the fact that Degas, Monet, and Renoir were all Impressionists.

Why didn't the thieves steal the portrait of Dante by Botticelli? Or the Egyptian Book of the Dead? Or the manuscript of the Gospel of Saint John?

It seemed to her that the thieves had eschewed the most valuable pieces in the collection in favor of the Impressionists. Perhaps there was more of a demand for Impressionist works on the black market. Perhaps the display cases that protected the manuscripts had been too difficult or time consuming to breach.

Acacia didn't have answers to her musings, but visiting the gallery with Nicholas, she'd caught a glimpse of the loss that had transformed him into the figure he now was—a man bent on justice.

She put her computer aside. She needed air and a diversion, or she'd end up pacing her room all night.

Nicholas had warned her to keep to the house, noting the guards and dogs that patroled the grounds. But Acacia was seized with the inspiration to take a moonlit swim.

Outside her bedroom, the corridor was empty and dark. She crossed to the staircase and quietly descended. She passed through a series of rooms before she exited onto the terrace.

The night was cool and still. She walked the length of the terrace to where steps led down to the swimming pool.

The pool wasn't enclosed. Dim lighting shone around the perimeter and illuminated the landscaped area and a series of lounge chairs.

She hadn't brought a bathing suit. But it was the middle of the night, and no one was around. She doubted the security guards would trouble her.

She quickly undressed to her bra and underwear, both of which were black, and slipped into the heated water. She was surprised to discover the pool was saline.

She swam from end to end, careful not to make too much noise, and reveled in the movement of her muscles. She floated on her back in the center of the pool and inspected the clouded sky.

She knew tragedy and loss. She understood the quest for justice. But she began to wonder about Nicholas's obsession and the lengths he would go to punish those responsible for his sister's death.

It didn't matter. She'd given him the journal. He was having her apartment repaired. She'd be able to return to Paris in a day or so and try to find another position. She'd never see Nicholas again.

When she was sufficiently exhausted, she climbed out of the pool and found a towel next to her abandoned clothes. She looked around.

No one was visible.

She picked up the towel and began to dry her body. She squeezed the water from her curly hair in an attempt to dry it.

A hand touched her shoulder.

Without thinking, she dropped the towel and grasped her assailant's palm in both hands. She wrenched it backward until he yelped.

The assailant twisted and slid behind her, then freed his wrist and placed his forearm under her chin.

She bumped her hip into his and used the movement to leverage his weight in order to throw him over her shoulder.

The assailant planted his feet and lifted her in return. "Rick was right. You can take care of yourself."

Nicholas placed her on her feet and stepped away.

She turned and found him grinning.

"I'm tired of being tested by you." She glared and placed her hand on her hip.

"How can that be when you keep passing every test?" He shook out his wrist with a grimace. "You nearly snapped it."

"You nearly deserved it."

Nicholas's gaze washed over her body—her high breasts encased in black, her thong underwear that showcased her toned thighs and curvy backside, and the pendant that swung from her neck.

She shook her head at him and retrieved the towel to shield herself from his perusal.

"You can't fault an art collector for appreciating beauty." He reproved her gently.

"I'm not eager to be collected."

"If a man were fortunate enough to win you, he'd give away his collection." Nicholas turned his back to give her privacy.

Acacia wrapped the towel around herself and removed her underthings. She dropped them to the patio. Then she pulled on her clothes and hid her wet things in the towel. "I'm decent."

Nicholas turned around, his hands thrust in his pockets.

She noticed he was still dressed. "You can't sleep?"

"I only sleep a few hours a night."

"Planning to swim?"

"Working." His expression shifted. He appeared tense.

"Thanks for the towel."

"You're welcome." He glanced around. "Do you want to walk?"

"No, I took a swim to tire myself. I'm ready to sleep."

"I'll walk with you."

Without another word, Nicholas accompanied her inside the house.

"Should I put those in the dryer?" He indicated the wet bundle she carried.

"No, I'll hang them up." She paused at the bottom of the staircase and waited for him to say something. Nicholas was at least six inches taller than her, his shoulders wide, his eyes piercing.

Her gaze dropped to his mouth — to his full lower lip and strong, stubbled chin. And then, as if her eyes had decided to sabotage her, her gaze drifted to the location of his scar.

Nicholas turned and walked away.

Chapter Twenty-Four

"I have to leave for Greece tomorrow."

Acacia looked up from her breakfast, her spoon in midair. "Sorry?"

Nicholas pulled out the chair next to her and sat. He placed a napkin across his lap. "I have to travel to Greece on business. I'd like you to come with me."

She shook her head. "I'm going home."

"Your apartment isn't habitable."

"I'll stay with a friend."

Irritation flared across Nicholas's face. "People are after you. Until we identify and neutralize the threat, you're in danger."

"What about Marcel's journal? Isn't it helpful?"

"I'm afraid not. I have someone analyzing it, but Marcel wrote in shorthand."

"Then why were those men so intent on recovering it?"

"I hope to find out." He cleared his throat. "You're welcome to stay here. But I could use your help."

"What kind of help?"

"As I said when we met at the KLH offices, my executive assistant can no longer travel with me. I could use an extra set of eyes and ears. I may need you to act as an interpreter.

"It will be a short trip—only a few days and a couple of meetings. But it will give you a chance to see what I do."

"You still want me to be your assistant?"

He frowned. "Of course."

She put down her spoon. "I don't think it's a good idea for us to work together."

He looked very displeased. "I thought we were allies."

"We are. But I need to focus on finding a job for the long term."

"I've just offered you one." He sounded exasperated.

Stubbornly, she continued to eat breakfast.

He leaned forward. "You know it's better for your curriculum vitae to resign a post than to be fired."

"Yes, I know that."

"You'll be paid well. My security team will travel with us. You'll have separate, private accommodations, and you'll probably have some time to explore while I'm in meetings."

It was her turn to frown. "I don't mean to sound ungrateful, but do you know when my apartment will be finished?"

"It will take a few days. They're going to need to repair the walls in addition to the damage to the kitchen. We can call the contractor after breakfast, and you can speak to him directly."

"Thank you."

Nicholas sat back in his chair and poured himself a cup of coffee from a French press. He peered over at the mocha-colored liquid in Acacia's cup. "I thought you drank your coffee black."

"Not at breakfast."

"Ah." He picked up a piece of brioche and began slathering it with butter and apricot jam.

Acacia lifted her coffee cup. "I don't think I can return to the Victoire after everything that's happened."

Nicholas chewed his brioche thoughtfully. He swallowed. "I think that's wise."

"I probably shouldn't press my luck by calling in sick again today, which means I'll have to send a letter of resignation."

"Tell them you've received a better offer from CI Paris and will be starting immediately."

"CI Paris?"

"The Paris office of one of our wealth management companies. Your contract will be with them. I'll have the director apply for your temporary work permit, as well as an EU Blue Card."

Acacia looked out over the grounds to where the Alps were visible above the trees. Majestic, snow-covered mountains rose against a blue sky, with only the barest wisp of cloud hanging above them.

Mountains didn't have to worry about employment, or supporting their mothers, or persistent Swiss businessmen who clearly had a weakness for brioche and apricot jam.

"You have a job offer on the table," Nicholas's low voice continued. "Working with me will buy us time to find out who is after the journal."

He cleared his throat. "You said last night I needed new friends."

Her eyes met his.

"Be my friend, Acacia."

"You're friendly with your assistants?"

"My current assistant has been with me almost ten years. I'm going to be the godfather of her first child later this year."

"You don't look like a godfather."

He lifted his arm over his head. "I'm not tall enough?"

She laughed. She couldn't help herself. At six-foot-three, Nicholas was tall. But not too tall in her estimation.

"We will make a good team, Acacia."

She sighed. "You helped me when I needed it. I'll help you in return. But after Greece, I want to go home."

"I'll take you to Paris personally."

"I'll sign a contract, but I'd like us to agree that Greece is a trial period. I won't accept any money, and we can both see if this is feasible longer term."

"That's ridiculous," Nicholas interrupted. "How will you —"

"It isn't ridiculous," she interrupted in return. "We might discover we don't work well together."

"I doubt it."

She frowned. "How can you be so sure?"

"Because I've seen your work ethic, and I've spent time with you. I'm a good judge of character, Acacia. I sized you up almost immediately."

She placed her coffee cup on its saucer with loud thump. "You sized me up and asked for Marcel."

"Because he was my contact." Nicholas tossed his napkin on the table. "You turned around and suggested I donate those ridiculous items I bought for Silke to benefit hungry children."

"And they did. I received an email from the organization telling me they raised thousands of Euros on your donation alone."

"Precisely. Don't you see? We already work well together."

"What about your current assistant?"

Nicholas rubbed his eyes. "She's on bed rest until the baby's born. She had a scare and was in the hospital."

"I'm sorry." Acacia turned in her chair. "I'll sign a contract, but I won't accept a salary until after Greece. I need a trial period."

"Fine," Nicholas said grumpily. "I'll have Madame Bishop send over your contract. Juliet has the number for the contractor in Paris. You can speak to him about his progress. After that, your first official task is to put together a wardrobe for a personal assistant. You'll need formal wear, in addition to business attire."

Her eyes narrowed. "Is that a typical task?"

"At the beginning, yes. My current assistant was given a clothing allowance when she started. We have to make a certain impression, but it's an impression I'll gladly finance."

"Really?"

"I thought you were a concierge, Acacia." The edges of his lips twitched. "Surely this can't be a difficult proposition?"

"Concierges don't usually act as personal shoppers for themselves."

His eyes twinkled. "Think of this as an opportunity to acquire a new skill set. I have a line of credit at several boutiques in Geneva. Juliet will give you the list, and she can accompany you, along with Kurt.

"I have to return to Zurich this morning. I won't be back until late tonight. We'll leave for Santorini tomorrow."

Acacia felt a sudden pang of…something, at the thought of rambling around the large estate without him. She hid her reaction behind a restrained smile. "Did you say Santorini?"

"I did. Be sure to include athletic wear, in case we go to the beach."

"The beach? Do you conduct business at the beach?"

He chuckled. "If I'm fortunate."

"While you're away, is there a place I can practice my martial arts?"

"Planning a work out, mademoiselle?"

She shrugged. "I try to practice every day. Don't you?"

"Good point. There's a small gymnasium that should suit your purposes. Juliet will show you where it is."

"Thank you."

Nicholas stood and touched her shoulder. "I'm looking forward to working with you."

Acacia turned in her chair to watch her attractive new employer walk away.

Chapter Twenty-Five

Late that night, Nicholas stood in the hall outside his bedroom at his parents' house.

It was late. He'd just returned from Zurich.

He'd visited the pool first, hoping to join Acacia for a swim. Sadly, she seemed to have retired for the evening.

He walked to her room and paused outside the door. No sounds were audible. Nicholas sighed in relief. He hoped she was sleeping well.

She was probably the strongest woman he'd ever met, with the exception of his sister.

Nicholas's gaze flickered to the next room.

Riva's room was adjacent to Acacia's. He hadn't been inside in years. But somehow, he found himself walking to the door and pushing it open.

He turned on the light.

He was surprised at how clean it was. Juliet and her staff kept all the rooms pristine, and Riva's was no exception. But they hadn't put away her things. Her artwork stood at the ready, as if it waited for her.

Nicholas carried several burdens, some of which had been placed on him by others. Some burdens he'd taken on himself. His sense of responsibility for his sister was something he'd felt since the night of her murder.

If he hadn't rushed her because he was so eager for her to meet his fiancée, she might still be alive. Perhaps the thieves would have left before she noticed them.

Thierry, the security guard, had survived his assault. Riva had not been so fortunate.

At least Thierry had provided information about the culprits.

Nicholas avoided looking at the portrait of Riva that hung on the wall of her room. Guilt kept his gaze averted as he walked to the door.

He'd sworn to avenge her death, and until he'd done so, he wouldn't look her image in the eye.

He switched off the light, closed the door, and strode past Acacia's room toward his own as he wrested his tie from his neck in frustration.

A tall, slim figure floated up the staircase.

Nicholas stopped short. He stared into the semi-darkness in confusion.

"*Maman?*"

Chapter Twenty-Six

The next morning, Acacia rose early. She ventured out to the pool in her new swimsuit and swam laps for thirty minutes. It was a warm, sunny day, and with the Alps as a backdrop, Acacia enjoyed her swim very much.

She returned to her room long before anyone else was awake to shower and pack. She dressed simply for the flight to Santorini — white pants, a yellow short-sleeved shirt, and bronze-colored sandals. To add more color, she twisted a multi-colored scarf through the belt loops of her pants.

She heard voices coming from the terrace as she approached the dining room. Through the open door she saw Nicholas at the breakfast table. This morning he wasn't seated at the head. She found that curious.

As soon as she stepped onto the terrace, she realized Nicholas was not alone.

"Acacia." He stood and gave her a restrained smile.

Seated next to him was a very attractive older woman with variegated strands of blond, shoulder-length hair. She turned her blue eyes to Acacia inquisitively.

Nicholas materialized at Acacia's side and pulled her chair out for her. "*Maman*, this is Acacia Santos. Acacia, this is my mother, Hélène Cassirer."

As soon as the import of Nicholas's introduction seeped into Acacia's consciousness, she smiled politely. "I'm pleased to meet you, madame."

"And you, mademoiselle." Madame Cassirer returned the smile.

Acacia looked up at Nicholas. "I'm sorry for interrupting. I'll just—" She gestured toward the house.

"We've been expecting you." Madame Cassirer nodded at the chair Nicholas pulled out. "I'm afraid my husband is still sleeping. We arrived from Tahiti late last night."

Acacia glanced at the empty chair at the head of the table and its untouched place setting. Nicholas's parents had come home.

She felt like a trespasser.

She sat down and carefully unfolded her napkin, placing it in her lap. When she lifted her head, Madame Cassirer's eyes were on her. They were curious.

Nicholas regained his seat next to his mother just as Gretle appeared. She served coffee and orange juice, along with champagne.

"I haven't seen my son in some time, so I insisted on a celebratory drink," Madame explained.

Acacia lifted her glass and clinked it against the others.

"We'll be delaying our departure until tomorrow," Nicholas announced. He gave Acacia an apologetic look.

She turned to his mother. "How were your travels?"

"Long. Tahiti is a magical place, but getting to and from it is something else altogether." She sipped her champagne.

"Thank you for your hospitality. You have a beautiful home."

Madame's expression brightened. "Every time I go away, I forget how lovely it is here. The house is usually empty, except for the staff. It's good to have company again."

Silence fell over the table as they ate their breakfast, though it eventually gave way to polite conversation.

Nicholas gave Acacia furtive glances, attempting to catch her eye.

Acacia didn't want to have a silent conversation with him in front of his mother, so she avoided his gaze.

She tried very hard to keep her tone light, but she felt incredibly tense. She didn't like surprises.

When they'd finished their meal, Madame Cassirer turned to her. "Would you like to accompany me on a walk?"

Acacia tried to hide her shock. "Yes, of course."

"Good." Madame stood and so did Nicholas, who pulled out her chair for her.

She patted his unscarred face and kissed him on both cheeks. "I'll see you later."

Nicholas came around the table to help Acacia with her chair. "I didn't know they were coming," he whispered.

Acacia knew she couldn't respond under Madame's watchful eyes. She gave Nicholas a small nod.

"I'll see you later?" His expression was hopeful.

"Yes." She smiled. She had no right to be put out because the Cassirers had returned to their home. She didn't want Nicholas to mistake her discomfort for peevishness.

She turned her head and caught Madame observing them, a smile at the edges of her mouth.

Nicholas stood aside as they crossed to the end of the terrace and down the steps.

At five-foot-eleven, Madame Cassirer was taller than Acacia. She was long legged and thin and elegantly dressed in a simple navy dress with a string of pearls.

"How are your sandals?" Madame stopped and inspected Acacia's footwear. "Are they comfortable?"

"Yes." Acacia eyed Madame's low-heeled navy and white shoes, with the interlocking gold *Cs* at the toe. They weren't exactly walking shoes, but they were handsome.

"There's a footpath. We won't have to worry about sinking into the grass." Madame forged toward a winding trail that was covered in pea-sized gravel. Her expensive shoes made a crunching sound.

Acacia followed and tried to think of appropriate subjects that would be safe for conversation.

"How did you meet my son?" Madame waited until Acacia was at her side before she continued to walk.

"We met at a hotel in Paris. I was the concierge." Acacia saw no reason to obscure the truth.

SYLVAIN REYNARD

"Ah. Which hotel?"

"Hotel Victoire."

"That's a lovely one. We have a flat in that neighborhood." Madame peered at her. "I've always felt that concierges were extremely well-educated. Did you study in Paris?"

"Yes, at the Sorbonne."

A look of sadness shadowed madame's face. "My daughter studied there. I don't suppose you knew her?"

Acacia shook her head.

"She was older than Nicholas, so probably she graduated before you started." Madame's face grew wistful.

"Nicholas took me to the gallery last night. You must be very proud of your daughter's work."

Madame turned to face her. "Nicholas took you to the gallery?"

"Yes."

Madame lifted the pearls she wore around her neck and pulled the strand back and forth. "He hasn't set foot in the gallery in years. None of us have."

Acacia wasn't sure what to do with that information.

Madame dropped her pearls. "I haven't been to Paris recently, although I always enjoy my visits. Do you live inside the city?"

"Yes, in the fifth arrondissement."

Madame smiled. "The Latin Quarter and the Sorbonne. I like that part of the city. It's very interesting."

They walked in silence as the path wound through an expanse of trees. Soon they could no longer view the house.

"How long have you been seeing my son?"

Acacia flushed. "We aren't seeing one another."

Madame stared at her critically. "But you're friends."

Acacia was at a loss for words. She wasn't sure what Nicholas had shared with his mother about her situation. It seemed Madame Cassirer had the wrong impression.

"I was in a bit of trouble, and Nicholas kindly brought me here while I sorted it out," she admitted.

"Good," madame said softly. "It sounds like my son has returned to the right path."

Acacia wondered how much his mother knew of his various activities. She must have had some awareness.

A lamppost came into view next to the path. As they approached, Acacia realized it was an old gas lamp, made of iron and glass.

When they reached the lamppost, madame stopped. "I have a confession to make."

Acacia steeled herself.

"When Nicholas told me he'd brought someone home, I was curious. When the staff told me the *someone* was an attractive young woman, I flew back immediately.

"Nicholas hasn't brought someone home in a very long time." Madame smiled. "You're even lovelier than I imagined."

Acacia grew flustered. "You're very kind. But I need to tell you that there isn't anything romantic between Nicholas and me. He's asked me to assist him with concierge services during his trip to Santorini, and I agreed. Our connection is professional."

"He wouldn't have taken you to the gallery if you were only colleagues," madame replied briskly. "The gallery represents too much sadness and loss.

"It's about time Nicholas became friends with a woman of substance. I'm delighted and will not be persuaded otherwise."

Acacia was too polite to argue. She liked Nicholas's mother. She couldn't help but contrast her behavior with that of the hotel guest from Lyon. Certainly Madame Cassirer had been most welcoming and gracious.

She gestured to the lamppost. "What do you think of this?"

Acacia gazed up at it. The lamppost was incongruous with the trees that surrounded it, as if someone had planted it in the middle of a forest in an act of whimsy.

"The lamppost reminds me of a children's story."

"Really? Which one?"

"*The Lion, the Witch and the Wardrobe.*"

"Just so." Madame looked at the lamppost thoughtfully. "My daughter was fond of that book when she was a child. She used to come here in search of Aslan. Many years ago, there was a driveway. When my husband's parents changed the location of the drive, they had the road dug up and planted grass. They left the lamppost."

"I'm so sorry, madame, for your loss," Acacia said gently.

Madame turned her head. Her face crumpled. But with a tremendous force of will, her features evened out. "Has Nicholas spoken to you of Riva?"

"A little. I was so impressed at how accessible the gallery collection is for people of varying abilities."

"Nicholas must have done that," madame whispered.

"Part of each exhibit has been reproduced in Braille, so the visually impaired can experience the artwork. And once a month, the gallery hosts patients with dementia or Alzheimer's and their caregivers. The gallery plays music and invites them to sit and enjoy the exhibits."

Madame closed her eyes briefly. "I didn't know." She opened her eyes. "When you lose a child, it opens a hole that will never close. In our case, I'm sorry to say that much of our lives center on Riva—on her absence. I avoid the gallery."

She lifted her head resolutely. "I need to visit it. What a wonder you are, my dear."

"I studied art," Acacia volunteered.

"Did you? Which period?"

"Impressionism."

"Oh yes, that's my favorite as well. We had a lovely Degas but..." She closed her mouth.

Acacia nodded. "Nicholas told me."

Madame gave her a funny look. "He told you about the artwork that was stolen?"

"Yes."

"There was a time I thought we'd never be able to speak about what happened. Nicholas must trust you to share such things." Madame came closer. She touched Acacia's cheek maternally. "You are a kind girl. I don't suppose I can persuade you to take tea with me this afternoon? It's been a long time since I've had a tea party."

Acacia smiled. "I'd be delighted."

"Good." Madame Cassirer smiled in return and they set off for the house.

Later that evening, after everyone else had retired, Nicholas and Acacia sat by the pool.

They'd dressed for dinner at the request of his parents. Nicholas had worn one of his black suits and now wore his dress shirt and trousers, his dark blue tie undone and askew around his neck. He'd shed his shoes and socks and was presently dunking his bare feet in the salt water.

Acacia sat next to him in a gauzy, peach-colored gown. Her high heels lay abandoned next to Nicholas's shoes, and she too immersed her feet in the pool.

It was a clear, starry night, and Acacia watched the heavens in breathless wonder. She could never have imagined her path in life would lead to this beautiful place. She could never have imagined such an enjoyable evening with someone else's parents.

A champagne bottle sat in a silver bucket nearby. Nicholas refilled their glasses from time to time as they sipped unhurriedly.

Nicholas broke the silence at last. "I didn't know they were coming."

The breeze lifted a lock of Acacia's hair and plastered it across her lips, where it stuck to her lipstick. Nicholas caught the hair between his fingers and pushed it behind her ear.

"Thank you." She saluted him with champagne.

"Thank you, Acacia. You've been very patient and very charming, despite being surprised by my relatives."

"Your parents are lovely. I enjoyed meeting them."

"Thank you for humoring my mother. She misses Riva." Nicholas's eyes met hers. They were filled with gratitude.

"It wasn't a chore. I haven't been to a tea party in years. Did you know your mother lent me a hat? It was a massive, elegant thing she'd worn to Ascot in England."

"The hat, the walk, the interior design of your apartment in Paris—these are all things she would have done with my sister."

"I know." Acacia's tone was sympathetic. "She misses her."

"I don't know how to talk to my mother." Nicholas lifted his foot from the water and dropped it, which caused a splash. "What's your mother like?"

"She's strict. She's serious, but she loves me fiercely."

"*Fiercely.*" Nicholas grinned. "I like that. My mother has been known to be fierce, too. She's a Rottweiler in Chanel."

Acacia threw her head back and laughed. The comparison of the elegant and refined Madame Cassirer to a Rottweiler was absolutely ridiculous.

"What a beautiful sound that is," Nicholas whispered.

"What sound?"

"Your laugh."

Acacia smoothed the skirt of her dress and took care that the hem didn't fall into the water. "It isn't for me to say, but I think your mother misses you."

Nicholas lifted his glass. "She knows where to find me."

"You know where to find her, as well. She rushed home because you were here."

"I think we both know why she rushed home," he remarked drily.

"When you danced with your mother after dinner, I could see she was happy to be with you again. She was smiling."

Nicholas glanced at Acacia from the corner of his eye. "You wouldn't dance with me."

Acacia stiffened. "I've already explained to your parents that I'm working with you. It wouldn't have been professional for us to dance."

"Perhaps not." He jostled her elbow. "But friends dance."

"We aren't really friends, Nicholas." Acacia kept her voice low so as not to give offense.

He looked down at his feet and moved them below the surface of the water. "Right."

She elbowed him in return. "For all you know, I have an incredibly long list of faults."

"I doubt that." He refilled their glasses.

"Your mother told me she didn't know about all the accessibility programs at the gallery."

"We stopped talking about the gallery after what happened. I continued my involvement, but my parents withdrew."

"You should be proud of what you've done."

Nicholas bobbed his head.

When he didn't comment, Acacia continued. "Art is for everyone, but without access, it becomes elitist."

"That's what my sister used to say. She thought art was a necessity, not a luxury. She instituted an open admission policy one day a month. We've continued that. One day each month we provide admission to everyone, free of charge."

"I wish other galleries and museums would be so open." Acacia put her champagne down and clasped her fingers in her lap. "I don't understand what it's like to lose a sister. You have my deepest sympathy."

Nicholas turned to look at her. "Thank you."

"A loss like that can't be repaired or forgotten. There will always be an absence. But my observation is that many people find meaning and purpose by focusing on a loved one's legacy, by ensuring she or he isn't forgotten.

"Whether or not your mother realizes it, you've been building your sister's legacy. You've expanded the programs she was committed to and added new ones as a tribute to her. You've devoted yourself to finding the artwork that was stolen. Your parents weren't able to do those things, so you did them. You should be proud not only of your family and your sister, but of yourself. Your devotion and hard work are very noble, Nicholas."

He frowned a little.

When his eyes came to hers, they were troubled. "I've failed."

"How have you failed?"

"I haven't found the artwork. I haven't brought her killers to justice."

Acacia sighed and looked up at the heavens again. She was quiet for a moment. "Do you know the story of Sisyphus?"

"I read Camus at university."

Acacia smiled. "Not that version. The ancient myth in Homer's *Odyssey*."

"No, I don't."

"I suppose the relevant points are the same. Sisyphus is condemned to roll a boulder up a hill. Zeus causes the boulder to fall to the bottom of the hill at the exact moment Sisyphus reaches the top. Over and over, Sisyphus exerts himself to roll the boulder up the hill, only to be forced to repeat the activity again and again for all eternity."

"You'll forgive me if I fail to see how this applies to our previous conversation." Nicholas gave her a half smile.

"It's the effort that's praiseworthy. It's Sisyphus's perseverance and resilience that we admire. I think we find something courageous and noble in the determination of others and ourselves." She turned to Nicholas. "I hope your quest for justice is successful. But even if it isn't, there is something courageous about the quest itself. I admire that."

"For God's sake, don't make me Sisyphus." Nicholas threw half his champagne back with one swallow.

"I can't make you anything," Acacia whispered. "But I recognize nobility and courage when I see it."

He sighed heavily and hung his head.

"Nicholas, you only fail when you give up. Every time Sisyphus places his shoulder against the boulder and rolls it up the hill, it's a victory over the gods. They cannot break him. In your mission to find your family's artwork, you honor your parents and your sister by not giving up. And that is a noble victory."

He nodded.

"Friends?" She placed her champagne flute next to his.

He looked her in the eye. "Friends."

They clinked their glasses together and drank.

"Thank you," Nicholas murmured.

"You're welcome."

Chapter Twenty-Seven

"With your knowledge of Homer, you must have been to Greece?" Nicholas's voice broke into Acacia's musings.

"Never." She looked across the aisle of the private plane to where her new friend and employer sat. His scar was visible, so she was careful to make eye contact.

Nicholas hadn't removed his prosthetic until after they'd boarded the plane. Acacia wondered if he always hid his scar around his parents. Surely they knew about it.

Madame and Monsieur Cassirer had breakfasted with them before they left for the airport. Apparently, the Cassirers had decided to stay in Cologny awhile longer.

During the previous afternoon, Madame had volunteered her design services to Acacia for her apartment, and she had gratefully accepted. She drew up an impressive plan and suggested fabrics and paint, to Acacia's delight.

Acacia hadn't expected to be treated with such kindness and generosity by Nicholas's parents. Their openness to her almost made her ashamed of how she'd mistrusted Nicholas.

But trust was earned. Acacia remained self-protective, but she'd begun to trust him a little. He'd sent Rick to watch over her when the BRB's protection had been compromised. He'd warned her to remove her valuables from her apartment, which enabled her to leave Claude with Kate. He'd whisked her safely to his parents' compound and offered her a job.

She'd done nothing to earn his favor, which made her begin to believe he truly was motivated by a sense of responsibility for her because of what had happened at the Victoire.

Nicholas's long legs were stretched out in front of him, and he sipped a vodka and tonic. He was the picture of ease, despite the fact that he wore one of his many restrictive black suits.

"We're approaching Santorini. Prepare for landing." The pilot reminded them to fasten their seatbelts, and the plane began its descent.

Nicholas leaned across the aisle. "You should be able to see the island."

Acacia looked out her window, over the vast expanse of blue sea. In the distance, she could see a crescent-shaped island, dotted with white buildings.

The plane adjusted its speed and continued its descent.

Acacia closed her laptop and placed it next to her new Chanel handbag—a handbag she'd balked at buying. Juliet, however, had insisted she needed something of the sort for her travels.

Acacia had conceded the point, once again keenly aware of how haphazard her packing had been the day she fled Paris. She did not have sufficient, appropriate clothing for professional engagements, and since she was representing Nicholas...

But there was another, far more secretive reason she'd agreed to buy the designer handbag. It was worth several thousand Euros, which made it a ready source of cash should she have need of it. Acacia was never without an exit strategy. Whether she trusted Nicholas or not was irrelevant to the other dangers lurking in the shadows.

She rubbed her eyes.

She'd sent a short but polite email of resignation to the human resources office at Hotel Victoire, informing them she'd accepted another position. She offered two weeks' notice, but the office replied that her resignation would be effective immediately. They were paying her for the next two weeks, though her presence was no longer required.

The speed with which they'd accepted her resignation had hurt. But Acacia hadn't risen through the ranks by nursing hurt feelings.

Something brushed against her forearm. "Remind me of the agenda?"

She turned to Nicholas. "Customs agents will meet us on arrival. A car will be waiting on the tarmac to transfer us to the villa. You'll have time to relax before your dinner meeting with Constantine Zervas."

"Rick?" Nicholas turned to view the man behind him and switched to English. "Do we need to go over the itinerary?"

"Negative." The bodyguard's response was more of a grunt.

Acacia took note of Rick's blank expression, which was mirrored by Kurt, who sat beside him.

Rick was now her protector, but she viewed him with skepticism. He'd captured one of her assailants, interrogated him, and then let him go on Nicholas's orders. The thought unsettled her.

Acacia tightened her seatbelt as the plane continued its descent. She heard the whir of the landing gear. A few minutes later, they landed on the small runway and taxied toward a silver Range Rover.

Acacia wrapped a silk scarf around her head and pushed the ends over her shoulders.

A chuckle sounded at her left.

She turned and saw Nicholas's eyes on her, his mouth wide with amusement. "You don't have to cover your head in Greece, except for inside the churches."

"I know. My research indicates that Santorini can be windy, especially up on the cliffs."

"You've made good use of your laptop during our flight."

"I take my work seriously."

Nicholas angled his head, and his eyes met hers. "I know."

He appraised her before he met her eyes again. "The scarf is very attractive. But I doubt any amount of wind could diminish your beauty."

Acacia's eyes widened. Before she could fumble a response, the plane came to a sudden halt.

Nicholas glanced over her shoulder, out the window. "As a reminder, Constantine is a business associate and not a friend. He knows me as Pierre Breckman."

Acacia nodded. They'd gone over the particulars just after takeoff. Nicholas had handed her a newly minted Swiss passport in the name of Andarta Silva.

"Globalization," he'd said with a wink. "You're part of a new wave of Brazilian immigration to Switzerland."

She hoped she'd remember her new name.

Acacia's skin grew warm as she repeated Nicholas's compliment in her head. She was darker than the fair, Nordic women he seemed to prefer.

Acacia set such inappropriate thoughts aside. Nicholas was her friend and her employer.

She switched on her cell phone and scrolled through the texts she'd sent and received from Kate. As promised, the contractor and his team had started work on her apartment. Madame Cassirer had been in touch with a designer in Paris, who was going to implement the scheme she and Acacia had agreed upon.

Kate had sent updates, including the following:

Holy shit. I didn't realize how much damage there was.

I am so sorry.

Claude says MEOW, which I think means he misses you.

Luc is looking for you.

"Andarta?" Nicholas called. Rick stood next to the now-open door, waiting.

She put her phone in her purse and gathered her things.

Rick exited the plane first and scanned the area before beckoning to Acacia. She descended the steps with Nicholas close behind.

The Greek customs agents seemed to remember him. They shook hands before checking his passport. They barely glanced at Acacia's.

Soon they were comfortably seated in the Range Rover, driving away from the airport and up the windy roads that led to the villa.

Nicholas was pointing out some of the places of interest when Acacia's cell phone rang. She removed the offending item from her handbag. A glance at the screen confirmed it was Luc. She quickly sent the call to voicemail, conscious of Nicholas's eyes on her.

"Is there a problem?" His voice rumbled.

"Not at all." Acacia slipped the phone back into her purse.

He gazed at her for a long moment before he turned his attention to the landscape.

The roads of Santorini were narrow and winding, and they challenged the width of the Range Rover as it ascended the cliff. Acacia gripped the armrest several times as cars whizzed past them, far too close for her comfort.

Finally, the car crested the cliff and approached a closed gate. Armed guards stood sentry at the entrance and waved them through.

"The villa is built into the side of the cliff, overlooking the sea. Only part of it is visible." Nicholas jerked his chin in the direction of the white, single-story building in front of them.

The driver parked and efficiently opened Nicholas's door, while Rick helped Acacia alight.

She recognized Wen as he exited the villa. Again, the young man greeted her warmly and scanned her for surveillance devices. Then he turned his attention to Nicholas, the bodyguards, and the driver. Thankfully, he didn't seem to find anything alarming.

As they entered the villa, a trio of household staff greeted them. An older woman stepped forward to pass Nicholas a note, which he read quickly.

"I need to make a phone call." He gave Acacia a small smile. "Make yourself comfortable; take a swim. I'll come find you later."

Acacia nodded and followed the young man who had her luggage to the back of the villa.

The villa had white-washed walls and windows that looked out over the cliffs and down to the sea. They took a steel staircase to the lower level and walked past an infinity pool and Jacuzzi to Acacia's room.

The young man placed Acacia's luggage in her closet and then lifted the house phone. He told her she should press zero if she needed anything. He pointed to a piece of paper that had the wireless password written on it.

The room reminded her of a cave. It had been hewn out of the rock and covered with plaster that had been painted white. A pale gray tile floor lay beneath her feet. There was a desk and chair, a walk-in closet, an expansive bed covered with mosquito netting, and an ensuite bathroom.

She removed her scarf and placed it next to her laptop on the desk. She retrieved her purse and walked outside, determined to familiarize herself with the surroundings.

A clear, Plexiglas barrier separated the pool deck from the precipitous drop below. She leaned over the edge and looked to see any points of egress, but there were none. No one could climb up the cliffs except an experienced, well-equipped mountain climber. Similarly, even if one wanted to climb down from the villa, there was nowhere to go but into the sea.

Three other doorways flanked the pool area, all of which she assumed led to bedrooms. *Probably Nicholas's room is the largest one, and Rick and Kurt are staying in the others.*

She climbed back up the staircase to the upper level and wandered through the living room, dining room, and kitchen. The dining room opened out to a spacious upper deck, shaded from the sun by a huge canvas canopy. The deck had a dining table that was already set for a meal.

Down the hall from the kitchen she found a home theater, library, laundry room, and a large bathroom with an adjoining steam room.

She noted that several of the windows on the upper level could be used for escape, but one would still have to climb the high iron fence that surrounded the property. She stood in the front doorway and looked at the gate, observing the security guards. She'd have to check the area after nightfall to see if it was illuminated.

Still carrying her Chanel handbag, she returned to her room. She had her Brazilian passport, along with the Swiss passport Nicholas had given her, and she had one thousand Euros she'd withdrawn from her savings account during her shopping spree in Geneva, along with a new burner cell phone she'd already programmed with all her contacts.

Leaving the island undetected in case of an emergency would not be easy. But at least she had the makings of an escape. So long as she had a plan, she could relax.

She opened all the windows in her room and bathroom, and welcomed the island breezes. She sat on the bed and pulled out her old phone.

Luc's voicemail was brief and to the point.

"Caci, where are you? Why are you ignoring my messages? Call me."

Acacia reclined on the bed and looked up at the white ceiling. She didn't want to speak to Luc, and she certainly didn't want to tell him where she was and with whom. But if she didn't reply, she was confident he'd dig harder—precisely what she didn't want him to do, for his safety as well as hers. It was possible whoever had pulled the BRB's surveillance of her could be watching Luc as well.

She sighed and tapped out a text.

I'm fine. Things at the hotel were brutal, so I quit. Taking a few days to visit friends. Back soon.

A gentle wind wafted in from the open door and caressed her face. She hoped the text would be enough.

An hour later, Acacia was relaxing in the Jacuzzi.

She'd spent thirty minutes swimming laps in the pool, pushing herself to the limit. Then she'd put on a pair of sunglasses, reapplied sunscreen, and climbed into the heated whirlpool.

The Jacuzzi was situated near the Plexiglas barrier and offered a view of the cliffs as they spread out on either side, and overlooked the sea. She wondered what it would be like to watch the sun slowly sink below the horizon. She imagined it would be breathtaking.

"There you are." Nicholas approached from behind. He'd forsaken his black suit and was dressed in a white linen shirt and khaki pants. His feet were bare, his hair slightly mussed, and he wore aviator sunglasses.

"I brought you a drink." He handed her a glass of white wine. "It's from a local vineyard."

They clinked glasses.

"You aren't wearing black." Mentally, she observed that his more casual clothes suited him immensely.

"It's too hot for black, and I find myself in a much better mood." He pointed to a deck chair. "May I join you?"

"Of course."

He dropped into it heavily and almost spilled his drink.

"Thank you." She sipped the wine and found it refreshing.

"You're welcome. Sorry I was so long. Constantine has invited us to dinner tonight at his villa in Oia. That's the favored location on the island to watch the sun set."

"Do you want me to go with you?"

He frowned. "Of course."

Acacia scratched her neck. "Concierges don't usually attend dinner meetings."

"You're more than a concierge, and you know it." Nicholas sipped his drink. "How's everything in Paris?"

"Fine." She deflected any follow up questions by pointing to the deck chair, which Nicholas had placed with its back to the sea. "You're facing the wrong way."

"I like where I am."

She shook her head. "You're full of surprises. I still can't believe you protected my cat."

"You're full of surprises as well." Nicholas lowered his voice. "Because we're dining out, I've sent the household staff home. The guards at the gate and the driver are local, but in my employ. Still, we should maintain our personas while we're here."

"Understood." Acacia moved closer to him, and Nicholas leaned in. "I thought Silke drew too much attention to this persona."

A wave of anger rippled across Nicholas's face. "I need Constantine's help. This was the only way I could ask for it."

He straightened and took a large drink. "The household staff will return tomorrow to prepare breakfast. My advance team swept the villa for surveillance devices and removed them before our arrival. They've rerouted the internet through our secure server, which means your email is safe."

"They found surveillance devices?"

"Remarkably, there were only four, and none of them were in your room."

Acacia placed her wine glass on the edge of the Jacuzzi. "Who do you think is behind it?"

"Constantine."

"Your contact has you under surveillance?"

"It's a game we play. He bugs me; I bug him. My team removed the bugs but didn't destroy them. They're feeding disinformation to Constantine, which is probably why he extended the dinner invitation to you."

"I don't follow."

"For the purposes of this trip, you aren't staff. You're my lover."

Acacia went very still. "That wasn't part of our agreement."

"No, but I'm asking you to play the role while we're in public." Nicholas took off his sunglasses. "Any information Constantine acquires can be sold for a price. If interested parties think you're my lover, and we go our separate ways, no one will follow you. If they think you're staff, they may approach you."

Acacia removed her sunglasses so she could see him more clearly. "That doesn't make sense."

"No one from my world has approached Silke since she took off with that American." Nicholas countered, his tone contemptuous. "Constantine's mistress is hosting tonight's dinner. She's Jordanian. Perhaps the two of you will hit it off."

Acacia froze. "Why do you think we'd hit it off?"

"You both speak Arabic. Constantine doesn't."

It took a moment for the tension in Acacia's shoulders to abate. She moved across the Jacuzzi and climbed out.

She wore a tangerine bikini that she knew looked very good against her tan skin. But she ignored her employer's perusal.

While she dried herself with a towel, he approached with a white terry robe. "Let me help."

She allowed him to assist her and then faced him. "I thought you were my friend."

"I am." His dark eyes blazed.

"You're putting me in an extremely awkward situation, with very little warning. That's not how friends treat one another."

Nicholas rubbed at his chin. "You aren't being asked to do anything illegal or scandalous. I'm just asking you to pretend for one evening. It will alleviate Constantine's suspicions."

"Why should he be suspicious of me?"

"You're new to his circle. You're intelligent and beautiful, with a talent for languages. A trained eye can discern that you practice martial arts. Constantine will assume you're Interpol."

Acacia scoffed. "You have an incredible imagination."

"I have an incredible ability for recruiting talent. My associates know this. No matter what we say, Constantine is already investigating you. It's possible he'll assume you're Interpol regardless. We need to misdirect him."

Acacia swore in Portuguese. "He's already investigating me?"

"Undoubtedly. But he won't find anything, of course."

Her hand went to her hair. "Did you plan this?"

"My meeting with Constantine was scheduled long before I met you."

"Really? What about his mistress?"

Nicholas shifted his weight. "What do you mean?"

"Constantine's mistress speaks Arabic. Did you recruit me so I could speak to her?"

"No," he replied smoothly. "Your departure from Paris was a last-minute development designed to keep you safe."

Acacia took a step forward, her eyes on his. "I'm not trained in espionage."

"That's not exactly true."

"Are you mad?"

"What is the motto of Les Clefs d'Or? *Service through friendship.* For one evening, I'm asking you to befriend another young woman who speaks a common language. That's all."

Acacia's hazel eyes flashed. "I'm not interested in becoming your mistress."

"Duly noted," Nicholas responded drily. "Allow me to emphasize that I wasn't extending an invitation."

"Duly noted," she snapped.

He grinned.

She placed her hand on her hip. "Why are you smiling?"

"You aren't afraid to tangle. I admire that."

"I'm Brazilian. We're all like this."

Nicholas brushed the edge of his thumb across his lower lip. "Brazil must be an incredible country."

She ignored the compliment and tied the belt of her robe more tightly. "When are we leaving?"

"An hour and a half. Is that enough time?"

"It's fine. Will dinner be formal?"

"No. I'll wear dress pants and a shirt, but no jacket or tie. A summer dress would be appropriate."

"All right. We agreed Santorini was a trial period. As your friend, I have to caution you that if you put me in a situation like this again, I'll be forced to resign." She tried to pass him but he caught her arm.

She looked up at a conflicted face. Nicholas's lips were pressed together as if he were angry. His eyes communicated something else entirely.

"I admit when I learned you spoke Arabic I hoped you'd be able to discover more about Constantine's mistress." He brought his face closer to hers. "I didn't realize…"

He released her arm and placed his hands at his sides. "My apologies. I'm grateful for your assistance, as always."

She stepped quickly to her room and closed the door behind her.

Chapter Twenty-Eight

"Ladies, if you'll excuse us." Constantine addressed the women in English, which had been the language of conversation for the evening. He pushed his chair back from the dinner table.

He was a handsome man in his late fifties. His dark hair, gray at the temples, brushed his shoulders. His blue eyes sparkled with intelligence, and he wore a day's worth of beard on his tanned face.

Like Nicholas, Constantine wore a light-colored shirt and darker trousers. Even in casual clothes, he spoke and moved with authority.

He stood behind Yasmin's chair and pulled it back, then reached to take her hand as she tottered on very high heels. "Enjoy the sunset. I'll have Theo bring champagne."

Yasmin smiled and kissed him, wrapping her arms around his neck.

Acacia averted her eyes from the intimate display as Nicholas pulled out her chair and helped her to her feet.

"Andy," he murmured a new nickname as he lifted her hand to his lips. He didn't break eye contact as he kissed her palm and the inside of her wrist. "I'll join you soon."

Out of the corner of her eye, she could see Yasmin and Constantine watching.

She touched Nicholas's cheek and stroked the area under his scar. "Don't keep me waiting too long."

His arm slid around her waist, and he caressed her exposed back with his fingertips. Acacia's nerves sparked to life under his touch and she shivered, her eyes fixed on his mouth. She wanted to kiss him.

He must have felt her reaction. He brought his lips to her ear. "Soon."

He stepped away, his dark eyes shining.

She blushed a little and followed Yasmin.

Acacia wore an indigo halter dress that fell to her lower thigh. Although high heels would not have threatened Nicholas's height, she'd eschewed them in favor of silver sandals that laced gladiator style to her knees.

Yasmin led her to a terrace below the dining area that looked out over the sea at the setting sun.

"How long have you been with him?" Yasmin reclined against the cushions of a comfortable chair, her gold dress billowing about her like a queen.

"Not long." Acacia sat opposite and set her bag to one side.

A servant appeared with an ice bucket and expensive champagne. He served them before disappearing back into the dining area, where the low voices of the men could barely be heard.

"Cheers." Yasmin lifted her glass, and Acacia returned her salute.

Yasmin appeared to be about ten years younger than Acacia, which would place her in her mid-twenties. She was petite with long, straight black hair and wide doe eyes. She was very, very beautiful.

"Does his scar bother you?"

Startled, Acacia almost choked. She swallowed her champagne in a rush. "No, why should it?"

"He'd be handsome without it. I suppose it gives him a dangerous look that's sort of attractive. Men from Monaco tend to be playboys." She fixed Acacia with a challenging eye.

Acacia shrugged, because she didn't know what to say.

"Every nationality has its drawbacks," the young woman continued. "Greeks have tempers, but they know how to relax. Not like the Germans."

Acacia was about to ask a question when Yasmin spilled champagne on herself.

She cursed in Arabic.

Acacia stood and wrested the cloth from the champagne bottle. She handed it to Yasmin. "I'm sorry about your dress," she said in Arabic.

Yasmin looked up at her in shock. "You speak my language?"

"Yes."

The younger woman took the cloth and dabbed at her dress before tossing it aside. "Sit down, sit down. I get so tired of speaking English. Constantine doesn't speak Arabic, and I don't speak Greek. Are you from Jordan?"

Acacia hid her face as she sat and rearranged her dress. "I'm from Brazil. But the man who taught me Arabic was Jordanian."

"I thought so. You sound Jordanian." Yasmin beamed. "Are you Muslim?"

Acacia blinked. "No."

Yasmin gestured to her hamsa pendant. "I know non-Muslims wear it for good luck, but when I saw it I wondered. Why did you learn Arabic?"

"I wanted to study international relations," Acacia lied.

"And did you?"

"Yes."

"Do you translate for Pierre?" Yasmin sipped her champagne again.

"No, I don't have anything to do with his work." Acacia mirrored Yasmin's movements. "Do you translate for Constantine?"

Yasmin laughed. "Never. I'm a trained engineer, and he doesn't let me do anything with that, either. But I find ways of amusing myself."

Acacia suppressed her surprise. "What kind of engineering?"

"Mechanical. I studied in Germany." Yasmin relaxed in her chair and rested her head on the cushions. "Most of Constantine's associates are so boring. They're all business types.

"Pierre is nice, of course. He's one of the few men who doesn't treat me as if I'm an idiot. He was with that Swiss woman before. The model."

"Yes." Acacia's tone grew frosty. She couldn't help it. The mention of Silke made her tense.

Yasmin wore a speculative expression. "Is he good to you?"

"Very." Acacia smiled.

"When you move on, avoid Russians." Yasmin finished her champagne and stood to pour another. "Let's get drunk. The men could talk for hours."

She filled Acacia's glass and placed the bottle in the bucket.

Acacia looked hard at the champagne. She had no intention of getting drunk. But perhaps she could distract Yasmin by persuading her to talk about herself.

"Do you mind if I ask about Russians? I haven't encountered any so far, but I'd rather be prepared."

Yasmin gave Acacia a searching look. Then she lifted her gaze to the dining area where Pierre and Constantine stood. They were deep in conversation, both held glasses of what looked like Scotch, and Constantine was smoking a cigar.

"I hate when he does that." Yasmin wrinkled her nose. "The smell will be all over him. And later it will be all over me."

She returned to her seat and took a long draught of champagne. "I was with a Russian before Constantine. He knows, but we don't discuss it."

Acacia eyed the men on the balcony. "Was the Russian bad to you?"

"You could say that. Of course, I didn't know what I was getting into. I met him at a club in Frankfurt." Yasmin turned to face the sunset.

When she didn't continue, Acacia remained silent, trying to figure out what to say next.

"He was a Philistine," Yasmin remarked. "Lots of money made quickly. No culture, no class. It was like living with a barbarian."

Acacia made a sympathetic noise.

"So I'm with him, and he takes me out. He buys me presents. He invites me to his home in Russia, and I go. Then I'm stuck in his house, outside Moscow, in the middle of winter.

"He has all this stuff, all these valuable things, hidden in a secret room. He won't let anyone look at them, not even me—well, not on purpose. He had a Fabergé egg. Do you know what that is?"

"I've only seen them in pictures. They're very rare."

"Exactly. It was small, but it was gorgeous. It was made of gold and had a large diamond on it. It sat on its own pedestal. But instead of displaying it in the open, he had it on a shelf in a vault, next to a pair of elephant tusks."

"Elephant tusks?"

"Yes." Yasmin laughed. "Can you believe it? Running from the floor almost to the ceiling are these ivory tusks and then a Fabergé egg. He had no sense of style, no concept of how to display art. I'm not even sure he knew what he had." She passed a hand over her eyes. "On the other side of the tusks was a drawing of a little girl having her hair done. And the room was full, floor to ceiling with all kinds of artifacts—just thrown into the room the way someone stores junk."

"Why didn't he have the items on display?"

Yasmin threw her hands up. "Exactly. He owned a huge, modern house with expensive décor. When we went out, he threw money around like he was a king. But then he had all these hidden treasures. I found the vault by mistake one day when I was in that part of the house and he'd left the door open. The asshole dragged me out by my hair and punished me."

Acacia inhaled loudly. "I'm sorry."

"That's when I knew I had to get out. I like sex, and I like to party, but I draw the line at punishment. Too bad it took me a few months to get away from him."

"He wouldn't let you go?"

Yasmin gave Acacia a hard look. "You know how it is."

Acacia nodded as if she knew.

"I bided my time, I saved all the money I could get my hands on, and I built a ladder so I could climb out the bedroom window."

"You're joking."

"No." Yasmin was triumphant. "I'm an engineer; I build things. I bribed one of the boys in the kitchen to smuggle me off the estate and into Moscow. Then I left the country. I was lucky. I heard rumors of other girls who were caught trying to escape." She drank more champagne.

"Were you worried he'd come after you?"

"Of course. That's why I went to the Jordanian embassy. I kept my mouth shut about what happened and told them I was a tourist who'd lost her passport. When I got back to Frankfurt, I hooked up with Constantine. I told him about the Russian, and he promised to protect me. I've been with him ever since."

"I'm glad you're all right."

"So am I." Yasmin gestured to the bottle. "Let's finish this so we can get another."

Acacia knew better than to try to keep pace with Yasmin's drinking. That's why at the end of the evening, she was still sober when she and Nicholas returned to the villa.

A security agent she had never met swept them for bugs, but found nothing. Acacia realized the world Nicholas inhabited was one in which trust was entirely absent.

He thanked her for accompanying him to dinner, but he was distant as he escorted her to her room. He didn't ask what she'd discussed with Yasmin. Instead, he bid her good evening and strode away without a backward glance.

Acacia assumed his meeting with Constantine had not gone as planned. Nicholas had been silent the entire drive home, almost grim. Perhaps the whole trip had been a waste.

She removed her makeup and was about to take a shower when her stomach growled. The idea of a midnight snack led to thoughts of eggs, which led to thoughts of Fabergé, which led back to her conversation with Yasmin.

Yasmin's Russian lover had been a collector. But he'd appeared to gather objects rather than artwork, with the exception of the drawing Yasmin mentioned — a little girl having her hair done.

Something about the description stuck in Acacia's mind.

She pulled out her laptop and clicked on an image she'd saved, *The Mante family* by Degas. The pastel drawing featured three females, including a young ballerina whose mother was fixing her hair.

Acacia closed her eyes and went over the evening's conversation in her head. Yasmin had described her lover's collection as a haphazard assortment, hidden in a secret room. She listed a Fabergé egg, elephant tusks, and a drawing of a little girl having her hair done.

Acacia racked her memory to think of another famous drawing that matched Yasmin's description. None came to mind.

On impulse, she accessed an online art database she'd used at the Sorbonne and typed "hair" into the search engine. She filtered the results, excluding sculptures and carvings. A few works remained, but many of them featured women and not girls. A painting from The Hague depicted a girl having her hair done, but according to the website, the painting wasn't missing.

Acacia drummed her fingers against the desk. It was probably a coincidence. The drawing Yasmin described could have been done by anyone, including a friend or relative of the Russian, which would explain why it didn't appear in the database.

Nicholas's sister had been murdered because of a similar drawing, and her murder remained unsolved. Certainly Nicholas deserved every piece of information related to the artwork, even if it was only coincidental.

Acacia closed her laptop and drew a deep breath. Nicholas wasn't in a happy mood. Despite keeping up appearances at the party, it was clear he was upset about something. She didn't relish bearding the lion in his den, but she felt honor bound to tell him what she'd learned.

It was dark, and the moon was high in a cloudless sky. She could see its reflection below on the sea and the surface of the pool. A breath of wind blew her curls about her face and floated over her skin.

Still dressed for dinner, she skirted the pool and walked to Nicholas's bedroom. She knocked on the door.

A moment later he emerged, his white shirt unbuttoned and untucked and his feet bare. Acacia couldn't help but notice his trousers. It looked as if he had just pulled them on — they were zipped but unfastened at the top.

Acacia felt her mouth grow dry.

He leaned a hand against the doorpost. "Can I help you?"

"Yes," she replied. "I mean no." She frowned. "I came to help you."

"I'm eager for help," he teased.

Her frown deepened.

He pushed himself off the doorpost. "Come in. Can I get you a drink?"

"No, thank you. I've had enough."

He chuckled and moved to a bar set against the wall. He poured a glass of tonic water and topped it with a wedge of lemon. "Dinner was delicious, don't you agree?"

"Yasmin said something I think you should know."

Nicholas's eyes lasered into hers. "What did she say?"

Acacia dug her fingernails into her palms, suddenly anxious. "You were right; she was eager for someone to talk to. We chatted in Arabic, and she told me about her ex-boyfriend, a Russian."

Nicholas put down his glass. His eyes grew alert. "Continue."

"She didn't tell me his name, just that he had an estate outside Moscow. Yasmin said his money was new and he'd made it quickly. He collected things, but she referred to him as a Philistine who had no idea what he had."

"And did she?" His tone was harsh.

"Not precisely. He had a secret room at the estate, where he kept everything. She only saw it once, but she described a Fabergé egg, a pair of elephant tusks, and a drawing."

"Acacia," he cautioned. "Forgeries are legion in the art world. It's very easy for the *nouveau riche* to be duped or to pretend to have an original just to impress."

She folded her arms across her chest. "He wasn't trying to impress her; she was already living with him. He kept the goods secret, even from her. But that's not why I'm here. She said there was a drawing of a little girl having her hair done."

Nicholas stared.

When he didn't respond, Acacia grew flustered. "I didn't think to ask her about it. It didn't occur to me until later that she could have seen your Degas. But I searched a fine art database for an image of a girl having her hair done. The only drawing I could find was the one stolen from you."

Nicholas's expression grew rigid. "You think the Russian has it?"

"I don't know. Yasmin didn't describe the girl as a ballerina, so perhaps the drawing is by someone else. But if her boyfriend was a collector, it's possible the items in his vault were genuine. It's possible he has your drawing."

"She didn't mention his name?"

"No. She said he punished her when he found her in his secret room. She escaped by climbing out a window."

Nicholas exhaled. "That's quite a story."

"I thought you should know."

"She could be lying."

"Certainly. But she says Constantine is aware that she fled from this Russian and has pledged to protect her."

Nicholas rubbed his chin. "He mentioned something about her having a troubled past."

"She's a Jordanian engineer who worked in Frankfurt. It sounds like her troubles began with the Russian."

Nicholas covered his face with his hands.

Acacia watched as his shoulders began to shake.

She touched his arm. "I'm so sorry. I didn't mean to upset you. I was only trying to help."

Nicholas threw back his head and roared at the ceiling. He lifted Acacia into his arms and twirled her around, laughing. "I knew you'd bring me luck. I knew it."

She gasped and clutched his shoulders. "What have I done?"

He stopped spinning and held her against his chest, her feet dangling above the floor. "I've been investigating the theft from various angles—the crew, the buyer, the artwork. I know the crew was Bosnian, but I don't know who the buyer was. Because the goods are tied to a murder, all my leads were quickly exhausted."

He placed Acacia on her feet, but kept his arms around her. "A few years ago, I heard rumors about a Russian collector with indiscriminate taste who's been buying up artifacts. I haven't been able to uncover his identity."

"You know about him?"

"I don't know if the collector I've been hearing about is Yasmin's Russian. There's a lot of money in Russia, much of it from the black market. The man I heard about is one of the top figures and very powerful. I had hoped my meeting in Paris would bring me closer to finding him. Then Marcel was attacked."

"The Russian had Marcel attacked?"

"Not the Russian, the dealer I was supposed to meet. He does business in Russia. But Yasmin's description and her connection may lead me to the man I'm looking for."

He twirled Acacia around again, grinning widely.

When he stopped, she was almost breathless. She remained wrapped tightly in his arms, lifted off her feet.

His eyes searched hers. He leaned closer, just an inch. "Acacia," he whispered.

She could feel his breath on her face.

He loosened his hold a fraction, and she slid down his chest. Yet when her feet found the floor, he didn't release her.

Her hands rested on his chest, the gap between the two sides of his unbuttoned shirt revealing a sculpted physique dusted with dark hair. She could smell his cologne and beneath it, the clean aroma of soap.

His left hand slid down the exposed skin of her back to span the hollow just above where the skirt of her dress began. He flexed his hand, and she felt the warmth of their contact ripple up her spine.

His other hand pushed the curls away from her cheek. "I didn't get a chance to tell you how beautiful you looked this evening."

Embarrassed, she wanted to look away, but found she couldn't.

His dark brows drew together. "You're so much more than a beautiful face. But can't I praise your beauty?"

She didn't answer.

He cupped her cheek. "You charmed Constantine and Yasmin. Your charm is why she took you into her confidence."

"Sometimes you long to be able to speak your first language with someone who understands."

He smiled. "I think it's more than just your facility with Arabic. It's you."

She leaned against his palm.

"Acacia, there's so much corruption in my world. Lies, betrayal, viciousness. You don't know how lovely it is to be in the presence of someone truthful and honorable."

She laughed softly. She couldn't help herself. It had been a long time since she'd received such compliments. She was out of practice.

"I like to hear you laugh." Nicholas tightened his hold and brought her chest against his. "Look at those eyes. A man could get lost in eyes like those."

He lowered his mouth to within a hair's breadth of hers. Acacia closed her eyes.

There was a pause, which seemed to last forever. Then something warm pressed against her cheek.

Nicholas repeated the embrace on her other cheek and released her.

Confused, she opened her eyes.

He stood a foot away, out of reach.

"Good night, Acacia," he said gruffly. "Rest well."

She stood and gazed up at him, baffled by what had just happened.

Nicholas's eyes were carefully guarded.

A wave of embarrassment washed over her, and she fled, her indigo dress fanning out as she ran like a deer to her room.

Chapter Twenty-Nine

This shall not stand.

It was a silly thing, really. On occasion a word or phrase would take residence in her mind, like the refrain of an annoying song.

What had happened with Nicholas the night before could not stand, which was why Acacia was typing up her resignation letter.

The door and windows to her cave-like rooms were open, and the bright sunshine poured in. An hour earlier, one of the household staff had brought a breakfast tray. It sat on its stand by the door, nearly empty. It had been a feast: coffee, fresh yogurt with honey, fruit, and bread and cheese. She'd awoken ravenous and slaked her hunger next to the pool.

She'd seen Rick and Kurt that morning, but Nicholas's bedroom door remained closed. She surmised he was still asleep.

She re-read her resignation letter and attached it to an email she'd drafted to Madame Bishop, blind-copying Nicholas. She didn't press send. Not yet.

She was attracted to Nicholas; there was no reason to deny it. He was handsome, intelligent, and charming, but much more. His devotion to his sister and her memory revealed a nobility of soul that Acacia admired. She also liked his parents and appreciated their kind hospitality.

She'd wanted Nicholas to kiss her and was sorely disappointed when he'd opted for her cheek instead. But he was her employer. It was highly unprofessional to become romantically involved with a supervisor, which was why she felt compelled to resign. She'd return to Paris and hopefully Madame Bishop could help her find another position as an executive assistant. Her hope of finding work as a concierge would have to be set aside, as least in the short term.

She wondered if her friendship with Nicholas would survive her resignation. Acacia felt a slight twinge, but it was a twinge she had no business feeling. Perhaps Nicholas was attracted to her. Perhaps not. He'd been emotional about the possibility of locating the stolen Degas. That emotion had likely translated into a momentary lapse in judgment. He would continue the quest for his family's artwork, and she would go home.

She checked her bank account balances and was gratified to see that the Victoire was still paying her, as they'd promised. She transferred the regular monthly amount to her mother's account in Brazil and tapped out a short email to confirm the transaction.

Her mother had to know she was avoiding her. Acacia hadn't returned any of her calls and had let her mother think she was still in Paris. She'd explain everything later, when she had more privacy.

She was in the middle of a text to Kate when a knock sounded. She turned to find Nicholas standing outside her open door.

"Good morning." His tone was warm, but his eyes were wary. "Did you rest well?"

She closed her laptop. "Yes, and you?"

"Tolerably, I suppose." He brushed his hair from his forehead. He glanced at the empty tray. "You've already had breakfast."

She nodded, still clutching her phone.

His attention focused on her phone for a moment. "Spend the day with me."

She looked at him with surprise. "Sorry?"

He entered her room. "We don't leave until tomorrow. Let's go to the beach."

"Why?"

He reared back and looked remarkably as if she'd wounded him.

She flushed. "I beg your pardon. That was rude. Nicholas, I've decided to resign my position with you."

His expression tightened. "If that's what you want…"

"I think it's best."

He paused. "Since you're resigning, I'm free to enjoy your company."

"As a friend?" Acacia asked in earnest.

"Is that what you want?" His tone was a challenge.

"It seems you can't decide what you want me to be."

He took a step closer. "Oh, I've decided."

Acacia placed her phone on her desk and changed the subject. "Were you able to find out more from Marcel's journal?"

"Not from the journal," Nicholas hedged.

"From some other source?"

"I was able to discover the name of the man I was supposed to meet in Paris. My team tracked one of your attackers, and he led us to a Parisian art dealer, who does a hell of a lot of work in Russia. Unfortunately, I can't confirm the dealer's identity with Marcel. So I can't be sure the dealer who sent men after you is the same person behind the attack on Marcel."

"Marcel is still unconscious?"

"No. He's dead."

Acacia made a horrified noise.

Nicholas took a step closer. "I'm sorry to tell you this. He died yesterday of his injuries."

She grabbed at her hair. "They killed him. They beat him so badly he died."

"Yes, I'm sorry." Nicholas placed his hand on her shoulder. "Can I get you something? A glass of water?"

"No. Can you give the dealer's name to the BRB?"

Nicholas squeezed her shoulder and moved away. "Given the fact that BRB surveillance failed you, I'm not in a hurry to trust them. I'll pass the name to the Minister of the Interior, but I'm going to warn him that some of his BRB agents may be compromised."

Acacia looked up at Nicholas. "The dealer shouldn't be allowed to get away with this."

"He won't," Nicholas replied firmly. "My team is already investigating the dealer's Russian contacts. We're going to cross-reference those names with Yasmin's description and see if there's any overlap."

At the same time, I'm going to approach Constantine to see if he can put me in touch with someone who has done business with Yasmin's ex-boyfriend."

"I thought your meeting with Constantine didn't go well."

Nicholas frowned. "What makes you say that?"

"You looked unhappy last evening. You didn't say anything in the car on the way back."

"My mind was heavy with…other thoughts."

She regarded him skeptically.

He cleared his throat. "In addition, the contact Constantine provided me with last night will not bring me closer to my goal."

"Yasmin is afraid of the Russian, and Constantine hates him, presumably. Why not ask them for his name?"

"Remember that Constantine knows me as Pierre Breckman. I can't tell him I'm looking for the Cassirer pieces. Also, names are rarely exchanged."

"What if the Russian is the one you're looking for?"

"Then I have to find another way of discovering his identity. Although Constantine may decide to put me in touch with someone who's done business with Yasmin's ex. That way, he remains at arm's length."

Nicholas gave Acacia a searching look. "We don't have to go to the beach. There's an art gallery I'd like to show you. Or we could visit the beach in the morning and the gallery after lunch."

She rubbed her forehead. "Of course I enjoy your company, Nicholas. But what will your other staff think?"

His brow furrowed. "I'm not inviting you to do anything outrageous. Please don't blame me for being attracted to you. Is that so great a fault?"

His voice and the look in his eyes were endearing. Acacia had to tamp down the thrill she felt at his admission. Perhaps he'd wanted to kiss her last night after all.

She wondered what had held him back. Perhaps he, like her, was conscious of the risk involved when one crossed a line.

"I need a few minutes to change and pack a bag."

"Good. We'll drive down to Red Beach, near Akrotiri. We'll stay as long as you like and then have lunch and visit the art gallery."

Nicholas bowed. "Bring a change of clothes for later tonight. I'll take you to dinner at a restaurant on the cliffs."

As she watched his retreating back, Acacia tried to take stock of her feelings. They were entirely too conflicted.

※ ※

"Why aren't we taking the Range Rover?" Acacia stood next to a Jeep, open at the top as well as the sides.

Nicholas wore sunglasses, a linen shirt, and khaki pants.

"I thought it would be fun to take the Jeep." He looked over his shoulder. "Rick and Kurt will follow us."

She turned to follow his gaze. The silver vehicle was parked behind them, ready to move. She scowled.

"I'm sorry." He eyed her reaction. "I can't travel without them."

"After what happened with Marcel, I don't blame you. I feel awkward around them, though."

"You'll get used to them. I pay them a tremendous amount of money to protect what I value." He gave her a look, heavy with meaning, before he helped her climb into the Jeep.

He crossed to the driver's side and took the wheel, then piloted the vehicle through the gates and onto the road.

Acacia rummaged in her bag for a scarf and tied it over her hair.

The sound of Nicholas's laughter rang out.

She gave him a sidelong glance.

"It should be a crime to look so fetching in a head scarf," he said. He bumped her elbow with his as he moved the gearshift.

"You don't have to worry about your hair." She eyed him behind her sunglasses. "Mine would be a mess if I let the wind get at it."

"You don't like my hair?" He pushed it back from his forehead.

She grinned. "Vanity, thy name is Nicholas."

"I'm far from vain." His tone grew serious. "How could I be?"

Something about the way he said the words warranted a response. Acacia looked at his profile while she spoke. "As your friend, I would tell you not to worry about such things. The people that count, the good people, will remember your words and your actions, and how you treated them. Over time, that's what forms our impression of beauty or handsomeness, not just the outward appearance."

A muscle jumped in his jaw. "Do you really believe that?"

"Yes." She turned in her seat so she could face him, even though he kept his eyes on the road. Mostly. "A lot of attractive and powerful guests came through the Victoire. I can't tell you how quickly my evaluation of attractiveness plummeted when someone was rude or condescending."

"What if the person apologized and was sorry for it?"

She turned to face the road again. It was extremely bumpy, and Acacia had to hold tight so she wouldn't bounce around too much.

"If the apology was sincere, I'd be inclined to forget it, provided the bad behavior wasn't repeated."

Nicholas remained silent.

Acacia felt compelled to break the silence at least once more. "I've done things I regret. I hope they won't be held against me forever. Keeping that in mind, I try to give a little latitude to others when they make mistakes."

"I'm very glad to hear that," Nicholas said.

He bumped her elbow once again, and Acacia couldn't be sure if it was intentional or not.

She picked at the hem of her short, bright pink sundress. "I'm wary of people who put too much value in someone's appearance. In a few years I'll be forty. I know I won't look like this forever. The people who are important to me value who I truly am, not just what I look like."

Nicholas released the gearshift and took hold of her hand. He brought it to his lips and kissed it. "I'm almost forty. It's just a number."

She changed the subject. "I wanted to thank you again for coming to my defense with the woman from Lyon."

Nicholas let go of her hand so he could downshift. "She was hateful to you."

"Not everyone likes Brazilians," Acacia observed.

"Obviously some people lack good taste."

She smiled. "It meant something that you defended me. The better I get to know you, the more it means."

"I'm glad." Nicholas gripped the wheel tightly. "You were very patient with that woman and also with me. You're much better at controlling your anger than I am."

"Years of practice."

"I'm sorry to hear that." His tone was sincere. "I'm sorry I contributed to that practice in Paris. I regret my behavior very much."

"You're forgiven."

"Thank you." His eyes met hers before he refocused on the road. "Why did you only buy a few things in Geneva? Juliet said you were frugal."

Acacia pretended to be fascinated by the straps of her sundress. "I didn't want to waste your money."

"Anything bought for your pleasure or comfort could hardly be a waste. You look lovely in that pink dress, by the way. Bright colors suit you."

"Thanks." Acacia folded her hands in her lap.

"What do you think of Yasmin and Constantine?"

"I don't judge."

"I'm not asking for a moral evaluation."

Acacia gazed down at her hands. "Yasmin is an engineer. But she has to stay with Constantine because she needs his protection."

"He cares for her."

"Maybe she cares for him. But she didn't seem content or in love." Acacia shrugged. "It's none of my business, but that is not the kind of life I want."

Nicholas remained silent for the rest of the drive.

They parked the Jeep at the top of the hill before hiking down to the beach, which was located in a small cove. High red cliffs stood over the dark volcanic sand that stretched toward the water.

Rick and Kurt accompanied them as they picked their way around the various sunbathers to an empty set of lounges next to a closed umbrella.

Nicholas turned and marked the location of the sun. "Is this all right?"

"It's good." Acacia placed her bag and beach towel on one of the lounges.

A man approached them and asked for payment to rent the chairs. Nicholas paid him, and he quickly put up the umbrella, adjusting it to provide only minimal shade.

"You want more shade?" The man addressed Nicholas in English.

Nicholas cast Acacia a questioning look.

"No, I prefer the sun." She unrolled her towel and arranged it carefully.

The man continued to the next sunbathers, and Rick and Kurt took their places in deck chairs behind the lounges.

Out of the corner of her eye, Acacia watched as Nicholas pulled his linen shirt over his head, revealing his muscled chest and abdomen. His khaki pants followed, leaving him in black swim trunks that fit very well.

While he slathered sunscreen on his arms and chest, she removed her sundress and adjusted her tangerine bikini. While many women were topless, as was common in Greece, she kept her top on.

She glanced over at Nicholas and discovered he'd abandoned his sunscreen to stare at her.

She lowered her sunglasses. "Something wrong?"

"Not at all. I was wondering if you'd help me." He waggled the sunscreen in his hand.

"Sit down."

He sat with his back to her, and she stood behind him. She squirted the white lotion into her hand and smoothed it over his broad shoulders.

Under her touch, his muscles tensed and then relaxed. She couldn't help but notice how fit he was.

"Your turn," he said thickly when she'd returned the bottle to him.

He rubbed the sunscreen into her skin. His touch was light but focused as he spread the cool substance all over. When he touched her lower back, she shivered.

"I should have warmed it first. I'm sorry," he apologized.

She felt his breath on her ear and the heat of his body so close to hers. "It's all right."

He smoothed over her shoulders, a last caress, before he sat back.

She thanked him and returned to her lounge where she lowered herself on her stomach.

A cell phone rang nearby. Nicholas muttered a curse and retrieved his phone from a beach tote he'd placed in the sand.

Acacia turned her head in his direction. "No rest for the weary?"

"I'm switching it off. They'll have to do without me for a few hours." He tossed the phone back into the bag. "You have my full attention."

She laughed. "Sorry to disappoint, but I'm taking a nap. You and your friends kept me out too late last night."

"Today is your day." He pulled out a Paris newspaper. "If you need anything, Andarta, anything at all, I'm here."

She started at the unfamiliar name, but recovered herself and returned his smile.

Nicholas's life was far from simple. She wondered how he could relax when there were so many dangers.

But Acacia couldn't deny that the beach was peaceful. She soon forgot about the bodyguards as she dozed in the hot sun. The gentle hum of the people around her combined with the sound of the waves lapping against the sand. The rhythm was soothing.

What seemed like hours later, Nicholas touched her shoulder. "I'm worried you're going to burn, *ma chère*. I think you should roll over."

Slightly hazy from her nap, Acacia simply nodded. It took her a moment to right herself and sit up.

"I'm going into the water. Join me?" Nicholas extended his hand.

She set her sunglasses down and placed her hand in his. Nicholas's hold was firm. He stroked her hand with his thumb as he navigated around the other sunbathers to the ocean.

When they reached the water, his grip on her tightened.

Acacia hesitated as the waves kissed her toes. The water seemed cool to her heated skin.

She looked over her shoulder and saw that the bodyguards had followed. As they approached, Acacia tugged Nicholas into the sea.

The water was at Acacia's waist when Nicholas released her hand. He immersed himself and then emerged from the surf and wiped the water from his face. "Much better."

Water droplets clung to his shoulders and chest and glistened in the sun like tiny jewels. Lower down, the droplets winked at her from a defined abdomen and the beginning of a trail of hair that disappeared below his waistband.

She looked away and surveyed the crowded beach and the looming bodyguards, who'd dipped their toes into the surf.

There were many beautiful women, almost all of them topless, who sunned themselves on lounge chairs and towels. A few had wandered into the water and looked like mermaids emerging from the foam.

Nicholas stood with his back to the mermaids, his eyes fixed on her. The realization sent a tingle down her spine.

She knew she was attractive. Her height stretched out her curves, but her breasts and her backside were generous. Her legs were long, and she had a narrow waist. Nicholas seemed to appreciate her bikini.

An arc of water sailed over her. She shrieked as the cold hit her skin.

Nicholas laughed. The bastard had splashed her.

Without hesitation, she used both hands to splash him back.

Nicholas held his arms up to block the spray, but was unsuccessful. With a roar, he charged, and lifted and spun her around.

Disoriented, she clutched at his shoulders and giggled.

"You are so beautiful." He stopped turning. They were at eye level, their faces very close. "I've seen you in a concierge uniform, a bikini, a formal gown, and jeans. No matter what you're wearing, you always take my breath away."

Nicholas's warm body pressed against hers, chest against chest. His arms wrapped around her. She felt safe, perhaps for the first time in years.

Nicholas's gaze moved to her mouth.

He inhaled slowly, as if he were exerting himself, and placed her on her feet. He released her upper arms. "I've laughed more the past few days than I've laughed in a very long time."

"I'm glad."

He lifted his dripping hand and pushed her hair back from her face. "I may be Sisyphus, but you are Euphrosyne, the goddess of laughter. She's one of the three Graces featured in Botticelli's *Primavera*."

Embarrassed, Acacia looked toward shore.

Nicholas took her hand in his. "We'd better return before Rick and Kurt show us what they look like in swimsuits. Do you think they wear Speedos?"

Acacia burst out laughing.

"So you grew up in Brazil?" Nicholas poured Acacia another glass of red wine.

They sat in a *taverna* built into the cliff, overlooking the sea. Their table stood next to the railing and afforded them an exceptional view. But again, Nicholas's attention was entirely fixed on her.

They'd changed for dinner. Acacia wore a knee-length, pale purple dress with high-heeled bronze sandals. Nicholas wore a navy linen jacket over a white Oxford shirt and dark-washed jeans.

"We lived in Recife. I tried to spend as much time as possible at the beach when I wasn't studying." Acacia sipped her wine.

"I bet you drove all the young men crazy."

She shook her head. "As I told you, my mother was strict."

"But not your father?"

Acacia placed her glass on the table to steady herself. "He was strict too. How about your parents? Were they strict when you were young?"

"Not really. You've met them, so you know they prize manners and deportment. Apart from that, we had a lot of freedom. Perhaps too much freedom."

"Did you go to boarding school?"

Nicholas gripped the stem of his wine glass. "No. I went to school in Geneva and lived at home until I went to university."

"What did you study?"

"Business."

"That's a surprise," Acacia teased. "I thought you were an expert in Lyonnais history and French existentialism. Did you attend the University of Zurich?"

"No, the London School of Economics."

Acacia couldn't hide how impressed she was. "Did you always want to go into business?"

"My parents expected us to be involved in the family business. Riva chose to curate the gallery. I decided to work for one of my father's companies in London. I've always been interested in history, but when I was young I wanted to be a tennis player."

"Really?"

"Yes. Do you play?"

"A little." She gave him a half-smile. "I wouldn't be a very good opponent."

"I doubt that." He tasted his wine. "Did you always want to be a concierge?"

"No, I wanted to be a curator and oversee an art gallery."

Nicholas's eyes widened. "Why didn't you?"

"I had a part-time job working at a hotel, and I kept being offered more work. I had difficulty finding employment in the art world. Finally, I gave up and took a few classes in hospitality."

Nicholas looked stricken. "Why didn't you tell me?"

"Why would I?"

"I can make an introduction. I'm friendly with the director of the Louvre, for God's sake."

She bristled. "I don't want a job at the Louvre because I know someone who's friends with the director."

"Why not?"

"Because I want to earn it."

Nicholas turned his head and looked out toward where the sun was setting.

I've offended his pride. She waited for him to turn to her once again.

The left side of his face was visible, and she studied it, noting that she'd become used to his scar. She'd been quietly upset when Yasmin brought it up, intimating that it was repulsive. It wasn't. It was just part of Nicholas, the way the scar near her temple was part of her. Over time, she doubted she'd notice it.

She reached out across the table to touch his fingers. He surprised her by twining them with hers.

He gave her a repentant look. "Can I interest you in more wine?"

"No." She squeezed his fingers. "I didn't mean to sound ungrateful. It's kind of you to offer, but I don't want anything from you."

"Perhaps that's why I want to give you everything."

Acacia rearranged the napkin in her lap, still holding Nicholas's hand across the table.

He waited until she lifted her head. "You are the only one who never wanted anything from me."

A long look passed between them, then Nicholas turned to look toward the sunset.

Chapter Thirty

They'd barely finished dinner when several of the waiters pushed empty tables aside in the center of the dining area to create a dance floor.

Music sounded from a pair of speakers. A group of men and women dressed in traditional costumes came out, bowed, and began a Santorini folk dance.

The restaurant patrons clapped their approval, and Acacia turned her chair so she could have a better view.

She glanced at Nicholas. Instead of watching the dancers, he was watching her.

When the first song ended, the performers approached the patrons and invited them to join the next dance. Acacia waved off the young man who spoke to her.

"You should dance," Nicholas suggested.

"I don't think so."

"Why not?" He looked at her feet, which were tapping against the floor. "You can barely sit still."

"I don't want some man I don't know touching me."

Nicholas gave her a curious look. "There is another option."

Acacia looked at the dancers and patrons lining up together, arms around one another's shoulders. "I can't dance in these shoes."

"That's easily fixed." Nicholas threw his napkin on the table and crouched in front of her.

"What are you doing?" she asked.

"Removing your shoes."

Discreetly, Nicholas lifted Acacia's foot and undid the strap around her ankle. He slipped off the bronze sandal and placed it aside. Then he repeated the procedure on her other foot.

He stood and offered his hand. "Let's go."

She hesitated, but then the music started, and she took his hand. He led her to the line of dancers and positioned her between a female dancer and himself.

Acacia's shoulders were bare in her pale purple dress. When Nicholas rested his arm across them, she felt a prickle of heat. Then they danced, mirroring the steps of the professionals as the music began slowly and increased its tempo.

Acacia could dance. She had innate rhythm and loved to move to music. She was amused as she watched Nicholas, who was a head and shoulders taller than everyone else, gamely trying to lift his long legs to keep step.

She smiled, she giggled, and she laughed until her eyes watered. It was so much fun. Almost the entire restaurant joined in the celebration.

When the dance was over, Acacia hugged the young woman at her side. Nicholas did the same. Then she looked up at him.

He'd been laughing and smiling too, but he grew contemplative.

She looked down at her brightly painted toes. "Thank you. You're a good sport."

He wove their fingers together and led her back to the table, where he helped her with her shoes. "Do you want to stay?"

"No." She gazed longingly at the sea. The sun had slipped just below the horizon. "I wouldn't mind a walk."

"I'll settle up." He waved over a waiter and quickly paid the bill.

"We can walk along the cliffs. There's a pedestrian path." They climbed the stairs that led to the Jeep, as Rick and Kurt followed close behind. Before they reached the parking area, Nicholas took a left turn.

"What do you call that?" He nodded vaguely at her dress.

"Call what?" She smoothed her skirt.

"The material at the bottom of your outfit."

In concert, they looked down.

Acacia laughed. "That's a ruffle."

"I like it."

"It's meant to be flirtatious."

Nicholas lifted their conjoined hands and kissed her knuckles. "And are you?"

"Am I what?"

"Flirtatious?"

"When I want to be."

Nicholas groaned, as if her answer pained him.

They walked slowly and admired the streaks of orange, pink, and purple that still lit the sky.

The wind began to rise and blew Acacia's curls across her face. She tried tucking them behind her ears unsuccessfully and finally gave up.

At the top of a staircase, Nicholas stopped and removed the navy linen jacket he'd worn to dinner. He placed it around her bare shoulders. "There." He pulled the lapels together, as if that would offer additional warmth.

She smiled up at him. "You noticed I was cold."

"I notice everything about you." He stood with his back to the sea and held her hand.

She looked down at their connection. It was a little thing—one set of fingers clasping another. But it was thrilling and comforting and strangely natural, given how little they knew one another. It was as if their hands had become acquainted long ago and were pleased at being reunited.

"What are you passionate about?" She lifted her gaze to his face. He watched her intently.

Nicholas's hands moved with hers, bringing her next to him, against the whitewashed concrete barrier that stood on the side of the cliff.

She frowned. "Perhaps my question was too intimate. I'm sorry."

"It wasn't, no," Nicholas responded. "You surprised me. There's one question I've been expecting, but as ever, you are most unexpected. In the best sense."

"What's the question?"

He gave her a half-smile. "If it hasn't occurred to you, I'll let it be.

"I used to be passionate about tennis, my work, my circle of friends. I'm afraid all those passions have given way to family concerns." His smile faded.

"Can I ask about your sister?"

"She was intelligent and funny. She was passionate about art. She always wanted to curate the gallery, even when she was a little girl."

"She must have been very gifted."

A fond expression came over Nicholas's face. "She was. I had a mind for numbers and problem solving. She had a mind for beauty. In many ways, she was closer to my parents than I was."

Nicholas exhaled slowly and looked down at Acacia. "Do you think if someone does the right thing for the wrong reason, the action is still right?"

"That sounds like a question for a prophet."

"What about doing the wrong thing for the right reason?" His eyes focused on hers.

"That question is easier to answer. I think it's clear that wrong actions are wrong, even if you have good intentions."

"Why?" He came a step closer.

She took a deep breath. "Because the rhetoric of racists, terrorists, and those that commit genocide always claims good intentions. The woman from Lyon claims to love France and wants to keep it strong. So she's determined to keep foreigners out. In the Rwandan conflict, the factions claimed to want to protect themselves. So they killed the men, women, and children of the other side."

Acacia shook her head. "Perhaps the real problem with the world is self-deception. People have evil intentions, believing them to be good."

Nicholas was silent. He drew her into his side and placed his arm around her shoulder. Together, they watched the light colors darken and fade from the sky.

Nicholas drove back to the villa, taking his time down the dark, winding roads.

When they reached their destination, he placed his hands on Acacia's waist and lifted her to the ground. She touched his chest to steady herself.

"I have to make a few phone calls." His face was rueful. "Thank you for today."

"Thank you. I had fun."

He lifted his hand to push the curls out of her face. "You didn't wear your head scarf."

She touched her hair frantically. "Is it a mess?"

"No. It's gorgeous."

She lowered her gaze. "I should give you your jacket."

She tried to remove the item but Nicholas stopped her. "I'll get it from you tomorrow."

He glanced over his shoulder. Rick and Kurt stood by the door to the villa.

Nicholas made an unhappy sound.

He touched her forehead, just the barest brush of the edge of his thumb, and stepped back. "I'm afraid they'll have to scan us in case we picked up any surveillance devices."

"All right."

"Good night, *ma*—" He gritted his teeth and cut off the last word.

Before Acacia could respond, he turned and strode away.

"Good night," she called to his retreating back.

Chapter Thirty-One

Things had changed.

Spending the day with Nicholas away from many of the trappings of his lifestyle had been one of Acacia's best days ever.

He'd been attentive and companionable, and of course, she was attracted to him. If they'd met under different circumstances, she would have been sorely tempted to see what they could become. But theirs was a relationship destined to end for several reasons.

Acacia counted herself lucky to have had such an amazing day and got ready for bed.

She took her time showering and doing her hair. She slipped into a pale green silk nightdress that looked lovely against her tan skin. She rinsed out her bikini and hung it to dry in the bathroom.

Loneliness washed over her as she turned out the lights.

The time she'd spent with Nicholas reminded her what it was like to have a boyfriend. Alone in her bedroom, she was confronted by how long and desolate nights could be.

It's just the darkness. Everything is worse at night. Tomorrow the sun will come out and you'll feel better.

She lied to herself because it would enable her to sleep. But the truth was, she'd be lonely tomorrow. And the day after that.

Loneliness, it seemed, was the constant companion of those who kept secrets. The realization didn't make the reality any easier.

She switched on the bathroom light and adjusted the door to ensure the bedroom was no longer completely dark.

A knock sounded.

At first she thought she was hearing things. Then the knock sounded again.

She padded over to the door.

Nicholas stood outside, his hair wet and carefully combed. He wore a white shirt, which was unbuttoned at the neck, and khaki pants. He wasn't wearing shoes.

Her heart thudded in her chest.

His dark eyes burned into hers. A question.

She stood aside.

Nicholas stepped into her room and closed the door. His gaze traveled to the shaft of light that shone from the bathroom to the bed.

Before she could draw breath, Nicholas strode toward her and cupped her face with his hands. Electricity charged between them. Nicholas's lips were firm and determined as they spread over hers.

She clutched his biceps and kissed him back. He made a noise in his throat that sounded like desire.

Nicholas kissed her, strongly and passionately, as if his desperation had reached a fevered pitch.

Acacia felt their connection all the way down to her toes. Thoughts of propriety and professional conduct were completely forgotten. There was just Nicholas and she, fused at the mouth.

Her loneliness fled as she wrapped her arms around his neck and luxuriated in the feel of his tall, strong body against hers.

His tongue slid against the seam of her lips and she opened, humming in satisfaction. Still he cupped her face, holding her firmly but gently as she welcomed him into her mouth.

She lifted onto the tips of her toes and stroked her tongue against his. He tasted of licorice.

With a groan, he withdrew to nip at her lower lip. Fire and heat exploded between them. She could barely draw breath as he angled his head to kiss her more deeply.

A few more beats and Nicholas's pace slowed. His hands found her hair, and he stroked her scalp.

She smiled against his lips.

Then his hands slipped to her shoulders and wound around her back. He held her so close all space between them was erased.

She leaned against him and traced the back of his neck and the tendons that led to his shoulders. All the while, their mouths and tongues explored at an unhurried pace.

Nicholas's fingers danced along her exposed back and down to where the top edge of her underwear should have been under her nightgown. And wasn't.

His fingers stilled.

There was a question in his eyes, but Acacia didn't answer.

His expression was raw as he scanned her face.

She smiled shyly.

Her smile, it seemed, was enough. Whatever concern he had retreated, and his face relaxed.

"I've wanted to kiss you for some time," he confessed. His large hands spanned her lower back, just above the curve of her backside. Acacia's skin tingled.

"You're beautiful and charming and good," he continued.

She rested her hands on his broad shoulders. "Don't put me on a pedestal. I'll fall."

Nicholas's dark eyes glittered. "I've got you, Acacia."

She read want in his eyes. His gaze was heated as he slid both hands beneath the silk of her nightdress to grip her naked backside. His touch was firm as he kneaded the flesh. He made a noise of appreciation.

She didn't protest. She raised herself up to capture his mouth in a brief, deep kiss before his lips moved to her neck. He was unhurried as he traced the column of her throat.

Her spine rippled in reaction. She placed gentle pressure on his neck and held him to her, as he ascended and descended her neck.

She reached around to kiss the shell of his ear. "Take me to bed."

"I won't deny you," he whispered against her skin. "But I want to take my time."

His nose skimmed her collarbone until it found the thin strap of her nightdress. He nudged it aside and pulled back so he could see her. The heat in his gaze flared at her exposed breast.

"Lovely."

Her breasts were full, and she knew it. But Nicholas stared as if they were a revelation.

He scorched a leisurely path with his lips from her shoulder to the top of her breast, and made an appreciative sound when he reached his prize.

Acacia tugged at his hair until his mouth found her nipple. He licked it, then teased and tasted before he sucked it into his mouth.

Acacia moaned.

Nicholas continued his adoration and slid her other strap over her shoulder. He tasted her other breast as her nightdress fell to her hips.

She gasped at the cool night air against her skin, but the jolt was soon forgotten. It was difficult to concentrate on anything other than pleasure. Nicholas had a talented mouth. His lips, tongue, and teeth played with her nipples, building and feeding desire.

She liked the way she felt in his large hands as he cupped her. She liked how he continued to caress her, even while his mouth was engaged.

Acacia inhaled the scent that lifted from his skin — a clean scent that reminded her of apples.

When he straightened, her fingers fell to the buttons of his shirt. He pulled it over his head and dropped it to the floor. Before his hands could move to his belt, she stopped him.

"I want to admire you." She covered his pectorals with her palms and kissed the space over his heart.

His skin was warm and stretched over lean muscles, with a light covering of dark hair. She took her time touching him, as if his body was a land to be discovered. Her fingertips roamed his shoulders, his biceps, and down his chest to the defined ridges of his abdomen.

She scorched a path above his waistband, and he reached for his belt. His trousers followed, which allowed her a closer look at the muscles in his quadriceps. Nicholas was unspeakably handsome.

He looked toward the bed, and then his eyes burned into hers.

Acacia nodded. Anticipation set her body on fire.

He lifted her into his arms and took her lips as he crossed to the bed. Gently, he set her in the very center.

He looked down at her in wonder. "I haven't wanted someone like this in a very long time."

"Then we are the same." She touched his face.

Nicholas grasped the edge of her nightdress, which had pooled around her waist.

Her hand caught his wrist. "You first."

Nicholas wore a look of pride as he stood and brought her hand to his black boxer briefs. He held his arms at his sides.

She rose to her knees.

He nodded, and she pulled the boxer briefs down, then waited as he tossed them aside before she touched him.

He stood with his legs brushing the side of the bed, and she wrapped her hand around his erection, full and hard. He closed his eyes as she stroked.

Blindly, he reached for her and fondled her breasts. His thumbs found her nipples.

Then he stopped her as he pressed his fists into the mattress and captured her mouth. He lowered her to the sheets and knelt between her legs, then wrested her nightdress and dropped it to the floor.

"It was beautiful," he murmured. His hands slid down her thighs and rested on her knees. "I liked the color. But don't answer the door in it for anyone but me."

His eyes traveled the length of her body from her head down to her toes. "You're like Euphrosyne reincarnate. A goddess with a pure heart."

Her breath caught. Her heart was far from pure. He'd never know how false his words were. But now was not the time for confessions.

Nicholas was very tall. She slid farther up the bed to give him more room, and he smiled his thanks.

His hands moved behind her knees and spread her legs. He placed an open-mouthed kiss just below her navel. Then his nose nuzzled her smooth skin until he descended between her legs.

Acacia stared in fascination as he lowered himself to the bed and licked and nibbled around her most sensitive areas. It had been so long…

He touched her with his tongue, finally tasting the place she wanted him most. She grabbed his head with both hands, holding him against her. Then, with embarrassing speed, she rocketed to orgasm.

Nicholas continued to lick her until she tugged at his hair. He sat back on his knees, a muscled, naked warrior, with a look of satisfaction on his face. He licked his lips and wiped his mouth.

She felt her face heat. "I…it's been…"

He stalked toward her and placed his forearms on either side of her torso, his body above her. "Don't apologize for catching fire. I like it. But I want to give you more. So much more."

She threw restraint to the wind and pulled him atop her. Their tongues meshed together as their skin collided.

Her hands slid across the muscles in his back before they came to rest on his backside. She squeezed him and felt taut, muscular flesh.

His hips nestled between hers and his pectorals brushed against her breasts. She felt his chest hair abrading her nipples.

He prodded between her legs, and she urged him on.

"There's no rush." He lifted up on an elbow. "I'm not leaving."

He lowered his mouth to her breast and teased it with his tongue, then took her nipple into his mouth.

Acacia let out a shaky breath and massaged his shoulders. She knew she was falling woefully short on reciprocation. "Let me touch you."

"I'll come in your hand." His tone was honest. "Just be present, in this moment, and let me please you."

Nicholas seemed to take delight in every caress, every inch of exposed skin. His expressions alternated between heat and joy.

The world they'd created in this bed was without rival, and Acacia knew it.

She pulled his face to hers so she could kiss him as her hand strayed over his scar.

He stopped moving. Vulnerability was present in his eyes, laced with worry.

Slowly and deliberately, she placed her lips to the deep furrow in his skin.

He leaned into her caress, and his breath left his lungs in a rush.

"You said this morning you were attracted to me." Acacia moved her lips to his ear. "I'm attracted to you as well. You're very handsome, and I like to look at you."

Nicholas lifted his head and traced her eyebrows, but did not meet her eyes. He touched the end of her nose with the tip of his finger.

"I don't have the words, Acacia. But I have actions."

Acacia felt satisfaction spread across her features.

He reached over the bed to pick up his trousers. He fished a small packet from one of the pockets and opened it with his teeth.

"Was this expected?" she asked.

"Nothing about you is expected." His eyes radiated sincerity. "When I said I wanted to be friends, I meant it. But I hardly dared hope..." He sheathed himself quickly and threw the wrapper to the floor. His eyes locked on hers as he angled himself at her entrance.

For a moment, he didn't move. He just looked down at her and waited as his finger traced the curve of her chin.

She touched his backside. An invitation.

He pushed forward and cursed obliquely. Despite her readiness, he didn't enter her fully.

She returned his look of intensity and bit back the urge to apologize.

"Am I hurting you?" His voice was hoarse.

"No, it's just been a while." She lifted her hips.

Nicholas moved forward and swore under his breath until he filled her.

She inhaled and held it.

"Incredible," he whispered. "Feel how we fit together. It's perfect."

She exhaled, and he fused their lips. Then he moved—a steady, intense rhythm like the rocking of a ship. His gaze never left hers.

She struggled to keep her eyes open as every movement brought pleasure. She set self-consciousness aside and moaned with each thrust. His eyes burned through her, opening her, reading her soul.

She couldn't hide, not from the emotion he expressed through his eyes or from the way she responded to the feeling of him inside her.

"Give me my name." His voice was breathy and uneven as he continued to move.

"*Nicholas.*" The tips of her fingers bit into his shoulder blades.

Her nerves sparked and caught fire, until the joy exploded and raced through her, bathing her body in heat.

Nicholas kept moving, but his pace slackened as he watched her reaction. A few more strokes, and he planted himself deeply, whispering her name as he climaxed.

Beyond speech, Acacia didn't react when Nicholas pecked her lips and withdrew from her body. He lifted the covers and pulled them over her, tucking them precisely under her sides before walking naked into the bathroom.

He was incredibly fit—tall and athletic, with powerful arms and legs. She touched the edge of the sheet to her mouth, overwhelmed.

She wondered what to say. What had just happened was unexpected and incredible, but they were still two people who walked very different paths. Perhaps it was best to wait to hear from him.

She leaned over the bed to retrieve her nightdress just as he returned from the bathroom.

"You don't need that, *mon coeur.*" He plucked the nightdress from her hand and threw it aside.

His skin was warm as he slipped in next to her under the covers. He wrapped an arm around her and tugged her against him.

"Sleep well." He yawned and kissed below her ear.

Acacia waited. She expected him to whisper things in the dark and clarify what had or had not happened. She expected his embrace to end and him to slide out of bed.

But he didn't.

Instead, Nicholas's grip on her tightened as they spooned. His warm breath blew across her neck.

She stared at the wall long after Nicholas's breathing signaled he was sound asleep.

Chapter Thirty-Two

Acacia awoke just as the sun peeked over the horizon.

Nicholas was in her bed, his face relaxed in sleep and shadowed with stubble. The sheets had fallen to his waist, exposing his upper body. One of his arms was tucked beneath the pillow, which showed his bicep and forearm to great effect.

Nicholas was a generous lover. It wasn't fair to compare him with Luc, who'd been her last. Both men had treated her well, which made her very fortunate indeed.

But something hidden had been unearthed the night before. She didn't remember ever having such an aching want or such intense, unbridled satisfaction.

Nicholas seemed more handsome to her that morning. She felt a tenderness toward him that made her reach out to touch his face. She kissed his pouting lower lip.

The previous evening had been incredible. But it was over.

She wondered why he'd stayed. She hadn't had a one-night stand before, but she'd discussed the subject with friends. Most of them declared it was better to end the evening amicably and awake, rather than awkwardly and sleepy.

But Nicholas had stayed. He'd fallen asleep with his arm about her, as if he'd wanted to remain there. He hadn't disappeared after she'd succumbed to sleep as well.

Acacia didn't flatter herself that he would think of their encounter as anything other than an enjoyable evening. A man like him would never be in want of female companionship. A man like him wouldn't become involved with a concierge.

But he was a good lover. He'd been unselfish and tender, and he'd made her feel special. Men like him were rare.

When they went their separate ways in a few hours, she would smile her goodbye and embrace him. She wouldn't begrudge him their single evening. She'd hide the memories among other mental treasures and think on them from time to time.

With an unaccountable tightness in her chest, she leaned down and touched her lips to his once more. She traced the sudden furrow of his brow and slipped out of bed.

Her shower was much longer than normal to allow Nicholas time to dress and depart. She only hoped for both their sakes he would not be surprised by one of the other staff on his walk back to his room.

The sun was rising in the sky when she emerged fully dressed from the bathroom, only to find Nicholas still asleep.

This was a surprise. Back in Geneva, he'd confessed he didn't sleep well. Yet he seemed to have slept soundly all night.

She contemplated walking up to the kitchen to eat her breakfast, but decided to check her email first.

She sent a brief message to her mother and responded to a couple of emails from colleagues at the Victoire, who notified her of Marcel's passing and the upcoming funeral mass.

She texted Luc and told him she'd be home in a day or so.

And she read the most recent texts from Kate.

Luc came by. Again. I need to wear sunglasses not to melt under his heat.

I've been checking your mail. A few bills arrived. The decorator came by yesterday to work on your apartment. She let me take a look. You'll love it. Come home.

Acacia was relieved. Now nothing was keeping her away from Paris, apart from her visa troubles. Nicholas's company would cancel the applications they'd begun on her behalf now that she'd resigned.

She suddenly remembered she hadn't sent her resignation letter.

She opened the email she'd drafted to Madame Bishop and Nicholas and quickly re-read it. She emphasized that her resignation was to take effect the previous day. Then she pressed send.

Somewhere in the room, a cell phone chimed.

Nicholas yawned.

He rolled over and squinted at her. "What are you doing way over there?"

She logged out of her email and closed her laptop. "Just catching up on a few things."

He patted the bed.

She shook her head. "I don't think that's a good idea."

He rubbed the sleep from his eyes and surveyed her freshly washed hair and floral dress. "Beautiful Acacia, please come here."

She found his tone irresistible. Vulnerability had crept into his voice, as if he were far from certain she'd acquiesce. His openness in that moment drew her like a magnet.

She crossed over to him and sat stiffly on the edge of the bed. He pulled her atop him and arranged her legs so they straddled his lower abdomen.

"I don't want…"

"What?" He put his hands on her hips. "You don't want what?"

She touched his naked chest and looked down into eyes that were suddenly alert.

When she didn't answer, he slid his palm underneath her dress to rest atop her thigh. His thumb ghosted over the crease between her torso and hip. "Are you sore?"

"No."

He cocked an eyebrow.

"A little tender," she admitted.

A look of what may have been triumph passed over his handsome features. It was replaced by concern. "You should soak in the Jacuzzi."

"Maybe later."

Nicholas's teeth marked his lower lip. "I'm going to sound like a bastard, but I'll ask anyway. Last night you said it had been a long time. How long?"

She sat back and dropped her hands from his chest. "That's none of your business."

"I know." He took her hand and kissed it. "But my inner Neanderthal is a curious beast."

She placed their conjoined hands against his chest. "I wasn't pining for someone. I went out on dates, but I worked a lot. I took language classes. I took courses in hospitality management."

"I'm glad you weren't pining." His voice gentled. "But people find time for sex. As I've recently discovered, Brazilians are very passionate."

Acacia sifted her fingers through the fine hair on his chest. "I'm particular about who I share myself with."

"Then I'm honored." He reached up to touch her face, tracing her eyebrows, her cheekbones, and her jaw. He looked as if he wanted to say more, much more. But he didn't.

She turned toward the window, where the sun was streaming in. "What time are we leaving?"

Nicholas lowered his hand. "That depends. I slept well last night, for a change." He caressed her thigh with his thumb. "What time is it?"

"It's early." She tried to move off him, but he kept hold of her hips.

His eyes blazed. "I can still taste you."

He slid his hands to her underwear. He plucked the side of it. "Take it off and come up here."

He shifted beneath her and pointed his chin at the ceiling.

"Are you sure?" Her voice was shaky.

He gave her a cocky smile. "I wouldn't invite you if I wasn't sure."

He tugged at her underwear again. She lifted and moved to the side so she could slip the silk down her legs.

He pushed her sundress up over her head and unfastened her bra with a flick of his fingers.

He grabbed the pillow from beneath his head and threw it across the bed, then settled himself flat on the mattress. He beckoned her with both hands.

Shaky with anticipation, Acacia straddled his shoulders and gripped the wall as she moved forward.

She raised herself over his face, and he wrapped his hands around her thighs and pulled her down to his eager mouth.

There were no words. There were no thoughts. Acacia's eyes closed as she swayed back and forth over him, palms against the wall for support.

Restraint had been abandoned. She writhed and panted, as loud utterances and exclamations fled her throat.

Nicholas was not in a teasing mood. He was single-minded in his focus and unrelenting in his movements.

Her orgasm spiraled out of control as she froze, leaning against the wall, holding her breath.

She sagged above him, and he lifted her to the side, watching as she lay very still.

He wiped his mouth with the edge of the sheet and looked over at her with a wide, satisfied grin.

"I can barely move," she whispered. She laughed softly.

She reached for his hand and wound their fingers together. "You have a very talented tongue."

"You have an exceptionally fine flavor."

She laughed again and shook her head. "I just need a minute to catch my breath."

"Take your time." He leaned over to kiss her. "I like where I am, very much."

When she'd recovered, she pushed him onto his back and held out her hand. "Condom."

He reached over the side of the bed and picked up another square packet. He held it in front of her, dark eyes dancing.

She took the packet and carefully sheathed him.

He fastened his hands on her hips. "Are you sure? You seem a bit fatigued."

"Arrogant." She returned his grin and lifted so she could position him properly.

When she sank down on him, he groaned.

"Are you all right?" She lifted herself and touched his chest for balance. "You seem fatigued."

"Minx." He gripped her hips to help her move. "Nothing will prevent me from answering your siren call."

She moved again and fell into a slow and even pace.

All of a sudden, he sat up against the wall.

The change in angle caused Acacia's eyes to close. She leaned her head back and rolled her hips.

He moved her faster and faster, and the sound of her moans combined with his harsh breathing.

She tensed and her body spasmed as another climax overtook her.

Nicholas followed, thrusting twice before he stilled. He clutched her hips and buried his face in her neck.

Without thought, Acacia kissed his scar and hugged him. Their bodies slid against one another, slick with perspiration.

Nicholas's fingers climbed her spine and came to rest on her shoulders. He eased her back, his eyes wide.

She kissed his brow. "Nicholas?"

His gaze remained fixed on her.

She tensed. "Is something wrong?"

"The fates have smiled on me." His head was lowered, his voice throaty.

"The Greek islands tend to have that effect on people."

"No." He pulled her into his arms and hugged her close. "It's you."

The embrace surprised Acacia, because the hug was not that of a lover. It was something greater. Something deeper. As Nicholas hid his face in her neck, she realized she'd never been hugged like this before. Not even by Luc, when he'd declared he loved her.

Nicholas's tenderness and affection awoke something in her that lay beneath the fear and caution. His touch was true. Her feelings for him blossomed, and she relaxed in his arms.

"What a beautiful heart you have," he whispered as he held her tightly.

"Oh, Nicholas," she murmured. "What happened to you?"

He opened his mouth as if he were going to answer; then he kissed her.

"I'll be back." He pressed his lips to one side of her mouth and then the other. He disappeared into the bathroom.

Acacia worried she'd said too much. His embrace had changed her. Her integrity would not allow her to hide that change. Inwardly, she squirmed.

"Sleep with me." Nicholas stood naked next to the bed.

"Now?"

"Yes." He reached into his trouser pockets and retrieved his phone. He switched it off without looking at it and placed it on the nightstand.

"The others will be getting up soon, if they haven't already."

"Last night was the first good night's rest I've had in a very long time. I could use a few more hours. Please." He positioned himself on his back and lifted his arm in invitation.

She went to him. He flicked the sheet over them.

She rested her cheek on the side of his chest as his arm curled around her. He blew a deep exhale across her hair.

The gentle tide of Nicholas's breathing slowly lulled her into sleep.

Chapter Thirty-Three

When Acacia awoke, the sun was in the sky, and Nicholas was gone.

Her stomach rolled. Their connection had deepened. She'd felt it, and she knew he'd felt it too. But perhaps he wasn't willing or able to deal with it.

She took a few minutes to tell herself she'd be all right — that she could be brave and survive the trip back to Geneva. That she could pretend his tenderness and vulnerability hadn't opened something in her that had always remained closed.

Even now she missed him, though she knew she shouldn't. They'd barely begun and it was over.

She tidied herself and spent a few minutes packing so she would be ready to leave at a moment's notice. She noticed with irritation that her breakfast tray hadn't been delivered.

When she opened the door and stepped out on the deck, she saw Nicholas sitting at a bistro table near the Jacuzzi. He was dressed in a button down shirt and suit pants and was typing on his laptop.

As soon as he spied her, his expression brightened and he walked over. Before she could speak, he wrapped his arm around her lower back and pulled her close, kissing her firmly on the mouth. "Just in time for brunch."

Acacia eyed Rick, who stood nearby, his eyes hidden by dark sunglasses.

"Can I speak to you inside for a minute?" She extricated herself from Nicholas's hold.

"We can talk over brunch."

Acacia lowered her voice. "I need to speak to you privately."

With a frown, Nicholas opened the door to her room and indicated she should go inside.

After he'd closed the door, she confronted him. "Please don't touch me in front of the other staff."

He lifted his eyebrows. "*Other* staff?"

"Yes, now Rick knows."

Nicholas shrugged. "Rick's job is to protect us. He doesn't care about anything else."

"Everyone will know I slept with you."

"Is that a problem?" His expression darkened.

"Of course it is." She huffed in frustration. "You're my employer."

"No, I'm not." His tone grew chilly. "You resigned as of yesterday."

She gestured to the door. "Rick doesn't know that."

"I'll speak to him." He reached for her hand, but she moved out of reach.

"What time are we leaving for Geneva?"

He frowned. "Why?"

She gritted her teeth. "Because I need to book my flight back to Paris."

Nicholas stilled. "You're going to Paris?"

"Of course."

He folded his arms. "So you've decided."

"I…" She hesitated, confused by his sudden hostility. "Decided what?"

Nicholas gestured to the bed, his face thunderous. "What do you think happened here last night? This morning?"

"Don't bark at me!"

He came a step closer. "So that's it? You're just going back to Paris?"

"It's where I live." She swallowed hard as angry tears pricked at her eyes. "Kate says my apartment is almost ready."

He brought his face within inches of hers. "Are you crying?"

"No." She blinked hard. "I'm fighting the urge to sweep your leg and punch you in the throat."

Nicholas stared at her. Then he burst out laughing.

She glared. "This isn't funny."

He grew solemn immediately. "No, it isn't funny. I'm sorry I barked at you."

He tried to put his arms around her, but she resisted.

"This is not how I wanted this conversation to proceed." His hand went to his hair self-consciously. "I didn't mean to make you cry."

"I'm not crying," she protested.

"I'm sorry." He stroked her cheek with his thumb. He inched forward, and she permitted him to wrap his arms around her.

Nicholas held her to his chest and rested his chin on top of her head. The strength of his hold and the tenseness of his muscles reminded her of how he'd hugged her earlier, when they were still in bed. When her world tilted on its axis.

This was not the touch of a man who'd made a sexual conquest, nor was it the touch of an amiable friend who'd shared his body casually. Nicholas touched her as if she were precious, as if he could hardly bear for her to be physically removed from him.

She exhaled her annoyance against his chest and kept her arms at her sides.

He kissed her hair. "Let's start again, shall we?

"Good morning, goddess. I've been sitting outside your door, like an eager boy, waiting for you."

"Why?" Her voice was muffled against his shirt.

"*Ma chérie*," he whispered. "Do you really have to ask that question?"

When she didn't respond, he pulled back. "Look into my eyes. Tell me if my feelings aren't returned."

Acacia searched his expression. In his eyes she read intense, hopeful longing. His brow was creased in worry, as if he were concerned about what she might say.

She exhaled and rested her cheek against his chest.

The tension in Nicholas's body dissipated. He pressed his mouth to her temple.

"That's better." He brushed his lips against her forehead.

"I wasn't prepared for this."

"I'm not a man who waits for what he wants."

"I'm not a woman who sleeps with her employer."

He squeezed her gently. "I want you to stop saying that. That isn't what happened."

"I didn't want to be presumptuous."

"Presume, Acacia. You've earned that right." Nicholas lowered his head to stare into her eyes. "Stay with me."

"For how long?"

"For as long as it's good."

"When I was in my room a few minutes ago, I told myself I'd have to be strong today. I thought you'd changed your mind."

"No." He touched her face. "We're allies. We're friends. Be my lover, Acacia."

"Is that what you want?"

"Yes. I want us to spend as much time together as possible, in bed and out of it. And I expect us to be monogamous."

Something jolted down Acacia's spine at his words. "You live in Zurich; I live in Paris."

"Leave that to me." Nicholas's lips came to hers, firmly and insistently.

She sighed against his mouth.

"I want your answer," he whispered.

Impulsively, she placed her hands about his waist. "My answer is *yes*."

"Yes, what?"

"Yes, Nicholas. I'll be yours for as long as it's good."

His arms tightened around her. "I'm sorely tempted to take you to bed."

"We can't delay our departure. I'm unemployed. I'm probably going to be deported."

"We've already secured a temporary work permit for you. That will buy you some time. Madame Bishop can help you find new employment. We can ask her to expand her search to include positions in the art world. I have every confidence she can find something for you."

Acacia shook her head. "I have to secure a position on my own merits. I'd welcome madame's help, but not if it means you'd be behind the scenes, pulling strings."

"If that's what you want, I won't interfere."

"Thank you. I learned a long time ago that no one else can save me. I have to save myself."

Nicholas gave her a pained look. "Wanting someone, needing someone, isn't a vice."

"I never said it was."

He rolled his eyes to the ceiling. "I'd move heaven and earth to help her. She doesn't want my help."

She reached up and kissed his chin. "You can help me by getting me to Paris. I have to find another job."

"All right." He gave her a repentant look and reached down to kiss her deeply. "I have to stop. Otherwise I'll be forced to show you how quick I can be."

She laughed. "If I wasn't worried about our flight, I'd take you up on that."

"Soon," he promised. "I'll escort you to Paris, but we need to make a stopover."

"Where?"

His mouth widened. "Dubai."

Chapter Thirty-Four

"I can't go to Dubai." Acacia pulled away.

Nicholas followed. "It's only for a few days. Three at most."

Acacia thought quickly. There were a number of reasons she shouldn't go to Dubai, but she wasn't in a position to share them. "I can't afford to go. I have to find a job."

"Three days won't make much of a difference," he insisted. "Even Madame Bishop won't be able to schedule an interview for you on such short notice."

"Why do you want me to go to Dubai?"

He kissed her knuckles. "For at least two reasons. First, I want you with me because I enjoy your company. Second, I need an interpreter who can speak Arabic."

"If your contact is conservative, he won't want to speak to a female interpreter."

"That's his problem."

"I don't have proper clothes for Dubai. They have a public dress code."

"Do you have something modest you can wear on the plane?"

She looked at her suitcase and garment bag, mentally cataloguing the items she'd brought. "Yes."

"Then we can either pick up things at the hotel or I'll take you shopping." He grinned. "Or better yet, you could use your concierge skills to have items waiting for you in our suite. We'll be spending much of our time at the hotel. Their dress code is more relaxed."

"You won't be able to touch me in public."

"I can be discreet."

She took his hand. "I'm serious. There are rules in Dubai. If we break them, we could be arrested."

"The hotel is less restrictive. In public, I'll be on my best behavior. I promise."

She sighed. "It's only for a few days?"

"That's right. My company will pay you a consulting fee for acting as an interpreter."

She released his hand. "I can't accept the money—not while we're together."

He regarded her for a moment. "The information you provided about Yasmin is valuable. I was able to verify part of her story, but the identity of her ex-boyfriend remains elusive. I called Constantine and persuaded him to put me in touch with a contact of his in Dubai who's done business with her ex."

"Isn't Constantine worried about what might happen?"

"He doesn't know my true identity or the nature of my quest, but he has plausible deniability."

"Isn't he worried the Russian will retaliate?"

"He hasn't given me a name, only an intermediary." Nicholas smiled. "I'm now one degree of separation from the man who may hold my family's treasures. A consulting fee is being transferred to your bank account to reward you."

"I didn't do anything."

"It's because of you my search has taken a substantial leap forward. I'm paying Constantine handsomely for introducing me to his Dubai contact. It's normal to pay for information."

"If we're together, I can't accept it."

"You earned it prior to us being together. I know you've paid a high opportunity cost by having your life and your job search disrupted. Justice requires you be compensated."

She bit her lip. What he said was true. But the true temptation of Dubai was to be found in Nicholas himself. Now that they were lovers, she was eager to stay with him.

"All right. I'll agree to be compensated for the work I did prior to my resignation, so long as the compensation is appropriate."

"Agreed." With a grin, he shook her hand. "Now, we'd best be having brunch. I want to leave as soon as possible."

He kissed her again before he opened the door and followed her onto the deck.

Chapter Thirty-Five

In her capacity as concierge, Acacia had previously spoken with her counterparts at the Hotel Dubai. The hotel was one of the finest in the world and stood like a gigantic ship made of steel and glass on the Arabian Gulf.

Since she was no longer his assistant, Nicholas insisted on making the local arrangements himself. But Acacia called one of her contacts at the hotel to arrange for the delivery of a series of clothing items better suited to Dubai for Monsieur Breckman's assistant, Andarta.

Acacia texted Kate the name of the hotel in Dubai and her expected dates of travel. She begged her not to pass the information on to Luc.

For travel, Acacia wore a very feminine black and white Chanel suit she'd purchased in Geneva. It was beautiful, but much too warm for Dubai, whose daily temperatures in summer reached forty degrees Celsius and above.

On the flight from Santorini, Nicholas insisted they sit together rather than across from one another. Rick and Kurt sat at the rear of the private plane. Nicholas worked on his laptop, answering emails in French, English, and German, and reading reports.

Acacia updated her resume to show her resignation from Hotel Victoire and her brief contract with one of Nicholas's companies. Madame

Bishop had agreed to help her. Truthfully, Acacia believed she would have to change fields and find another line of work once Monsieur Roy began to share his opinion of her with other hotels in Paris.

Nicholas moved his left arm to the armrest between them and discreetly placed his hand over hers. She looked over at him and smiled.

On instinct, she peered over her shoulder and found Rick staring at her. She turned back around as her face heated.

Nicholas had kept his promise to speak to Rick and Kurt about the change in her employment status. But Acacia knew how things appeared.

She'd loved Luc when they were together. Their intimacy had grown and deepened over time. But she'd ended things with him when he decided to enter law enforcement.

She had no illusions about her relationship with Nicholas. They were attracted to one another. They were affectionate. But Acacia believed it would be short-lived — perhaps a month or two at most.

"You look unhappy." Nicholas's dark eyes radiated concern.

"Just lost in thought." She squeezed his hand.

He turned to look at Rick and Kurt before leaning toward her. "Forget about them."

"Theoretically, I'm sure that's possible. Not in practice."

Nicholas's lips twitched. "Theoretically, it's possible to be near you and not touch you." He touched her chin and angled her face toward him. "Not in practice."

He brushed his lips against hers. When he pulled back, she was smiling again.

"Forget about them," he repeated. "We'll have privacy at the hotel. We should arrive at five o'clock local time, which means you have time for a nap." He traced a line down her neck. "You need to conserve your strength."

"Oh, really?"

His tongue peeked out from between his perfect lips. "Now that I know how you taste, I'm eager for more."

Acacia felt her face flame.

He kissed her shoulder. "Rest up."

She chuckled and closed her laptop. She felt the sudden urge to nap.

When Acacia awoke, they were preparing for landing. She'd fallen asleep against Nicholas's shoulder. Remarkably, he'd been able to work without the use of his left arm.

After they landed at Dubai International Airport and taxied to the area that catered to private aircraft, they deplaned. As she stepped down the staircase to the tarmac, the heat hit Acacia like a wave. The sun was bright in the sky, and the temperature hovered at forty-six degrees Celsius, which was one hundred fifteen degrees Fahrenheit.

"Are you all right?" Nicholas looked up at her as she descended the stairs. He'd deplaned first, and she'd played the role of the dutiful assistant and trailed behind.

She nodded and smiled brightly at the uniformed staff from Hotel Dubai who waited a few feet away.

The staff escorted Nicholas and his entourage into a private lounge where they spoke with customs and had their passports stamped. While Nicholas exchanged pleasantries in English with the government officials, Acacia noticed a large, flat crate had joined their luggage. Two men in uniform accompanied the crate, along with an airport official.

The government official pulled Nicholas aside, and the two men approached the crate.

"Of course you can examine it." Nicholas reached into the interior of his jacket and withdrew an envelope. He handed it to the official. "All the particulars are there. Can one of my staff oversee the examination?"

The government official nodded.

Nicholas gestured to Kurt, and the bodyguard stood next to the crate. The uniformed men, Kurt, and the government official accompanied the crate behind a set of doors.

When Nicholas returned to her side, Acacia resisted the urge to ask questions. There would be time for that conversation at the hotel.

One of the hotel staff piloted the rest of the luggage out a side door, while the other staff member led Nicholas and Acacia outside. A helicopter and its pilot stood nearby.

"Sir?" Acacia gave Nicholas a questioning look.

"The hotel sits on the Arabian Gulf. Although you can book a car service, I thought it would be more interesting to fly. We'll have a brilliant view of the city as well as the water." Nicholas stood a few feet away and clutched his briefcase tightly. It appeared his fingers were itching to touch her.

She gave him an appreciative look. "I've never flown in a helicopter before."

"Prepare to be impressed." He gestured for her to precede him.

One of the staff members escorted her to the helicopter, helped her inside, and closed the door firmly. Nicholas entered the helicopter on the other side.

Acacia's heart raced as the helicopter lifted into the sky. Although the flight to the hotel was only ten minutes, it seemed longer. In the late afternoon heat, a kind of haze hung over the sprawling city and its skyscrapers. The blue-green water of the gulf dazzled her. Then she saw the hotel.

Hotel Dubai reminded her of part of a ship. It was a magnificent structure that rose high out of the water, linked to land by a palm-tree-lined causeway.

The helicopter circled the hotel once before it landed on a helipad on top of the building. Within minutes, they were met by more hotel staff who guided them into an elevator and down to their suite.

"Magnificent," Acacia said as they exited the elevator. A large central atrium ascended to the highest point of the hotel. Glass allowed the sunlight to pour in, reflected by the white balconies that ringed every floor. Aegean blue and an abundance of gold, black, and red were featured in the décor.

When they arrived at their suite, the door stood open. Six staff members, some of whom wore national dress, formed a receiving line in the entryway. Acacia accepted a hot towel to wash her hands before she retrieved a glass of champagne from a silver platter.

"They pride themselves on seven star service," Nicholas murmured as he saluted Acacia with his drink.

She sipped champagne as she followed Nicholas and the private butlers assigned to the suite. There was a dining room, a private kitchen and pantry, a sitting room, and an entertainment room in addition to the bedrooms.

Rick and Kurt's bedrooms were on the first floor. Acacia's room was situated across a wide hallway from Nicholas's on the second story.

The butlers unpacked Nicholas first before they moved to Acacia's room. They hung her clothes in a large dressing room and showed her the items she'd ordered through the concierge.

Nicholas dismissed the hotel staff as soon as possible and stood with Acacia in the front hall.

Before she could say anything, Nicholas placed a finger to his lips and crossed to the dining room.

Wen emerged from the doorway. He gave Acacia a wide smile and a wave.

She smiled and waved in return.

He scanned her with a metal wand and paused at her left arm. He opened his silver briefcase, removed a pair of magnifying glasses, and stared at her elbow. Then he used tweezers to remove something from the fabric of her jacket.

He placed the item, which looked like lint, in a small box. Then he finished scanning her from head to foot, along with the contents of her handbag, before he repeated the process on Nicholas.

Acacia observed the procedure anxiously.

After he finished, Wen pointed to the room he'd just vacated and gave Nicholas the thumbs-up.

Nicholas piloted Acacia into the dining room and closed the door. "Wen has already scanned in here, so we can talk now."

He placed his hands on her forearms and rubbed gently. "My advance team scanned the suite before we arrived, but then the hotel staff came in to deliver your clothes and a few other items. They're re-scanning everything."

"What did he remove from my elbow?"

"A surveillance device."

"From where?"

Nicholas shrugged. "It could be from one of the staff. It could have been placed in the helicopter and you brushed up against it." He pulled her into his arms. "You're safe. Don't worry about it."

Acacia's forehead creased.

He brushed his lips against the creases. "I'm sorry to say this is a way of life for me."

"I don't know what people hope to accomplish by eavesdropping." She touched his jaw, underneath his scar. "Please be careful."

"I am always careful, *mon trésor.* Now that you're with me, I'll be careful with you, too. I swear it."

He kissed her hungrily and lifted her arms so they wrapped around his neck.

When they parted, he pushed a few curls away from her face. "What do you think of the suite?"

"It's incredible. Do you always stay here?"

"No." He grinned sheepishly. "I wanted to impress you."

His confession took her aback. He looked boyish and eager to please at that moment. She found his expression endearing.

"The suite is beautiful. Thank you." She touched his chest. "But I was impressed first by your character."

"Would that I would find myself worthy of you," he whispered.

She frowned. "I'm as good as anyone, but not better."

"That's where you're wrong." His thumb stroked her lifeline.

She tugged his head down and kissed him. Nicholas responded by bending her backward and pressing his body against hers.

"Your guest room is only for appearances." His mouth moved to her neck. "Tonight, you'll be in my bed."

"I hope so." She clung to his shoulders as his lips slid to her jaw.

"The dining room table looks sturdy." He nipped her ear and pulled her upright.

Acacia looked over her shoulder at the large, gleaming mahogany table. "It's about the right height."

Nicholas laughed.

He gave the closed door a baleful look. "I wouldn't want you to feel embarrassed."

Acacia followed his gaze. She thought of the staff on the other side of the door. At the moment, at least, she didn't care.

She removed her jacket and draped it over one of the chairs. Then she hopped up on the edge of the table and grabbed his tie. She pulled him between her knees.

"Brazilians are incredible," he whispered.

She kissed him intensely and teased his tongue with hers. But when she loosened his tie, he caught her wrists with his hands.

"What's the matter?" she asked.

"This isn't…" He halted, his gaze on her hands.

"Did I do something wrong?"

He lifted his head. "No, you're magnificent. And I'm hard and wanting."

"Good." She tugged, and he released her hands.

"This isn't what I want for us—hiding from the staff, a brief liaison on a table."

"We were just being playful," she said quietly.

"Of course."

He touched her cheek, and Acacia was sure he could feel her blush through his fingertips.

"I want to be playful. But I'm concerned about the timing."

Acacia caught the edge of her tongue with her teeth. She shifted forward to move off the table, but he stopped her.

He placed his palms flat on the table on either side of her hips. "You're insulted."

She maintained eye contact. "Maybe you can explain what just happened."

"I'm trying to tell you I brought you here because I enjoy your company. I don't want you to think you're here simply for sex."

Her puzzlement lessened somewhat. "I was under the impression we'd become friends, as well as lovers. A spontaneous encounter on a table could be considered friendly." She pressed down on the table experimentally.

"Then I'll make sure it happens. But later." He moved the back of his fingers across her jaw. "I'm supposed to have a conference call in about ten minutes. You deserve far more attention and far more time than that."

He kissed the corner of her mouth, then the other corner. Finally, he kissed the center of her lips and tugged her lower lip into his mouth.

"Your wish, your pleasure," he whispered.

Acacia shivered and pulled him closer.

Tulsa City-County Library

Broken Arrow Library

Items that you checked out

Title: The man in the black suit / Sylvain
Reynard
ID: 33345080304862 0
Due: 3/19/2020

Total items: 1
Account balance: $0.00
3/5/2020 4:32 PM
Checked out: 1

To renew:
www.tulsalibrary.org
918-549-7323

We value your feedback.
Please take our online survey.
www.tulsalibrary.org/Z45

Her cell phone rang, but she ignored it. Eventually, the call went to voicemail.

When her phone rang again, Nicholas stepped back. "I think you'd better check that."

She scowled at the interruption, and with a curse, hopped off the table. She retrieved her phone from her handbag and looked at the screen. Two missed calls from Luc. One voice message.

One text from Kate, which read:

> **Luc is looking for you. He's worried, and so am I.**
> **Please keep checking in so I know you're okay.**

"I need a moment." Acacia crossed to the other end of the dining room as her thumbs tapped against the screen.

> *At hotel in Dubai. I'm fine. I'll let Luc know I'm okay,*
> *but I don't want him to know where I am. Thanks.*

She sent the text to Kate and checked her voicemail.

Luc sounded agitated. *"Acacia, where are you? Have you been getting my messages? Your colleague Marcel is dead. The Paris police are conducting a murder investigation. Call me."*

Acacia lowered her phone and stared at it.

"Something wrong?" Nicholas approached her.

She tapped the screen and turned the phone off. She skirted Nicholas to return the item to her handbag. "Luc keeps calling me."

Nicholas followed. "What does he want?"

"He wants to know where I am. He heard about Marcel. He said the Paris police are investigating the murder."

"As expected." Nicholas drew near and looped his arm around her waist. "Luc needs to be told you're seeing someone."

Acacia lifted her chin. "I'll handle it."

Nicholas's eyes searched hers. He released her and took a measured step back. His expression grew blank as he moved to the large, well-stocked bar. "Can I get you a drink?"

"No, thank you." Acacia watched him, confused. His reaction was subdued but the air between them was unaccountably tense.

Slowly and meticulously, he poured himself a Grey Goose vodka and tonic. He sipped the drink thoughtfully. "We'll need to vacate the suite while my team goes over everything. Would you like to visit the spa?"

"With you?"

"I'm sorry." He gave her an apologetic look. "I have a conference call and a few other things. You could take a swim, if you like, and visit the steam room. Or have a massage?"

Acacia looked down at her hands. His offer was thoughtful, but clearly he was still irritated about Luc. "I'm not with him. I haven't been for years."

Nicholas inhaled. "I know."

"You know?" She lifted her head. "How long have you known?"

"I knew you two had history. I wasn't sure what your feelings were for him."

Acacia's eyes narrowed. "How did you know we have history?"

"It came up in my investigation."

She cursed in Portuguese. "Do you investigate everyone?"

"I wanted to know if Luc was clean or on the take. When I met you, I was concerned you were involved in the same illegal activities as Marcel."

Despite her best efforts, Acacia felt the muscles in her shoulders grow tight. "What did you find when you investigated me?"

Nicholas's features softened, and he put his drink down. "That you were intelligent and industrious. That you were well respected and had won awards and commendations for your work, prior to joining Hotel Victoire. That you had a few friends but spent most of your time alone."

"This isn't fair." She crossed her arms.

"It isn't," he admitted. "I began investigating you after our first interaction at the Victoire. I had no idea one day I'd have to look into those beautiful hazel eyes of yours and apologize for breaching your privacy."

"Are you apologizing?"

"Absolutely, but only for investigating you. Luc looked into me; it was only fair for me to look into him."

"How do you know he looked into you?"

"My people have put certain markers in place that indicate when someone, especially law enforcement, takes an interest in one of my identities. I knew a few minutes after he'd typed my name into the BRB database."

"That's frightening."

Nicholas came a step closer and brought his chest in contact with hers. "Is it?"

"Knowledge is power. But it comes with tremendous responsibility."

"I don't disagree." His expression grew thoughtful. "I'm sorry I can't accompany you to the spa. But this evening, you'll have my full attention."

She rubbed her eyes. "Maybe a visit to the spa is a good idea. I wasn't able to practice my martial arts this morning. I'll work out my frustrations in the pool."

"I'd rather you work them out with me." Nicholas's voice was close to a growl.

Acacia jerked her chin toward the dining room table. "We've had that conversation."

Nicholas lowered his head and his eyes leveled with hers. "Please be patient with me. We're new. We will both make mistakes. But we have something special, and I want to explore it."

"All right."

"Thank you for telling me about Luc."

"You could have asked."

He frowned. "I've been referring to him as your boyfriend. You never corrected me. You told me it was none of my business."

She set her chin defiantly. "It wasn't. Things have changed."

He smiled. "Yes. Which reminds me, I have something for you."

He returned to the bar, where a large black box sat. He presented it to her.

She gave him a questioning look. When she opened the box, she found folds of ivory silk. Nestled against the silk was a necklace, formed of large blue globes.

"I wanted to give you something to commemorate our time in Santorini." Nicholas carefully removed the necklace from the box. "This is lapis lazuli. It matches the blue from the buildings on the island."

Acacia touched her hamsa pendant. As she looked at Nicholas holding the beautiful necklace, she unfastened it and wound it around her wrist, turning it into a bracelet.

"You don't have to take off your pendant," he whispered. "You could wear both."

She reached out and touched the large lapis beads. "I wouldn't want them to get scratched."

He indicated she should turn around. Carefully, he placed the necklace around her throat and fastened the large, gold clasp. The globes were cool and heavy against her skin.

Her fingers coasted over the smooth beads. "It's exquisite."

Nicholas turned her and took a step back. He smiled. "It looks wonderful."

"Thank you." She touched the necklace again. "I love it."

His smile widened. "Good."

She reached up and moved her lips to his, gently stroking the back of his neck. "Do I have to go to the spa? I'd rather stay here."

He touched the curve of her cheek. "I need you to work out some frustration. But save some for me."

"I'll try." She winked.

"Rick will go with you."

"That's hardly comforting."

Nicholas chuckled. "Poor Rick."

With one final kiss, Nicholas pulled away. "Enjoy yourself. I'll meet you here before dinner."

He opened the door. Rick stood in the entryway to the suite.

Nicholas followed Acacia into the hall. "Rick, please escort Miss Silva to the spa."

Rick grunted and opened the door to the suite. He checked the hallway before he stood to one side, waiting for Acacia.

She smiled over her shoulder at Nicholas before she followed Rick into the hall.

Chapter Thirty-Six

The two-story hotel spa was lavishly decorated, with windows that looked out over the gulf. Acacia enjoyed a swim and a visit to the steam room before her massage treatment.

Although Rick haunted her like a distant ghost, Acacia spent most of her time by herself. She enjoyed the solitude, for it gave her time to think.

The angry and exacting Monsieur Breckman had turned into the noble and passionate Nicholas Cassirer. He was jealous of Luc. Acacia was certain of that. She had to smile at the odd symmetry of the two men investigating one another while trying to protect her.

She was attracted to Nicholas and cared for him. But as always, she was conscious of the fact that she must conceal things from him. If he were to uncover the truth, their relationship would be over.

But Acacia was determined to live in the present, enjoy Nicholas, and not worry about the future.

Two hours later, she returned to the suite, escorted by Rick. The spa had been incredible, and she was undeniably relaxed. But Rick had not spoken a word to her.

Wen scanned Rick and Acacia as they re-entered the suite, finding nothing.

SYLVAIN REYNARD

Acacia turned to Rick as Wen retreated into the room that had become a command center.

"Thank you," she said in English.

Rick's face was impassive. Then, to her surprise, he spoke. "I don't care who he fucks."

Acacia reared back.

Rick's expression remained unchanged, as if giving further weight to his words.

She took a moment to count to ten. "That's good, Rick, because it's none of your business."

"My job is to protect him. Even from his women." Rick's American accent grew more pronounced. His expression was unchanged, but something glinted in his eyes.

She refused to take the bait.

"Thank you for protecting him."

Rick's carefully controlled expression slipped. He looked shocked.

"We both want the same thing." Her voice was low but firm. "We want him to be safe. I'd like to see him happy as well. I doubt that signifies for you."

When Rick didn't respond, she continued. "It would be better if we could co-exist peacefully and professionally. But I don't want or need your approval."

She took a step forward, and her body relaxed, arms slack at her side.

Rick glanced down at her arms, as if assessing a threat.

She made eye contact. "Just to be clear, I know you carry a weapon. I'm still not afraid of you.

"Thank you for escorting me to the spa. Have a good evening."

She turned and ascended the staircase, feeling Rick's gaze follow her.

It was after nine o'clock before Acacia and Nicholas went to dinner. Nicholas dressed in a bespoke suit he'd purchased during a previous visit to Paris. He paired the black suit with a crisp white shirt, gold cufflinks, and a pale blue silk tie.

Acacia wore a crimson silk suit. The jacket fastened with a black satin bow and had notched collars. Both the jacket and matching skirt were covered with a subdued black floral pattern. She was grateful the hotel was well air-conditioned.

They dined at an intimate table in one of the hotel's lavish restaurants, with an incredible view of the water. Then they returned to the suite, where he escorted her to the second floor.

It had been a very long day, but Acacia's nerves tingled with anticipation. She noticed that the crate she'd seen earlier at the airport was now leaning against the wall between her room and Nicholas's. "What's in the crate?"

Nicholas scratched his chin. "It's something that might come in handy when we meet Constantine's contact tomorrow. You've seen it before."

Her eyebrows shot up. "I have?"

"It's the Matisse reproduction you saw back in Paris."

Acacia's eyes widened. "Why is it here?"

"I use it as a way of moving art through customs. I bring it into a country, such as Dubai, and ensure that it's declared when I arrive and that the papers are stamped. Then, if I happen to purchase a stolen painting during my visit, I hide it in a secret compartment at the back of the crate. When I return to Europe, customs sees that I declared the painting on arrival in Dubai and waves it through."

"Does that work?"

"Every time. However, I'm cautious about where I travel. With the support of the French Minister of the Interior, landing in France is preferable to other locations. If customs were to detain me, the Minister would intervene."

Acacia stared at the crate. "It's so simple."

"The simplest solutions are usually the best solutions." He crooked a finger and moved to the open doorway of his bedroom. "Come here."

Acacia glanced down the staircase to the front hall, where Kurt stood sentry. He didn't make eye contact.

"Come here," Nicholas repeated. He drew her attention away from the bodyguard.

She pushed aside any twinges of embarrassment and smiled as her high heels clicked across the beautifully tiled floor.

Nicholas waited for her to enter his room before he closed and locked the door behind him. "Are you tired?"

"No." She examined the four-poster bed. It was very large and sat on a raised, purple velvet platform. A circular, tasseled canopy hung over it, and heavy red and gold silk curtains draped the sides. It was the bed of a king.

Nicholas stood between her and the bed. "It's interesting, isn't it?"

"Very."

"Would you mind if we delayed our enjoyment of it?"

At the tone of his voice, Acacia's mouth went dry. "All right."

He kissed her hand and led her to the opulent marble bathroom. "I've had the bath butler draw a bath in the Jacuzzi."

"Bath butler?" Acacia repeated.

She took in the low, cushioned benches stacked with white towels that flanked the raised Jacuzzi. She noted the generous assortment of Hermès amenities on the vanity. The Hotel Victoire offered a bath butler service, but only by request. Acacia had never experienced such luxury herself.

Nicholas watched her eagerly. "Take your time getting in. I'll join you shortly."

He kissed her and returned to the bedroom.

Acacia touched her mouth with her fingertips. Nicholas was a gentleman, but he was certainly skilled in the erotic arts. His manners and thoughtfulness made him even more attractive.

He'd seen her naked and had entered her body. Yet he still offered her privacy while getting into the bath. She found herself strangely appreciative of it.

Nicholas certainly knew how to feed desire.

The music of Miles Davis wafted from speakers set into the ceiling. Acacia recalled from the Hotel Victoire's records that Nicholas enjoyed jazz.

She surveyed the room. The bath butler had been busy. The lights were dimmed, and pillar candles had been placed artfully around the space. The scent of roses and sandalwood hung in the air. The Jacuzzi's bubbling water echoed in the large space.

Acacia carefully unfastened the necklace Nicholas had given her and arranged it on top of a folded towel. The smooth blue globes gleamed in the candlelight. She slipped out of her suit and hung it on an obliging hanger.

She stood in her underwear in front of the several mirrors that lined the bathroom. She tossed her undergarments aside, climbed up to the Jacuzzi, and carefully stepped into the steaming water.

She sat on one of the benches inside the tub and leaned against a cushioned headrest. It was heavenly.

As she watched rose petals dance across the surface of the water, images from the night before crowded her mind. Nicholas had suggested she use the Jacuzzi early that morning because she was tender from their activities. Now, with the aid of the bath butler, Nicholas was insisting.

Men like him were rare. She wondered at Silke letting him go.

The thought that he'd brought Silke to similar places and wooed her in similar fashion rankled her. He deserved to be with someone who cared for him and wouldn't run off and humiliate him in front of tabloids and the world.

A few minutes later, the door to the bathroom opened and closed. Nicholas approached the Jacuzzi, clad in a white bathrobe.

He stared, his gaze drawn to her bare shoulders. "May I join you?"

"Of course."

Nicholas undid his bathrobe and set it aside. This gave Acacia a moment to appreciate his form.

As he leaned against one of the marble pillars that flanked the Jacuzzi, his bicep flexed. He was in very good shape. Everywhere.

He stepped into the Jacuzzi, and Acacia found herself hungry for him.

She drew him onto the seat next to her and looped her arms around his neck, bringing her breasts to his chest.

His hands slid down to cup her backside as their mouths fused.

"That's quite a welcome." He tucked one of her long curls behind her ear.

"I wanted to thank you."

He slid his nose along hers. "You don't need to thank me with your body, although it's a welcome gift."

"You care about my comfort. That means something to me."

He pushed another disobedient curl aside. "How do you feel?"

"Relaxed. I enjoyed my visit to the spa. Thank you."

His thumb traced the crease between her hip and thigh. "And here?"

She rolled her eyes. "Perfectly fine."

"Certainly perfect." He touched her chin. "You don't know how you appear with those eyes of yours, surprised that someone would want to spoil you." He looked at her resolutely. "I'm eager to do more."

She gave him a half smile. "I just want your company."

Nicholas sat back on one of the benches and pulled her to straddle him. He spanned her hips with his hands, under the water. "Kiss me."

She tilted her head to take his mouth and tasted his lips leisurely before she pushed her tongue inside.

His palms slid up her back and crushed her against his chest.

She inclined her head the other way and tugged at his upper lip.

Nicholas kissed his way to her chin and down to her neck. He licked at the skin and pulled it into his mouth.

Acacia exposed her neck even more.

He nipped a path to her collarbone and traced it with his finger. When she shivered at the sensation, he cradled her breast above the water and wrapped his mouth around her nipple.

Acacia hummed and squirmed in his lap at the sensation. She could feel him lift between her legs, hard and wanting.

He pulled on her nipple until she groaned. Then he took the other breast with his eager lips.

Acacia massaged his scalp as he licked and sucked. She brought her knees to either side of his thighs on top of the bench.

"Wait." He rubbed his stubbled chin against the center of her chest. He placed a kiss over her heart. "Are you ready?"

She nodded and reached between them.

His fingers had already dropped between her legs. He touched her tentatively at first. When she began to lift up and move her hips, he applied more pressure.

She kissed him deeply. "I'm ready."

"Let me open you a little." Gently, his fingers quested her entrance and moved inside.

He curled his fingers, and Acacia gasped.

With a smile, he reached behind him to a discreetly hidden box. He dried his fingers on a towel before he retrieved a condom.

"I'm afraid I'll have to move you." He placed her next to him on the bench and stood. The water rolled off his chest and abdomen as if he were a sea god emerging from the surf.

Quickly and efficiently, he rolled on the condom and sank below the water once again.

"Now." He smiled and lifted her by the hips, positioning her over him.

She sank down slowly, eyes closed. When the backs of her thighs met the top of his, she moaned and raised herself. Up and down, up and down, she moved against his exquisite fullness.

"How do you feel?" he whispered.

"Incredible."

He gripped her hips and pushed and pulled. She had to place her hands on his shoulders to steady herself.

"Mmmm," she hummed.

The water bubbled and sloshed around them, and rose petals gathered around their bodies.

Nicholas nosed a petal aside as he lowered his mouth to her breast.

"Yes." Her voice was a throaty groan.

She wasn't going to last. He was positioned just right, and the pleasure began to build.

Her up-and-down motions stuttered, and he drew back. His grip tightened as he maintained a steady motion while she orgasmed.

The sensations were so intense, it felt like diving off a mountain. Acacia was in free fall as her body tightened and a wave of euphoria overtook her.

"That's it." His voice spurred her on as he continued to move her up and down. "Magnificent."

She opened her eyes as the orgasm began to wane. Nicholas's mouth was open and he breathed heavily, still raising her up and pulling her down. The cords of his neck stood out, and the muscles in his arms bunched and flexed.

His eyes burned into hers.

"Now," he groaned as she sank down on him. She ground her hips as his body tensed.

He continued to stare into her eyes as he pulsed inside her, his mouth going slack.

She blinked against his intense gaze, the moment heavy between them.

His expression changed. Somehow, it grew fierce. His hands squeezed her backside. "Incredible."

She collapsed against him and rested her head on his shoulder. Her hands drooped at her sides. "You slayed me."

He hugged her. "So sweet."

She breathed a happy sigh.

He kissed her forehead. "*Mon trésor*. We're good together, no?"

"Very good." She closed her eyes.

"Are you going to fall asleep?" His voice was tinged with amusement.

"Maybe."

His mouth grazed the shell of her ear. "I'm still inside you."

"Yes." She shifted on his lap. "I like you there."

"Good." He chuckled. "I like it there too.

"I'm sorry it was such a long day. Tomorrow will be better." He kissed below her ear.

She didn't open her eyes.

"Just a minute." He withdrew from her body and moved her to the bench. Quickly, he disposed of the condom. Then he sat next to her and whispered a kiss against her shoulder. "I think it's time for bed."

"The way you looked at me at the end. It's almost as if you—" Abruptly, Acacia closed her mouth. Her face flamed.

Nicholas stiffened. "I almost what?"

"Nothing." She climbed onto his lap and nuzzled his neck. "I'm in the afterglow and babbling."

"I doubt you've babbled a day in your life." He played with her hair, sifting through the black curls.

Acacia decided to change the subject before she said something foolish.

"Can I ask you about this?" She touched his scar.

Nicholas froze.

She pulled back. She'd let her guard down and was forcing intimacies that weren't warranted.

She cursed herself.

Nicholas fished her hand from under the water. "I'll tell you some day. Not tonight."

"I'm sorry for prying. It doesn't matter."

His head shot up. "It doesn't?"

"No." She straightened on his lap. With her other hand, she lifted the curls that framed the right side of her face, twisting the strands to expose a two-inch slash of skin where hair no longer grew.

"What's that?" Nicholas dropped her hand and angled her head so he could see.

"I had stitches when I was young. My curls hide it."

Nicholas traced the area with his thumb. "How did it happen?"

"A fight between my father and mother. I was caught in the middle." Acacia adopted a stoic expression. "The hair never grew back."

Nicholas's eyes met hers. Slowly and deliberatively, he pressed his lips to the raised skin. "Are there more?"

"None that you can see." She smiled a little too brightly.

His expression darkened. "I meant what I said in Cologny. Anyone who fucks with you, fucks with me."

"There was a time when I couldn't take care of myself. That time has passed."

Nicholas looked as if he were about to give voice to his disagreement, but thought better of it.

"Our scars don't define us," she said simply.

"I'm afraid you're wrong, *chérie*, at least in my case." He released her hand.

Water droplets fell from her fingers as she breached the water. She traced his scar, barely skimming the surface of the furrowed skin. Then she kissed it, inch by inch.

He caught her fingers and brought their connection to his heart. "What sweetness I hold in my arms."

"You have a noble soul, Nicholas. You've been thoughtful and generous. I'm very lucky."

He cupped the back of her head with his hand. "You wouldn't think I was noble if you knew what was in my soul."

"I'm not saying you're perfect. But whatever imperfection you have, it's marked by nobility."

He groaned. "If you only knew…"

"I have my own darkness, Nicholas. I'm not inclined to discuss it, but you should know it's there."

He regarded her thoughtfully.

Acacia noticed he didn't appear surprised.

He shifted on the bench and he lowered his hand to cup her breast. "Let me take you to bed. I want to taste you."

"Now?" She blinked, surprised by his sudden change.

"Yes."

"Okay." She ducked her head and made a show of examining her hands. "My fingers are starting to wrinkle anyway. I need to get out."

She extricated herself from his embrace and lifted a thick, white towel from a nearby alcove.

"*Acacia*." He touched her wrist. "You can always refuse."

She looked down at the towel. "Why would I refuse, when you offer me pleasure?"

"Because we're equals." He rubbed his face. "Because we're friends as well as lovers, and I would never take advantage."

Acacia sighed. The power differential was there. It could not be denied.

His expression was almost pleading. "Patience."

She wasn't quite sure why he asked for patience or why he'd looked so guilty when she praised him. There would be time enough to ponder those questions later.

She gave him a smile. "I think you owe me an encounter on a dining room table."

He gaped at her for a moment. Then he grinned.

Chapter Thirty-Seven

Acacia refused to be embarrassed as she and Nicholas passed Kurt's evening replacement in the downstairs hall.

"Don't disturb us," Nicholas called over his shoulder. He followed Acacia into the dining room and switched on the lights.

A large, ornate chandelier swung over the table. Nicholas adjusted the dimmer switch until he was satisfied with the soft lighting.

Acacia hopped up on the mahogany table.

He closed the door and stood before it. He stared at her legs as they hung over the end of the table.

Excitement, mixed with apprehension, coursed through her. Even though he'd just had her in the Jacuzzi upstairs, Nicholas looked hungry.

"Take off the robe."

Acacia unfastened the knot at her waist. She gave him a questioning look.

He nodded.

She pushed the robe off, and it fell around her. Now she was naked.

She bit her lip. One of the bodyguards was just beyond the door. He would know what they were doing.

"Forget about him," Nicholas commanded. He pushed off the door and moved in her direction. "Are you cold?"

"No."

He eyed her breasts suspiciously. "If you get cold, tell me. You look beautiful." He caressed her naked shoulders and cupped her breasts. "You look absolutely perfect."

Her skin heated under his undisguised appreciation. "Thank you."

He stroked her knees. "I'm in the mood to feast."

Nicholas knelt in front of the table and pulled her legs over his shoulders. "Lie back."

Acacia reclined and stared up at the chandelier as Nicholas massaged her calves.

He nuzzled her inner thigh before he kissed the top of her hip. He repeated the actions on her other leg.

Acacia reached down to touch his head. She ran her fingers through his damp hair.

Then he touched her with his open mouth.

His tongue tasted and retreated and tasted again. He nibbled at her skin and teased her with his lips.

She tugged on his hair to pull him closer.

Nicholas chuckled and began to lick.

Acacia couldn't keep her eyes open. She flattened her hand against the top of his head and urged him forward.

He licked in an alternating pattern, before he touched the flat of his tongue where she desired him most.

She let out a loud moan and brought her ankles to his shoulders. The leverage enabled her to lift her hips and drive herself into his open mouth.

He applied more pressure with his tongue, and she soared as inchoate sounds escaped her lips. Her back arched off the table as she held his mouth to her.

He continued to taste her until her legs began to shake and she released his head.

"It's too much," she whispered. She shifted backward.

Carefully, Nicholas removed her feet from his shoulders. He stood between her legs and wiped his mouth on the sleeve of his bathrobe.

Almost dazed, she looked up and fanned a hand over her lower abdomen. "I can still feel you."

"Good." He gave her a devilish grin.

His eyes devoured her. Then he grasped the edges of her robe and draped them over her. "I don't want you to catch cold."

"Come here." She lifted her arm to beckon him.

He placed his hands on either side of her hips and leaned closer.

She kissed him deeply.

When they parted, he slid his hands around her back and assisted her to a seated position. He drew the robe around her shoulders and tied the belt at her waist.

"Was that playful enough for you?" He kissed her nose.

All she could do was grin.

Chapter Thirty-Eight

Attraction. Anticipation. Satisfaction. Comfort.

Acacia was naked with Nicholas, her head resting on his shoulder.

He reclined on his back in a bed designed for a king. His arm curved around her shoulders, and his fingers made lazy patterns on her arm.

She touched his abdomen and rested her hand above the valleys of his muscles.

"Are you awake?" His voice was just above a whisper.

She nodded.

He chuckled. "I thought you'd fallen asleep."

"You woke me up."

His fingers brushed her elbow. "I could say the same."

"These moments are dangerous." She yawned in spite of herself and nestled against his shoulder again.

"Why?" His movements stilled.

"It's peaceful and cozy. These are the times people are tempted to say grand things they don't mean."

"Like what?"

"Oh, I don't know." She slid her hand up to his chest, near his heart.

Nicholas continued stroking her arm. "I don't say things I don't mean."

"Good."

His right hand came up to cover hers at his chest. "I'm serious."

She kissed his shoulder.

"So when I tell you we are good together, Acacia, I mean it."

She grinned. "You aren't wrong."

He brought his lips to her hair. "I asked you to be patient with me. But you should know, I can be patient too. Very, very patient."

She lifted her head from his shoulder so she could see his eyes. "What would you need to be patient for?"

He smiled slowly, and Acacia's heart skipped a beat.

He guided her mouth to his and kissed her. "Sleep, *mon ange.*"

Acacia rested her head next to his on the pillow and closed her eyes.

Chapter Thirty-Nine

The next day, Nicholas and Acacia were accompanied by Rick and Kurt to one of the restaurants in the hotel atrium. They were scheduled to have afternoon tea with Constantine's contact at two o'clock.

As ever, Nicholas was dressed in a bespoke black suit. On this occasion, he paired the suit with an equally fine black shirt and monochromatic silk tie.

He and the contact shook hands and exchanged polite greetings.

"And this is my interpreter." Nicholas gestured to Acacia, who stepped forward.

She wore a conservative black dress that fell to her knees. A short, emerald green silk jacket covered her arms. Black stockings and high heels completed her ensemble.

They stood in a private corner of the restaurant that faced the enormous windows looking out over Dubai.

Constantine's contact stood aloof, flanked by four bodyguards. He wore a navy blue suit and tie. His hair was gray, and he wore a full beard. His dark eyes gazed at Acacia skeptically.

He returned his attention to Nicholas.

"I was under the impression this was a private meeting." The man spoke flawless English.

"I brought my interpreter as a courtesy. I'm afraid my Arabic isn't equal to your English." Nicholas tried to make light of the situation.

The man's eyes darted to Acacia's. He switched to Arabic. "I doubt this woman's knowledge of the language is equal to mine."

"That is probably true, sir," Acacia replied, also in Arabic. "But I am always eager to practice and improve."

The man studied her.

He gave her a brief nod and continued to speak to Nicholas in English. "There's no need for an interpreter. We can speak English. But I prefer privacy." The man waved a hand at his bodyguards, who withdrew to a few feet away.

Nicholas made eye contact with Acacia. She read an apology in his expression, one he could not give voice to in present company.

She wanted to volunteer the fact that she didn't care that she'd been dismissed. But in the role of his assistant, she couldn't. She gave him a small smile instead.

Nicholas inclined his head. He gestured to Rick and Kurt and turned back to Acacia. "You're free to go. Security will escort you."

He gave her a look, heavy with meaning.

"Very good, sir." Acacia bobbed her head.

As she'd suspected, Constantine's contact was traditional, if not paranoid. He didn't want an audience for his conversation. Acacia also noted that names had not been exchanged.

She walked with Kurt across the expansive atrium toward the elevators. She was deep in thought, not just about Nicholas's meeting but also about her activities with Nicholas the night before.

After their encounter on the dining room table, he'd carried her to bed. They'd both slept well, naked and wrapped around one another.

In fact, it had probably been the most restful sleep she'd ever had. She smiled and thought of the delights that awaited her in Nicholas's arms.

Then something caught her attention.

She turned and saw an older man in a finely tailored gray suit, surrounded by black-suited bodyguards. The man walked swiftly across the atrium.

She stopped and stared.

Another similarly suited man who was much younger greeted the man. They clasped one another's arms. She caught a glimpse of the older man's face.

Her heart seemed to pause in her chest. Time grew elastic and slowed to a crawl.

The man had aged, of course, and his black hair was now mixed with white. But she would know his face anywhere. And if that were in doubt, she recognized the signet ring he wore on his right hand as he released the man he'd greeted and smoothed his gray tie.

Acacia put her head down and walked as fast as she could toward the elevator.

Behind her, Kurt hastened to keep pace.

Her heart thumped wildly, and the blood sang in her ears.

She resisted the urge to run but was careful to face the elevators, her back toward the man. She pressed the elevator button.

"What's wrong?" Kurt asked in French.

"Nothing," she lied. "Let's go."

When the elevators opened, she rushed in and kept her back to the atrium. She touched the hamsa pendant at her wrist and prayed with all her might the man hadn't seen her.

When the doors closed, she sagged against the wall and covered her face with her hands.

"What just happened? Do I need to call the boss?" Kurt bent over her.

She lowered her hands. "No."

He looked concerned. "Are you sick?"

"No." She eyed the security camera in the top corner of the elevator. "I'm fine."

When the elevator opened on their floor, she crossed the threshold and broke into a run. She hurled herself across the thick carpet to the suite and quickly swiped her key card.

Kurt followed.

Acacia pulled off her heels as she entered the hall and tossed them aside. She climbed the stairs to her room as fast as she could.

"What's going on?" Kurt entered her room, just behind her.

Acacia didn't turn around. "There are security cameras in the elevator and probably audio surveillance. You know that."

She jogged into the massive dressing room that adjoined her bedroom.

Kurt stood in the doorway. "What are you doing?"

She picked up a pair of sensible, flat shoes and slipped them on. "I'm going to the airport and taking the first flight out. I don't care where it goes."

"I have to tell him." Kurt's voice was firm.

Her eyes flashed. "Tell him after I'm gone."

Kurt frowned and disappeared from view.

She punched a security code into the dressing room safe and opened it. She grabbed her passports, her cash, and her burner cell phone and threw them into her handbag. There was no time to pack clothes.

Then she remembered the necklace.

It would take precious minutes to retrieve it. But Acacia wasn't going to leave it behind.

She threw caution to the wind and flew across the hall into Nicholas's room. She raced past the bed and into the bathroom. The lapis necklace was still where she'd placed it the night before.

She picked it up and quickly put it on. Her fingers shook as she tried several times to fasten it. Finally, the catch caught, and she was able to close it.

She ran back to her room and unplugged her laptop, then tossed it and its cord into a tote bag. She looked around anxiously for her cell phone. Then she realized it was in her jacket pocket.

She pulled out the phone and switched it off, in case someone tried to use it to track her. She didn't have time to remove the SIM card. She'd have to do it at the airport.

Acacia swung her handbag over her shoulder and grabbed her tote bag.

"You're leaving?" Nicholas's voice came from behind her.

She whirled around. "Yes."

"Were you going to tell me?" His tone barely concealed his anger.

She kept her head down and moved toward the door. "There isn't time."

He slammed the door shut behind him and stood in front of it, fists clenched.

"Why?"

"I have to go." Her voice was pleading. "I'm in danger here."

Nicholas's eyes narrowed. "Not from me."

She tried to move past him, but he blocked her. "Tell me what's going on."

Her hands went to her hair and pulled. "I saw someone in the atrium."

"Who?"

"Omar Zaid Hirzalla," she whispered. "I have to get out of here."

Nicholas took a step closer. "Who is he?"

"Nicholas, please!" she begged.

"I can't help you if you won't tell me what you're afraid of."

Frightened tears formed in her eyes. "He's an arms dealer. He's dangerous. Please, let me go."

Nicholas looked stunned. "How do you know an arms dealer?"

She hesitated.

"Acacia." He bowed his head and almost brought their noses together. "Tell me who this man is, right now."

She swallowed the lump in her throat.

Her gaze darted to the door. She was wasting precious time.

She looked back at Nicholas.

"He's my father."

Chapter Forty

Nicholas's head jerked back. "Your father?"

"I need to get out of the hotel before he comes for me."

Nicholas passed a hand over his mouth. "Then you aren't leaving because of me?"

"Of course not." She wiped a tear away. "But if you don't get away from that door, I'm going to remove you."

He lifted his hands. "Let me help you. Tell me what happened."

"There's nothing you can do." She pushed past him and opened the door. "I saw my father. I don't think he saw me, but if he did, he'll come after me. He'll find my mother. I need to go to the airport."

"Slow down." He caught her elbow. "Where's your mother now?"

"Recife."

"Are you sure it was your father?"

"I saw his face. And the ring he always wore."

Nicholas led her into the hall. "You can call your mother on a secure line. I'll arrange to move her to safety."

"You can do that?" Acacia sniffled and wished she had a tissue.

He touched his lips to her forehead. "We'll move her temporarily, until we decide what to do next.

"No matter who your father is, he won't make a move inside the hotel. I'll arrange for additional security. I'll notify hotel security as well."

Acacia pulled on his arm. "If you raise the alarm with the hotel, he'll find out."

Nicholas surveyed her tears. "I'll speak with my security team, and we'll come up with an alternative."

As they approached the staircase, Acacia caught sight of Kurt.

His eyes were alert. He followed Nicholas and Acacia down the stairs and into the media room that had become a security hub.

As soon as Nicholas entered the room, Wen and Rick stood at attention. "Wen, I need a secure line. Acacia is going to call Brazil."

Nicholas guided her to a low couch. He pulled her handbag and tote from her shoulders and placed them next to her.

He withdrew a silk handkerchief from his breast pocket. Tenderly, he wiped her face.

"You need a drink." He deposited the silk into her hand. "I'll be right back.

"Rick, come with me."

The bodyguard stepped forward, his eyes narrowed at Acacia. She ignored him, her mind racing.

Rick and Nicholas walked across the hall in the direction of the dining room. Acacia heard them talking, but couldn't make out the words.

Kurt stood in the doorway and looked over his shoulder, as if determining Nicholas and Rick's location. He approached the couch. "I had to tell him. I work for him."

Acacia nodded and clutched the handkerchief.

Kurt crouched down in front of her. "I wouldn't have let anyone get near you. My job is to keep you safe. Understand?"

"I understand," she replied dully.

"But you have to disclose any and all threats to us. We can handle surprises, but we don't like them. Neither does the boss." Seeming satisfied, Kurt returned to his position in the doorway and watched for his employer's return.

Wen handed her a phone and addressed her in English. "This line is secure. Do you know the number?"

She nodded. She dialed with trembling fingers.

When her mother answered, Acacia breathed a sigh of relief. Immediately, she switched to Portuguese. "*Mãe?* Where are you right now?"

"I'm in bed," her mother answered, sounding sleepy. "What time is it?"

"It doesn't matter. Listen, *Mãe*, you have to get up. I saw him."

There was a pause on the other end of the line. "What did you say?"

"Him, *Mãe*. I saw *him*. I don't know if he saw me, but I can't take that chance. You have to get up and pack a bag."

Acacia heard the rustle of bedclothes.

"Where are you?" her mother asked.

Acacia shut her eyes tightly. "Dubai."

"Dubai?" her mother shouted. "What are you doing in Dubai?"

"I'm here with a friend. We've arranged for someone to come and get you. They'll take you to a safe place."

"You stupid girl! You knew better than to go to that part of the world. Are you crazy? Now we have to start all over again." Her mother swore.

Acacia stifled a sob. "I'm sorry, *Mamãe*."

Nicholas stood over her and gestured to the phone.

Acacia handed it over.

"Mrs. Santos, this is Nicholas Cassirer." He spoke in English.

Acacia overheard her mother replying in English.

"I'm Acacia's boyfriend. Pack a bag and be ready to leave your apartment in less than an hour. I'm sending someone to get you. You can ask him for the password. The password is Santorini." Nicholas's eyes met Acacia's.

She heard her mother haranguing Nicholas in a mixture of Portuguese and English.

"Mrs. Santos," he interjected, "you need to get ready now. Take everything you value with you, including your passport. Call me at this number if there's a problem."

He waited for her acquiescence.

Acacia heard her mother agree tersely before hanging up.

Nicholas pulled the device from his ear and frowned. He handed it off to Wen before he retrieved a drink from a nearby table.

"You look like you need this." He placed the glass in Acacia's hands. "I'll make another."

She sipped the vodka and tonic gratefully as her mother's curses echoed in her ears.

Acacia opened her eyes.

She looked up at the canopy that hung over Nicholas's bed. Confused, she turned to her side; Nicholas watched her from a nearby armchair.

He'd removed his suit jacket and tie and rolled up the sleeves of shirt. His expression was subdued, his eyes wary. "How are you feeling?"

"Disoriented." She sat up and noticed she'd shed her green jacket, but was still in her dress and stockings. "What time is it?"

"It's after five."

"I've been asleep for two hours?"

"Yes." He crossed over to the bed and sat next to her. "You were in shock. Your adrenaline crashed, and you fell asleep on the couch downstairs."

"Maybe it was the vodka and tonic." Acacia rubbed her head. "You didn't give me something, did you?"

"Certainly not." His temper flared. "I admit the drink was strong, but you needed it. You were shaking like a leaf."

She lifted her head. "My mother."

"She's in a safe house in Manaus. She's fine."

"Can I speak to her?"

Nicholas frowned. "You could, but I wouldn't recommend it. She isn't in the best of moods at the moment."

Acacia brought the heels of her hands to her eyes. Her mother blamed her for what had happened. She'd never forgive her.

"I put her life at risk by coming here," she groaned.

"Nonsense. How could you have known he would be here?"

"We avoided this part of the world intentionally. I knew better."

"It wasn't your fault."

Acacia picked at the sheets. "What about your meeting with Constantine's contact? Did you go back?"

"Don't worry about it. How do you feel?"

"Drained. Upset." She brushed the sleep from her eyes.

"I need to tell you a few things." Nicholas's tone was grave. "Are you feeling up to it?"

She nodded.

"My team made inquiries, and you're correct; the man you saw is Omar Zaid Hirzalla."

A feeling of horror rose in Acacia's chest. "Is he here now?"

"No. I'm told he left the airport in a private plane about an hour ago. Apparently, he's flying to Morocco." Nicholas pried her fingers from the sheet. "I owe you an apology."

"For what?"

"For shouting at you. I'm sorry."

"Apology accepted."

His gaze dropped to their hands. "I thought you were leaving me."

"I was trying to escape *him*."

"Next time, let me help."

She set her teeth. "There won't be a next time. I don't ever want to be that close to him again."

Nicholas's eyes lingered on hers before they lowered to the large, azure globes around her neck. "You weren't wearing those at the meeting."

"No." Instinctively, her hand covered the necklace. Her hamsa pendant swung from her wrist.

"You stopped to take my gift with you?"

She changed the subject. "Were you able to reschedule your meeting?"

His expression tightened. He shook his head.

"Nicholas, I'm so sorry. Were you able to get any information at all?"

"We'd barely begun."

"Oh, no."

Nicholas lifted a shoulder. "In life there are detours."

Acacia winced. Nicholas couldn't hide his disappointment. It was evident in his eyes and on his face. "You gave up your chance to find your family's paintings because Kurt told you I was leaving?"

Nicholas didn't answer. The searing intensity of his gaze was its own response.

"I'm so sorry," she whispered.

"When you're feeling up to it, I'd like you to tell me how a Brazilian concierge ended up related to a Jordanian arms dealer."

Acacia leaned back against the pillows.

Nicholas was conflicted; that much was obvious. Clearly he was upset about what had happened to her. But there was a hint of censure in his voice she didn't like.

"I don't like things hanging over my head," she said heatedly.

"Nor do I," he challenged.

"Fine." She fixed him with a defiant look. "The story is simple. I was born in Jordan to a Brazilian mother and a Jordanian father. My mother converted to Islam when she married my father."

"I take it Acacia Santos isn't your real name."

"No. My name is Hanin. Hanin Hirzalla."

"Hanin." Nicholas pronounced her name as if it were a caress.

"It means longing or yearning in Arabic."

"It suits you."

She looked down at the sheets. Nicholas was from an old and prominent European Jewish family. She had been worried about how he'd react to the revelation that she was Muslim. But he seemed untroubled. And the way he pronounced her birth name...

"We lived in Amman until I was ten, and then my mother took me and fled. I haven't seen my father since."

"If you hadn't seen him in so many years, how did you recognize him?"

"I know what my father looks like. Besides, the man downstairs was wearing the same signet ring he always wore."

"So you fled Jordan and went to Brazil?"

"That's right."

Nicholas smoothed the wrinkles from his suit trousers. "Why are you afraid of him?"

She lifted her hair and exposed her scar.

"That's reason enough." Nicholas's eyes met hers. "Is there more?"

"He sent a man to Brazil to kidnap me when I was fifteen. But by that time, I had enough martial arts training to get away."

Nicholas's eyebrows shot up. "What happened?"

Acacia looked at the floor. "We were living in Rio. I was on my way home from school. Someone grabbed me and started speaking in Arabic about my father. He didn't expect me to fight, so I surprised him."

Nicholas chuckled. But when he saw Acacia's expression, he sobered. "I'm sorry. It isn't funny. But there's something wondrous about the thought of you beating up a grown man when you were a teenager."

"My mother and I had to leave everything behind and flee Rio for Recife. We had to change identities. Again." Acacia tugged at her hair. "That isn't the worst of it."

"What is?" Nicholas whispered.

"My father sold bomb-making materials to the people who bombed Damascus in 1986. They killed civilians."

Nicholas blinked. "That wasn't in the dossier I was provided."

"You have a dossier on him?"

"Once you gave me his name, I had Wen reach out to some allies. The dossier said your father is a wealthy Jordanian businessman who travels a lot, doing business all over the Near East and North Africa. It's widely known he's an arms dealer, but no one has been able to tie him to a specific terrorist attack or incursion."

"Try the March 1986 bombing of Damascus. He admitted it to my mother, along with supplying materials for the April bombings."

Nicholas's eyes narrowed. "If you were ten years old in 1986, then you can't be thirty-five."

"We didn't know about the bombings until years later, just before I turned ten. By that time, he was trading arms all over the region. He'd kept his activities secret from us, but my mother found out.

"When we fled to Rio, we adopted new identities and changed our birth dates. I'm thirty-seven." She fanned a hand over her forehead. "Where did you say my mother was?"

"At a safe house in Manaus. She's in the care of a former CIA agent. You can speak to her again tomorrow." He paused, his brow wrinkled. "In the dossier, you and your mother are recorded as deceased."

"How good is your intelligence?"

He adjusted the rolled sleeves of his black shirt. "Let's just say I have friends in America."

Acacia's stomach flipped. "Please tell me you didn't give them our names."

"Of course not." Nicholas's eyebrows knitted together. "Your father is the person of interest. Let me add that our American friends were grateful for my report. They've been tracking your father for some time."

Acacia's hands went into her hair. She rocked back and forth and tugged.

"Don't." Nicholas's hands covered hers. "You're hurting yourself."

She allowed him to unwind her fingers from her hair and lower her hands to the mattress. "The CIA has my mother."

"No." Nicholas returned his hands to his knees. "I have your mother. The ex-agent and his team are simply the ones on the ground."

"My father will find her."

"No, he won't. The extraction was done quickly and quietly." Nicholas touched her hand. "I should tell you that there were death certificates in the dossier, one for you and one for your mother. Anyone who has access to the dossier will think you and your mother died long ago."

"My father must have reported us dead after we fled."

"The death certificates looked official. Your new identities are solid. My best people investigated you, and there wasn't even a hint of your true background."

"My mother bribed a government official in Rio. She cut ties with her friends and family in Minas Gerais before we left Jordan. We've never contacted them."

Nicholas gave her a thoughtful look. "Your fingerprints aren't linked to another identity."

"I was so young when we went to Brazil, I hadn't been finger-printed. And then afterward, when we changed identities and moved to Recife, my mother bribed the same official."

"I'm sure it was very confusing for you while you were growing up."

"Hatred is the only thing I find confusing."

"You lied to me." His voice was sad.

She pulled the sheets back and swung her legs to the floor. "I lied to everyone. Just like you lied to me and the rest of the staff when you walked into Hotel Victoire."

He watched her for a moment. "Now that we're telling the truth, is there anything else I should know?"

"My mother found weapons in our apartment in Amman. When she confronted my father, he became violent." Acacia gestured to where her scar was hidden beneath her hair. "I tried to protect her, and he beat both of us. He threatened to kill us if we told anyone about the weapons. My mother bided her time and was able to pay a man to smuggle us out of Jordan. We've been in hiding ever since."

Nicholas's face darkened. "He beat you?"

Acacia jerked her chin.

"You were ten years old." Nicholas lowered his voice. "He beat you?"

"I have the scar to prove it."

"Jesus," he swore.

Slowly, he stood.

She remained perched on the edge of the bed. "If he finds me, he'll find my mother. There are too many ties between us—emails, phone calls, money transfers."

"You're assuming he'd recognize you after all this time."

"I can't risk it."

Nicholas made eye contact with her. He stepped closer. When she didn't move away, his fingers sought her hair. He pushed back her curls and regarded her scar.

"I've dealt with arms dealers before. I'm not afraid of your father."

"You should be."

Nicholas withdrew his hand. "He's no different from others I've encountered in the art world over the years. The question is, what do you want me to do about him?"

"Protect my mother."

Nicholas half-smiled. "You didn't even take time to think before answering. Your mother will remain in the safe house until we assess the threat. I've demanded updated intelligence on your father and his people. We'll see what we find out. What do you want me to do for you?"

She hesitated.

"Acacia?"

She wrung her hands. "I'll need a new identity."

"You want to keep running?"

"No." She clutched at her chest; the weight of her decision made it difficult to breathe. "I have no choice."

"If you want a new identity, I can secure one for you. Wouldn't you rather stand your ground? Keep the life you've worked so hard to build?"

"I may not have that luxury." She inhaled slowly. Her eyes pled with him. "No matter what happens with us, promise me you'll keep my secret."

"Are you anticipating us parting ways?" His tone was cautious.

She ducked her head. "My father is a terrorist. I lied to you, about everything."

Nicholas was silent for a few seconds. He lifted her chin. "Did you lie to me in bed?"

She blinked, confused. "No."

"Did you lie when you said you cared for me? That we would be monogamous lovers, as well as friends?"

"Of course not."

"When you said I had a noble soul?" he whispered.

"Your soul *is* noble." Her voice wobbled.

"You thought I'd send you away because you and your mother ran away from your father?"

"I lied about who I am. I'm a Brazilian Jordanian Muslim, Nicholas."

"You think I'd stop caring for you because you're Muslim?" He shook his head. "Muslims and Jews have their differences, but we are not natural enemies. We live in peace in many parts of the world. You know that. You also know I am not a racist."

"I know." Acacia swallowed noisily.

"You knew I was Jewish probably from the moment Madame Bishop gave you my real name."

"Of course. The Cassirers are a famous Jewish family from Germany."

"So my religion wasn't a barrier to your affection."

"I don't choose my lovers on the basis of their religion. I choose them on the content of their characters." She sniffled.

"Then we are the same. Don't you see? We have our differences, but we share the same ideals.

"Acacia, if a woman who'd been beaten by her husband came to me and asked for a new identity, I'd do anything I could to help. I'd be on the right side of justice in doing so. Of course your mother gave you a new identity when you were a child. She was protecting you."

Acacia covered her mouth with both hands as years of emotions flooded her. The strain of keeping so many secrets finally gave way.

Nicholas wrapped her in his arms before the first tears fell.

Chapter Forty-One

Acacia couldn't sleep.

Nicholas held her in his arms, but her mind would not rest.

She was afraid her father had seen her. She was afraid he'd find her mother. She was afraid her mother would never speak to her again.

She was also afraid she'd cost Nicholas closure to his family's tragedy.

"I'm sorry," she murmured to the semi-darkness.

Nicholas had insisted on leaving the bathroom lights on. Their warm glow spilled onto the bedroom carpet. On Acacia's side of the bed, he'd lit a small oil lamp that flickered on her nightstand.

His arm tightened around her. "Sorry for what?"

"Everything." She bit her lip.

He kissed her temple. "That's too much to be sorry for, *mon amour*."

Sorrow, keen and sharp, pierced her. She placed her hand over her mouth and willed herself not to cry.

Nicholas drew her back toward him, his naked chest flush against her shoulder blades. "Hanin, you are safe now," he whispered in Arabic.

Acacia held her breath. "You speak Arabic?"

"No." He hugged her. "This afternoon I asked the staff to translate for me, and then I practiced saying it."

"You did that for me?"

"I'll continue calling you Acacia, unless you tell me otherwise. But I want Hanin to know she is safe." He kissed the back of her head.

"Hanin is lost." Her voice was hoarse.

He pressed a kiss to her hair. "You aren't lost. You're right here."

"I don't know how to feel. I've kept secrets so long…"

He squeezed her gently. "Now you have someone who cares about you who knows the truth."

"But I've put you in danger."

"Don't worry about me. Who else knows the truth?"

"My father, my mother, the government official she bribed in Rio, and you and your people."

"I haven't shared. My trusted team members know your father is a potential threat to you and your mother, but I've concealed as much as I can."

Acacia sighed in relief.

"Does Luc know?" Nicholas's tone was anything but casual.

"No. When he decided to join the BRB, I ended things. I was afraid of what would happen if he found out the truth."

Nicholas's body grew rigid. "What, specifically, were you afraid of?"

"I was afraid the truth would end his career. I thought it would put him in danger. I also worried someone would investigate me because of him."

"But he knows you're Muslim, and he accepted it."

She shook her head. "I hid my faith when I came to France. I was afraid of my father, but I was also afraid I'd be discriminated against. I practiced my religion in secret, but I always wore my hamsa pendant."

"Did you love him?"

"My father?"

"Luc." Nicholas's voice grew tight.

"Yes."

Nicholas rolled her to her back and hovered over her. "Do you still love him?"

"No."

Nicholas brought his forehead to hers. "Are you sure?"

"Yes."

Nicholas brushed his lips across hers, feather light. "The truth changes things."

She looked away. "I understand."

"Do you?" He caressed her cheek. "What I meant was that I'll need to be careful to keep you away from the media. I don't want your photograph splashed around."

"How did you avoid having your picture taken as Pierre Breckman?"

"I avoided places where the paparazzi were known to congregate, and if a stray photo was taken, I bought it." His thumb moved over her eyebrows. "You could have told me before. It wouldn't have made a difference."

She grabbed his hand and pulled it away from her face. "You can't say that. You have no idea what you would have done had I told you."

Artfully, he moved his hand so he held hers instead. "I know myself. That's all I need to know."

She lowered her gaze to their hands. "Why aren't you afraid of my father?"

"Why should I be?"

"He's a terrorist."

"As I said, I've dealt with men like him before."

She lifted her eyes to meet his. "He could kill you, Nicholas, or have you killed."

Nicholas didn't respond.

Acacia's breath seemed to catch in her throat. "Doesn't that trouble you?"

"My sister was murdered. I'm on a mission to find her killer. I have an elaborate network in place, designed to protect me and those I care about. That network wouldn't hesitate to eliminate a threat."

Her gaze slid to the side, toward the lamp that shone from her nightstand.

"Acacia," he rumbled. "Stay with me."

Her eyes moved back to his.

He touched her cheek once again. "While my network is different from your father's, I'm confident it can protect us. I not only trade in artwork and antiquities, I trade in information."

"What does that mean?"

"It means I have contacts in various intelligence agencies around the world. I provide them with information, on occasion, and they do the same for me."

"So you're a spy?"

"No." His denial was firm. "I'm only an asset to those agencies, as they are to me. I choose when to share information and what information I share. They do the same. Thus far, these relationships have been profitable for both sides."

"You're scaring me," she whispered.

"Your father may be a threat to you, but I am a threat to your father. If he were to discover your identity, he'd find me as well."

Acacia let out an unsteady breath.

"*Mon amour*, I'm not telling you this to frighten you. I'm telling you this to reassure you. You're safe with me."

"I want to go back to Paris."

"Tomorrow. I've already made arrangements." His hand slid down to her hip. "I have one request to ask of you."

"What?"

"If the time comes for you to leave me, tell me before you go."

"Nicholas, I—"

His dark eyes glittered. "Promise me."

"I promise."

He squeezed her hip. "I've got you, Acacia. I've got you, Hanin. Anyone who wants to get to you will have to go through me."

She screwed her eyes shut and buried her face in his neck.

Chapter Forty-Two

"How do you feel?" Nicholas traced the back of her hand with his thumb.

"I'm all right." She gave him a brave smile and turned to look out the window.

They were in Nicholas's private plane and had almost reached Paris.

In the hours before they left Hotel Dubai, they'd agreed Acacia wouldn't change her identity. According to Nicholas's sources, there'd been no chatter about her or her mother. It seemed her father hadn't seen her.

Acacia was cautiously optimistic. It was still possible her father had seen her and was simply lying in wait. Just to be sure, her mother remained in hiding, and Acacia had promised to be shadowed by Kurt at all times. Nicholas offered to take her to his home in Zurich, but she'd refused.

He'd disappeared into the lavatory about an hour after takeoff to apply the prosthetic he wore to cover his scar. When he emerged, it was so artfully done, Acacia couldn't even see where the prosthetic began and his real skin ended.

"What will you do next?" he asked.

"I need to find a job." She shut her eyes quickly and opened them. "I need to let Luc know I'm back."

"Be careful."

Acacia faced Nicholas. "If I cut him off, he'll be more suspicious."

Nicholas scowled. It was clear he wanted to protest, but he held his peace.

She changed the subject. "I should probably call Madame Bishop tomorrow."

"That's a good idea."

"The Paris police might want to interview me again." Acacia shuddered. "More attention I don't need."

"I have a contact in the police service. The investigation is focused on linking Marcel's murder to other assaults in the area."

Acacia stared. "But Marcel's assault was premeditated. You figured it out."

"Yes, but I was aware of Marcel's underworld activities. Obviously, Monsieur Roy has pointed the police in a different direction. I've kept Marcel's journal as insurance, so the police are missing that as well."

"Shouldn't we hand over the journal?"

"We'd be putting ourselves at risk."

"But what about Marcel's killers?"

"They came after you once. We have something they want, which means we have leverage."

Acacia rested her head against the seat. "Do you think they'll try to get the journal back?"

"Not if their employer is as smart as I believe he is."

She drummed her fingers against the armrest. "How can you be so sure?"

Nicholas shifted in his seat. "Because like anyone involved in the black market, he doesn't want exposure. At the moment, we have a détente. Marcel, for whatever reason, was a threat to him. Marcel has been eliminated. The dealer wants the journal, presumably to clean up loose ends, but he knows we have it. He also knows we haven't turned it over to the authorities. If he's smart, he'll leave us be and move on."

Acacia looked at Nicholas carefully. "Just how involved in the black market are you?"

He gazed straight ahead. "The black market took my sister. I'm as involved as much as I have to be to find the ones responsible."

Acacia exhaled loudly.

Nicholas leaned closer. "I know you're feeling upset about the meeting I had to cut short. But I've already made progress. My analysts are cross-referencing the Paris art dealer's associates with associates linked to Constantine's contact in Dubai. It's only a matter of time before we narrow the pool to a few wealthy Russians who've done business with both dealers. Then we'll focus on that list and see if they can be linked to Yasmin. It may take time, but the leads are much more promising than anything I've had before."

"I don't know how you can cross-reference leads when names are never exchanged."

Nicholas gave her a half-smile. "We have ways of uncovering identities."

"When you find Yasmin's ex, you'll be able to get your family's artwork back?"

"Perhaps." Nicholas's expression wasn't precisely happy.

Acacia wondered why.

"I'm gratified you're still wearing my gift." He touched one of the beads of her necklace.

"It means something to me." She reached up to draw Nicholas's mouth to hers.

She kissed him slowly and let the affection she felt for him in her heart lead her.

"Thank you for protecting my mother," she whispered.

He deepened the kiss.

When they parted, he looked down at her, his eyes on fire. "You're mine this evening. I'm taking you to dinner, and then I'm taking you to bed."

"Is that a promise?" She tugged on his tie.

"It's a vow."

She smiled and snuggled closer into his side.

Nicholas and Acacia were whisked through customs in Paris before being transferred to a large Range Rover. Nicholas gave Acacia's address to the driver.

A short time later, they pulled up in front of her building.

As Kurt helped her step onto the curb, she looked up at the stone structure. It seemed so long since she'd been home. Indeed, she felt like a different person.

She was conscious of the fact that although Nicholas knew her secrets, she was still obliged to keep them from others. The duality felt curious.

Kurt guided her into the building quickly. Like most bodyguards, he didn't like his client being out in the open. Rick followed with Nicholas.

There was a brief exchange with Madame Ouellete, the superintendent of the building, who provided Acacia with new keys. The locks had been changed on the front door to the building as well as her apartment.

As they ascended the staircase, Acacia craned her neck to see her doorway. It was freshly painted and stood apart from the other ivory-colored doors and walls.

"Wen is waiting for us," Nicholas murmured as he took Acacia's elbow. "He's already scanned the apartment, and he'll scan us as well."

Acacia sighed. Wen's presence was a constant reminder of possible threats.

She used her new keys to unlock the two new locks on her door. Slowly, she opened it.

The studio apartment had been repaired, but it had been no ordinary renovation. The space had been entirely transformed into a peaceful haven. Madame Cassirer's design plan had been implemented to the letter, and it was far more beautiful and functional than Acacia had imagined.

"Hi." Wen greeted her from the kitchen.

"Hi." She smiled and crossed the threshold.

Wen completed his surveillance, and when he didn't find anything, waved his goodbye.

Now she could truly admire the renovation.

SYLVAIN REYNARD

The kitchen had been completely redone with white, glass-doored cabinets and stainless steel hardware. New stainless steel appliances and a marble countertop gleamed under task lighting. The parquet flooring had been refinished and shone a warm honey color.

The sleeping area now featured an expanded closet with built-in shelves and cubbyholes. Her old twin bed had been replaced by a white, wrought iron day bed, dressed in azure and blue.

Nicholas frowned darkly at the bed. "It's far too small."

Acacia laughed. "It pulls out into a queen. It was part of the design plan I worked on with your mother." She tugged at Nicholas's hand so he could take a closer look.

He breathed a sigh of relief. "I knew my mother adored you." He kissed the top of Acacia's head.

"Does she know about us?"

"I called her this morning and told her we were returning to Paris. She wormed the information out of me."

Acacia felt the edges of panic begin to close around her.

Nicholas touched her face. "What's that look for?"

Acacia's gaze flickered to the bodyguards, who acted as if they weren't eavesdropping.

Nicholas stroked her cheek with his thumb. "Look at me."

When she made eye contact, he continued. "She doesn't know about your past. That's your story to tell, when and if you choose. But you should know she and my father are very happy for us. You have no reason to fear their approval; you have it. Not that it matters."

"Family is important."

He touched her chin. "Yes. But by way of contrast, I don't have the approval of your mother. And I'm afraid I don't care."

Acacia smiled. "Right now I don't have the approval of my mother. I'm not sure I'll ever have it again after Dubai."

"Which illustrates my point. Family can be a blessing, but they can also be a curse. We shouldn't allow our happiness to be tainted by their disapproval."

She nodded.

"Now, let's admire your collaboration with *Maman*. She said you and she worked together very well." Nicholas placed his arm around Acacia's shoulder, and they surveyed the apartment together.

Acacia's attention was drawn to the lamps and new light fixtures, the cozy area rug in front of the day bed, and the floor-to-ceiling bookshelf that stood on a side wall.

She noticed that her copy of Monet's *Twilight, Venice* had been repaired and framed. And to her surprise, next to it hung a large, framed copy of Monet's *Gare Saint-Lazare*, which was one of her favorite paintings.

"*Maman* mentioned she had a gift for you," Nicholas explained. "You and she share an admiration of the way Monet painted light."

"I have to thank her. It's such a beautiful copy. The original hangs in the National Gallery in London, but I've never seen it." Acacia stepped closer and reached a hesitant hand to the painting.

"We'll call her later. The contractors did excellent work, but you and *Maman* have an eye for design. I see you picked Santorini blue and white as your colors." Nicholas caressed Acacia's shoulder.

She wrapped her arm around his waist and hugged him. "It's wonderful. Thank you."

His chin came to rest on top of her head. "You're welcome, *amour*."

"Hello, Acacia? Are you home?" Kate's voice carried from the hall.

Acacia turned to see her friend at the door, her view partially obscured by the bodyguards.

"Whoa." Kate lifted a finger to point at Nicholas. "Who's that?"

Acacia laughed. She took Nicholas's hand and led him past the bodyguards, who crowded the doorway and blocked Kate's entrance.

"Kate, this is Nicholas. Nicholas, this is my neighbor, Kate."

Kate pulled Acacia away from Nicholas and hugged her. She switched to English. "I'm so glad to see you. I was worried."

Acacia squeezed her back. "I'm fine. How are you?"

"Jealous. You flee the city and end up coming back with someone even hotter than Inspector What-A-Shame. I need to take Brazilian lessons."

Acacia laughed again. "He speaks English, Kate."

"Excellent," she murmured.

"Pleased to meet you." Nicholas extended his hand and shook Kate's with a smile. He turned to Acacia. "*Inspector What-A-Shame?*" he mouthed.

Acacia shook her head.

"I wasn't sure I'd be home when you got back, so I gave the keys to Madame Ouellette. I guess she handed them over?"

"Yes."

"Good. You didn't have to wait." Kate tugged on Acacia's arm. "Claude is in my apartment. And I have your mail."

Kurt insisted on preceding Acacia and Nicholas to Kate's apartment. He carried the cat carrier and bag of accoutrements as they escorted Claude back to Acacia's.

"So this is your cat." Nicholas peered down at the ball of fur in Acacia's arms.

The cat looked up at Nicholas and hissed.

"Claude," Acacia scolded him. He wriggled free, leaped to the floor, and ran under her new bed.

Nicholas frowned. "That went well."

"Claude doesn't like people."

"Just like his namesake. He seems to like you and Kate well enough," Nicholas observed.

Kate put Acacia's mail on the kitchen counter.

"Thank you." Acacia hugged her friend again. "Thank you for looking after Claude and picking up the mail."

"No problem."

"I'll take you to lunch."

"That sounds great. I have a meeting with my thesis advisor tomorrow morning. We could have lunch after?"

"Sure. Meet you at Café Mirabel?"

"Perfect." Kate peered around the apartment. "It looks so much better than before. Do you like it?"

"I love it." Acacia took Nicholas's hand.

"Bernard is having a party tonight. I don't suppose you two want to come?" Kate looked at Nicholas dubiously.

"I'm afraid we have plans." He kissed Acacia's knuckles and smiled down at her.

"Right. Poor Bernard." Kate stared at Nicholas, who gazed longingly at Acacia, and jerked her thumb at the door. "I'm just going to go now. See you."

Nicholas's eyes moved to hers. "Nice to meet you."

"You too." Before Kate entered the hall, she made eye contact with Acacia. "Call me." Then she closed the door.

Nicholas looked in the direction of the bed. "I don't suppose the cat will be coming out anytime soon."

"Not with so many people around." Acacia looked at Rick and Kurt balefully.

From their body language, they had no intention of leaving.

"Welcome home," Nicholas said. "We have a reservation at Le Jules Verne, but it's not until sunset. You have plenty of time to settle in."

"Le Jules Verne?" Acacia gasped. "I thought we'd be staying in. Wouldn't that be safer?"

He turned to the bodyguards. "Wait in the hall, please."

They exited the apartment and left the door ajar.

Nicholas gathered Acacia in his arms. "You've spent a lot of years hiding. With me, you don't need to hide."

"I've always had to look over my shoulder. I don't think I'm capable of living any other way."

His expression was grave. "I know what that's like. There was always the possibility my sister's killers would try to end me as well."

Acacia's arms around him tightened.

"But Acacia, those who wreak terror and trade in fear want us to cower. They want us to hide. It's time for you to reclaim control.

"Now you have the resources to protect yourself and your mother. You have the resources to fight back."

"I don't want to fight. I just want to live in peace."

Nicholas's expression hardened. "Sometimes the war comes to you."

She frowned. "If I rely on you for my protection, I'll be living Yasmin's life."

Nicholas released her, his face angry. "What are you talking about?"

"Nicholas, please don't be cross with me." She reached for his hand, but he evaded her. "I met you, and you're wonderful. You're generous and noble and thoughtful. But wouldn't you have me with you because I want to be and not because I have to be?"

"I'm sorry, I thought that's what was happening." He folded his arms over his chest, his eyes thunderous.

"Right now, it's both." She touched his arm. This time he didn't withdraw. "We need to find a way for me to be safe without relying on your protection. Then you'll know I'm with you solely because I want to be."

"What's wrong with protecting those you care about?" He made a sweeping gesture to the room. "What's wrong with offering resources as well as your heart? If you were part of my family, it wouldn't even be a question."

"But I'm not, Nicholas."

Nicholas opened his mouth. He shut it abruptly.

"Fuck." He took her hand. "Our connection makes you family. I protect those I care about, Acacia. I'm not going to compromise your safety."

"This is how you want to bind me to you?"

Nicholas looked stricken. "No," he admitted. "I'd rather have you with me only because you want to be."

Acacia wrapped his hand in both of hers. "Then we're agreed."

"I hadn't thought of it that way," he said almost sorrowfully. "I didn't think you'd see our situation as resembling Yasmin's."

"We have to find a way forward that allows me to continue living my life."

"Am I part of that?" Nicholas's eyes were earnest. But something lurked in their depths. Something that appeared to Acacia like anxiety.

"I'd like you to be."

His shoulders relaxed. "Good. It will take some time to find our way. I'm hoping you can give me that time."

"I can."

"Thank you. Now, are you coming to dinner with me this evening or not?"

She cocked her head to one side. "Is that an invitation or a command?"

He smiled repentantly. "I would be honored if you'd accompany me to dinner, *mademoiselle*."

"Thank you. I accept."

"I'll leave Rick with you. Kurt will come with me to the hotel, and we'll come back in about two hours to pick you up."

"Not Rick."

Nicholas lifted his eyebrows. "Why not?"

"He doesn't like me."

"Rick doesn't like anyone. Then again, neither does your cat."

Nicholas's attempt at humor was entirely lost on Acacia. She pondered whether or not to mention the exchange she'd had with Rick in Dubai and decided against it. "I'd prefer Kurt."

"Very well." Nicholas gave her an assessing look. "Can I invite myself to stay tonight?"

"Here?" Acacia looked over at the bed. "But you booked rooms at the Ritz."

"Were you planning on returning to my hotel with me?"

"I just got home."

"Precisely." He placed his arms around her and drew her into his chest.

"We won't have privacy if the bodyguards are here. It's a studio." She leaned her cheek against his heart.

"They can stand in the hall." Nicholas tipped up her chin and brushed his lips across hers. "I'll see you in two hours."

"Hurry back."

Nicholas rewarded her with a blinding smile, and then he was gone.

Chapter Forty-Three

Le Jules Verne was a famous restaurant located on the second floor of the Eiffel Tower, which afforded an incredible view of Paris as night began to fall. Nicholas had ensured his reservation coincided with the setting sun.

They sat at an intimate table next to the windows. Parts of the tower's elaborate metalwork framed their sightline. The chef himself came from the kitchen to shake hands, clapping Nicholas on the shoulder and addressing him as an old friend.

Acacia was grateful for her training in hospitality, which gave her a quiet poise she could adopt whenever she was nervous. Of course, her clothes helped, too. She was grateful for the limited wardrobe she'd bought when she'd become Nicholas's assistant, as it was tailored for special occasions such as this one.

She wore a cocktail dress of black lace embroidered with brightly colored flowers. Her hair, as always, hung in dark curls to her chin. Her black high heels saved Nicholas from having to bend his neck too far in order to kiss her. Her hamsa pendant hung from her wrist, and she wore Nicholas's necklace at her throat.

After the chef returned to the kitchen, Nicholas gazed at her appreciatively. "You are very beautiful."

"Thank you." Her eyes sparkled as she turned to the skyline. The lights of Paris had begun to shine; both skyscrapers and historical buildings were illuminated. The beautiful Seine, her lucky river, flowed in the distance. Acacia had a difficult time tearing her eyes away.

"I've made many reservations at this restaurant, all for other people," she mused. "I never expected to dine here."

"I wanted to lay Paris at your feet." Nicholas reached across the table to take her hand.

"It's breathtaking."

"Good. And how is Claude?"

Acacia smiled. "He's happy I'm home. I hope the two of you will get to know one another."

"I'm not really a cat person. For your sake, I'll try." Nicholas sipped his champagne. "Have you spoken to Luc?"

Acacia stared into her champagne glass. "I texted him, telling him I was home."

Nicholas frowned. "And?"

"He wanted to come over. I put him off until tomorrow."

Nicholas's expression soured.

Acacia glanced around. The restaurant was full. Although the other patrons were speaking at reasonable levels, she was conscious of the fact that she and Nicholas could be overheard.

She lowered her voice. "I'm not looking forward to seeing him, but he's been worried about me. When I was at the Victoire and wondering what to do about the painting I saw in your suite, I called him. He came right over."

At that moment, a waiter appeared to top up their champagne glasses. Another waiter served the *amuse bouche* of marinated white fish with radish.

Nicholas lifted his fork and stabbed the fish. "He's BRB. He was doing his job."

"I can handle Luc." Acacia tasted the fish. It was incredible — buttery and flavorful.

"You shouldn't have to handle him. He needs to remember his manners."

Acacia dabbed at her lips with her napkin. Her annoyance flared. "You know everything about me and Luc. Tell me about Silke."

Nicholas's eyes burned into hers. "Why?"

"I'm curious."

"It isn't a pleasant tale," he warned.

"You know my secrets."

"That's true." He peered out the window, looking very upset.

A waiter removed their empty plates while another served the next course: blue lobster with a vinaigrette.

"Nicholas?" she prompted.

Nicholas slid his palm over the tablecloth, as if he were smoothing out wrinkles. "You saw the photographs of Silke with that American."

"I did. They were disgraceful."

Nicholas's eyes seared into hers. "Ours was a business relationship. Silke was part of my cover. I needed someone who could move in and out of social events. I paid her a salary and secured an apartment for her. She traveled with me a few times a year."

Acacia's fork clattered against her plate.

A number of patrons turned to look.

She flushed and brought her napkin to her mouth. "You paid her?"

"She wouldn't have considered me otherwise." Nicholas laughed without amusement. "One of my associates introduced me to her in a different guise." He gestured to where his scar rested beneath the prosthetic. "She tried to back out of our arrangement when she saw the true me. She said she couldn't bear to look at me."

Acacia cringed. "Oh, Nicholas."

"Despite her mercenary heart, Silke had at least one loyalty. She works in intelligence."

"For whom?"

"I can't tell you." Nicholas's expression was serious. "She never disclosed who she was working for, but I investigated her before our arrangement took effect and found out."

He looked down at the table. "During one of our trips, one thing led to another. We started a sexual relationship that continued until she decided to take up with that American."

A feeling of horror passed over Acacia. She hadn't given his previous relationship sufficient attention when she considered becoming involved with him. Clearly, his wounds were fresh.

Nicholas glared into his champagne. "She broke our agreement, and she didn't even have the courtesy to tell me herself. She engineered the paparazzi photos in order to break things off with me. I don't know if the American is an asset she's working, or if her heart, such as it is, is involved. I suspect the former."

Nicholas threw back his drink in a single swallow. He signaled for a waiter and ordered a vodka and tonic.

"I'm sorry," Acacia whispered. The feeling of horror grew. It was now resident in her stomach, twisting her insides.

When the waiter returned with Nicholas's drink, she placed her napkin on the table. "Please excuse me."

The waiter pulled out her chair, and Nicholas stood, his eyes stormy.

Kurt followed as she exited the dining area and walked toward the ladies' room. He waited outside the door.

Inside, Acacia leaned against the vanity.

What the hell am I doing?

Nicholas had just confessed to hiring a spy to be his mistress. He'd continued paying her a salary after they started having sex. Acacia thought back to the Hotel Victoire's guest records and the names of the women who'd accompanied him over the years. Had they been high-priced escorts, too?

Acacia turned. In the mirror she could see the dress Nicholas had bought. She was living in an apartment he and his mother had renovated and decorated. She was eating a dinner he'd be paying for. What was the difference between she and Silke? Or she and Yasmin?

Affection. You care for Nicholas, and your affection is given freely.

In her reflection, she saw a woman who'd lived a life of fraud. A woman who lived in fear. Even so, she'd tried to find a way to be with Nicholas as an equal and not a dependent.

She could tell herself she'd been lonely when Nicholas came to her room in Santorini. But that wasn't the only reason she welcomed him. She wasn't ready to call it love, but whatever she felt for Nicholas was powerful and deep. He was in her heart now. And the thought that Silke had wounded him so cruelly made her angry.

You want him to be happy.

The truth about Silke stung. But Nicholas's shame and pain at being thought ugly was far more troubling. He'd obviously developed some feelings for Silke, or else he wouldn't have been so incensed by her betrayal.

Acacia had no right to be angry with him. In judging Nicholas, she'd have to judge herself. They'd both hidden and tried to find human connection while preserving secrets.

She fixed her makeup and combed her hair before exiting the ladies' room.

Kurt reached for her elbow. "Are you all right?"

His evident concern touched her. "I'm all right. Thank you."

"If you're ill, I can take you home. I'll tell Rick."

"No, I'm going to finish dinner. Thank you, Kurt."

He stood aside and shadowed her back to the dining room.

Nicholas moved to his feet as soon as he caught sight of her. His mouth and jaw were tight.

He came around the edge of the table to pull out her chair, waving the waiter aside.

He placed his hands on her shoulders as she sat and bent toward her ear. "I wasn't sure you were coming back."

"I needed a minute." She replaced her napkin in her lap.

Nicholas sat across from her. He waited while the waiter took away their plates and served the next course, a stuffed zucchini.

"It's a shameful thing," he said in a low voice. "Much as I'd like to pretend otherwise, she was a hired companion. It's embarrassing and humiliating. Imagine what my parents would say, if they found out."

Acacia slid her hand across the table. "Nicholas."

He took her hand, but didn't lift his eyes. "My previous relationships were normal. Nevertheless, I assure you that I always wore condoms with Silke. And I'm tested regularly."

Acacia wound their fingers together. "I believe you."

He lifted his head. His dark eyes were filled with regret. "I would never put you at risk."

"I know that." She swallowed. "That isn't what upset me."

"If I could do it over, I would."

Acacia nodded. "I can't help being jealous."

"Jealous?" His tone was incredulous.

"Whatever else she is, Silke is very beautiful."

"I never had a moment of levity with her. She didn't make me laugh or tell me I needed better friends. She was indifferent to art

272

but extremely interested in valuable, costly things. I was foolish to get involved with her at all, and even more foolish to sleep with her."

Acacia lifted Nicholas's hand and kissed his knuckles. "She doesn't appreciate beauty; that much is true."

"No one has called me beautiful in some time."

"You need new friends."

Nicholas threw his head back and laughed. Other patrons once again turned their heads toward the sound.

"Why is it, *ma petite*, that you have this ability to make me laugh just when I want to smash something?"

"You should laugh more. Your eyes brighten, and your face crinkles. I love hearing you laugh."

"Then I shall endeavor to laugh more," he vowed. "I'm sorry to have sullied our beautiful evening with confessions of my frailty."

"Although the story is unpleasant, I'm glad you told me."

"I'm grateful you didn't walk out on me forever." His gaze deepened in intensity.

"I'm sorry you've experienced so much hurt because of your scar. You're handsome, Nicholas, with the scar and without it. You don't have to wear the prosthetic. Not with me."

"You mean it," he murmured.

"Of course. You have to know how much I care for you. All of you."

His smile was dazzling.

"But Nicholas, this reinforces what I was saying earlier about finding my own way and not being dependent on you."

His smile faded. "Our relationship is entirely different."

"Which is why I need my independence." She drew a deep breath. "I checked my bank statement today. I can't accept the money you transferred as a consulting fee."

He smiled at her wistfully. "Somehow I knew this conversation was coming. Would it help if I told you that sums like that are transferred every day to contacts of mine around the world?"

"No, it wouldn't."

"I know better than to argue, especially after what I've just revealed." He scratched his jaw. "I don't suppose you'd consider it a loan, just until you find another job?"

"No." She sighed. "And there's something else. I received an EU Blue Card in the mail today."

Nicholas rubbed the back of his neck. "As soon as you agreed to work for me, I instructed the Paris office to file the paperwork. As you know, I have friends in the French government. Obviously, they did me a favor."

"I'm in a difficult position. I don't want to be deported. I love my apartment and my friends, and I don't want to be separated from you."

Nicholas nodded. "But?"

"I don't want to accept it, but I feel like I have to. So I owe you." Acacia wore a strained look.

"When they applied for it, I didn't know about your past. I can understand you don't want to do anything to jeopardize your residency or to invite scrutiny. All I can do is apologize." His expression was sincere.

"I hope there will come a time when I can do a great kindness for you."

"You already have." His voice grew thick.

She scored a pattern on the surface of the linen tablecloth with the tines of her fork. "To summarize, I'm going to return the commission to you, but I'm going to accept the Blue Card—with the hope that someday I can do something grand for you. The only thing that remains is for me to find a new job. And I need to do that on my own."

He studied the skyline for a moment. "I'd like to see you work in the art world, on your own terms."

"I became a concierge partially to hide."

Nicholas turned to her. "How so?"

"People who work in hospitality tend to be invisible. We work long hours in service, and many guests don't even bother to learn our names. I think of it as hiding in plain sight."

"I never thought of it like that." Nicholas frowned.

"I told you about the kidnap attempt in Brazil when I was a teenager. After that, we fled to Recife. A year later, my mother sent me here on a study abroad program. I worked hard on my French, and after I returned to Brazil and finished my schooling, I came to the Sorbonne. Paris was a good place to hide, we thought. Hospitality was even better. But I always intended to work in the art world. I was waiting until more time had passed."

"Don't put it off any longer, Acacia. You should ask Madame Bishop to help you find employment in a gallery. I won't interfere, I promise."

Acacia smiled. "All right."

"Good." Nicholas lifted her hand. With his eyes on hers, he pressed his mouth to her palm. "I knew when you reported me to the BRB you were an amazing woman."

Acacia closed her eyes and grimaced.

Nicholas chuckled. "You have to admit, it's a very funny story."

She opened her eyes. "I never thought of the BRB as a group of matchmakers. I suppose I'm lucky."

"I'm the lucky one. You're intelligent and attractive. You're incredibly gifted, and yet you're jealous of Silke for my affections."

Acacia squeezed his hand. "I'm angry at how she treated you. I don't care if she is a spy, she'd better stay far away from me."

Something pulled at the edges of Nicholas's lips. "Or what?"

"I'd give her a lecture on true beauty. I'd tell her to grow up and look inward before her interior ugliness defaced the rest of her. I'd trip her as she walked by."

Nicholas sat back in his chair.

Acacia frowned. "Too much?"

He grinned. "Never."

She lifted her fork. "Now that we've had our serious conversation, I propose we enjoy the rest of our dinner and the fantastic view."

"Your wish, your pleasure," he whispered.

She smiled. "Thank you."

Chapter Forty-Four

After dinner, Nicholas and Acacia retired to her apartment, while Rick and Kurt's overnight replacements guarded the hallway.

After such an intense evening, Acacia was desperate for him. But Nicholas took his time lighting candles around the studio to the music of Anne Ducros.

"Where's the cat?" he asked.

"Hiding in the bathroom."

"Finally, we have privacy." Nicholas smiled and assisted Acacia in transforming the day bed to a queen-sized bed.

She removed a pair of pillows from her reorganized closet. "The look on your face when you saw the bed this morning was priceless."

"I know my mother likes you. I know she likes us together. I couldn't believe she'd sabotage me by incorporating a single bed in her design."

Acacia laughed.

He removed his suit jacket and hung it on a chair. Just like that, the mood in the room shifted.

Acacia watched, mesmerized, as he slowly unfastened his tie and placed it over his jacket. He gazed at her while he unbuttoned his white dress shirt and removed the cufflinks, setting them on her nightstand.

He took her hand. "You are my reward." He kissed her fingers, one by one.

"I'm a reward that comes with a tremendous amount of baggage. But I care for you."

"That's all I ask." He touched her face with both hands, lowering his mouth to hers.

When their lips touched, the energy between them sparked. Nicholas tugged her lower lip into his mouth and drew on it.

His thumbs passed over her cheeks, and Acacia leaned into him. He released her lower lip and angled his head, smoothing his mouth across hers.

Her arms lifted to clasp around his neck. She brought their bodies together, sighing into his mouth.

His tongue slid against hers, and she tasted cinnamon.

"You don't have to hide yourself." Acacia reached a tentative hand to his prosthetic.

He caught her hand. "It doesn't repulse you?"

"It troubles me because I know someone hurt you. Others continued to hurt you because of it. But it's part of you the way my scar is part of me. It's evidence of your strength. Your courage."

He kissed her hand and turned around.

She was about to call him back when she realized what he was doing. He'd positioned himself in front of the mirror that hung near the front door.

She gave him privacy by fussing with the pillows.

A minute later, his hands were on her shoulders.

She turned. His eyes were cautious.

She touched her lips to his scar. "I'm not hiding from you. You know who I am and who my father is. You know I accept you as you are."

He took her mouth fiercely. Then he unzipped her dress and watched it fall to the floor. "It was a lovely dress."

"I'm glad you liked it." Gingerly, she held onto his shoulder as she took off her heels.

He caressed her neck and nudged her bra strap aside to taste her skin. He plied kiss after kiss across her collarbone.

"I love your curves." His hands covered her breasts, over her black lace bra.

"Good. I like to eat, so despite the time spent at the dojo, I'll always be curvy."

He pulled the cups of her bra down. Then with murmured appreciation, he bent to take one of her nipples in his mouth. He teased the other with his thumb.

She fanned a hand against his neck, urging him on. She kissed the shell of his ear and nibbled at it with the edge of her teeth.

With a growl, he released her. He tugged his shirt out of his trousers and threw it aside. He stepped out of his pants, and his belt buckle clanged against the floor.

They came together again with urgent kisses. Nicholas's hands slid to her backside and he lifted her, wrapping her legs around his hips.

He carried her to the bed and looked down at her with longing.

"I delight in you," he whispered. "What you say, your laughter, the way you speak."

He rested his hand on her abdomen. She felt her insides flutter.

"Come here." She tugged his arm, pulling him atop her. "I like your weight."

"That's good." He chuckled, bracing his forearms on either side of her shoulders. "Because I like how my body feels against yours."

She parted her legs, and his hips nestled between them.

His fingers quested the catch to her bra and unfastened it, dragging it over her heated skin.

"You're lovely in everything." He dropped the bra to the floor. "But you have a beautiful body. Look how your skin glows in the candlelight."

He blew across her nipples and watched them constrict. He teased them, catching them between his thumb and his forefinger. Pleasurable sensations shot across her body, increasing her desire for him.

She didn't want to be selfish. She traced the ridges of his abdomen above the waistband of his dark blue boxer briefs.

He pushed himself against her hand, and she stroked him firmly.

"Delicious." He licked her breast and transferred his attention to her nipple.

She reached around him to push his underwear over his hips.

It took a moment for him to free himself. Then he sheathed himself with a condom and moved between her legs.

He caressed the curves of her cheeks, his gaze watchful and serious.

"Aren't you happy?" Her finger traced his dark brows.

"Happy to be with you, of course. But I'm afraid I'm out of practice at being happy, *mon amour*."

Her hand rested on his backside and she pressed, nestling him more tightly between her legs. "Do you feel this?"

"Yes." His expression brightened.

"We create something together we don't have apart."

"That makes me happy." His mouth slid against hers, and his tongue dipped inside.

She lifted her hips in encouragement, and he thrust forward.

"I need a moment," he said roughly, tearing his mouth from hers.

She touched his face. "You feel so good."

They moved in concert, and she lifted her hips to meet every stroke. But Nicholas was determined to make their connection last. He would not rush.

Her hands traced his strong shoulders and the bumps of his spine. She clutched his backside with both hands and squeezed.

"Look at me," he demanded when her eyes fluttered closed.

She saw a slight vulnerability in his eyes — something in that moment he could not hide.

"It's good," she panted. "So good." Her head lolled back and her eyes closed.

His pace quickened and pushed more deeply. She met him stroke for stroke.

He kissed her neck, tonguing the skin wetly and catching it with the edge of his teeth.

He went deeper inside her, and she felt the pleasure build. Building. Building.

"Please," she begged. Her eyes flew open. "Please."

"What do you need?" He almost stuttered. He clenched his jaw as he quickened his pace.

"More." Her fingers dug into his backside.

He lengthened his strokes, entering her more deeply and moving faster. Faster.

He angled his upper body and lifted her breast to his mouth. He tongued her nipple and sucked hard.

"*Yes.*" She released with a cry.

He kept moving, extending her pleasure.

She wrapped her arms around him and hid her face against his neck.

He pulsed inside her. Then he grew still.

She touched his cheek, below his scar. "Are you all right?"

"I was just thinking about the fireworks that always seem to explode when we're together."

"We're lucky."

"Yes, we are." He paused and lifted his head. "The way we are together is very different from how it has been for me in the past."

"For me as well."

He brought her hand to his chest. "You've stolen my heart."

"An even exchange." She smiled. "You have mine, as well."

Chapter Forty-Five

The following morning, Acacia awoke to the sound of her front door opening and closing.

She cursed at the intrusion and pulled the covers over her head. Underneath the sheets, she was wrapped around Nicholas's naked body, her head resting on his chest. They'd made love many times the night before, their romantic activities extending well into the morning. She was far too tired and too comfortable to be disturbed.

"I'm sorry, boss, but there's a BRB agent who wants to speak with mademoiselle." Kurt's voice cut through her sleepy haze.

"Damn." Nicholas's hand flexed against her backside, below the sheet. He squeezed her affectionately and kissed her hair. "I'm sorry, *amour.*"

She groaned and carefully extricated herself, taking care to keep her body covered with a sheet.

Nicholas sat up. He looked as if he was going to answer the door.

"I'll handle it." She reached down to kiss him.

As she approached the entrance to her apartment, Kurt opened the door.

"Caci." Luc's eyes met hers. He wore jeans and a black leather jacket. His face was unshaven, and he looked tired.

His mouth curled in disapproval as he took in her mussed hair, sleepy face, and bare shoulders. He eyed the sheet in disgust.

Her irritation flared, and she pulled the sheet more tightly around her. "I texted you. I said we'd talk later today."

"You've been saying that for days. Who's here?" Luc looked over her shoulder, into her apartment.

She followed his gaze as he found Nicholas sitting on the edge of the bed, his upper body bare.

Luc's face reddened, and he gave her an accusing look. "What's he doing here?"

"I'm not dressed." Her voice was firm. "I'll explain everything later."

He grabbed her arm. "Caci, come into the hall."

"No touching." Kurt intervened, placing his hand on Luc's arm.

"I'm BRB," Luc said angrily. "Get your hand off me, or I'll have a dozen agents here in five minutes."

Acacia stood between the two men. "It's all right, Kurt."

She pulled her arm free of Luc, and Kurt released him.

"Now isn't a good time," she said. "I'll call you later."

"Time to go." Kurt moved back, taking Acacia with him.

"Wait." Luc moved to block the closing door, but Kurt stood in front of him. Luc's blue eyes blazed. "Caci, come into the hall. He can't stop you."

"The owner of the apartment has asked you repeatedly to leave, and you've refused." Nicholas walked to the door, a blanket wrapped around his hips.

"I know all about you, Breckman." Luc's eyes narrowed. "I'd recognize that Frankenstein face anywhere."

"*Connard*," Acacia swore at Luc, pushing him back before anyone else could move.

"Caci." Luc looked wounded.

"Don't speak that way to him." Her voice shook.

"Are you joking?" Luc's nostrils flared. "This guy is an arms dealer. You asked me to protect you from him, and now you're fucking him?" He shook his head. "How do I know he isn't holding you against your will?"

"Because I'm telling you he isn't," Acacia snapped. "Speak to Kate. She came over to see us yesterday. Speak to Madame Ouellete, downstairs."

"I came here to speak to you."

"Yes, and as you can see, I'm fine. I'll explain everything later. But don't insult the man who has my heart."

Luc passed a hand over his mouth. "I can't believe this. You know what? We don't need to talk. Not now." He muttered a curse. "Call me when you get your head together."

He turned and walked swiftly toward the staircase.

Kurt entered the hall and closed the door behind him. Nicholas locked and bolted the door from the inside.

Acacia sank into his arms. "I'm so sorry. What he said was terrible."

"He lost you. That's enough to make a man forget his manners."

She looked up at him. "How can you be so calm? I wanted to punch him."

"It's a good thing you didn't." Nicholas lifted her hand and formed it into a fist. He kissed it, a wicked gleam in his eye. "My legal team might have difficulty making that charge go away."

She cursed in Portuguese.

Nicholas gave her a half-smile. He examined her knuckles. "Did you mean what you said?"

"Did I mean what?"

"That I have your heart?"

"Of course."

Nicholas puffed out his chest. "See? I'm calm because I won. And my woman can swear in at least six languages."

"I'm working on Japanese." She lifted up on tiptoes. "I'm going to make coffee and *pão de queijo*."

"What's that?"

"Fantastic Brazilian cheese bread."

"To the winner goes the spoils." He bent her backward to kiss her.

"He showed up at your apartment when your new, hot man was there? Holy shit." Kate turned to face Acacia as they walked under the great glass pyramid at the Louvre. Kurt followed.

"Then what happened?"

"Luc insisted I speak to him. I wasn't even dressed; I was wrapped in a sheet. Then he insulted Nicholas."

"Saying what?"

Acacia shook her head. Kate had been introduced to Nicholas when his scar was covered. She couldn't mention it. "It doesn't matter. I told Luc I was with Nicholas. Then Luc told me to call him when I got my head together."

"Wow. That was awkward."

"Incredibly."

Acacia and Kate had had lunch at a quiet café in the Latin Quarter before traveling on foot to the Louvre. As ever, Acacia didn't go anywhere without Kurt.

"He isn't going to tell Nicholas everything, is he?" Kate whispered in English as they waited under the pyramid.

"No," Acacia replied. "But because of what happened at the Victoire and…other things, Nicholas has insisted I have a bodyguard."

"Cool." Kate bobbed her head. "I should have brought you and your bodyguard to my meeting with my thesis advisor. He's a jerk."

"I'm sorry."

"I'm sorry I spent our entire lunch complaining about him. Thanks for agreeing to come here. I thought this would be a quiet place to talk."

There are several adjectives one might apply to the Louvre, Acacia thought, *but quiet is not one of them.*

She looked at her friend in concern. "Will things be all right with your thesis?"

Kate frowned. "I don't know. But I'm not giving up."

They stood admiring the pyramid that rose above them, as well as the pyramid that hung from the ceiling, bathing the underground entrance in bright Parisian sunlight. Tourists crowded the area taking photographs and selfies.

"Luc showing up and being a jerk was a dumb move on his part," Kate observed. "Do you think you'll be able to talk to him after he cools off?"

Acacia glanced over her shoulder at Kurt, who wore a blank expression. "I think I owe Luc an explanation. I'm the one who involved him in my life again. But I don't want a repeat of what happened this morning."

A man in a very handsome dark green suit rounded the corner and walked toward them, flanked by a smartly dressed woman on one side and a uniformed security guard on the other.

Acacia swore under her breath.

Kurt stood in front of Kate and Acacia as the entourage approached. Kate leaned sideways so she could see around Kurt's massive body.

"Mademoiselle Santos?" The green-suited man stuck out his hand and smiled. "Louis Richard."

Acacia shook hands, trying to recover her manners. The man in front of her was the director of the Louvre.

"This is Danielle DuBois, the director of guest relations, and Étienne Gauvin, the head of security," he said.

Acacia shook hands and quietly introduced Kate and Kurt.

"Nicholas called," the director explained, smiling broadly. "I didn't realize he was in Paris."

"He just arrived." Acacia forced a smile, still feeling tense.

"I'll need your bodyguard to sign in with security. Then you'll be free to enjoy the museum. Would you care for a personal tour? Madame DuBois would be happy to be your guide."

"That's very kind." Acacia gave Danielle an appreciative look. "But we're here simply to explore a few rooms."

"Of course." The director rubbed his hands together. "We'll just step into Madame DuBois's office to complete the paperwork."

Acacia looked at Kurt, who nodded encouragingly. "It's all right. Rick texted me about the protocol."

Acacia's smile slipped.

They followed the Louvre staff to Madame DuBois's office and completed the paperwork. Kurt was required to show several pieces of identification along with his permits.

The director shook Acacia's hand once again. "Please give Nicholas my best greetings. I hope I can prevail upon you both to come to the opening of our new antiquities exhibit in September."

Acacia's heart leaped. "I'd like that very much."

"Excellent. I'll be sure to send Nicholas's assistant the particulars. Enjoy your visit."

With another smile, Acacia, Kate, and Kurt departed the office with the head of security, who escorted them through the checkpoint and into the museum.

Acacia noticed they'd skipped the metal detectors. She'd forgotten that Kurt, like Rick, always carried a sidearm. Yet the director hadn't insisted he surrender it. She found the fact curious.

"You didn't tell me you had connections like that." Kate took Acacia's arm after they passed through the entrance. She spoke in English because of Kurt, although Acacia was fairly certain he knew English, too.

"I didn't know," Acacia said. She eyed Kurt, who seemed unperturbed by the entire situation.

"Getting back to Luc." Kate released her friend's arm. "It's obvious he's hung up on you. He kept coming by the apartment while you were gone and seemed genuinely concerned. I'm sure he was shocked that you returned from your 'vacation' with someone new."

Acacia nodded.

"I'm sorry it was awkward. But I want to hear about Nicholas, the new guy."

For reasons known only to Kate, they decided to venture toward the *Mona Lisa*, braving the crowds headed toward the Denon Wing.

The friends quickly moved past the Decorative Arts exhibit and entered the cavernous room that displayed the *Mona Lisa*, along with works by Botticelli. Acacia kept close to Kate, and Kurt kept close to both of them.

Acacia spoke in Kate's ear so she wouldn't have to shout above the din. "Nicholas was a guest at the Victoire. His security team intervened when someone attacked me. He was worried the assailants would come to my apartment, which is why I left."

"Why does he have a security team? And how is he so cozy with the director of the Louvre?"

Acacia hesitated. "He's a businessman. I think he's a patron of the museum."

Kate gave her a suspicious look.

They approached the *Mona Lisa* from the side in an attempt to inch their way forward for a better look. The crowds were almost impenetrable.

"Did Nicholas go with you when you left Paris?" Kate raised her voice so they could be heard over the chattering of the crowd.

"Yes. He was traveling on business anyway."

"Sounds awfully coincidental."

"Yes." Acacia couldn't dispute the fact.

"Come on, there's an opening." Kate pulled Acacia forward through a gap between two separate clusters of people. They were now a few feet in front of the famous painting.

"It always appears smaller than I remember," Kate mused.

"And darker." Acacia regarded the masterpiece with a critical eye. "But the perspective is amazing."

"I wish I could paint." Kate sighed.

"You can. Just buy some art supplies in the Latin Quarter and set up an easel by the Seine. Everyone else does."

Kate frowned. "I'm not talented."

"Have you seen some of those paintings? Lack of talent doesn't stop others from trying. You don't know if you're talented until you try."

"Acacia, you're someone who can do anything."

"I can't do everything. I can't make a soufflé, and I can't do a cartwheel. But I never know what I can and can't do until I try."

"That should be on a T-shirt." Kate moved forward a few steps and pulled out her phone. She snapped a few photos. "Do you want to take a picture?"

Acacia shook her head. "Not today."

"We can explore the other rooms. Thanks for humoring me. I like to visit her when I'm stressed."

Acacia grinned. "I understand. *Mona Lisa* is nonjudgmental, and she always has a smile."

They weaved their way back through the massive crowd and into the hall.

Acacia breathed a sigh of relief. She didn't like crowds, even with a security guard blanketing her like a coat.

Kate guided her to the French art exhibit nearby. "So you went away with your wealthy businessman. Where did you go?"

"Switzerland first. That's where he's from. Then Santorini."

"Santorini? That doesn't sound like business."

"It was, but he took me to the beach and..."

Kate moved closer. "And?"

Acacia lifted her hands. "And we happened."

"Huh. Well, Santorini is the place for something to happen. But I bet he was smitten with you when you met him."

"He didn't like me at first." Acacia made a face. "He was used to dealing with a different concierge."

"Sexual tension." Kate winked. "It's a powerful motivator. I'm glad you have a new man. You've been alone since I met you. Nicholas is hot."

"But?" Acacia looked at her friend curiously.

Kate gave Kurt a look designed to intimidate him, but to no avail.

"Nicholas seems sad to me," she whispered. "He doesn't fit the profile of the tortured artist, but take him out of the black suit, and that's what I see."

"He lost his sister. It...marked him."

"I'm sorry." Kate stopped, facing her friend. "That explains it. Just be careful. If he's an unhappy person, eventually he'll make you unhappy too."

Acacia stopped, stunned.

Her eyes found Kurt's. He gave her nothing by way of a reaction.

Acacia turned around and fell back into step with Kate, her words of warning ringing in her ears.

Chapter Forty-Six

That evening, Acacia and Nicholas opted to have dinner in his suite at the Ritz. In the privacy of his rooms, he forewent the prosthetic and left his scar uncovered.

Acacia was noticeably quiet. Kate's words had chastened her and made her wonder about her rapidly developed feelings for Nicholas.

He'd noticed her change in disposition but hadn't commented on it.

Later, they made love on the floor by the fireplace. Without words, they'd communicated through their bodies, their pleasure deep and intense.

Afterward, they lay in a naked tangle of limbs on the floor. They hadn't even bothered with a sheet. A light sheen of sweat covered their skin.

Acacia's leg was thrown over his, her arm across his abdomen. She rested her head near his heart, while his arms wrapped her shoulders.

"I love you."

His words came out of nowhere. Acacia lifted her head in shock.

Nicholas looked pained. His dark eyes were worried, his brow furrowed.

He touched her lips. "There's no need to reply. I've been bursting to say the words for some time. I'm afraid they just slipped out."

"You love me?" Her lips moved against his fingers.

He withdrew them. "Yes. I've loved you almost since the moment I saw you at the Victoire. You're incredible, Acacia. I'm mad about you."

"You love me despite my complicated past?"

"You told me you accepted me, scar and all. That's how I feel about you, but much more deeply."

"I love you, too," she confessed. "I realized it last night. *I love this man. I can see his heart and his soul in his eyes, and I don't ever want to be without them.*"

Nicholas brought his mouth to hers and kissed her.

"I didn't know," he said as he brought their lips together over and over again. "I was afraid if I told you, I'd lose you. But the words could not be contained."

"I've been afraid for so many years. I'm not afraid anymore, not while we're together. I've waited a long time for you."

"And I for you," he pledged. He touched her face in wonder. "You love me."

"With all my heart." She touched her hand to her chest, just below the necklace he'd given her, and then brought the same hand to his heart.

He gave her a blinding smile. "I'm very relieved to know my feelings are returned."

She tilted her head to the side. "You couldn't tell? Every time you touched me, I felt I was giving up my secrets."

"You're very expressive during sex; that's true." He kissed her nose playfully.

"So are you." She straddled him and began tickling his ribs.

He howled with laughter and tried to bat her hands away.

She laughed with him.

"And of course, you told your ex-boyfriend I had your heart. That made me brave."

"Good."

"I've got you now." He clasped her hands together, binding her wrists.

"No more tickling." She gave him a look that was meant to be sincere.

"Liar." He kissed her palms. "This is one of the reasons I love you. You make me laugh."

She smiled down at him.

They were quiet for a moment. Acacia took that opportunity to examine his face.

"Will you tell me about your scar?" Her voice was gentle.

Nicholas released her hands, and they rested on his chest.

"You already know about my sister. Her death threw my life into chaos. I didn't have the network I have today, but I had some wealth and some influence. I began my own investigation.

"A group of men had been seen in the gallery on two separate occasions prior to the robbery. They didn't act like art enthusiasts. I followed their trail into Bosnia, but they found me first."

"What happened?"

"They gave me this." He pointed to his scar. "They told me the next time we met, they'd kill me and my parents. I vowed at that moment I would become someone they could not kill."

"Nicholas." She touched his face. "You're lucky to be alive."

"I came back to my family disfigured. My own mother couldn't bear to look at me."

"I'm sure that's not true."

"It was. Although perhaps she's come to terms with it," he conceded.

"You didn't want to have the scar removed?"

Nicholas gritted his teeth. "I wanted to stand in front of the man who gave it to me and do the same to him.

"I wore a prosthetic. I lived in my parents' house, obsessed with finding the person who'd bought the artwork from the Bosnians. I lost my fiancée because of my obsession."

"I didn't know you were engaged." Acacia's voice was quiet.

"I was working in London at the time. We met there. I had brought her home to meet my family the night Riva was killed."

"Oh, Nicholas." She touched his shoulder. "What happened to your fiancée?"

He scrubbed his face. "She lived in London, where she was working. I took a leave of absence to live in Cologny. She didn't want to let me go, but I didn't have it in me to continue with her. I'm the one who ended it."

"Did you ever think of reconciling?"

"Years later I tried, but I'd hurt her so deeply she couldn't trust me."

Acacia's sigh matched his own. "You know who killed your sister."

"I know the men involved, yes. They boasted about working for someone powerful. But then they disappeared, and I was never able to pick up their trail."

"Do you think they worked for Yasmin's Russian?"

"They were wise enough not to say. In the beginning, we didn't know if the thieves had been commissioned by someone to steal the artwork or whether they were opportunists who would look for a buyer. But when I found them, they made it clear they'd been commissioned. Unfortunately, Riva surprised them the night of the robbery. They said her death was an accident. They'd only meant to knock her out."

"I'm so sorry."

Nicholas's expression grew fierce, dark fire burning in his eyes. "When I find them, I'm going to stand in front of them with this uncovered." He gestured to his face. "And I'm going to put a bullet in their brains."

Acacia stilled.

Nicholas's eyes glinted. "Returning the art to my parents is important, but I can never give them back my sister. I'm going to find the man who ordered the theft, and I'm going to kill him and his crew."

"But that's…" Acacia swallowed. "Wouldn't it be better to turn them over to Interpol?"

"So the crime boss can deny involvement? So he can plead guilty to charges of possession of stolen property? No." Nicholas's voice grew harsh. "They all need to pay."

"That's murder."

Nicholas's gaze was cold. "No, Acacia. It's justice."

She sat back and stared. "I thought you wanted to get the art back."

"It isn't enough. That man destroyed my family. My parents can't bear to be in the house we grew up in because of the memories."

"You think killing him will give them closure?"

"Yes."

"Nicholas." She bent over him. "Listen to me. Killing just brings more killing. It will never end."

"What do you know about it?" he spat.

Carefully, she moved from atop him. "Think about the part of the world where I was born. Think about my brothers and sisters in that region. I know all about killing."

Nicholas sat up. "This is different. This isn't terrorism."

"Terrorism is an act of violence brought about by someone who is a law unto himself. What's the difference between the Russian and my father? What's the difference between you and the Russian, if you do this?"

"Acacia," Nicholas warned.

"You're both powerful. You have intelligence networks and security guards. You have political power. What's the difference?"

"I'm not corrupt. I didn't start this."

"If you are a law unto yourself, then you are just like them. You can't decide who lives and who dies. You can't become the law."

"No, but I can be the agent of justice."

"Whose justice? Yours? Your sister's?" She came closer to him. "Would your sister want you to become a murderer?"

Nicholas stood, his hands clenched in fury. "Look what they did to my face! Look what they did to my sister!"

Acacia covered herself with a sheet and stumbled to her feet. "Nicholas, listen to me. You want justice. You deserve to have it. But an eye for an eye makes us all blind.

"Killing broke my family apart. We couldn't stay with a man who had become a law onto himself."

He jerked his head in her direction. "I am not your father."

"But you will become him, if you do this."

"Acacia." Nicholas lowered his head so their eyes were at the same level. "Once this is done, I'll be free. Free to live. Free to love."

"Once this is done, you'll wear the chains of killing. The Russian's people will come after you, or your family, or me. Don't you see? You'll be placing all of us at risk."

He took her hands in his. "You said you loved me. You have to understand why I must do this."

Her eyes searched his. She saw desperation and desire, force of will and affection. But it wasn't enough.

"If you love me, don't do this."

He released her. His expression was resolute. "I must."

"I love you, Nicholas. The thought of being without you tears me here." She pushed her fist against her heart. "But if you do this, if you kill that man, I can't be with you."

He grabbed her fist between his hands. "Acacia, if you were to think about it more, you'd realize I'm right."

"I've been thinking about revenge and death for almost thirty years. I know you're wrong. Promise me you won't kill anyone."

His spine straightened. "I can't."

She extricated herself from his grasp.

"Then I have to go." Acacia picked up her clothes, strewn across the floor.

"We can talk about this."

"There's nothing to discuss. You've said it all." She fled to the bathroom.

"Acacia, wait!" He followed her.

But the door was already locked.

Chapter Forty-Seven

As soon as Acacia stepped out of the bathroom, Kurt was at her side. She deposited the necklace Nicholas had given her on a table in the suite's front hall. She scribbled a quick note and told him she didn't think it was right to keep his gift.

She retrieved her purse and shoes as quickly as she could and headed to the door. Evidently Nicholas had shut himself in his bedroom.

Without a word, Kurt escorted her to the elevator and down to the front door of the hotel. He hailed a taxi and rode with her to her apartment. He made a call along the way, but Acacia blocked out the words. She was too busy bleeding inwardly.

When they arrived at her apartment building, she paid the driver, and Kurt helped her out of the taxi. He preceded her into the building.

Shots cracked just as Acacia crossed the threshold.

Kurt fell to the floor before he could retrieve his sidearm. Blood pooled on the front of his dark shirt.

Acacia screamed. She tried to flee, but a masked man with a rifle grabbed her arm. She struck him in the throat and kicked the side of his knee, sending him crumpling to the floor.

She pushed open the door and stumbled onto the sidewalk. But before she could get her bearings, something heavy and wide struck her across the lower spine. She pitched forward and crashed to the ground.

Winded, she gasped for air. Someone grabbed her by the hair, and something sharp pierced her neck.

Her heart thumped irregularly as darkness took her.

Chapter Forty-Eight

Acacia came awake with a start.

She'd been dreaming she was drowning; water filled her lungs and made it impossible to breathe. She gasped. The hot, humid air was stifling. No wonder she'd found it difficult to catch her breath.

She sat up and instantly regretted the decision. A dull ache in her lower back flared to a sharp pain that wrapped around her middle. She fought back nausea and examined the small, square room. Bright sunshine streamed in a small window set high in the cinderblock wall, indicating it was midday or later. She'd been unconscious for hours.

She breathed slowly, in and out, trying to manage the pain while ignoring the heat.

A steel door presumably led to the outside. Unfortunately, the door lacked a doorknob. Another door opened into a bathroom.

The only furniture in the room was the cot she was sitting on and a small side table. A pitcher of water stood on the table next to a small metal cup. She poured water and drank it greedily, though it was warm.

Acacia examined the ceiling. The overheard lights were off, probably because of the stifling heat. She was sweating and she'd barely moved.

She closed her eyes and listened for traffic or any other recognizable sounds. She could hear the pathetic ventilation system rattling through the covered shaft above her, but nothing else.

She opened her eyes. She wondered if the ventilation shaft was wide enough to afford her a means of escape.

But first, she'd try the window. The cinderblocks had shallow grooves between them, some shallower than others.

Years ago, she'd taken a rock climbing class. She hadn't climbed since then, but she knew the basics. The difficulty of climbing the wall was much greater than her skill level, but she had nothing to lose.

Her back complained as she lifted herself from the cot. She looked in vain for her purse, but of course, whoever had taken her had likely taken it as well.

She was still dressed in the previous night's clothes—white jeans that were now filthy and an orange silk long-sleeved top. A large rip in the silk opened below her right arm. She wore black leather shoes with no heel. At least the shoes were suitable for climbing.

She hobbled to the wall and stretched her arms upward, fingers questing for depressions she could hold. Then she lifted her left foot, ignoring the complaints from her spine, and found a toehold. Carefully, she transferred her weight to her left foot and lifted her right. She had difficulty finding a hold for the right and flattened the side of it into the deepest groove before transferring her weight to her left foot again.

Her hands sought and found higher holds, her stomach scraping against the wall as she lifted her right foot still farther, searching for a place that would take her weight.

She pulled herself up, adjusted her weight into her right foot, and began the process again with her left. Bit by bit she climbed, not giving up until finally her right hand reached the windowsill.

Straining, she pulled herself up.

There were bars on the window, covering what seemed to be Plexiglas. Outside, beige pillars topped with arches lined the courtyard, which featured a central fountain. Part of the courtyard floor was an intricate mosaic of small tiles, but the courtyard was dirty and dilapidated. Many of the tiles were broken.

A doorway stood to her left and one to her right, but there were no other visible windows on the main floor. Shuttered windows dotted the second floor, and two massive palm trees stood at the opposite end of the courtyard, flanking a tall double door with rusted iron hinges.

Acacia's arms and legs began to shake, and she quickly retraced her moves, climbing down to the concrete floor. Based on the architecture and palm trees, she was likely somewhere in the Middle East. As if in confirmation, she heard the sound of the muezzin leading the call to prayer.

Her father must have kidnapped her.

She covered her face with her hands and took a long, deep breath. Instead of praying, she ignored the muezzin and tried to organize her thoughts.

Rick would have gone looking for Kurt. She thought of his vacant stare as he lay on the floor of her apartment building, blood staining his chest. He'd promised to protect her when they were in Dubai. He'd died protecting her in Paris.

She knew so little about him. She wondered if he had a family.

Acacia stifled a sob.

Think, she told herself. *You can grieve for Kurt later. Now you have to find a way out.*

She surveyed the room and looked for anything that could be used as a weapon or a means of escape. The cot had a simple steel frame and slats overlaid with a thin mattress. She had sheets and a blanket, as well as a pillow. If the window were large enough, she could climb out and lower herself with a rope made of sheets. But the window was far too small for her to pass through, and it was barred with iron.

If she stood the cot on its end, she could use it as a ladder to the ventilation shaft. She wasn't sure how steady the cot would be on the uneven concrete floor. And she'd have to figure out a way to remove the cover to the ventilation shaft. As an escape plan, it held promise. She could try after dark.

The door to the cell didn't have a doorknob or a lock she could pick, and the gap between door and doorframe was exceptionally slim. Even if she could remove one of the metal slats from her bed, it would probably be too wide to pry open the door. But again, it was something she could try.

Acacia crossed to inspect the bathroom. It had a shower stall, toilet, and sink. She turned her back to the mirror and lifted her shirt. A long horizontal bruise of dark purple and blue cut across her lower back. She pushed at it and winced.

If she smashed the mirror, she could wrap the shards of glass in strips torn from the bed sheet and use them as a weapon.

She didn't want to kill anyone. As she'd learned in martial arts, her goal was to escape an attacker by disabling him. But if a shard of glass was the only means of escape she had, she'd use it.

She inspected the shampoo in the shower. The Arabic and French label declared it had been made in Morocco.

Morocco.

Of course she had no idea where she was in Morocco. Without money or a passport, returning to Europe would be difficult. She didn't have Nicholas and his myriad of contacts and diplomatic passports to rely on.

Nicholas.

She wondered where he was and what he was doing. She wondered if he was searching for her.

She'd left him, so if he washed his hands of her, it would be her fault. But the man she knew, the man she still loved, would not do that. Acacia believed down to her soul that Nicholas's love for her and his nobility of character would not allow him to surrender her to her fate. Somewhere, he and his people were looking for her. The thought bolstered her hope.

She heard a door open.

Acacia stood in the doorway of the bathroom and stared straight into the eyes of a young, dark-skinned man dressed in loose-fitting, sand-colored clothing and carrying a military rifle.

He spoke Arabic. "Your father returns tomorrow. Do you need anything?"

"I don't understand what you're saying," she answered in French.

The man scowled and continued in his own language. "I was told you know Arabic."

"I don't understand what you're saying," she repeated. She hunched over dramatically and placed her hand at her lower back. "I'm in pain. I need a doctor."

The man gave her a confused look and exited. The door clanged shut behind him.

He hadn't seemed angry or aggressive, despite his weapon. He'd held the door to her cell open while he spoke to her. She wondered if he'd return. If he did, she'd be ready.

She stood behind the cell door and waited. And waited.

More than an hour passed before something clanged against the door and metal scraped against metal. The door swung inward. Acacia grabbed the edge of the door with both hands and pushed as hard as she could. The door caught someone and knocked him to the floor. She leapt over his sprawled body and wrested his gun from his hand.

A guard shouted at her from the other end of the hall.

Acacia didn't know how to use a rifle. She squeezed the trigger but the gun didn't fire. Frustrated, she hoisted the rifle over her shoulder and ran.

A doorway at the far end of the hall opened into what looked like the courtyard. But just as she approached the threshold, someone stepped into her path.

Acacia continued running, then, at the last minute, she executed a roundhouse kick to the guard's head.

He fell to his knees.

She struck him in the head with the butt of the rifle and kept on running.

Outside, the sun shone bright and hot. Her steps echoed across the mosaic tiles as she ran past the fountain and toward the high, wooden doors. She yanked the door handle, but it wouldn't budge. Furiously, she searched for a lock.

She heard footsteps and turned around, but before she could defend herself, something struck her from the side. For the second time in less than twenty-four hours, everything went dark.

Chapter Forty-Nine

The ache in Acacia's back had been replaced by a dull throbbing in her skull. She lifted her hand to probe her head injury. It came away with traces of blood that must have seeped through the bandage.

The room spun. She closed her eyes.

"He will be punished. We had orders not to touch you." A man's voice spoke Arabic.

"I speak French," she whispered.

"I know what languages you speak, Hanin." The voice radiated contempt.

Acacia moaned. "Can I have a glass of water?"

She heard movement and the sound of liquid sloshing. A metal cup was placed in her hand.

She opened her eyes and lifted the cup. She downed the water in a few swallows.

"Don't you recognize me?" The voice mocked.

Acacia's gaze lifted to her captor, a man with black hair and eyes. He wore a dark beard, carried a rifle, and wore military fatigues.

"Hello, cousin. It's Ibrahim."

Acacia carefully schooled her reaction, determined to give away nothing.

Ibrahim pointed to her head. "There was a lot of blood. Sayeed got carried away, but that won't happen again."

"What do you want?" she asked in French.

The man walked to the wall near the door. He leaned against it. "Are we really going to play this game? I know you understand me. You look like your mother, Hanin. That's how we knew it was you."

Acacia bit her tongue. She wondered if they had her mother, but was too afraid to ask.

"Your father has been planning this for days. But he was called away before you arrived. He'll be back tomorrow." Ibrahim lifted his chin in the direction of the table. "There's food."

"Please," she asked in French. "I'm hurt. Can I see a doctor?"

"No. Fatima is a healer. She bandaged your head."

"Can I have a pen and paper? Something to read?"

Ibrahim shook his head at her and left.

Acacia closed her eyes and tried to ignore the dizziness. She had a concussion; she was sure of it. The room continued to spin.

The door opened again.

Acacia opened her eyes and saw Ibrahim place a pen, a piece of paper, and a Qur'an on her bed. He left without a word.

She snatched up the items and examined the pen to see if it could be useful.

The scent of food wafted from the nearby table. She was too nauseated to eat, but she noticed a metal spoon sitting next to her meal. She picked it up, turning it over in her hands.

They'd given her a weapon.

Despite her concussion, Acacia wasted no time before trying to escape.

By the light of the bathroom, she took the ballpoint pen apart, placing the pieces on a towel on the floor.

Try as she might, she couldn't envision a way to use them to pry off the cover to the ventilation shaft. It seemed to be affixed from the inside.

She'd even tried hanging on it. But the cover remained firmly in place.

The slats attached to the underside of the cot with metal screws. She used the handle of her spoon as a screwdriver to remove one of the slats. But it was too wide to slip between the door and the doorframe.

She hid the slat and screws underneath her thin mattress, hoping she could find some use for them.

Sitting on the closed toilet and contemplating the pen pieces, her thoughts strayed to Nicholas. Rick and his team would scour the crime scene for clues, if the Paris police didn't get there first.

Perhaps Luc would be there as well. Although it wasn't likely, given what she'd said to him at her apartment.

In the small, dank bathroom, Acacia allowed herself the luxury of a few tears. She cried for Kurt. She cried for Nicholas and the love she felt for him. While her opposition to killing remained unchanged, she regretted her decision to leave him, and not only because she'd been kidnapped shortly thereafter.

She loved him, and he loved her. She even liked his parents. And she believed they could build something extraordinary together. Rather than issuing an ultimatum and running off, she should have stayed and worked hard to present him with an alternative to the path of death he seemed hell bent on. She should have tried harder rather than giving up.

Sitting in the mysterious compound in Morocco, Acacia made a vow. When she escaped, she would return to Nicholas and try to work things out. The thought fortified her.

She dried her eyes and hid the spoon in her sleeve, determined to use it to attack one of her guards the next morning. Yes, her sensei had told her she was the weapon. But in this situation, she believed she needed something in addition to her physical skills to escape men with automatic weapons.

She was against killing, but she was not against hurting someone in self-defense.

Acacia slept fitfully. Her head hurt, and the wound seemed to be on fire. She'd checked the bathroom, but there was nothing she could use as an antiseptic.

She was awoken very early by the first call to prayer. She went back to sleep until the call was repeated.

She groaned and sat up slowly. She felt tired and dizzy. Nevertheless, her mind continued to devise escape plans.

A short time later, the door opened and someone flicked the lights on. A short, rotund woman wearing a black headscarf and black robes appeared, clucking at Acacia. The door slammed shut behind her.

"You need to clean up." The woman spoke Arabic, carrying a bundle of fabric in her arms. "Your father will arrive soon. He wants to see you."

Acacia decided to give up the pretense that they'd kidnapped the wrong woman. Her father wouldn't be fooled. Undeniably, she looked like her mother. If necessary, her father and his men could take blood and test her DNA.

"I have a concussion," she said quietly in Arabic.

"I'm Fatima, the one who bandaged your head. We can't wash your hair because of the wound, but I can help you shower."

Acacia bristled. "I can shower myself."

"What if you fall?"

Acacia allowed her shoulders to slump. "All right. But I need something for the pain."

The woman nodded and rapped on the door. It opened, and she departed.

Acacia quickly slipped the spoon under the mattress. She could overpower the woman, but she'd still be locked inside the cell. She needed to find a way to take the spoon with her to meet her father.

A short time later, Fatima returned with fresh water and white tablets that she said were for pain.

Acacia had no way of knowing what the pills were, but she downed them with a glass of water. They must have been something strong, because her pain diminished within twenty minutes.

"Are you my father's wife?" Acacia asked.

"I only keep house. My husband is dead, and so are my sons." Fatima was matter-of-fact as she ordered Acacia to the bathroom.

Soon she was clean and dressed in a long-sleeved T-shirt and pants, along with a traditional caftan. Fatima re-bandaged her head, exclaiming in horrified tones how ugly the wound was.

Acacia contemplated the ugliness that could be wrought on a carotid artery by a spoon.

The woman helped affix a headscarf over Acacia's bandage, hiding her hair. When Fatima's back was turned, Acacia slipped the spoon from under the mattress and into the long sleeve of her T-shirt, under her caftan.

Ibrahim entered the cell and told Fatima to leave. She scolded him in Arabic, telling him Acacia was hurt and needed rest, before lumbering off.

Ibrahim brought Acacia into the hall. No less than three men stood guard, each carrying a rifle.

She elected not to try to overpower them and run, conscious of her dizziness, as well as the fact that she didn't know the layout of the compound. The more they showed her, the better her escape plan would be.

They marched her through the courtyard and into a side door. They rounded to a set of stairs and climbed to the second floor, stopping in front of a wooden door.

Ibrahim knocked.

A faint voice ordered them to enter.

When Ibrahim opened the door, Acacia could see sunlight shining from a large window on the far side of the room. An older man sat behind a large desk, a laptop computer in front of him.

The room was ordinary and dilapidated, as was the furniture, although the laptop appeared new. Whatever opulence her father had displayed in Dubai was now muted. He wore his signet ring and an ordinary set of white robes.

Acacia was struck by the banality of his appearance and his office. She was struck by the banality of terrorism.

"Leave us," he ordered Ibrahim.

The men closed the door securely on their way out.

Acacia looked at her father.

He pointed to a chair. "Sit down."

She sat.

He regarded her for some time. He resembled the man she used to know in some respects, but his eyes were dead. Whatever warmth she'd once seen there or in his expression had now vanished.

"You look like your mother," he observed in Arabic.

Acacia didn't respond.

His eyes narrowed. "Where is she?"

"She's in Brazil."

"Where in Brazil?"

Acacia shrugged. "If you found me in Paris, you should be able to find her in Brazil."

Her father lifted from his chair and came around to the front of his desk. Before Acacia could react, he struck her across the face.

In a flash, she was a little girl in Amman again. Her mother was on the floor, crying, and Acacia was hanging off her father's arm, trying to stop him from hitting her.

"Where is your mother?" Omar's voice was low, controlled.

Acacia lifted her hands to protect herself. "I don't know."

He stood over her.

Then for no reason she could discern, he returned to his seat. He stared at her from behind the desk.

As the shock of being struck faded, so did her memories. While she inhaled and exhaled deeply, she studied him. If he came at her again, she'd take him to the floor.

He appeared to be unarmed. Yet even if she made it to the window and dropped down to the courtyard below, it was far from certain she'd be able to make it out of the compound before his men caught up with her. Her dizziness would hamper her ability to run and defend herself.

So she sat where she was and seethed with anger. This man, who stared contemptuously from across a desk, was lucky he didn't have a spoon sticking out of his neck.

His eyes became slits. "I wasn't sure if you saw me in Dubai. Obviously you did and warned your mother. You look like her. You even walk like her."

"What do you want?" Acacia redirected the conversation. "Why am I here?"

He crossed his arms and ignored her questions. "Your mother had an apartment in Recife. It looks like she left in a hurry. She hasn't contacted you since then, and you haven't contacted her."

"I don't know where she is."

"Perhaps." He waited, as if anticipating a response.

"Father, please. I want to go home."

"You are home."

"I live in Paris."

"That life is over." He gestured to her head. "If you try to escape again, you will be beaten."

Her gaze flicked to his desk. "Can I have access to a computer?"

"So you can contact Mossad?" He spat on the floor. "No."

"Mossad?" Her eyebrows shot up. "What are you talking about?"

"The man you whored for." Her father's low voice dripped with poison. "The rich Jew you were with in Dubai. He's Mossad."

Acacia shook her head. "He's a businessman. He isn't a spy."

"He's Mossad." Omar's voice was contemptuous. "You've shamed me and your family. You've abandoned the true faith. You will be punished, and so will your mother. How long has it been since you've seen her?"

Acacia's throat felt dry. She could hardly manage to swallow. "Not since December."

"Where did you see her?"

"Recife."

"You will tell me where she is, and you will tell me how you've been contacting her."

Acacia moved forward on her chair. "Please, father. I don't know where she is. She lives in Recife. If she isn't there, she's run away."

Omar slapped his hand on top of the desk, making Acacia jump. "Until you tell me where your mother is, you won't receive any food or medicine."

He pressed a button on his desk and Ibrahim opened the door. He took hold of Acacia's elbow.

Acacia stood, but before she turned to go she looked at her father.

"I loved you once," she said in Arabic. "And you loved me. I know you did. Where is the man who protected me from monsters in the dark? What did you do to him?"

Omar gazed up at her and cursed. "That man is dead."

He waved a hand to Ibrahim, who escorted Acacia from the room.

A short time later, Acacia sat on her cot and removed her headscarf.

Fatima had insisted on slathering a foul-smelling poultice over her head wound before re-bandaging it yet again. Given the scent, Acacia didn't know whether to thank her or curse her.

To her surprise, Ibrahim had followed her into the cell. He stood guard, his gun slung over his shoulder.

She groaned and touched the side of her head. The pain had returned, but she knew there would be no more relief.

Acacia knew her mother was in a safe house in Manaus, but she didn't have the address. She believed Nicholas would have moved her mother from Manaus to a different city once he realized she'd been kidnapped. Or so she hoped.

"Tell me where your mother is and I'll give you something for the pain." Ibrahim spoke after Fatima had left the cell. His gaze fixed on the large bruise that covered Acacia's cheek.

She hugged her knees into her chest, taking care not to brush against her injured face. "Do you expect me to believe you?"

"Yes."

Acacia closed her eyes. She sifted through her memories, trying to find something she could use to influence her father. Since he'd become radicalized, it appeared the man she knew was gone.

"I remember you." Ibrahim's voice was contemplative.

She opened her eyes. "I remember you, too. We lived in the same apartment building in Amman."

His eyes met hers, and he adjusted the gun on his shoulder. "Why don't you tell your father where your mother is? It isn't you he wants."

Acacia blinked. "Are you so sure?"

"Of course."

She fixed him with a stony glare. "Ibrahim, I'm as good as dead. You know that. My father thinks I've shamed him. That's why he wants my mother—so he can kill us both to recover his honor."

Ibrahim's expression remained unchanged. "He just wants your mother."

Acacia cursed in Arabic. "You can tell him you tried. You can tell him I know he's going to kill me. I don't know where my mother is, and I can't tell him what I don't know."

She closed her eyes.

Ibrahim made a noise of exasperation and knocked on the cell door. The door opened.

For some reason, Ibrahim closed the door and remained in the cell. "Do you remember when the boys from the neighborhood caught me by the fence? They were throwing stones."

Acacia didn't respond.

Ibrahim came a step closer. "You came to find out what was happening."

"They were bullies."

"I was four. You were my big cousin, even if you were only a girl."

Acacia snorted and opened her eyes. "I was six. I think."

"You pushed the boys out of the way and called them cowards." Ibrahim gave her a serious look. "The boys were much bigger than you, but you stood in front of me."

She peered up at her cousin suspiciously. "You were crying. I didn't want them to hurt you."

"The ringleader, Hassan, pushed you to the ground. You got up. You dusted off your dress and stood, your head held high. So he pushed you again. You got up. Over and over he pushed you down, and you kept getting up."

She shrugged. "I was stubborn."

"He screamed at you to stay down. You kept standing up."

"I didn't know what to do," Acacia admitted. "They had us against the fence. They could have thrown stones at any moment."

"The others pulled Hassan away. He was screaming, and they were afraid their parents would hear. You took me home."

"I can't believe you remember that. It was a lifetime ago."

"'Whoever does an evil deed will not be recompensed except by the like thereof; but whoever does righteousness, whether male or female, while he is a believer—those will enter Paradise,'" Ibrahim recited.

Acacia recognized the words from the Qur'an. "Are you telling me I did a righteous thing?"

Ibrahim didn't answer.

"I've read the Qur'an, too." She retrieved the book from the table next to her bed and flipped through it. "'And if any one of the polytheists seeks your protection, then grant him protection so that he may hear the words of Allah. Then deliver him to his place of safety. That is because they are a people who do not know.'"

"You know, Hanin. You were raised Muslim."

"I am Muslim. I never left the faith. Look." She held up her wrist and showed him the hamsa pendant. "I wear it for protection."

"You whored for a Jew," he spat.

"My father is going to kill me. But I protected you when you were a child, Ibrahim. Now I'm asking for your protection. If the Qur'an commands you to protect non-Muslims who seek your help, how much more should you protect one of your own?"

"'He it is who gives life and causes death; and when He decrees a matter, He but says to it, "Be," and it is,'" Ibrahim countered. "It is the will of Allah that you return to the truth faith."

"'Grant him protection...Then deliver him to his place of safety,'" she repeated. "I'm a Muslim. I'm asking for your protection."

Ibrahim's expression shifted. He moved closer to the door. "You fornicated with Mossad."

"How do you know? Because my father told you?" Acacia's anger flared. "What else did he tell you? That bombs don't kill people, people kill people?"

"We're fighting a war."

"A war with whom? Other Muslims?"

Ibrahim glared. "Some of the governments are corrupt."

"My father gets to decide who's righteous? He isn't an Imam. He isn't a holy man."

Ibrahim stepped forward. "You don't know what you're talking about."

"I do." She lifted the Qur'an. "I've read it in Arabic, the same as you. Are you going to tell me that saving you from those boys wasn't a righteous deed?"

He didn't answer.

"I'm not the one with the gun, cousin." She pointed an accusing finger. "You accuse me of fornication, but are you guilty of murder?"

She flipped through the pages of the book. "'Whoever kills a soul — it is as if he had slain mankind entirely. And whoever saves one — it is as if he had saved mankind entirely.'"

Ibrahim spat out a curse. "You aren't worthy to recite it."

"Why not? The Qur'an tells me to read it. You're going to tell me to go against the Qur'an?"

"You aren't reciting all of it. You're picking and choosing."

"Are there passages that contradict what I've recited?" she challenged.

He crossed his arms. "The Qur'an is truth."

"Then there won't be a contradiction. When my father kills souls — Muslims, Jews, and Christians — it is as if he has killed the entire world. And when he stands before Allah, he will be judged."

Ibrahim took a step forward, his face angry. "If we don't protect our people, they will be slaughtered. Someone has to defend them."

She took a deep breath. "How are you defending them? You can't be in favor of killing Muslim children, Ibrahim. That's what my father's weapons do. They kill mothers and children."

He waved his hand dismissively. "Propaganda. You're Mossad."

"I'm Muslim. I work at a hotel in Paris, and I'm certainly not a spy. I speak the truth." She pointed to the Qur'an. "When my father murders me, I will stand before Allah and be judged. And I will stand as one who did a righteous deed. When you enter the afterlife, you will be a murderer."

Ibrahim cursed her, loudly and angrily.

But Acacia wouldn't stop. "Ask my father about Damascus, when he sold bombs to Muslims so they could kill other Muslims."

Ibrahim passed a hand over his beard. His hand was trembling.

"You didn't know about that, did you?" Acacia quieted her voice. "Why do you think my mother and I left Jordan? We loved our friends and neighbors. We loved our community. We didn't want to stand by and watch my father deliver weapons that would kill."

Ibrahim shrugged unconvincingly. "In war, there are casualties."

"But the casualties aren't supposed to be Muslims, are they? You shouldn't kill the righteous, the people of faith."

"Shut up!" Ibrahim's face darkened with anger, and he spat at her.

Acacia lifted her hands in an expression of surrender. "Ibrahim, where are your mother and sisters?"

"Jordan."

"Are they well?"

He jerked his head.

"Please greet them for me, cousin. May peace be upon them."

Without acknowledgment, he strode to her cot and picked up the Qur'an. "You're an apostate. You don't deserve to touch this!"

"You would take away a Muslim's holy book?"

Ibrahim scowled. "You left the faith for a Jew."

"I protected you. I did a righteous deed. Will you stand by and watch while my father throws stones?"

Ibrahim avoided her eyes. Carrying the book reverently, he went to the door and knocked.

"When you stand before Allah, you will have to answer for your actions," Acacia called after him. "What justification will you give for killing your own people?"

The door opened and slammed shut, leaving her alone.

She curled into a ball on the cot.

It was likely she'd worsened the situation and that Ibrahim would run and repeat everything to her father. But since her father intended to kill her, she had nothing to lose. Better that he fly into a rage and murder her than starve her to death or force her to watch him murder her mother.

She closed her eyes and prayed she'd have the strength to make her escape the next day. Time was running out.

Chapter Fifty

A hand covered her mouth.

Acacia jerked awake and drove her fists into the dark figure bent over her.

The room was black. Not even the lights from the courtyard were shining through the window.

The figure batted away her blows. "We're here to rescue you. Keep quiet. Injuries?" he whispered in English.

"Concussion," she whispered. "Bruised back. But I can walk."

The man wore combat gear, which she could barely make out. He seemed to be accompanied by others. She wondered if they'd cut the power to her father's compound. They appeared to be wearing night vision goggles.

The man lifted her to his shoulder and began to move. Acacia bounced as they exited the cell and jogged down the hall. He picked his way around a couple of bodies on the floor. She couldn't tell if one of them was Ibrahim.

She heard a shout in the distance and the rattle of gunfire.

The man clutched her more tightly and began to run. Boots pounded against the concrete floor and over the mosaic tile in the courtyard.

Gunfire split the silence and a spray of bullets flew through the air. She heard the cries of someone who was hit and loud cursing in Arabic.

She heard more gunfire, and the man carrying her went down.

Acacia landed on the soldier, who tried to cushion her blow. She rolled off him and ducked for cover. "Are you all right?" she hissed in English.

The man swore and grabbed his thigh. Blood poured from underneath his fingers. "Goddamn it!"

A flashlight shone in her eyes. Someone grabbed her hand and jerked her to her feet.

She planted her feet, squinting to see who held her hand. As soon as she realized it was one of her father's men, she didn't hesitate.

She withdrew the spoon she'd hidden in her sleeve and jammed the handle into the side of the man's neck. Blood spurted in a wide arc as he screamed in pain. He released her and fell to his knees as blood continued to spurt from his wound. He covered his neck with his hands, gurgling and gasping.

Acacia stared, frozen.

Another soldier began dragging her toward the door. "We gotta go. Now!"

Acacia turned to see the wounded man slump to the floor. He didn't move.

Bullets whizzed by, and two other solders approached from in front of her, trying to provide cover to their fallen comrade.

Acacia struggled to keep up with the soldier who gripped her bicep. He pulled her out of the courtyard and toward a waiting Humvee.

Acacia vomited next to the vehicle.

"Jesus," one of the soldiers said. He grabbed a cloth from inside the Humvee and handed it to her. "Is there more?"

Acacia didn't answer. She vomited once again and doubled over.

"We gotta go," another voice said from inside the Humvee.

"I'm okay," she whispered, swallowing bile. She wiped her mouth with the towel.

"Are you sure?" the soldier asked. He examined her quickly.

She climbed into the Humvee, and he followed.

The armored vehicle pulled away, speeding down a rough, uneven trail.

"*Status*," the man in the front passenger seat barked.

"The raven is here. She just emptied her stomach, and she's covered in blood." The soldier who'd helped her replied. He had an English accent and began running his hands over her arms and legs.

"It isn't my blood," she replied in English.

The soldier took note of her bandaged head and facial bruising. "She's going to need a medic."

"Copy that. There's one waiting." The man in the front sounded American. He seemed to be the officer in charge.

"Drink this." The soldier on Acacia's right handed her a bottle of water. He didn't sound American.

She tasted the water gratefully, but was careful not to drink too much.

"Innis is down," the English soldier announced.

"Is he the soldier who was carrying me?" she croaked. "Is he all right?"

"We'll find out in a minute." The officer's tone was grim.

"I'm sorry." A wave of emotion hit her.

"Honey, you got nothing to be sorry for." The officer turned in his seat. He made eye contact. "This is our job."

The communication link in the vehicle crackled to life. "Innis needs a medic. Taking him back to base."

"Copy that. Out," the officer responded.

He turned to the driver. "Location?"

"Out of range."

"Good." The officer hit a couple of buttons, and the com link crackled once again. "Ranger one to S-one. We're out of range. Go get them."

"Copy that, Ranger one," a voice came over the com link. The accent was Middle Eastern, but Acacia couldn't place it.

"Good luck, S-one. Over." The officer pressed a button again, and the com link fell silent.

"Is there a NATO base nearby?" Acacia asked.

"Negative," the Englishman clipped.

She was alarmed. "Then who are you?"

"Private contractors," the man sitting on her right said.

Now she recognized his accent. "Israeli?" she whispered.

He nodded.

"Mossad?" she asked.

"Ex-Mossad."

"They thought I was Mossad."

"No, they didn't," he scoffed. "If they had, they'd have tortured you and put you out to bid."

Her eyes met his. If her father had captured him, things would have been far worse for him than for his American and British colleagues.

"I think I killed someone." She spoke to him in Arabic, hoping he could understand.

The Israeli's eyes flashed to hers. "Better him than you," he replied in Arabic.

"I didn't mean to kill him. I was trying to get away."

He made a horizontal motion with his hand. "Someone puts a gun to your head, someone threatens you, you do whatever you can to stay alive. That's self-defense."

Acacia took a drink of water, trying to process everything that had just happened. She thought of the man in the courtyard, blood spurting from his neck. She thought of the soldier who'd carried her, clutching his thigh and swearing.

Her father had caused this. He'd kidnapped her from her home and killed Kurt, her protector, in the process. The killing and injuries that resulted from the kidnapping were her father's fault.

Damn his soul, she thought. Her body shook.

She put her hand over her heart. "Thank you for rescuing me," she said in Arabic.

"You're welcome."

Acacia was grateful they could understand one another. She didn't want a large audience for her words. "May peace be upon you and your household."

"Peace be upon you, as well."

"What are you saying?" the officer broke in sharply.

"She's giving me beauty tips," the Israeli replied in English.

Laughter erupted in the Humvee.

"Injuries?" He leaned closer, still speaking Arabic.

Her hand touched her bandage. "Concussion. Head wound. Facial bruising. Blunt force to the lower back. I think they hit me with a rifle when they kidnapped me."

The Israeli's expression tightened. He shifted the gun that rested on his lap.

Three military vehicles appeared out of the darkness and sped past them, heading in the opposite direction.

"There won't be anything left by the time they're done." The Israeli jerked his chin in the direction of the other vehicles, speaking to Acacia.

"Who are they?"

"Syrian special forces." He turned to face forward.

Acacia hugged herself in an effort to stop her body from shaking. If the Syrians knew about her father's connection to the Damascus bombings, they'd kill him.

She remembered Nicholas telling her about the intelligence he'd acquired about her father. The Damascus bombings had not been included in the dossier.

She clapped a hand over her mouth.

She'd been the source of that information. She'd only passed it along to one person, which meant…

She removed her hand from her mouth. "Are the Syrians going to kill everyone in the compound?"

The Israeli turned his head. "I don't know their rules of engagement."

Acacia felt like she was going to be sick again. She covered her mouth.

"Put your head down." Careful to avoid her bandage, the Israeli guided her head between her knees. "Breathe in through your nose, slowly." His hand rested lightly between her shoulder blades.

Acacia did what she was told. She put her guilt and horror aside to focus on her breath, visualizing her emotions like a wave that crashed over her and spilled onto the floor of the Humvee. In her mind's eye, she watched the waters recede.

"If it's either you or them, you choose yourself," the Israeli whispered. He kept his hand to her back and lowered his head so he was almost at eye level. "Every time."

"I didn't want anyone to die," she whispered.

"They chose death when they kidnapped you and killed your bodyguard. Actions have consequences.

"They can't bomb people into oblivion and turn around and expect judicial process. That is not justice."

She breathed in through her nose and out through her mouth, her lungs the only thing tethering her to the moment.

"Everyone wants justice," she mumbled. "But does anyone know what justice really is?"

The Humvee made a sharp turn and increased its speed. The Israeli withdrew his hand.

Acacia lifted her head. Lights in the distance lined what appeared to be an airstrip. She saw a small jet.

The Humvee pulled alongside the jet, near another Humvee. Several armed soldiers were guarding the plane.

"There's your ride," the officer announced over his shoulder.

The Israeli helped her out of the vehicle and held her arm as he escorted her to the plane. Her legs shook, and she stumbled.

A man stood at the foot of the staircase that rose to the jet's door.

Rick.

Without a word, she went to him and wrapped her arms around his waist. She hugged him as if he were a long-lost friend.

To her surprise, he enveloped her in a bear hug.

Tears pricked her eyes. She'd never thought she'd be so happy to see him.

"I'm sorry we're late." He released her.

"Concussion, head wound, facial bruising and lacerations, and blunt trauma to the lower back. She vomited on the way out," the Israeli reported. His expression was stoic.

Acacia had forgotten he was there. "Thank you. Thanks to all of you. I'm so sorry about what happened to Innes."

"He's going to be fine." The officer stepped forward. He shook hands with Rick. "You need to get out of here."

With a nod, Rick walked Acacia up the stairs and into the plane. He lifted the staircase and closed the cabin door.

Acacia quickly surveyed the inside of the cabin.

She turned to Rick. "He didn't come?"

Rick shook his head, his face blank.

"But he sent you for me?" Her voice grew hoarse.

Rick nodded. He looked uncomfortable.

"My father thinks Nicholas is Mossad." Acacia blinked back tears. "Others may think the same thing. You have to warn him."

Rick's eyebrows shot up. "Your father mentioned Mossad?"

She nodded.

Rick cursed and pulled out his cell phone.

A middle-aged woman wearing surgical scrubs moved from the back of the plane. "I'm Doctor Büchi, from Geneva. Let's take a look at you."

Acacia sat on a low couch and turned to look out the window. In the light provided by the makeshift landing strip, the soldiers clustered around the Humvees.

She said a prayer of gratitude for her rescuers before taking a moment to mourn the loss of life at her father's compound.

"Whoever kills a soul—it is as if he had slain mankind entirely. And whoever saves one—it is as if he had saved mankind entirely." She recited the words from the Qur'an in her head.

A tear fell.

Chapter Fifty-One

"It's infected." Doctor Büchi paused her examination of Acacia's head. "I'm going to clean the wound and leave it open to the air so it can heal."

"That's fine." Acacia was having difficulty staying awake.

"I'm going to start an IV with fluids and an antibiotic. How's your pain?" The doctor continued speaking in French.

"It hurts, but I'm so tired."

"I'll give you something for the pain. Just stay with me for a few more minutes, then you can lie down." The doctor set up a portable IV and uncovered a surgical tray. "I'm going to have to cut your hair a little in order to deal with the head wound."

"I don't care." Acacia's blinks became longer and longer.

"Acacia." The doctor took her hand and prepared to administer the IV. "Do you speak Italian?"

"No, Spanish and Portuguese."

The doctor switched to Italian. "If I ask questions, can you understand? I can understand Spanish, but I can't speak it."

"I think I can." Acacia looked at the doctor curiously.

"You're my patient," she continued in Italian. She gave a sideways glance to Rick. "Anything you say will be kept private unless you direct me otherwise. Do you understand?"

"Yes," Acacia responded in Spanish. She wondered why the doctor didn't want Rick to understand their conversation.

"Tell me how you got your injuries."

"The bruises on my back happened in Paris. Someone struck me from behind." Acacia pointed to her bruised face. "My father hit me. Someone hit me in the head, probably with a rifle. That's where the wound came from. They put some kind of a poultice on it."

"I saw that." The doctor wrinkled her nose. "I think it made it worse. You have other bruises on your body." Efficiently, she administered a peripheral IV line and taped the connection to the back of Acacia's hand.

"I fell in Paris when they hit me from behind. I fell just now when the soldier was carrying me. He was shot." Acacia swallowed a sob as she recalled Innes crying out in pain.

The doctor gave her a sympathetic look. "Did anything else happen?"

"No. They gave me something for pain, but I don't know what it was. The pills were white. Can I lie down now?"

"In a minute. Acacia, were you raped?"

"No."

"Were there any other assaults?"

"No."

"Did you lose consciousness at any time?"

"In Paris. They must have knocked me out before taking me to Morocco. And then I lost consciousness when they hit me on the head. I think that was yesterday." She thought hard. "I don't know what day it is."

"When you went to the bathroom, was there any pain or bleeding between your legs?"

"No." Acacia shook her head vehemently.

"All right." The doctor switched back to French. "I'm going to help you lie down so I can work on your head wound. You can sleep if you like. Just remember you have an IV in your hand. Don't thrash around."

Acacia allowed the doctor to help her recline on the couch. She started to shake uncontrollably and the doctor covered her with a blanket.

"It's shock," the doctor explained. "You're going to be all right, Acacia. Just get some rest."

It took a while for Acacia to stop shaking. She closed her eyes.

When Acacia awoke, she was in Geneva. An ambulance waited at the private airport and transferred her to a nearby hospital, with Rick and Doctor Büchi at her side.

Acacia had no idea how she'd been able to enter Switzerland without a passport or without even speaking to a customs agent. She was too weary to worry about it.

A team of doctors examined her, and then a group of nurses tidied her and helped her change into a hospital gown. They scanned her body to determine the extent of her injuries and to look for possible brain damage. Finding none, they sedated her, and she fell into deep, dreamless sleep.

Chapter Fifty-Two

Nicholas sat next to Acacia's hospital bed and lightly stroked her arm. He'd showered and shaved for the first time in days and now wore dark jeans and a blue shirt. He hadn't slept much since Acacia's disappearance. Purple smudges lay below his eyes.

"I was afraid you were dead," he whispered.

He knew she couldn't hear him. That's why he was there.

He bowed his head, and his damp hair brushed her hand.

"The doctor wouldn't tell me about her injuries," Rick said in a rough voice. He faced his boss from the other side of Acacia's hospital bed. "I just know what the contractors told me when we picked her up in Tangiers: concussion, head wound, facial bruising, and trauma to the lower back."

Nicholas lifted his head. "I've known Doctor Büchi for years. She won't betray a patient."

"I assume she asked about rape. I don't know what was said."

Nicholas looked stricken. He pushed a curl from Acacia's face and tucked it reverently to the side. "This is my fault. If we hadn't argued, she would have stayed with me."

"Put the blame on the animals who took her." Rick swore. "They would have made their move eventually. They would have tried to kill you to get to her."

Nicholas let out a tortured exhalation. "Look at her face. They've done God knows what to her, and it's all on me."

"You should have seen her, calmly thanking the contractors for rescuing her, as if they'd taken her out for pizza."

Nicholas smiled a half-smile. "That's my girl. But she shouldn't have to be brave. I was supposed to protect her."

"You did. You got her out of there."

Nicholas's hands folded into fists. "One bruise is one too many. At least her father isn't a threat to her now. The Syrians made contact with the contractors. It's done."

"Justice," Rick murmured. "I would have liked a crack at him. He's the one who did her face."

Nicholas bent to kiss Acacia's forehead. "When she wakes up, let her know her mother has been moved, and she's safe. She's worried, understandably. Wen can arrange for them to talk."

"Done. How'd Mossad take the news?"

Nicholas clenched his jaw. "As well as could be expected. Their deal with the Syrians was profitable, I'm told. They promised to disavow me, as I requested."

"You might as well have been an agent for all the trouble it caused you."

"Which is precisely why I'm not an agent." He rubbed his forehead. "Did I ask you to warn Silke? I can't remember."

"Her handlers already got to her. She's gone underground for a little while."

"Mossad will regret recruiting her. I'm sure of it."

Rick looked at his employer more closely. He gestured to his face.

Nicholas reached up and touched his scar. His dark eyes widened. "I forgot. Have I been without my prosthetic all this time?"

"You had it when we left Paris. After that..." Rick shrugged. "I don't remember."

"My parents never mentioned anything." Nicholas paused. He looked down at Acacia in wonder. "She made me forget."

"She has that effect on people." Rick's tone was dry.

Nicholas's gaze sharpened. "You've changed your opinion of her?"

"She's got a will of iron. I respect that."

"Jesus," Nicholas whispered.

He kissed Acacia's forehead once again and walked over to Rick, extending his hand. "Thank you, my friend."

"Don't mention it." Rick's voice was gruff as they shook hands. "Are you still going?"

"I have to see it through."

Rick thrust his hands into the pockets of his jeans. "That's the wrong move."

"What did you say?" Nicholas's eyes narrowed.

"Look at her." Rick pointed to Acacia's serene form. "Your girl needs you. You should stay."

"She doesn't need me, Rick. She left me." Nicholas sounded bitter.

"She asked for you. She didn't ask for food or water or a fucking doctor. She asked for you."

Nicholas looked at Acacia, lying peaceful and quiet in her hospital bed. "I spoke with Kate. She's booked on a flight from Paris tomorrow afternoon, with the cat."

"A fucking cat," Rick mumbled. "If that ain't love…"

"What's done is done," Nicholas said softly. "I turned her father over to the Syrians. In her eyes, I'm a killer."

"You did what you had to do. The guy was a terrorist."

"It doesn't matter if my intentions were good. She's against killing." Nicholas turned his back on her. "Take care of her and Kate."

Rick nodded.

With one last look, Nicholas left the room.

Chapter Fifty-Three

"Will he come to see me?" Acacia asked Rick as soon as he entered the room.

It was more than twenty-four hours after she'd arrived at the hospital. Her head still ached, but the nausea had subsided.

Rick had absented himself while Doctor Büchi examined her during morning rounds. He remained in the hall while the nurses tidied her and dressed her wound. When he returned, Acacia was nibbling at her breakfast.

"The boss has already been here." Rick sat next to the bed. He was casually dressed in jeans and a black shirt. But for whatever reason, he wore combat boots.

Acacia dropped her fork on the breakfast tray. "When?"

"While you were asleep."

"Will he come back?"

Rick shook his head. "He's gone."

"Where?"

Rick leaned forward and rested his arms on his knees. "He's flying Kate from Paris. She'll arrive this afternoon. She's bringing your cat."

Acacia leaned back on the pillow. "He wanted to see that I'm all right, but he doesn't want to talk to me."

"Fuck," Rick swore under his breath. "He wants to talk to you, but he had something to take care of."

"Has he found the man who took his family's artwork?"

"How are you feeling this morning?" Rick asked in response. "What did the doctor say?"

"I want to see him," she whispered.

"Acacia, I don't think—"

"I need to see him." She lifted her voice.

Rick hesitated. "I'll call him. You can speak to him on the phone."

Rick walked into the hall.

Acacia waited on tenterhooks for him to return. She tried to formulate sentences in her mind, but had difficulty deciding what to say.

A few minutes later he returned. His face was impassive. "The boss is busy at the moment. He wants you to rest and take care of yourself."

Acacia's eyes filled with tears.

Rick lifted his hands. "Don't cry. Kate will be here soon. When you're discharged from the hospital, I have orders to take you both back to Paris. And, uh, your cat. What's your cat's name? Ned?"

Acacia pressed the call button for the nurse. She threw the covers back and shifted to the edge of the bed, near her IV stand.

Rick moved forward. "What are you doing?"

"I'm leaving." She wiped her eyes with a napkin.

"You can't leave. You have a head injury."

She turned furious eyes on him. "Why didn't you stop him from going after the Russian?"

"What makes you think that's where he's gone?"

"Because he's obsessed with getting justice for his family. I know his team was working on finding Yasmin's ex-boyfriend. I know he wouldn't want me to know he's in Russia."

"Listen, you need to rest. I'll call the nurse."

"No. I'm not going to lie here while he destroys himself."

Rick skirted the bed to stand in front of her. "There's nothing you can do."

"I have to try."

He rubbed his face with both hands. "Get back into bed. Kate has your cat. Don't you want to see your cat?"

"Tell Kate I'm sorry. I'm going after Nicholas."

"No, you aren't."

Acacia leaned forward at the waist. "I'm not asking for your permission. I killed a man in Morocco. Did you know that?"

Rick's expression didn't change.

Her shoulders slumped. "You already know. But what you don't know is that I have to pay for that. I have to pay for taking a life by saving a life. And I'm going to save Nicholas."

"That's the nuttiest fucking thing I've ever heard." Rick glared at her. "Some terrorist tried to kill you, and you severed his artery with a spoon. I should give you a fucking medal. Do you hear me? You don't need to save anyone for protecting yourself. It was self-defense."

"I didn't mean to kill him, but I did. I accept the consequences."

"You need to have your head examined."

"What's going on?" A nurse stood in the doorway. "Why are you sitting up?"

"I'm leaving. Please remove the IV." Acacia held out her hand.

"You aren't going anywhere until you're discharged by the doctor." The nurse pushed Rick aside. "And who are you? Why are you shouting at her and using foul language? I'll have security remove you."

Rick folded his arms over his chest. "Lady, I am security."

"Tell Doctor Büchi I'm signing myself out. If you don't remove the IV, I will." Acacia gave the nurse a determined look.

"Just wait. Okay? It's dangerous to try to remove an IV when you don't know what you're doing." The nurse gave Rick a severe look. "Both of you, just stop. I'll find the doctor."

She scurried into the hall.

"If you cared so much about him, why'd you leave him?" Rick spoke.

"If he didn't care about me, why did he hire a team of commandos to rescue me?" Acacia countered, slipping off the bed.

She was unsteady on her feet and had to grip the railing for support.

Rick touched her elbow. "You need to lie down. You can't even stand up."

She pulled away from him and fell against the bed, almost toppling her IV stand.

Rick caught it just in time. "Fuck. Will you just sit down?"

She leaned heavily on the mattress. "One way or another, I'm getting out of here, and I'm going after him. Are you going to help me or not?"

Rick pulled out his phone and tapped at the screen. "You aren't going anywhere without clothes."

Acacia looked down at her hospital gown and bare feet. "I can't wear this?"

Rick's face reddened. "Are you nuts?"

She frowned. "It was a joke, Rick."

He crossed the room, speaking into his phone in hushed tones.

Doctor Büchi bustled into Acacia's room a few minutes later. "The nurse said you want to go home."

"That's right." Acacia held her hand out. "Please remove my IV."

The doctor turned to Rick. "Could you wait outside, please?"

Rick made eye contact with Acacia, who nodded at him. He withdrew and placed his cell phone to his ear.

"Why don't we talk for a moment?" The doctor pulled a chair closer to the bed and sat down. "Tell me what's happening."

"I need to go. I'm feeling better, and I have things to do."

"You have a concussion that needs to be monitored. You have a head injury that's open so we can irrigate it to fight the infection. You need to stay here."

Acacia was contemplative for a moment. "If I hire a private nurse to deal with the head wound, can I leave?"

"You aren't a prisoner, Acacia. But you've just had a traumatic experience. I understand you want to go home, but I'd like you to speak with one of my colleagues first."

"A psychiatrist?"

"Yes. Doctor Aswan has worked with newcomers to Switzerland, some of whom experienced trauma in their homelands."

"I'm not crazy."

"I didn't say you were." The doctor's expression grew reproving. "That's a very unkind way to refer to another person."

"I don't mean to be unkind." Acacia felt guilty. "But I'm not ready to speak to someone about what happened."

"Healing is a process. Doctor Aswan won't make you speak about anything you don't want to, but she will be able to help you make sense of your feelings."

Acacia elected to adopt a conciliatory expression. She lowered her voice. "Doctor Büchi, I know you have my best interests in mind. I realize I need to speak to someone. But right now, the only person I want to talk to is Nicholas, my partner. He's away on business, and I can't wait until he comes back."

The doctor studied her. "If you want to leave, you're free to do so. You'll need to sign some paperwork, however, since you'll be signing yourself out of the hospital against medical advice."

"I'll sign," Acacia volunteered quickly.

The doctor studied her for a moment. Whatever she saw on Acacia's face seemed to decide matters.

The doctor stood. "I'm going to send you with some prescriptions. I'm going to give you Doctor Aswan's information, too. I'd like you to make an appointment with her."

"I will."

"I'll be back shortly. Please wait for me."

Acacia reclined back on the bed to rest. She closed her eyes as a wave of dizziness passed over her.

Her thoughts turned to Nicholas. She hoped she wouldn't be too late.

Chapter Fifty-Four

"Madame Cassirer wants to see you." Rick sat next to Acacia in the back of the limousine. Another bodyguard named Frank sat in the front seat next to the driver.

"Please give her my regrets. I'm going to Nicholas." Acacia gazed out the window and marveled at how green and full the trees were. It was such a contrast to Morocco and its sparse palms.

"You can see Madame Cassirer while you wait for Kate. And your cat."

She turned her head. "Take me to the airport, or let me out of the car. I'm not going to ask you again."

"Fuck." Rick rubbed his chin. "You only have the clothes on your back. You don't even have a passport."

Acacia looked down at the clothes Madame Cassirer had sent over for her. A pair of dressy black pants, an ivory blouse, and Chanel shoes that matched the ones she'd admired during their walk.

"I don't care about clothes. And I know damn well you and your team prepare for every contingency. How did you get me into Switzerland without a passport?"

Rick had the decency to look sheepish.

"I thought so." She held out her hand.

Rick withdrew a Swiss diplomatic passport from his pocket.

She checked the photograph and the name. It was her picture, and the name read *Andarta Silva*. She clutched it to her chest.

"I'm not taking you to Nicholas without a doctor." Rick's tone was final.

"You aren't taking me anywhere except to the airport. I'll fly back to Paris and ask my friend Luc to help me."

"That fucking guy?" Rick growled. "You do that, the boss will lose his mind."

"He can't refuse to see me and then get jealous because I ask an old boyfriend for help."

"Just go back to the house. I'll call him again when things have settled down. He'll talk to you."

She rounded on him. "If you want to help, get me to Nicholas as quickly as possible. Otherwise, shut the hell up and let me out of the car."

Rick gave her a look that would have caused a grown man to shake.

Instead, she moved closer. "My own father kidnapped and threatened to kill me. You think I'm afraid of you? I have nothing to be afraid of. Not anymore."

Rick smacked his hand on the car seat in between them, causing Acacia to jump. "You can't save the whole world."

"He who saves one soul, it is as if he has saved the whole world."

Rick gave her a hard look. "Even if I take you to him, he doesn't want to see you. What then?"

"He'll see me." Acacia was defiant.

"You can't assume that. You need a plan."

"I'm open to suggestions." She adjusted the bandage around her head. "You're the security specialist."

"Ex-Navy SEAL," he clarified, a look of pride in his eyes.

"I don't really know what that means, since I'm not American."

Rick drew a deep breath, as if he were trying to control his temper. "I have to tell him we're coming. Then he's going to fire me."

"So I'll hire you to take me to him."

"With what?"

"A Chanel handbag."

Rick snorted. "You're going to hire me with a purse?"

"It's worth several thousand Euros. It's sitting in my apartment in Paris. You can have it."

"I'm fucked. I am absolutely fucked." Rick shook his head. "Frank, make the call. We're going to Helsinki."

"Helsinki?" Acacia blinked. "Why is Nicholas in Finland?"

Rick wore a sour expression. "You can ask him when we get there."

"Thank you." Acacia put her head back and closed her eyes. The pain medication had begun to wear off, and a headache threatened at her temples.

"Madame Cassirer packed you an overnight bag, just in case," Rick whispered. "It's in the trunk. And before I forget…" He placed a cell phone in her hand. "We weren't able to recover your purse, but we found your phone just inside your apartment building. The kidnappers must have dumped it."

She opened her eyes.

"Thank you for helping me." Tentatively, Acacia slid her hand across the car seat. She touched his little finger.

He squeezed her hand before pulling away.

Chapter Fifty-Five

The black Range Rover pulled through the iron gates and entered the estate just outside Helsinki.

The grounds were heavily forested, which meant the main buildings couldn't be seen from the gates. The car slowly climbed the hill and turned onto a circular drive in front of a large, three-story country house. The house itself was made of stone and featured a red tiled roof.

"This is it," Rick announced as the driver halted the car.

Acacia turned to inspect the building. It was early evening and still light outside. Yet every lamp in the house appeared to be on.

"He knows we're here. The guard at the gate called him," Rick warned her.

Acacia's heart changed rhythm — five quick beats — before returning to its usual pace. The result was panic. She touched her chest and closed her eyes.

"Are you okay?" Rick spoke next to her ear.

"Yes." She opened her eyes. "Let's go."

He came around to help her out of the car and escorted her up the stairs to the front door.

The house was furnished sparsely with modern furniture. Hardwood floors gleamed in the front hall and led to a large living room on one side and a closed door on the other. Acacia could hear voices coming from behind the door.

Nervously, she adjusted her bandage. Despite her clothes, she knew she looked a fright. Her face was bruised, her head bandaged, and she was very much in need of a bath. Her curls, which were unruly at the best of times, were a riot barely contained by the white gauze that wrapped around her head like a band.

"Hi, Acacia." Wen entered the hall from the living room. He smiled at her shyly. "It's good to see you."

"You, too." She returned his smile, eying the equipment he was carrying.

"You know the drill. I'm just going to scan you for bugs." He lifted the wand and paused.

She nodded and stood very still as he scanned her.

"All clear." Wen smiled again before approaching Rick, Frank, and the driver, who had assembled behind Acacia in the front hall.

The door opened and Nicholas strode out wearing jeans and a white button-down shirt. He looked as if he hadn't slept much.

Acacia noticed he wasn't wearing his prosthetic.

He stopped short when he saw her. His face crumpled into an expression of shock mixed with pain.

Acacia made eye contact before the room began to spin. She fell to the floor.

Chapter Fifty-Six

One minute Acacia was looking at Nicholas's face and the next she was on her hands and knees. Dazed, she didn't move, but distributed her weight to all four limbs. Something buzzed loudly in her ears.

She recognized Rick's combat boots as he crouched in front of her. He put his hand on her shoulder, but she couldn't make out his words over the noise.

Nicholas stood over her and pushed Rick aside. The two men had an angry exchange before Nicholas scooped her into his arms.

It was no easy feat. Acacia was tall, and she knew she wasn't slight. Still, he lifted her and quickly climbed the central staircase to the second floor.

She closed her eyes and leaned against his chest. There was no point in being brave.

She inhaled his scent. The buzzing in her ears subsided, but she didn't open her eyes until he placed her on a large bed.

"I'm getting a doctor." Nicholas's hand lingered beneath her shoulders.

As he withdrew, she caught his hand. "Don't leave me."

"You just fainted. You need a doctor."

"Please." She tugged on his hand.

"What do you want?" His voice was a tortured whisper.

"I'm all right. I just felt light-headed. Lie down next to me for a minute."

Nicholas screwed his eyes shut.

When he opened them, he withdrew his phone and spoke in hushed tones to someone.

After he disconnected, he climbed onto the bed and lay on his side. He wrapped himself around her.

She exhaled in his arms.

"You should be in the hospital," he whispered.

"I wanted to see you. You wouldn't even talk to me on the phone."

His arms tightened around her. "Rick's fired."

"Don't blame Rick. I signed myself out."

"That's why he's fired. And since when are you Rick's ally? I thought you disliked him."

"I need all the friends I can get. Doctor Büchi is more worried about my mental state than my concussion."

Nicholas stilled. "What did she say?"

"She wants me to see a psychiatrist who works with trauma victims."

"Wouldn't it help to talk to someone?"

"That's why I'm here."

Nicholas made a pained noise. "I'm sorry. If I'd known you were going to sign yourself out, I'd have spoken to you on the phone."

"So tired," she murmured. In Nicholas's arms, her body and mind relaxed. The reaction had been almost instantaneous.

She felt herself drift. "Don't leave."

"When you left, I felt as if my heart had walked out the door. I couldn't leave you, Acacia, even if I wanted to." Nicholas kissed her forehead and held her close to his chest.

Chapter Fifty-Seven

A few hours later, Acacia sat up in bed and picked at her dinner. She'd been seen by a doctor, who examined her and told her she should be in a hospital. Acacia dismissed him and his nurse.

Nicholas had only left her side while she was in the bathroom.

"Now will you talk to me?" Acacia pushed her dinner tray aside.

"I'm worried our conversation will place additional stress on you." Nicholas removed the tray and placed it in the hall. He closed the bedroom door and stood next to the bed. His expression was wary.

"I guess we can postpone our talk until after I have a bath."

"That's easily done. I'll fetch the nurse."

"You can help."

Nicholas hesitated. "Are you sure?"

Acacia sighed. "Send in the nurse, if you must. But I'd rather have you."

"I would do anything to help you." His tone was insistent. "But we've gone our separate ways, remember? You left me."

"I did." She gave him a tremulous look. "But I'm here now. I'm not feeling well, and I need a bath. Are you going to make me beg?"

"Of course not." Nicholas ducked his head guiltily. "I'm sorry."

He helped her climb off the bed, but she insisted on walking to the ensuite bathroom unassisted.

She sat on the closed toilet while Nicholas fussed. He filled the large Jacuzzi tub with hot water and bath salts. He shook out a pair of large, white bath sheets and a face cloth and arranged them next to the tub. When she unbuttoned her blouse, he turned away, an act that made her heart clench.

Acacia thought for a moment that perhaps she did need to see a doctor. Perhaps her hope that she and Nicholas could reconcile was entirely delusional.

She climbed carefully into the tub. When she was safe beneath the bubbling water, he perched himself on the closed toilet.

"I thought you'd gone to Russia," she said softly.

He folded a towel and placed it behind her head, so she could lean back.

"No. I'm confident I'm being watched, so I've avoided any incursions." Nicholas rested his elbows on his knees and wrapped his hands around the back of his neck. He stared at the floor.

"My father thought you were Mossad."

"Rick told me. I'm not, but I passed information to them from time to time." He rubbed his neck.

Acacia's eyes widened. "If you passed information to them, then you're Mossad."

Nicholas leaned forward. "I need you to hear this, because it's very important. As I've repatriated stolen art over the years, I've come into contact with crime bosses and arms dealers. On some occasions, I acquired information that would be valuable to law enforcement and other agencies. From time to time, I've passed that information on. I've worked with Mossad, Interpol, the CIA, and others. So no, I'm not Mossad, just as I am not Interpol or CIA."

"What you're doing is dangerous."

"Yes, which was why I was cautious about what information I shared and with whom. But the contacts I made and the favors I curried have more than paid off. Mossad shared intelligence that enabled me to pinpoint your location. We made an agreement that my team would extract you and Mossad would give your father's location to the Syrians."

"Why would Mossad do that?"

"There are surprising and uneasy alliances all over the world. No one does anything for free, however. The Syrians wanted your father for the Damascus bombings, and Mossad wanted something from Syria. I wasn't told what that was."

"I was worried if they thought you were Mossad, then someone would…" She trailed off. Her emotions bubbled to the surface.

"I have more allies than enemies. But I'm beginning to realize how much I want out of that world.

"I'm the one who failed you, Acacia. You were under my protection when your father's men kidnapped you."

"I never should have gone to Dubai. That's how my father found me."

Nicholas sighed. "You could have run into him in Paris or Geneva or a thousand other places he did business.

"He traced us to Paris and bided his time until you were alone. I believe the taxi driver who drove you and Kurt to your apartment was in on it."

"Kurt," she whispered.

Nicholas grimaced. "I attended his funeral."

"Did he have a family?"

"Just his parents."

Her eyes began to water. "Could I write a letter to them? He died trying to protect me."

"I'll have my assistant get you the address."

"I guess she hasn't had her baby yet."

Nicholas gave her a half-smile. "You remembered. No, she hasn't."

"When your men came to get me, the soldier who was carrying me was hit. We went down, and one of my father's men grabbed me. I killed him." She covered her mouth with her hand.

Nicholas's dark eyes blazed. "I know."

Acacia began to sob. As soon as the tears began, she knew this was a deluge that could not be controlled. She didn't have the energy to visualize a wave or anything else. Her reserve of inner strength was gone. All she could see was the man she'd killed, lying on the mosaic tile, blood pouring from his neck.

Nicholas wrested his jacket and threw it aside. He kicked off his shoes, peeled off his socks, and climbed into the tub with her.

Acacia looked at him in shock. "What are you doing?"

He shifted so he was behind her, and wrapped his arms and legs around her body. "I'm not going to sit there and watch you cry."

"You're fully dressed." She hiccupped. "You'll ruin your clothes."

"I don't give a fuck." Nicholas placed his chin on her shoulder. He hugged her as she sobbed in his arms.

When her tears were spent, she rested her head against his chest.

"The nurse will have to change your bandage." Nicholas kissed the top of her head.

"I sent her away, remember?"

"She's downstairs. I told her she was staying the night."

"Thank you."

"Acacia, I need to send you back to Geneva. It isn't safe for you here."

She gripped his forearm with both hands. "I'm not leaving."

"You need time to recover from your ordeal."

"Are you returning to Geneva?"

He exhaled loudly. "No."

"Then I'm not either."

Nicholas huffed in her ear but didn't argue.

"Your mother invited me to see her after I checked out of the hospital. I didn't respond to her invitation. I'm sorry."

"Don't worry about it. I kept your personal details private, but she knows you were kidnapped. She'll understand you weren't ready to see people."

"I didn't have any clothes. She sent me the outfit I was wearing, along with a bag of brand-new things."

Nicholas stroked Acacia's hair. "She cares for you."

"Does she know you're here?"

Nicholas gently extricated himself from her grasp and stepped out of the tub. He stood on the bathmat, dripping wet.

He ran his fingers through his hair.

"You've ruined your watch." She pointed to the gold timepiece that sat on his wrist.

He shrugged. "To answer your question, no. My mother doesn't know I'm here. I've been avoiding her calls."

He unfolded a bath sheet and held his hand out toward her. She took it gratefully.

He wrapped her in the bath sheet and helped her out of the tub. Despite the fact that his clothes were soaked, he took his time toweling her. Then he retrieved a bathrobe from a nearby hook. "We have a lot to discuss, but now is not the time."

"We can talk tomorrow."

He made an exasperated noise. "You know why I'm here. I have to see this through."

She looked up at him. "I love you."

He tugged at his hair in frustration. "But you know what I'm going to do. You told me you couldn't stay with me."

"I'm sorry I left you. That was a mistake."

"I'm probably not well, Nicholas. The doctor is sure I have post-traumatic stress disorder. But somehow I see things much more clearly than before I was kidnapped."

"And?" he interjected, his eyes guarded.

Acacia was quiet for a moment. But when she spoke, it was from the heart. "I'm not here to prevent you from seeking justice. I want the people who killed your sister to be punished. And I want your family to have their artwork back. I just don't want you to kill anyone." Her voice wavered. "I say this as someone who has."

"Acacia." He gripped her arms. "Look at me. No one blames you for that. You were trying to escape."

"But it's a choice I wish I hadn't had to make. And I will have to live with that choice for the rest of my life." She sniffled. "I'm not leaving you. I'm going to stay at your side and work like hell to keep you from making a mistake."

His eyes bored into hers. "There have been some developments."

"What happened?"

"We'll talk more tomorrow. It's getting late and you should rest."

She took his hand. "Promise me you won't do anything until we talk."

He looked down at her hand. He rubbed his thumb across her knuckles.

"I promise. I'll get the nurse so she can see to your bandage." He kissed her forehead and left the room, still soaking wet.

Chapter Fifty-Eight

Acacia stood next to the overnight bag Madame Cassirer had packed for her, and held up an elegant nightgown. The gown had a plunging neckline and was made of ivory silk.

Acacia sighed. This was not what she wanted to wear to bed.

A knock sounded at the door.

"Come in," she called, hastily placing the nightgown on top of the bag.

Nicholas peered around the edge of the door. "What did the nurse say?"

Acacia waved him inside the room. "She said the wound is beginning to heal. I still have to be careful. I'm still taking antibiotics." Acacia frowned. "She reminded me that antibiotics render birth control pills inert."

When Nicholas didn't comment, she cast the nightgown a baleful look. "I don't have anything to wear to bed."

"I thought my mother packed a bag." Nicholas looked around until he spied the luggage.

"She packed that." Acacia pointed to the gown. "It's lovely, but inappropriate."

Nicholas's expression tightened when he saw the ivory silk. "I see."

"Can I borrow one of your shirts?"

Nicholas turned to look at her. "Of course." He crossed to the wardrobe and opened it. He went through the hanging clothes and finally settled on a pale blue dress shirt. He brought it to her. "Here."

"Thank you." She gathered the shirt to her chest, surreptitiously inhaling the scent that lifted to her nostrils.

"I came to say good night." Nicholas stood next to her.

"I thought this was your room."

"It is. I thought you'd want space."

Her forehead crinkled. "I want space. I just want you to be in that space."

He grinned. "All right. I'm going to be working late, so don't wait up. But I'll join you later on."

"Thank you." She reached up to kiss him, and he kissed her back.

His kisses, however, were restrained.

"Sleep well," he whispered.

She watched his retreating back as he walked to the door.

❈ ❈

"Acacia, wake up." Nicholas's voice invaded her darkness. His hand rested lightly on her shoulder.

Acacia opened her eyes and blinked against the light that shone from the nightstand.

Nicholas raised himself up on an elbow and leaned over her. "You were speaking Arabic and groaning."

"What was I saying?" She lifted a hand to block out some of the light.

"I don't know." He smiled patiently. "I don't know Arabic, but you sounded upset."

"I was back in Morocco." She covered her face with her hands, and a shiver passed over her.

Gently, Nicholas pulled her hands away from her face. "You aren't in Morocco. You're in Finland. And you're safe."

Impulsively, she tugged on his arm and drew him atop her.

"What are you doing?" he asked, his voice thick. He held himself over her, shifting his weight to his forearms.

"I miss you." She gazed up at him, at the face that had become so dear to her—a face she had thought she might never see again.

He stroked her hair. "*Ma choute*. My beautiful, brave girl."

"I don't feel very brave. I feel small and scared."

"But you aren't." He spoke forcefully. "It's natural to feel frightened, but you're strong and determined. Even Rick is in awe of you."

Acacia rolled her eyes. "He wasn't going to bring me to you. I told him to let me out of the car and I'd find my own way."

"See? I've seen men quake in their boots on the receiving end of one of Rick's glares. You almost reduced him to tears."

"He needs a good cry. It releases tension."

Nicholas laughed and brought their foreheads together. "A woman who wasn't brave couldn't laugh in such situations. And you make me laugh, when I've gone years without any mirth at all."

"Kiss me," she whispered.

Nicholas cupped her face with both hands, taking care to avoid the bruise on her left cheek.

Acacia could read his hesitation. But she also saw love, shining in his eyes.

He stroked her jaw. "I thought I'd lost you."

"I regret giving you an ultimatum."

"We'll talk tomorrow," he vowed. "But tonight, at least, you're mine."

"You have my heart, Nicholas. I don't want it back."

He brought his mouth to hers and kissed her tentatively.

She touched the back of his neck and opened her mouth.

Nicholas would not be rushed. He pecked at her lips at an unhurried pace before swiping his tongue across her lower lip.

Acacia reacted hungrily.

Nicholas gently entered her mouth and savored her tongue.

Her fingertips glided to his shoulders and across the strong muscles of his back. Nicholas hadn't worn a shirt to bed and as usual, his skin was warm. She was grateful for his heat.

"My shirt looks good on you," he murmured as his lips dropped to her neck. He kissed the indentation at her throat before he nudged the placket aside, exposing the tops of her breasts.

"I missed your scent," she said shyly.

He lifted his head and gave her a blinding smile.

Her fingers moved to his shirt and removed it, exposing her breasts.

Nicholas gazed down in appreciation. He touched her nipples, his eyes moving to hers for approval.

"Yes," she whispered.

He continued fondling her and bent to kiss the tops of her breasts.

Her hands moved to his lower back, and she traced his spine. He responded by taking one of her nipples into his mouth.

Pleasure, sweet and raw, filled her.

Nicholas took his time. He murmured his appreciation against her skin and used his skillful tongue and lips to build the joy within her.

Then he kissed his way down the center of her body to the edge of her underwear.

She placed her hand on his shoulder and stilled him. "I just want you inside me."

He regarded her carefully. "We'll use a condom, but remember the nurse said your birth control pills aren't working right now."

"I don't care."

He was quiet for a moment. "Okay." He left the bed, walked into the bathroom, and switched on the light.

Acacia could hear a drawer open and close.

Nicholas padded back to the bed, offering her the glorious view of his almost-naked body, clad only in blue boxer shorts.

He removed the shorts and opened the condom as he stood next to the bed.

She watched, eager with anticipation, as he rolled on the prophylactic.

Then he was next to her on the bed, his hand on her abdomen. "Wouldn't you rather be on top?"

"Not tonight. I like how you feel on top of me."

Nicholas looked at his hand. His face grew troubled.

"What's the matter?" she asked, suddenly worried.

"I don't want you to feel trapped or anxious." His eyes met hers.

"I'm not broken, Nicholas. I'm just bruised."

He winced and reached for her cheek, his thumb hovering over the place her father had struck her.

"How can you love me?" Nicholas whispered.

"How could I not?" She gripped his wrist and squeezed. "I see you as you are, but I also see you as you will become. I think you saw the same spark in me, even when I was hiding who I was."

"Nothing could hide your spark. It was one of the first things that drew me to you."

"And nothing could hide your commitment to justice. You came to my aid even when you were suspicious of me, back at the hotel."

He kissed her reverently. "How about side by side?"

"As long as you're holding me."

"Of course." He kissed her deeply and wrapped his arms around her. Their lower bodies moved toward one another.

Acacia threw her leg over his hip, and he brought his hand to her backside. Their chests pressed together, and Nicholas sought her eyes.

She smiled.

He engaged her slowly and when he was fully seated within her, he closed his eyes.

She could see the emotion on his face. It was beautiful.

They began to move together, a gentle rhythm that slowly increased in pace. In time their desire outstripped their restraint, and they moved more quickly.

"This is worth fighting for," he groaned.

"Yes."

Acacia's hand slid to Nicholas's backside as she urged him forward. Then she arched her neck as her orgasm raced through her.

Nicholas continued to thrust, his movements jerky and rapid. Without warning, he stilled within her and buried his face against her shoulder.

"Thank you," she murmured. She felt as if she were floating, her body finally relaxed.

Nicholas kissed her neck. "Why are you thanking me? I should be thanking you."

"I'm just happy to be back in your arms."

Nicholas pulled back so he could see her eyes. "Your love is a gift. I promise I won't take it for granted."

Acacia closed her eyes and wrapped her arms around him.

Chapter Fifty-Nine

The following morning, after breakfast, Nicholas and Acacia sat in a brightly lit sunroom on the ground floor. Acacia curled up on the sofa with a cup of coffee, and Nicholas sat across from her in a chair.

His laptop rested on the table nearby, along with a large green box. He opened the box to reveal two matching gold watches.

He retrieved the women's watch. "After you were kidnapped, I realized that locating you would have been easier if you'd worn a tracking device. You don't have to accept this, but my team has suggested we both wear them. If, for someone reason, we're separated, we will always be able to find one another."

Acacia didn't hesitate. She held out her arm, and Nicholas slipped the watch over her wrist. He fastened it carefully.

"I wasn't sure you'd accept it," he murmured, slipping the men's watch on his own wrist.

"My perception of the world is somewhat altered." She touched the Rolex in wonder. "No one would know by looking at it that it has a tracking device."

"Exactly." He clasped his hands together. "As I mentioned last night, there have been some developments. I was able to uncover the name of Yasmin's ex-boyfriend. My people hacked his security system and accessed the video feed from inside his house. We've been monitoring him. But I'm sure he has his own hackers who are now hunting mine."

"What does that mean?"

"It means time is running out. Either he knows we've hacked him and he's trying to uncover the identities of the hackers, or he will soon. We have surveillance near the house. The Russian isn't there. My team is waiting for him to return."

"What will they do when he returns?"

"They'll go in after dark, disarm him and his men, and secure the art. Then I'll go in."

"Do you know for sure he has your artwork?"

Nicholas shook his head. "Not without examining it in person. I'm relying on Yasmin's testimony, along with what I've been able to uncover about the Russian's taste for expensive art.

"Through the video feed, I've been able to see inside his vault. What appears to be our Degas is visible. Some of the items are covered or positioned behind other objects, so I can't be sure what he has. We pulled stills from the video, and I'm having them analyzed."

"Can I look at them?"

"Shouldn't you be resting?"

"I can rest and look at photographs."

"Then be my guest." Nicholas retrieved his laptop and opened a few files. He handed it to Acacia.

She clicked through a series of black and white screenshots of what she presumed was the vault inside the Russian's house. It matched what she could remember of Yasmin's description — piles of art and artifacts crowded into a room. She saw elephant tusks, what looked like a gold Fabergé egg, and the Degas drawing.

Acacia gasped. She pointed to a painting that hung on the wall, to the left of the elephant tusks. "Is that…?"

Nicholas's face was grim. "That's the missing Matisse from the Musée d'Art Moderne. I've been searching for the original for years. Now I know who has it."

"Have you told the BRB?"

"Not yet. If I'm able to secure it, I'll hand it over to the Minister of the Interior. I won't even involve the BRB."

"Why not?"

"If they were to take over the recovery, they'd have to work with the Russians. Serge Kuznetsov, Yasmin's ex-boyfriend, seems to have paid off every high-ranking law enforcement official in Moscow. He's untouchable."

"What about the Russian bureau of Interpol?"

Nicholas shifted in his seat. "I have a contact in that office. They are suspicious of Kuznetsov and his activities, but they haven't had any evidence linking him to art theft."

"What about these photos?" Acacia tapped the screen of the laptop.

"I haven't shared them, since they're the product of an illegal hack." Nicholas pointed at his computer. "Look at the rest."

Acacia clicked through images of a palatial estate and its interior. A few of the photographs showed armed guards and dogs patrolling the grounds.

She clicked on another photograph and gasped. "What are these?"

Nicholas looked at the screen. "Weapons. Grenades. Ammunition. Bombs."

"Why does he have a stockpile of weapons?"

"He's probably dealing them."

"And the Russian police don't care?"

Nicholas's expression tightened. "They probably don't know. But again, I uncovered evidence that Kuznetsov has been bribing officials. Perhaps they're looking the other way."

Acacia closed the laptop and placed it on the coffee table. "After you have the artwork, what will you do?"

"I'll punish the collector and find out where his Bosnian team is. Then I'll go after them."

"Why haven't you told your parents about this?"

Nicholas frowned. "I don't want them involved."

"You don't want them involved because you know part of what you're doing is wrong."

"I want justice."

"Justice means the man who ordered the robbery must be punished. It doesn't mean he has to be killed. If the artwork is returned to your parents and they discover who killed your sister, it will give them closure."

"It won't be enough."

Acacia stilled. "Did your parents ask you to kill him?"

"No."

"Nicholas, not even killing the man who did this to your sister will be enough. You could kill him a thousand times and it still won't bring your sister back."

"I owe it to her to avenge her."

Acacia cleared her throat. "I say this with love and respect. Nothing I have learned about your sister or your parents suggests to me that they want you to do this."

"I have to see this through." Nicholas stood and began to pace across the room.

"I thought I was going to die." Acacia's voice broke on the last word. She cleared her throat and tried to regain her composure. "My father threatened to kill me, and I believed he was going to carry out that threat."

Nicholas stopped pacing. "Do you blame me for killing him? I was the one who turned over the information you gave me to Mossad, who in turn, told the Syrians."

"No, I don't blame you. The Syrians made their choice; his blood is on their heads. But Nicholas, you have a choice now. You can choose freedom."

"I will never be free so long as the men who killed my sister are still alive."

"And if you kill them, you will never be free."

Nicholas let out a shaky breath. His body seemed to deflate. "How can I face my parents and tell them I let the man who killed my sister go?"

Acacia went to him and wrapped her arms around his waist. "You won't be letting him go. We have to find a way to have law enforcement punish him, and that means involving them somehow. And you won't be standing in front of your parents by yourself. I'll be with you."

"I don't see how we can persuade the Russians to prosecute someone who has been bribing them for years."

"There has to be a way. You don't want to appear before the Minister of the Interior of France and hand him the Matisse after killing the man who stole it. You don't want the celebration of the recovery to be clouded by that. And the same is true of recovering the paintings owned by your parents.

"We have this second chance. We are both alive. We can both be free, together. You told me once that you took pride in being able to look at yourself in the mirror. I'm asking you to continue being the same noble man I fell in love with."

He placed his hands on her shoulders. "I'm sorry, Acacia. There's no way out."

She reached up and touched his face. "I couldn't find a way out of the prison my father put me in. But there was a way out. You sent people to show me the way. Just because you can't see the way out, doesn't mean it isn't there."

He regarded her for a moment. "You'll stay?"

She lifted on the tips of her toes to bring their foreheads together. "I love you, and I'm not leaving. But I'm asking you to work with me to find another way."

Nicholas closed his eyes.

When he opened them, he wore an expression of defeat. "I can try. But if it looks like he's going to escape, I'm going to do everything in my power to prevent that from happening. *Everything*, Acacia."

She searched his eyes. She recognized that he was conceding a great deal to her, even though it wasn't exactly what she wanted.

"All right." She wrapped her arms around his neck.

Chapter Sixty

"Boss, there's something you need to see."

A man Acacia didn't recognize interrupted their tender moment. He was young, bearded, and had carefully oiled and combed hair. He reminded her of some of the Sorbonne students who hung out in cafés on the Left Bank of Paris.

"I have to go." Nicholas kissed her firmly and released her. He followed the young man into the hall.

She returned to the couch and gazed out the window, admiring the sunny day and the beautiful fir trees that encircled the house.

"How are you feeling?" Rick called from the doorway.

She looked over at him and smiled. "Much better, thanks."

He entered the room. "So you and the boss?"

"We're working things out."

Rick nodded. "Good."

"Thank you for bringing me," Acacia said quietly.

Rick smiled, which was, in Acacia's experience, a rare occurrence. "You're welcome."

At that moment, Acacia's cell phone rang. She gave Rick an apologetic look and looked at the screen. It was Kate.

"I need to take this." She picked up the phone as Rick left the room to give her privacy. "Hello?"

"Hello. Claude and I are at this very posh house in Switzerland, about to have to tea with Nicholas's mother. Where are you?"

"Oh, Kate." Acacia sank back down on the sofa. "I'm so sorry. I'm with Nicholas."

"Yeah, his mother told us that when we arrived yesterday. She's been spoiling us, you know—fancy meals, sightseeing in Geneva, and shopping. She bought Claude a new collar. He adores her."

Acacia laughed. "It's so good to hear your voice."

"You, too. Listen, what's going on? Mrs. Cassirer said you were kidnapped. And I know one of Nicholas's bodyguards was killed. The Paris police were all over the apartment building for days."

"I'm all right." Acacia's voice was shaky. "It's a long story, and I promise you, I will tell it all one day. But the short version is that my father and my mother were estranged, and my father kidnapped me. It was a very bad situation, and I'm lucky Nicholas was able to rescue me."

Kate was silent for a moment. "The strangest, most dangerous shit happens to you. Are you sure you aren't Brazilian Secret Service or something?"

Acacia laughed. "No, I'm not. It was rude of me to leave Geneva before you arrived, without explanation. I'm so sorry. But Nicholas and I had a falling out, and I went after him."

"Well, good for you." Kate paused. "Did you get him?"

"Yes," Acacia said softly. "I got him."

"Good. Claude and I have decided to live it up in Cologny for a few more days. The Cassirers are really nice, and I needed a vacation. When are you coming home?"

Loud, quick footsteps echoed in the hall, and Nicholas reappeared, his expression tense.

"I'm coming home soon. I just don't know when. Do you mind taking care of Claude for me?" Acacia looked at Nicholas, who nodded at her.

"No problem. I'm kind of fond of the little guy. I'm thinking about getting a cat myself." Kate sighed. "I'll let you go, but please, take care of yourself and your hot guy. No more dangerous shit."

"No more dangerous shit."

"See you soon."

"Bye, Kate." Acacia ended the call.

Nicholas moved toward her. "I need to go to Moscow."

Acacia stood. "What's happening?"

"Kuznetsov returned to his house. My team is going in after nightfall. I want to be nearby."

"Then I'm coming with you."

"What about what you just promised Kate? This will be dangerous. Once we enter the country, we'll be at risk."

Acacia squared her shoulders. "I don't care. I'm not being left behind."

Nicholas exchanged a look with Rick, who shrugged.

Nicholas rubbed his forehead. "I'm not making the same mistake. But I'd like you to see the nurse first. She may have to travel with us."

Acacia nodded and went in search of the nurse.

❈ ❈

The flight from Helsinki to Moscow was less than two hours. Acacia and Nicholas checked into the opulent five-star Red Square Hotel around five o'clock in the evening. Nicholas and his team had chosen the hotel for its security, as well its location.

Acacia stood in the bedroom of their suite, next to the floor-to-ceiling windows that looked out over the Kremlin. While she'd had contact with the concierge staff when she worked at the Victoire, she'd never visited Russia before. It was an entirely new experience.

She could see the elegant domes of Saint Basil's Cathedral and the red brick Kremlin walls. If their visit had been personal in nature, she would have liked to walk around Red Square.

Nicholas materialized at her side. They'd entered the country with fictitious Swiss diplomatic passports, but he'd been determined to display his scar. He wanted to face the Russian and his Bosnian team and show them what they had done.

Nicholas placed his arm around her shoulder. "I love you," he whispered.

Acacia lifted her eyes to his. He hadn't said the words since she'd returned. In her heart, she'd feared he might not say them again.

"I love you, too, *mon coeur*." She reached up and kissed him.

He held her in his arms and kissed her deeply.

"I have something you left behind." He gave her a searching look.

"What is it?"

He crossed to his briefcase and retrieved a black box. Acacia recognized it.

Nicholas stood in front of her. "I don't want to assume anything."

"Of course I want it back," she whispered. "I never should have left it behind."

Nicholas opened the box and retrieved the lapis lazuli necklace. He placed it around her neck and fastened the clasp.

"That is where it should always be," he said, stroking the column of her throat.

A knock sounded, and they turned toward the open door.

Rick wore a very unhappy expression. "Someone wants to talk to you." He held out a cell phone to Nicholas.

Nicholas crossed toward him and placed the phone at his ear. "Go."

He strode into the living room, and Acacia followed. Several more security agents were there, along with the nurse.

"Repeat that," Nicholas barked into the phone, in English.

Acacia couldn't hear what the voice on the other end of the line was saying, but clearly something was wrong.

"Fuck!" he exploded. "I'm putting you on speaker so my head of security can hear you." Nicholas pressed a button on the cell phone. "Go, blue leader."

"Target has entered an armored car and is in a three-vehicle convoy driving from the house to the gates." A male voice with an American accent filled the room. "Either we ambush them outside the gates, or we let him go. Awaiting instruction."

Nicholas looked at Rick.

Rick shook his head. "Too noisy and too open. It isn't dark yet, so there wouldn't be much cover. It's possible Kuznetsov knows our guys are out there, and he's attempting to draw fire."

"Damn it." Nicholas made a fist. "Blue leader, an ambush will draw too much attention. Hold your positions and wait for further orders."

"Copy that," the voice replied.

Nicholas ended the call, his face thunderous.

Acacia touched his arm. "What's going on?"

"Kuznetsov is leaving the compound. We lost our window."

Acacia couldn't help but feel relieved. "What are you going to do?"

Nicholas looked at Rick. "We need to have Kuznetsov detained. Call Wen and try to have him put eyes on the convoy.

"Activate the secondary incursion team and have them meet me here. I want to be with them when they close in on Kuznetsov. Have Wen reach out to our contact in Russian Interpol and patch him through to my cell phone."

Rick's gaze moved to Acacia and back to his employer. "You can't wear a suit with the incursion team."

Nicholas shrugged. "I'll change. Tell them to bring an extra set of gear."

With a last look at Acacia, Rick pulled out his cell phone and made the call.

Acacia took hold of Nicholas's hand. "What about the artwork? Why not send your team in after dark to recover it?"

"If I do that, I'll have lost Kuznetsov. And probably started a war." Nicholas led Acacia into the bedroom and closed the door. He took off his suit jacket and placed it on the bed. He sat down and removed his shoes and socks.

Acacia came to stand in front of him. "I don't want you to go."

"I can't let him get away."

"Then I'm going with you." Acacia kicked off her shoes and reached under her dress for her stockings. She began to roll them down her legs.

Nicholas stared. "What are you doing?"

"I told you." She threw the stockings aside and unzipped her dress. "I'm going with you."

Nicholas moved to his feet. "You can't go with me. It's dangerous. You still have a head injury, for God's sake."

"Where you go, I go. If it's too dangerous for me, then it's too dangerous for you. Unless you intend to have your men restrain me or knock me out—the way my father's men did when they kidnapped me—I'm coming with you."

Nicholas's expression shifted from determined to surprised to anxious. He took her hand. "I've hurt you enough."

She lifted his palm to her heart. "Can you feel that?"

He nodded.

"My heart is still beating. I'm alive, and so are you. If you kill Kuznetsov, I'll still love you, Nicholas. But you'll kill part of my heart."

Nicholas screwed his eyes shut.

"Talk to Interpol. Send your team to retrieve the artwork. Follow Kuznetsov. But don't go with the incursion team, unless you're prepared to kill him in front of me. Because I'm not letting you go." She covered his hand with hers. "Not now. Not ever."

Nicholas swallowed hard. He opened his eyes. "All right."

With a deep, shuddering sigh, he sat back on the bed and replaced his socks and shoes. "Put your clothes back on. I'm going to speak to Rick, and I'll head over to the surveillance center."

Acacia nodded.

Nicholas stood. "Stay with Steve and Ray. I'll be next door."

"I'll come over shortly."

Nicholas touched her cheek. "You haven't had dinner."

"Neither have you."

"Order room service for both of us. It's going to be a long night." He kissed her and exited the bedroom.

Acacia hugged herself and sat on the bed. She knew she'd done the right thing, but she also knew that in acceding to her request, Nicholas had foregone part of the closure he thought he needed.

She took her time getting dressed, trying to process what had just occurred.

A short time after she finished dressing, Acacia unpacked her suitcase. She was hanging the clothes Madame Cassirer had given her when someone knocked on the bedroom door.

She opened it.

Rick stood in the doorway, speaking hurriedly into his cell phone. "He isn't there? He left ten minutes ago with Jeff and Kevin.

"No, he told me to redirect the incursion team to Kuznetsov's coordinates. I thought they were patched in to your guys." Rick looked at Acacia. His normally calm demeanor had vanished. "Check the feed to see if he went down to the parking garage. Maybe he changed his mind." Rick disconnected the call.

"What's going on?" Acacia asked.

Rick was already running toward the suite's entrance. She followed, with Steve and Ray. The long corridor outside the suite was empty.

"Damn it!" Rick ran toward the service elevator, his eyes on the carpet. He crouched down and touched a few spots. "Blood."

Cursing, he stalked past Acacia and the other two bodyguards to the room next to the suite. He swiped his security card and led the small group into the surveillance room.

Acacia stepped to the side. The large conference room was filled with tables and chairs and an abundance of laptops and machines. Ten men and three women hunched over separate workstations. Many of the agents wore headsets.

The curtains to the room were drawn and the lights dimmed. A large screen had been suspended from the ceiling; a series of video feeds were projected on it. Acacia surmised the feeds came from the Russian's compound. She recognized the interior of his vault.

Rick went to Wen, who was standing and typing on a laptop. "Talk to me."

Wen's fingers flew across the keyboard. "We're pulling up video from the exits on this floor, including the service elevator."

Acacia stood next to Rick. "You don't think Nicholas decided to go with the incursion team?"

Rick frowned. "No. That wouldn't explain the blood in the hall."

Wen turned to a woman sitting behind him. "Olga, put the video feed for this floor on the main screen. Play back the past fifteen minutes."

"I didn't see anything," Olga protested. "The boss didn't even enter the hall."

"Did you see Rick and Ms. Santos?" Wen asked, focusing on the main screen as the images changed.

"Negative."

Wen turned to Rick. "We've been using the hotel's security system to monitor access to this floor. Olga should have seen you and Acacia enter the hall. She should have seen the boss too, but she didn't."

"What does that mean?" Acacia gazed at the main screen, which showed an empty hotel corridor.

"There!" the bearded young man Acacia had met in Helsinki shouted from the front of the room. "There's a loop. Someone hacked the system and looped an image of an empty hall."

"Fuck," Wen swore. "Olga, bypass the loop and get the actual feed.

"Everyone except Jim, focus on the feeds for all entrances and exits to the hotel. Jim, try to reach Jeff and Kevin."

Rick straightened and addressed the room. "The hotel has been compromised. We're dark as of this moment, so no information-sharing with hotel security. Wen, the secondary incursion team should be on its way, but let them know they'll be stationed here. We'll need them for additional security."

Rick gestured to Steve and Ray. "We're going to sweep the floor, the elevator, and the stairwell. Wen, call me when you've got something."

"I ordered room service," Acacia said quietly.

Rick nodded at Wen. "Cancel that order."

Rick drew his gun and the other guards followed suit. They exited into the hall.

Acacia stood behind Wen as he canceled her room service order. The air in the room was tense as the analysts scanned their computer screens.

"Jeff and Kevin aren't responding via com link," Jim announced. "Their cell phones are on, but they aren't answering. I've traced the phones to the parking garage downstairs."

"Copy that." Wen quickly relayed the message to Rick.

"I found something." Another woman stood next to her laptop.

"Put it on the main screen," Wen ordered.

Acacia gazed in shock at images of Nicholas being bustled out of an elevator by a group of masked men and entering what looked like an underground parking garage. He was pushed into a waiting van, and the limp bodies of his security guards were loaded into the back. The van sped off.

"God damn it." Wen lifted his voice over the cacophony that erupted in the room. "Liz, I want you to analyze the video and pull everything you can. Try to get a license plate. Everyone else, divvy up the video feeds to see if we can find out where the van is going.

"Dave, I need you to hack into the Moscow streetlight and security cameras. See if you can pick up the van."

"We've got the feed to the floor," Olga interjected.

"Main screen," Wen ordered. "Rewind the past thirty minutes."

The command center grew silent as they watched Nicholas and his security guards being ambushed by a group of six masked men, armed with automatic weapons, who'd been hiding in the service elevator.

"Shit," said Wen. "They've got eyes inside the hotel. The service elevator opened as soon as the boss entered the hall. They were waiting for him."

Wen quickly relayed the findings to Rick. Acacia could hear him swearing over the com link.

Acacia clasped a hand over her mouth as Olga played the images of Nicholas's capture over and over again. His security guards had been struck in the head, knocking them out. Their bodies had been carried into the elevator.

Nicholas had attempted to wrest one of the guns from an assailant, but another masked man had placed his gun to Nicholas's temple. After they'd restrained him, they'd punched him in the face. Acacia saw blood spill from Nicholas's mouth.

As his hand covered his mouth, she saw something glitter at his wrist.

"The watch," she croaked, touching Wen's elbow. "Nicholas is wearing his watch, the one with the tracking device."

"Right," Wen muttered. Again, his fingers flew across his keyboard. "Dave, I'm sending the link to the tracking device in the boss's watch. I want you to pinpoint his location and report back."

"Affirmative," the bearded man replied. He tapped several keys on his laptop.

"Where are they taking Nicholas?" Acacia whispered.

"Dave, status," Wen called out.

"Okay, I've got eyes on the watch. He's still in the city," Dave replied.

Acacia closed her eyes and said a prayer. Kidnappings took extensive planning, especially inside what should have been a secure hotel. If the Russian had Nicholas, he would probably kill him. They needed a rescue plan, and they needed one fast.

"Where's Rick?" she asked.

"On his way back up."

"We need to contact the incursion team at the Russian's house and send them after Nicholas." Acacia spoke to Wen quietly.

He gave her a quizzical look.

"You know who I am to Nicholas," she continued. "I'm not going to hamper your efforts; I'm here to help."

Wen frowned. "The boss wanted the team to go in."

"If the Russian isn't in the house, the incursion is pointless. Nicholas told me that. Right now, his safety should be our first priority."

"No argument there, but we have a protocol."

"And that is?" Acacia lifted her eyebrows.

"Rick's in charge."

"Fine." Acacia crossed her arms. "Call him."

As Wen did as she asked, she stood and surveyed the room and all the computer screens. "Can you patch the incursion team into the surveillance on Nicholas's watch?"

"Yes." Wen looked toward the door. "Rick's back."

The door to the conference room opened and all eyes swung to the door. Rick, Steve, and Ray entered.

Acacia went to Rick. "I want Wen to activate the incursion team to rescue Nicholas."

Rick frowned. "The boss isn't going to like it, but I was thinking the same thing. Russian law enforcement isn't an option, not with the operation we have going on here."

"What about hotel security? Will they call the police?"

Rick scoffed. "Someone paid them off. The extraction team drove right into the parking garage and took the service elevator to this floor. They'd have to have an elevator key to do that. I doubt the hotel will call the police, but just in case, I'll activate one of our contacts."

Rick walked over to Olga and began speaking to her in low tones.

Acacia followed. "Nicholas is wearing his watch, and Dave is tracking him. How can we find the Russian?"

"The boss was supposed to speak to a contact in Russian Interpol." Rick looked around Acacia to Wen. "Did you make the call?"

"Yes. When the boss was delayed, the agent hung up."

Acacia chewed at the edge of her lip.

"Kuznetsov knows we're here," Rick mused. "Look at the timing. He leaves the house, knowing it will provoke a reaction from us. Then his guys jump the boss. Kuznetsov must have people inside the hotel." He turned to Wen. "Patch the incursion team into our surveillance on the boss. Tell them to get ready for an extraction."

"Affirmative," Wen replied. "Rules of engagement?"

"Tell them not to leave a large footprint," Rick replied. "Obviously, we want the boss unharmed, but they're going to take fire getting him out."

"Copy that," said Wen. He began speaking into his headset in a low voice.

"We need a diversion," Rick muttered. He approached Wen and waited until he'd finished speaking. "Tell the incursion team to trip the security system at the compound. That will bring out the cavalry, and it will buy us some time."

As Wen followed orders, Acacia turned to Rick. "Kuznetsov probably has Nicholas, but without involving law enforcement, we may not be able to tie him to the kidnapping. If we let the artwork go, Nicholas will have failed."

Rick looked at her keenly. "I think we agree the boss's safety is our first priority."

"Of course. But I want to tie Kuznetsov to the stolen art. It may give us some leverage if the incursion team runs into problems."

Rick shook his head. "We have two teams. The first is going to get the boss, and the second is on their way here. We need them for security. I'm surprised Kuznetsov didn't try for you, too."

Acacia's heart leapt into her throat. A wave of anxiety washed over her, and she was suddenly in Morocco, sitting in her cell in the dark. She found it difficult to breathe.

"You need to sit down." Rick took her elbow and led her to a chair. "Do you want me to call the nurse?"

She shook her head.

Steve quickly retrieved a glass of water and handed it to her.

Her hand shook as she took the glass.

"Take a deep breath," Rick ordered, "but don't close your eyes. Look around you. We're doing all we can to help the boss. Don't fall apart on me."

Acacia kept her eyes open and visualized her panic attack as a wall of water. She imagined it crashing over her from head to toe and then disappearing into the carpet. She drew a deep breath.

"Do you want to go back to the suite and lie down?" Rick's face creased with concern.

"I want to help." Shakily, she sipped the water.

Rick placed his hand on her shoulder. "We've got this. You should go. This will take time."

"The artwork," she managed, tasting the water again. "We have to find a way to tie Kuznetsov to the artwork. Then we have something Russian law enforcement can prosecute."

Rick shook his head. "The boss has a contact in Russian Interpol, but his hands are tied. He doesn't have legal grounds to search."

"Sure he does," Olga called from across the room. Her face reddened as Rick and Acacia scrutinized her.

She left her workstation and walked over to where Acacia was seated. "Olga Ivanova," she introduced herself. "I'm the Russian specialist. Russian law requires only that law enforcement have the *suspicion* of the presence of weapons on private property to justify a search. If you can provide Interpol with video of weapons in Kuznetsov's compound, it's enough for *suspicion*."

"That's risky," Wen interjected as he walked over to the huddle. "The video is illegally obtained. Kuznetsov can challenge the search."

"Not if Interpol sees footage of an armed response to a security breach," Olga countered. "Rick called for the incursion team to trip the security system. If they can lure Kuznetsov's men outside the walls of the compound and videotape them, the footage wouldn't be the product of an illegal wiretap."

"That may work," Rick admitted.

"Please," said Acacia. "It's worth a try."

Rick nodded at Wen.

"Okay, Kris, get eyes on the compound so we can get footage of their response." Wen looked over at the analyst seated next to his workstation.

"Copy that," said Kris.

"Dave, location," Wen barked.

"Still in Moscow," Dave reported. "The boss is on the M-9, which is the Baltic Highway. It looks like they're headed west, outside the city."

"Possible destinations?"

"The highway runs all the way to Latvia. But settlements outside the city include Golyevo, Novyy, and Voronki."

"What about Kuznetsov?" Rick asked.

"The convoy disappeared," Dave admitted. "Several of the side streets in his neighborhood don't have cameras on them."

"Start pulling up aerial views of the settlements you mentioned," Wen instructed, "but keep an eye out for the convoy."

He turned to Rick and Acacia. "We just received some good news. Nicholas is on the M-9 heading west. That's in the general direction of the Barvikha area, which is where the compound is. Our incursion team won't be too far away."

"Have they tripped the security system yet?" Rick asked.

"Kris, status," said Wen.

"Nothing yet," Kris reported.

"Okay, tell the team to breach security in such a way as to draw Kuznetsov's men outside the compound. Then they need to get the hell out," Rick instructed. "Since Nicholas is traveling toward them, they should be able to catch up with him."

"Affirmative." Wen spoke into his headset in hushed tones.

"I need my cell phone. It's in my purse, which is in the suite," Acacia said quietly to Steve, who stood next to her.

He turned and exited the conference room.

She moved to sit next to Wen. "Does Nicholas's Interpol contact know him as Nicholas or one of his aliases?"

"Pierre Breckman. Why?"

"I'd like to speak to the Interpol contact."

Wen looked up at Rick and lifted his eyebrows.

Acacia frowned. "I speak Russian. I know about the stolen art, and I've seen photos of Kuznetsov's vault."

"That's not a good idea," said Rick. "You're under a lot of strain. And we've got the incursion team poised to trip the security system. Let's see what they can do first."

"I'll wait a few minutes, but I want to talk to the contact." Acacia was determined. "I'm going to call Paris first."

Rick shook his head. "That's the wrong move. We need to work with the Russians."

"The French may help us motivate the Russians," Acacia explained. "You said yourself that Nicholas's contact hasn't been able to help. Maybe the BRB can persuade him."

Rick frowned. "Who are you going to call? Luc?"

She nodded.

Rick's frown deepened. "He isn't going to help us."

"He's BRB," Acacia argued. "He knows the agent who is hunting the stolen Matisse we saw in Kuznetsov's vault. It's the best lead they've had in years."

At that moment, Steve returned and placed her cell phone in her hand. She thanked him.

She took the phone to the far corner of the room and dialed Luc's number. She rubbed her hamsa pendant, praying he would answer.

"Do you have your head straight?" Luc's voice was cool.

Acacia closed her eyes. "It's an emergency."

Luc's tone changed and grew alert. "Where are you?"

She opened her eyes and faced away from Rick and the others. "I'm in Moscow."

"What are you doing in Moscow?"

"It's a long story. Listen, we found the Matisse, the one that was stolen from Musée d'Art Moderne. It's here."

There was silence on the other end of the line.

"Luc?" She grew panicked. "Are you there?"

"Is this some kind of a joke? Do you and your new boyfriend make up these games just for laughs?"

"This is not a joke. I called you first, but his security team is also calling Russian Interpol."

"Good. Tell them I said hello."

"Wait!" She lifted her voice. "Don't hang up."

Luc huffed into the phone. "I'm here. But Caci, you're trying my patience."

"I need your help. The man who has the Matisse is Serge Kuznetsov. He's Russian mafia, and no one will touch him. Not even Russian Interpol."

Acacia heard footsteps on the other end of the line and the sound of a door closing.

"This is out of my jurisdiction. I'm not even assigned to the Musée case."

"I thought you could speak to Philippe."

Luc made an exasperated noise. Then Acacia heard the sound of fingers on a computer keyboard. "What else can you tell me?"

"Kuznetsov has other stolen works in his vault. Our security team was able to hack into their system. We have video surveillance."

"Can you send it to me?" Luc rattled off his BRB email address.

"Of course." Acacia crossed over to Wen and scribbled Luc's email on a piece of paper. She quickly listed the files she wanted Wen to send and pointed to them with the end of her pencil.

Wen nodded.

"We're sending them. But Luc, I need the BRB to do something now."

There was silence for a moment.

"That's not possible." Luc breathed heavily into the phone. "We'd have to coordinate with Russian Interpol, as well as local law enforcement. It will take days. Maybe weeks."

"We don't have that kind of time!" She raised her voice, at the edge of tears.

"Why isn't your boyfriend handling this?"

"Because Kuznetsov has him." She barely restrained a sob. "He was kidnapped from our hotel. I'm with what remains of his security team."

"Call the police. Caci, I'm in Paris. What the hell do you expect me to do?"

"I expect you to help me. Not for his sake, but because I'm asking you." She sniffled. "I'm asking you. Please."

"I'll look at what you have, and if it seems credible, I'll pass it on to Philippe." Luc's voice was low and gravelly. "I get that your boyfriend is in trouble, but there's nothing I can do about that."

"Can you at least speak to Russian Interpol?"

"No. I'll look at what you send me, but there's no way I'm putting my ass on the line for this."

"Why? Because I don't have my head straight?" Acacia's temper balanced on the edge of a knife.

Luc blew out a breath. "I'm sorry. I shouldn't have said that. But this is my career. After what happened last time, you can understand my hesitation."

"This is his life," she whispered.

"Call the police," Luc repeated firmly. "Report the kidnapping, and contact your boyfriend's embassy."

"Fine. Goodbye."

"Caci, wait!" Luc raised his voice.

"What?"

He sighed deeply. "I'm sorry. I'll look at what you gave me and see what I can do. But I'm not making any promises."

"Thanks." Acacia hung up.

She pressed her cell phone to her forehead and closed her eyes. Time was running out, and she'd just wasted precious minutes on someone who she'd thought was going to help.

She'd never make that mistake again.

Chapter Sixty-One

"My name is Acacia. I'm Pierre Breckman's girlfriend. He's been kidnapped." Acacia spoke in Russian through Wen's headset. Olga sat next to her, listening silently to the exchange through her own headphones.

The Interpol agent on the other end of the line cursed. "Now there's a war."

"A war you can end. We will rescue Pierre. We're asking you to help us track down Kuznetsov."

"Do you have evidence Kuznetsov is behind the kidnapping?"

"Pierre was kidnapped inside a secure floor at the Red Square Hotel," Acacia grew testy. "You tell me—who else could be behind it?"

"It's after hours. You're talking about a full-scale operation that requires extensive planning."

"I have something to offer in exchange." Acacia signaled to Olga. "Let's hear it."

"Kuznetsov is stockpiling weapons, grenades, and bombs inside his compound."

The agent paused. "How do you know?"

"We have video footage. I can send it to you."

The agent rattled off an email address, which Olga quickly copied down.

"The address is secure," the agent assured Acacia. "Send it over."

Acacia locked eyes with Olga. "Email the weapons footage," Acacia instructed in English. "Send the stills from inside the vault, too."

"Can you see the images?" she asked the agent in Russian, nervously tapping her foot on the floor.

"Opening now." The agent swore. "These are in his house?"

"Yes. I've also sent images of stolen artwork and antiquities from his vault. One of the pieces is very important to Pierre."

The agent exhaled heavily into the phone. Then Acacia heard a furious tapping sound and a low expletive.

"What is it?" she asked.

"Hold on." The agent seemed to put the phone down. Acacia heard footsteps and the sound of what could have been a filing cabinet opening.

She heard papers rustle through the telephone line, and then the agent spoke again in her ear. "There's something else of interest in that vault."

"What?"

"There's an Imperial egg."

"A Fabergé egg. Yes, I saw it."

"It looks like the Third Imperial egg, which belonged to the Tsar and his wife. After the revolution, it was seized by the Bolsheviks and placed in the Kremlin Armoury Museum."

"I don't follow," Acacia confessed.

"The egg is a national treasure. It was on loan to the Hermitage in St. Petersburg a number of years ago when it was stolen. Law enforcement all over Russia has been looking for it."

"So you'll help us?" Acacia held her breath.

"Everything takes time. But this, coupled with the weapons, should be enough for me to get some support. The Russian President is friendly with the Director of the Hermitage Museum. He pledged the stolen treasure would be found."

"What can you do?"

"Let me speak to your head of security. I'm going to approach my superiors." The agent paused. "And thank you."

"Any help you can offer will be appreciated, Agent. But you know time is of the essence." Acacia tried to keep the emotion out of her voice.

"I understand."

"In case your superiors need further motivation, I should mention that in addition to the stolen Degas and the Imperial egg, it looks as if the missing Matisse from the Musée d'Art Moderne is in the vault as well. I have the contact information for the BRB agent in Paris who is in charge of the investigation."

"Send it over."

Acacia placed her cell phone on the table next to Wen's laptop and gestured to the screen. Since Luc had been unwilling to help, she would pass along Philippe's contact information herself. She pulled up his profile from her cell phone, silently grateful she'd met him.

"I will. I'm turning you over to our head of security." She murmured her thanks and handed the phone to Rick.

"Thank you, Olga." Acacia touched the agent's arm.

"You're welcome," she replied, removing her headset. "We've been working with that contact for some time, but the boss wasn't able to get anywhere with him. Lucky for us, the weapons and egg seemed to have swayed him."

"Kuznetsov must have a lot of influence if Interpol was willing to turn a blind eye for so long."

"He has an incredible amount of influence," Olga agreed. "He rose to power by killing his rivals and anyone he felt was a threat. They call him Serge the Terrible."

Acacia shivered. Serge the Terrible had Nicholas. They had to find him as soon as possible.

"What's happening?" She turned to Wen.

He pressed a few keys and a black and white video popped up on his laptop. "The incursion team cut the power to the compound." He pointed to some movement on the lower part of the screen. "They started a bonfire outside the walls of the estate. Kuznetsov's men opened the gates to check out the fire."

"So the compound is without power?"

"They must have a backup generator, because the lights came back on." Wen gestured to an image of the mansion, which was illuminated. "As you can see, he's got the equivalent of a small army in there. He was waiting for us."

"Send the footage to our Interpol contact." She pulled on Rick's arm.

"One minute," Rick said into the phone. "Yes?"

"Wen is sending over footage of Kuznetsov's men leaving the compound. Interpol will be able to see how well armed they are."

"Copy that." Rick returned to his phone call.

"What about Nicholas?" Acacia asked Wen.

"Dave, status," Wen ordered.

"The van got off the M-9 and onto the A-109, which is taking the long way round to Barvikha, if that's their destination," Dave replied. He projected an image of a flashing light traveling on a roadmap of Moscow onto the large screen.

Wen stared at the screen. "The incursion team is on the move. Is there a possible intercept point?"

Dave studied his laptop. "The A-109 turns into the A-106, which is the road into Barvikha. If the incursion team hops on the A-106, they may run right into them."

"What about Kuznetsov? Any sign of the convoy?"

"Negative." Dave shook his head. "I'll keep looking."

"Copy that." Wen spoke into his headset, passing information on to the leader of the incursion team.

"Wait a minute," said Dave. "The boss has stopped. It looks like he's in a forest."

A hush fell over the room. The light on the main screen continued to flash, but it had moved off the A-109.

Dave tapped on his computer, and an aerial view of the area appeared on the screen. "He isn't in a forest; there's a house."

"Could be one of Kuznetsov's safe houses," Wen observed.

"So close to his compound?" Olga interjected.

"That could be why we lost the convoy," Dave suggested. "Maybe the house was Kuznetsov's intercept point."

At that moment, Rick stood behind Acacia's chair. "Okay, everyone. I want everything you can get on that house, including property registry, security systems, and schematics. Go!"

The team scurried into action.

"How far away is the incursion team?" Rick walked over to Dave.

"They're about five minutes from the safe house," said Dave.

Wen gestured to Rick and pointed to his laptop. "The secondary incursion team just entered the lobby. They're on their way up." He pointed to images from hotel cameras on the ground floor.

"Good. Send everything you can get to the primary incursion leader." Rick straightened and rubbed a hand across his mouth.

Acacia looked up at him. "Now what?"

"Now we pray."

She touched her hamsa pendant. "That isn't good enough. I want to go after him."

Rick rounded on her. "After who? Kuznetsov?"

"No, Nicholas." She stood, clutching her cell phone. "I want the backup team to take me to wherever Nicholas is."

Rick stood over her, hands on his hips. "No. No way. The incursion team is going to handle the extraction. The backup team is here for our safety. You aren't going anywhere."

"I'm not asking for permission." She held up her wristwatch. "Wen will be able to track me. But I'm not going to sit here and wait."

Rick scowled. "This is the safest place for you. We have no idea if Kuznetsov has other agents in the building or nearby. They could ambush you."

"Then it's a good thing I'm with a group of professionals." She moved toward the door.

Rick followed. "Once the incursion team has Nicholas, he's going to want to see you. You don't want to be stuck in traffic in the middle of Moscow."

"It will take time for the incursion team to study the schematics and plan their attack, correct?"

Rick nodded.

"If I want to see Nicholas as soon as possible, I'd better get going."

"God damn it." Rick scrubbed at his face. He turned to Wen. "I'm going with her. I want constant updates."

"Copy that." Wen looked from Rick to Acacia. "Stay safe."

"I will." She opened the door to the hall and Rick passed through it. She followed and closed the door.

Chapter Sixty-Two

The men dragged Nicholas from the van in handcuffs. He'd suffered a split lip and bruised jaw, but luckily hadn't lost any teeth.

Two burly men carrying automatic weapons—who Nicholas had seen take down his security team at the hotel—now held him by the arms. The security guards remained unconscious, lying in the back of the van.

He knew better than to take on his assailants. He was outnumbered and without a weapon. But he wasn't outsmarted. They hadn't scanned him for tracking devices. He flexed his wrist against the handcuff. His Rolex was still there.

As the men pulled him into an opulent, three-story villa, he thought of Acacia. It was possible his attackers had captured her as well. He prayed she was still alive.

He marched down a long hall and into a massive library. At the far end of the room, next to a black marble fireplace, stood a man.

Nicholas recognized him immediately. "Kuznetsov."

The man turned. He held a crystal glass in his hand. He took a sip of amber liquid. "Cassirer."

Serge Kuznetsov was of medium height and appeared to be in his fifties with a shaved head and peering blue eyes. His barrel chest and squat physique reminded Nicholas of a bulldog. He wore an expensive-looking tailored navy suit without a tie.

He gestured to his men, and they settled Nicholas in a leather armchair near the fireplace.

"Would you mind removing the handcuffs?" he asked in English, lifting his arms behind his back.

Kuznetsov nodded to one of the men. He produced a key and undid the cuffs.

Nicholas rubbed his wrists.

"A drink?" Kuznetsov approached the bar that stood in front of a large window.

"Vodka," Nicholas replied.

Kuznetsov retrieved a bottle from a small freezer and poured two fingers of the spirit into a glass. He handed it to one of his men, who delivered it to Nicholas.

Nicholas sipped the liquid, but he didn't take his eyes off his enemy.

"This is all very unfortunate." Kuznetsov sat opposite Nicholas, his men standing nearby.

"Since I am your prisoner, I would have to agree." Nicholas's tone was wry.

Kuznetsov's eyes grew sharp. "You attacked my home."

"You murdered my sister."

"No." Kuznetsov lifted a finger and wagged it in Nicholas's direction. "A Bosnian named Luka murdered your sister."

Nicholas threw back more of his vodka. It tasted expensive but still produced heat in his throat. "You gave the order."

Kuznetsov raised his shoulders. "I placed an order for rare artwork. I didn't give an order to kill. Luka got carried away."

Nicholas began to argue, but Kuznetsov spoke over him. "I've killed before, and so have my men. This is not a secret. But I did not kill your sister."

Nicholas's hands began to shake, he was so angry. "Where's Luka?"

"He gave you that scar." Kuznetsov made a slashing motion across his face. "I wonder, why didn't you have it removed?"

Nicholas curled his hand into a fist. "I'll have it removed after I have justice."

"Justice." Kuznetsov gazed at him. "I'm afraid you've traveled a long way, only to be disappointed."

Nicholas ground his teeth together. "What do you mean?"

"Luka is dead."

Nicholas stared daggers at his enemy. "What?"

Kuznetsov sipped his whisky, purposefully delaying his response. "After you found Luka and the others, they came to me. I dealt with them."

Nicholas stared at the Russian in shock.

In a haze, he lowered his head to look at the glass in his hand. It was heavy and probably crystal. The vodka was expensive. And he and his enemy were sitting across from one another, calmly discussing life and death.

It was possible Kuznetsov was lying. But the fact the Bosnian and his crew had disappeared seemed to lend credence to the Russian's account.

This was not an outcome Nicholas had anticipated. He had envisioned confronting Kuznetsov and moving on to confront the Bosnians. Now the latter might never happen.

He felt as if he'd been marched onto a scaffold, only to have the floor give way under his final step. He was falling through space and time, entirely adrift.

And Riva...

He choked back his anguish. He'd never be able to look her killer in the eye and demand retribution.

Nicholas stared at the vodka in his glass. The clear liquid taunted him. He was somewhere outside Moscow, having a drink with a man who referred to the Bosnian thieves as if they were an annoyance—a group of flies he'd swatted, not a group of human beings he'd murdered.

Nicholas blinked. In his mind's eye, his free fall came to an excruciating halt at the bottom of an abyss. He felt the impact as if it were physical, and his heart thumped irregularly.

The absurdity hit him with all the force of a fall from a great height. Kuznetsov showed absolute indifference to human life as he sat in the large villa drinking thousands of Euros of whisky.

"It will never be enough," Nicholas muttered, looking at his enemy. He could kill Kuznetsov, if he was able to escape and get hold of a weapon, but it wouldn't take away his grief for Riva. It wouldn't heal his loss. If anything, it would sink him even further into darkness. He would become the man he hated, the figure who had haunted his dreams and the lives of his parents since Riva's murder.

"The man who scarred you is dead," Kuznetsov continued. "The other members of his team are dead. The dead bury the dead."

"Perhaps." Nicholas's voice was hoarse. "But you're still in possession of my family's artwork."

"And you think you can take it back?" Kuznetsov chuckled. "Advice is wasted on the young, but let me give you some. You need to know your enemy better than you know yourself, if you want to win. I've followed you for years."

Nicholas's eyebrows lifted. "Years?"

"When you went after Luka, I knew you wouldn't rest until you found me. I followed you. I watched your progress. I monitored your aliases and trailed your mistresses."

Nicholas's face grew alert.

Kuznetsov smiled. "The model was interesting enough, but your latest mistress is far more compelling. You agree, don't you? You seem to be willing to do anything for her."

Nicholas unclenched his fist. Kuznetsov's attempt to rattle him had succeeded, but he forced himself to remain calm.

"You have the Matisse from the Musée d'Art Moderne," Nicholas changed the subject. "The government of France is very interested in recovering it."

Kuznetsov stood and returned to the bar. "France is used to disappointment." He refilled his glass with whisky and brought the bottle of vodka to Nicholas. Kuznetsov poured for him.

"Have you checked your house recently?" Nicholas watched his enemy as he placed the bottle in the freezer and regained his seat.

Kuznetsov's eyes darted to Nicholas. "Another piece of advice, my young friend. Never attempt to invade Russia. Your people cut the power to my estate, but it was back on within minutes.

"Ivan," Kuznetsov beckoned one of his men.

The man stepped forward. He hadn't removed his mask.

"Ivan, have there been any reports of a security breach at the estate?"

"Just the power outage, sir," Ivan replied. "And a bonfire outside the gates."

"A bonfire." Kuznetsov smiled smugly. "Your team has failed."

Nicholas tensed. He didn't understand why the incursion team hadn't followed orders and breached the compound. Unless...

He redirected his attention to the man who was smiling at him. "Did you order the attack on the concierge at the Hotel Victoire in Paris?"

"I know of no such attack. I did business with a dealer in Paris. He ran into some trouble and handled it clumsily. But his trouble was not from me."

Nicholas narrowed his eyes. He wasn't sure what to believe. "What are you going to do now?"

Kuznetsov tasted his whisky again. "I'm going to kill you. I'm going to send someone to retrieve Yasmin from Greece. She kept her mouth shut when she left, so I let her go. Now she's going to be punished. Since Yasmin will be unavailable, I've decided to take your latest mistress as my own. I've never fucked a Brazilian."

Involuntarily, Nicholas's fingers curled into a fist.

"That will never happen." He looked into the eyes of his enemy.

Kuznetsov laughed. "In Russia, I am king. Why should today be any different?"

Nicholas smiled.

Kuznetsov's expression darkened. "Why are you smiling?"

"Have you studied Russian history?"

"What do you mean?"

Nicholas's smile broadened, and he leaned forward in his chair. "What do you think happened to the kings of Russia?"

Kuznetsov threw his crystal glass at Nicholas's head, spraying whisky through the air.

Nicholas caught the glass and in one smooth motion, flung it back at the Russian.

Kuznetsov lifted his arms to shield his face, and the glass shattered as it hit his forearm.

Nicholas ducked to avoid the flying debris. Kuznetsov's men closed in on him, but at that moment the lights went out.

Nicholas dropped to the floor and maneuvered himself under the armchair. He could hear the sound of boots in the hall and shouts in Russian and English.

Then someone opened fire.

Chapter Sixty-Three

"He did it." Rick turned from his position in the front passenger seat, his cell phone pressed to his ear.

"Who?" Acacia asked.

She was sandwiched between two armed soldiers. Three more sat behind them in the large utility vehicle.

"The Interpol agent," Rick explained. "Russian Interpol just busted into Kuznetsov's compound."

"Can Wen send photos?"

"Send me stills from the compound," Rick ordered. When the text was received, he clicked through a series of black and white images. He handed his phone to Acacia.

In the photos, she could see the Interpol team working their way through Kuznetsov's house. One photograph showed a couple of bodies on the floor.

"Does Interpol have enough men?" Acacia gazed in disgust at a photo of what looked like Kuznetsov's soldiers preparing an ambush at the top of a staircase.

"Rick, we got a problem." Wen's voice came through the phone.

Acacia handed it back to Rick.

"Go ahead," Rick said.

Acacia couldn't hear what Wen was saying.

Rick's body jerked. "Location?"

Again, Acacia strained but couldn't make out the words.

"Make sure they go to the closest and most advanced medical facility. Text me the location." Rick looked over his shoulder at Acacia. "Yeah, we'll meet them there."

Rick disconnected the call and faced Acacia.

"What is it?" she whispered.

"The team went into the villa. It was supposed to be a snatch and grab, but Kuznetsov's men opened fire. Our team engaged, and the boss was hit." Rick spoke slowly, keeping his voice calm.

Acacia didn't react. She just repeated his words in her head.

"How bad?" the soldier to Acacia's right asked.

Rick's gaze flickered to Acacia before returning to the soldier. "Gunshot wound to the chest. One of the guys is also a medic, so he's administering first aid. They're on their way to the hospital."

The world seemed to slow down. Acacia saw movement through the car windows, but everything seemed wooden.

Rick touched her hand.

She looked up at him. His lips moved but she couldn't understand what he was saying.

She closed her eyes and opened them. "Take me to him."

"Of course." Rick faced forward. His cell phone chirped with an incoming text, and he rattled off the location to the driver.

The driver sped through the streets of Moscow, and Acacia focused all her mental energy on Nicholas. There were so many things she wanted to say.

Chapter Sixty-Four

"Can he hear me?" Acacia turned anxious eyes on the surgeon, who'd just finished explaining the surgery he'd performed on Nicholas.

"He can hear you," the doctor replied in Russian. "He's going to be sleepy. I think he'll make a full recovery. As I said, the bullet went through the trapezius muscle above his clavicle, not the chest. It was a clean shot, no bullet fragments. But the bullet nicked the clavicle."

"Thank you." She shook the surgeon's hand, and he smiled at her.

"I'll return for rounds tomorrow," he explained before passing Rick to approach the exit. "If the night nurses give you trouble, you can tell them I thought your presence would be good for the patient."

"Thank you," Acacia whispered.

She went to Nicholas and took his hand in hers. She lifted his fingers to her face. She'd been so afraid she was going to lose him. The past few hours had been the worst of her life. Worse even than being a prisoner in Morocco.

"Acacia," he murmured. He had a sleepy, confused look on his face. "Are you okay?"

"Me?" She shook her head. "I'm fine. I'm worried about you."

"Don't." He closed his eyes. "I thought they had you. Kuznetsov said…"

Acacia waited for Nicholas to finish his sentence, but he didn't. She cleared her throat. "I'm fine. I was in the car with Rick when we got the call you'd been shot. I came as soon as I could, but they took you right into surgery."

Nicholas hummed. He opened his eyes and for a moment, the grogginess seemed to leave him. "Kuznetsov?"

Her eyebrows drew together. "He's still alive, but he got caught in the crossfire as well. He's at another hospital."

"He isn't dead?"

"No, but he's going to be arrested. Interpol went into the compound and seized a cache of weapons and bombs, along with stolen treasures from around the world. Kuznetsov had an Imperial egg in his vault that belongs to the Kremlin Armoury Museum. The Russian media is hailing Interpol as national heroes."

"Russian Interpol?" Nicholas murmured. "They refused to help us."

"The suspicion of weapons gave them grounds to search the property. The news is already reporting that Kuznetsov is an arms dealer. He's been selling weapons to terrorists."

Nicholas closed his eyes. "He told me he killed the man who murdered Riva."

Acacia gasped. "He said that?"

Nicholas nodded.

"Do you believe him?" she whispered, moving closer.

"I don't know. It would explain why we couldn't find them."

"I'm sorry, Nicholas. But I'm so glad you're all right. You could have been killed." Her voice shook.

Nicholas exhaled loudly.

She leaned closer and brushed his hair with her fingers. "Wen spoke with the Interpol agent. They think they recovered all three works that belong to your family. They're waiting to have the artwork authenticated before they release them."

Nicholas didn't reply.

She continued to caress his forehead. "I called your mother after you came out of surgery. She and your father are on their way."

"All right," he slurred.

He seemed to fall asleep. Acacia continued touching his face, relief causing tears to flow.

"You were right," he whispered. He opened his eyes. "I looked him in the eye, and I imagined killing him. It wouldn't have been enough."

Acacia reached over to kiss his lips, careful not to jostle his bandaged shoulder. "Don't think about it now. You succeeded. You got the artwork back for your family. It's over."

Nicholas made a sound in the back of his throat and drifted off to sleep.

Acacia stayed with him, while Rick watched over them both.

Chapter Sixty-Five

"I called Constantine." Nicholas stood on the terrace at his parents' home and looked up at the incredible view of Mont Blanc.

"What did he say?" Acacia asked.

"He thanked me for warning him about Kuznetsov. He's going to take extra measures to keep Yasmin safe, even though Kuznetsov is in prison."

"Good." Acacia touched Nicholas's arm.

"I feel lost."

Acacia wrapped her arm around his waist, careful not to jostle his left shoulder and arm in a sling. "I think that's a normal reaction."

"Is it?" He turned questioning eyes on her.

She gave him a half-smile. "I've only met with Dr. Aswan once. But she stressed how normal my feelings were, even though they're all over the place."

Nicholas turned back toward the Alps. He clenched his jaw.

"I don't pretend to understand your loss or the loss felt by your parents. But I love you, Nicholas, and I welcome you, no matter what your feelings are."

"Thank you." His dark eyes met hers, filled with affection. "I've had this burden for so long. Now that it's gone, I feel bereft. I keep checking to see if I still have my wallet and my phone. But I know that's not it."

"No, it's not." Acacia was sympathetic. "I keep looking over my shoulder, even though the man who haunted me and my mother will never trouble us again."

Nicholas placed his uninjured arm around her shoulder and kissed her temple. "I'm so glad you're in my arms again. And you're safe."

She snuggled into his side and took his hand in hers. Her hamsa pendant clanked against his watch, along with another, larger pendant.

Nicholas looked down at their connection. "When you told my mother you were Muslim, what did she say?"

"She was horrified she hadn't been offering me halal food. But she was relieved I wouldn't be asking for pork."

"My parents don't keep kosher."

"I don't think pork is in their future."

Nicholas laughed.

Acacia lifted her wrist to show him the new silver bracelet and pendant she wore. The pendant was a large disk, inscribed with Hebrew. "Your mother gave me this today."

Nicholas squinted at the writing. "I left off studying Hebrew after my bar mitzvah. What does it say?"

"It's a quotation from the book of Ruth. It says, '*The Lord deal kindly with you, as you have dealt with the dead, and with me.*'"

Nicholas frowned. "That's morbid."

"Naomi says those words to Ruth after the death of her husband, Naomi's son. Your mother said she wanted to offer me a blessing, in gratitude for what I've done for your family."

Nicholas's frown morphed into appreciation. "She's right. We are all grateful."

"I didn't do anything but love you."

"That isn't true, but your love is certainly the greatest gift I've ever received." He smiled. "Do you like my mother's gift?"

"I think of it as a blessing, too. Ruth wasn't Jewish, and neither am I. This is your mother's way of welcoming me."

Nicholas brought his mouth to her ear. "I have another, better way of welcoming you into the Cassirer family. But we agreed we'd speak about that later."

Acacia reached up and kissed him.

He returned her embrace, his arm wound around her waist. His thumb brushed her cheekbone as his lips moved over hers.

When they parted, his expression grew grave. "You did it, you know."

"I did what?"

"You saved a life."

Acacia lowered her head, her heart full.

"It's true, *mon amour*. I was so fixated on revenge, I didn't see what it was doing to my family or myself. I didn't see what I was becoming. You helped me see. You saved my life." Nicholas lifted her chin with his finger. "'And whoever saves one — it is as if he had saved mankind entirely.'"

"Thank you," she whispered. "I don't think the guilt of taking a life will ever leave me."

Nicholas's forehead creased. "We both have regrets. But we also have a second chance."

She hugged him tightly.

Nicholas touched the tip of her nose. "We need to have a serious conversation about something."

Acacia drew in a breath. "What?"

"Claude Monet, your cat. Are you sure you want to keep him? This morning he used my best dress shoes as a litter box."

Acacia looked up at Nicholas and saw longsuffering amusement in his twinkling eyes.

She burst out laughing.

Chapter Sixty-Six

Cassirer Foundation Museum
Cologny, Switzerland
One year later

"**M**y friends, I give you the Riva Cassirer Memorial Hall." Nicholas cut the ceremonial ribbon, officially opening the exhibit hall. His shoulder had healed, and he was able to use his arm with ease.

Applause erupted from the audience. Photographers took pictures as Nicholas and his parents shook hands with the curator of the museum.

Standing a short distance behind them, Acacia joined the applause. She wiped a tear from her face as she watched Nicholas embrace his parents.

He still had his scar. But he'd decided to have it removed. A plastic surgeon in Zurich had examined him and declared he could fix it. Surgery was scheduled in two weeks.

Nicholas caught her eye and smiled. She smiled in return.

He extended his hand, and she stepped forward. He kissed her chastely and rested his arm around her shoulders.

From her other side, Madame Cassirer placed her arm around Acacia's waist and hugged her.

Acacia looked around the hall to see the Degas drawing, the Monet, and the Renoir, all displayed in their rightful places.

She admired the portrait of Riva Cassirer that now hung in the center of the hall. It was the portrait from Riva's room in her parents' house. She smiled down at all who passed.

Acacia saw Kate, giving her two thumbs up, standing next to her mother, Marileia. This was only Acacia's mother's second trip outside Brazil since she'd traveled to Jordan on a teacher's exchange, before she met and married Acacia's father.

Acacia sobered at the memory of her father and her cousin, Ibrahim. Her mother's face had been lined with worry for years. Now, she was relaxed and happy. She no longer had to live in fear. She no longer had to hide.

Acacia touched the blue globes at her neck, and her hamsa pendant and the Hebrew pendant clinked against them. She was never without those three items, along with the watch Nicholas had given her.

He'd told her early that morning when they'd awoken and made love that he had another gift to give her after the exhibit opening. He'd held her left hand and kissed it, his lips lingering on her fourth finger.

"Happy?" Nicholas took her hand and squeezed it.

"Yes. And you?"

Nicholas's gaze moved to the portrait of his sister. He could look her in the eye now. "Since she's at peace, I feel like I can finally find peace as well."

Acacia nodded, and Nicholas kissed her temple.

Acacia stood encircled by her new family and looked up at the portrait of Riva Cassirer. In life there was love and loss. There was faith and doubt. There was hope and regret. But Acacia believed in her heart that, just like Sisyphus, humanity was at its best when it confronted adversity with determination and courage. And she realized the support and love of a family made life's burdens much lighter.

Acacia bowed her respect to Riva, touching the pendants she wore at her wrist. She prayed Riva would be at peace and said a silent prayer of gratitude for Nicholas and her new family.

Fin

Acknowledgments

I owe a debt to Paris, Geneva, Cologny, Santorini, Helsinki, Dubai, Morocco, and Moscow. Thank you for your hospitality and inspiration.

I am grateful to Kris, who read an early draft and offered valuable constructive criticism. I am also thankful to Jennifer and Nina for their extensive comments and corrections.

I've been very pleased to work with Cassie Hanjian, my agent. I'd like to thank Kim Schefler for her guidance and counsel.

My publicist, Nina Bocci, works tirelessly to promote my writing and to help me with social media, which enables me to keep in touch with readers. I'm honored to be part of her team. She is an author in her own right and I heartily recommend her novels.

Heather Carrier of Heather Carrier Designs designed the book's cover. She did a beautiful job. I would also like to thank Jessica Royer-Ocken for copy editing and Coreen Montagna for formatting the novel.

I am grateful to Erika for her friendship and support and I am so thankful for the kind words of Deborah Harkness. I also want to thank the many book bloggers who have taken time to read and review my work.

I especially want to thank my Brazilian readers from around the world and the administrators of SRFansBrazil and the Noites em Florencia podcast. You have been such a supportive community since the publication of *O Inferno de Gabriel* several years ago. This book was written for you, with thanks.

I want to thank the Muses, Argyle Empire, the readers from around the world who operate the SRFans social media accounts, and the readers who recorded the podcasts in English, Spanish, and Portuguese for *The Gabriel Series* and *The Florentine Series*. Thank you for your continued support.

Finally, I would like to thank my readers for continuing this journey with me. We form a diverse, supportive community that spans the globe. I am so grateful to be part of this community.

*SR
Feast of the Archangels, 2017

About the Author

New York Times, USA Today
and #1 International Bestselling Author

I'm interested in the way literature can help us explore aspects of the human condition — particularly suffering, sex, love, faith, and redemption. My favourite stories are those in which a character takes a journey, either a physical journey to a new and exciting place, or a personal journey in which he or she learns something about himself/herself.

I'm also interested in how aesthetic elements such as art, architecture, and music can be used to tell a story or to illuminate the traits of a particular character. In my writing, I combine all of these elements with the themes of redemption, forgiveness, and the transformative power of goodness.

I try to use my platform as an author to raise awareness about the following charities: WorldVision, Alex's Lemonade Stand, and Covenant House.